a **Ewing** is a New ZͼSERVED). ͺhor who
ͺnd works in London. She has a ͻR REGISTERͼ in English
Ʌaori, and won the Bancroft Gͻ ͼ the Royal
ͼmy of Dramatic Art.

'ͺliantly evocative and superbly researched re-creation of a
ͺ fascinated by the Rosetta Stone and the decipherment of
ͺnt Egyptian hieroglyphs. For Barbara Ewing, history is not
ͺ a decorative background for romance, but the very centre of
ͺonate and enthralling intellectual adventure.'

Assistant Keeper, Department of Ancient Egypt and Sudan,
The British Museum

Also by Barbara Ewing

The Actresses
A Dangerous Vine
The Trespass
The Mesmerist

Rosetta

Barbara Ewing

sphere

SPHERE

First published in Great Britain in October 2005
by Time Warner Books
This paperback edition published in 2007 by Sphere

A CIP catalogue record for this book is
available from the British Library.

ISBN 978-0-7515-3761-1

Typeset in Palatino by M Rules
Printed and bound in Great Britain by
Clays Ltd, St Ives plc

Sphere
An imprint of
Little, Brown Book Group
Brettenham House
Lancaster Place
London WC2E 7EN

A Member of the Hachette Livre Group of Companies

www.littlebrown.co.uk

To Fatma Moussa
who gave me an English history lesson in Cairo.

. . . And this decree shall be inscribed on a stela of hard stone in sacred writing, and native writing, and Greek writing . . . and live for ever.

The Rosetta Stone
196 BC

1795

Sentimental stories, and books of mere entertainment . . . should be sparingly used, especially in the education of girls. This species of reading cultivates what is called the heart prematurely . . .

MARIA EDGWORTH
(*Practical Education*, 1798)

That summer the old men appeared at the top of Vow Hill as usual, carrying small telescopes. They were waiting, they said, to see His Britannic Majesty's glorious fleet appear in the English Channel, returning from heroic battles against the French and the new general that everyone had begun to speak of, General Buonaparte. Sometimes there was no sign of any fleet at all, yet the old men with their telescopes were still to be seen on Vow Hill, arriving early on fine mornings for the best position. Just above the bathing machines.

The bathing contraption for containing ladies had been wheeled out into the sea. Rose and Fanny wore large swimming gowns which tied under their chins, and bathing bonnets. First they had been dipped into the calm, sparkling water by the female bathing attendants; now, on the beautiful, still summer day, they drifted further from the shore in the dark gowns. Small waves sighed and whispered and enfolded them. Rose's hair was dark and Fanny's hair was red; much of it had escaped from the bonnets and become caught up in tendrils of floating seaweed, as if they were mermaids. Their laughter and their voices echoed along the sand and up to Vow Hill where old gentlemen may, or may not, have been loitering.

Long afterwards Rose remembered the summer day when she and her cousin had drifted in the English Channel, where forbidden France with its rumours still of terror glittered in the distance; and the way the coldness of the water had made them catch their breath as they laughed, so that their laughter had a breathless, astonished quality of surprised joy.

Later they were lifted, shaken and dried by the female bathing attendants, and transported back to the shore; that night there was a ball and both the cousins, the laughing dark-haired one and the short and serious red-haired one, displayed hair that had not been quite tamed by the maid, Mattie; that escaped and fell and curled round their young faces.

Some of His Britannic Majesty's officers were at the ball; blue and red uniforms shone brightly for the young ladies. That night Miss Rose Hall, beloved daughter of the naval hero Admiral Arthur Hall, met Harold Fallon, a rather dashing young naval captain (not yet a hero but with high hopes); they danced a mazurka and then a reel. The musicians played, the violins and the harpsichord and the clarinet, and people laughed and talked very loudly and the summer room became unbearably hot as summer ballrooms were inclined, became filled more and more with the extremely strong smells of humanity. Spices in bowls and pomade and perfume and powder disguised what they could; ladies hid behind fans to conceal the problems of teeth and breath; strong eau de Cologne was liberally applied by everybody; gentlemen sucked scented pastilles. Despite the heat, when Captain Harry Fallon (it was only the following day she understood he was also the Viscount Gawkroger) kissed her young hand, Rose felt – again – that surprised breathlessness she had felt in the sea, though she could not possibly have put the feeling into words. Her cousin Fanny Hall, whirling past, observed Captain Fallon bending absurdly low over Rose as he twirled her about. He reminded Fanny at once of the handsome but untrustworthy gentlemen that appeared in all the new novels, and she knew that Rose, who had read all the new novels also, would see it too. And Fanny put her hand over her face, to stop herself from laughing aloud.

A week later the cousins were perambulating the circulating library near Hanover Square, quite their most favourite place in London (mostly for acquiring the new novels; occasionally for observing visiting gentlemen), when suddenly Fanny Hall, beloved eldest daughter of a manager in the

East India Company, almost swooned at the sight of an extraordinarily handsome man of the cloth who had been critically studying the wide variety of books available and who smelt not of sweat and bad teeth and pomade but, just delicately, of lavender.

'I would not like my wife to read Tom Jones, he said, and Fanny (who with Rose had of course read Tom Jones and Pamela and Clarissa and Evalina and, indeed, Fanny Hill) blushed prettily and knew that this man would read Locke, and Hume, and Pope, and Milton. The clergyman, whose name was Horatio Harbottom, smiled at the blushing Fanny, admired with charm her beautiful red hair, and gave her his arm to continue her perambulations. (As he was a man of God, this did not seem presumptuous.) The Reverend Horatio Harbottom had just received, through family connections, a rich parish as his own and was looking for what he now needed to complete himself: a wife. He had the most melodious voice, and the voice spoke of philosophy and history and God, a seemingly bottomless explosion of knowledge to Fanny, who at once imagined him standing handsomely in a pulpit dispensing wisdom. Rose dropped back and pretended to peruse a volume but, observing the handsome but ridiculously pompous clergyman talking to Fanny, she put her hand over her face, to stop herself from laughing aloud.

At Rose's home, just around the corner in Brook Street, they talked over the gentlemen they had thus encountered with Mattie the maid, who made them cooling lemon drinks. They whispered the word 'love'. Mattie was ten years older than both of them and had once been married herself, and so knew about such things.

'Make sure you like them as well as love them,' said Mattie drily. 'You might as well have got a lifetime in prison if you don't like them!' Rose and Fanny listened without understanding, for Mattie was old. But they pronounced the word love with awe, for they had read of it often, in the new novels. They had not heard that many people criticised these new novels and felt they were a bad influence on young girls: trivial novels, it was said, were much too seductive and delusional.

In hardly more than six months the two young, novel-reading cousins aged seventeen who had bathed in the sea that summer afternoon had been given away in holy matrimony. To obtain wedding dresses Fanny's mother had taken them to Bond Street: wonderful, swirling, glamorous Bond Street, with its shining big lamps and its exciting new glass shopfronts and the swinging shop signs and the elegant carriages rattling by and the shoes and the clothes (and the hawkers and the traders and the boxing saloon and the petty thieves and the open stinking gutters and the noise). In Bond Street the two virginal young ladies were dressed in flowing white and prepared themselves with wild excitement, adamantly refusing warm undergarments: they declared they would rather be cold than lumpy on their wedding days. Mattie the maid gave them hot chocolate in the evenings, to calm them. This beverage was also given to Fanny's mother (with a tot of brandy added), for she was quite red-faced with the excitement of it all. The two girls put pineapple juice on their faces before they went to bed, to prevent wrinkles.

Rose was married (with much naval attendance from both families) at a society wedding in St George's Church, Hanover Square, whence she emerged as Viscountess Gawkroger and as a member of the somewhat illustrious Fallon family of Great Smith Street. (The mother-in-law looked imperiously sour: she had hoped for at least a minor princess.) However, this event merited mention in several of the London newspapers beside naval dispatches from the wars against General Buonaparte, and a report that James Preston (70) and Susannah Morton (24) were executed the same day as the wedding, for the murder of their bastard male child. Further paragraphs declared that two gentlemen returning home at midnight in a post chaise were robbed of watches and money near Uxbridge; and that worms could not breed in the bodies of those who frequently took Dr Anderson's Genuine Scots Pills. There was also a report of the court hearing regarding the Countess of Pugh, who had run away from the Earl of Pugh and now pleaded in vain to be allowed to see her children: the court was resolute, the law was clear: fathers alone owned their children. In nearby Conduit Street the print shop had in its window an unflattering cartoon of the Prince of Wales, fat and bejewelled and portrayed as a pig.

Fanny's marriage took place in the pretty little market town of Wentwater, where Horatio Harbottom (whose uncle was a bishop) had obtained the aforementioned financially advantageous ecclesiastical preferment and an extremely pleasant country vicarage. He was a man with prospects, it was clear. And he had absolutely insisted on being married among his parishioners; he knew it was his duty as their vicar to do so. Fanny's family were bemused by his decision – it was indeed a perplexing

4

matter to get her brother and all her sisters to Wentwater – but to Wentwater they must: mother, father, and the five other children. The connections of Montague Hall, Fanny's father, to the East India Company meant an extremely generous settlement on the young couple and Horatio's relations were well satisfied, including the uncle who was a bishop. Fanny's family and friends (especially her father, who had arranged the purchase) were a little disconcerted nevertheless at the refusal of the bridegroom to drink the health of his new wife in the old Spanish sherry especially obtained for the momentous day. 'God's pure water will be my choice,' he was heard to say, perhaps a little sonorously, as the faint scent of lavender drifted; nevertheless all were soothed by the fact that he was an extremely handsome and sweet-smelling man of God – and as God moved in mysterious ways it was no doubt useful to have one of his representatives in the family. The Wentwater Echo wrote of the marriage of their new vicar in glowing terms alongside a report of a carriage accident in the town; also one of Horatio Harbottom's sermons was reproduced in the same edition, and this (and other religious tracts) were offered for sale. The Countess of Pugh (the Wentwater Echo also reported) had now run screaming along the main street of Oxford in her night attire, crying for her children, and had been removed to Bedlam. The rest of the news was naval dispatches from the wars against General Buonaparte.

In Wentwater market square a lone dissenter stood on a small stool and spoke of God.

If the two cousins had any reservations about each other's choice of husband, they were hidden. For they loved each other dearly and hoped only for each other's happiness.

On Vow Hill the old men had long put away their small telescopes; they sat now by winter fires and hoped they would live to see another summer and perhaps one more glimpse of youth and joy and a young ankle, all the things they once had known.

ONE

When Rosetta Hall, daughter of the naval hero Admiral John Hall, was a little girl she believed that she was named after a princess in a child's fairy story: Princess Rosetta who married the King of the Peacocks and lived happily ever after – her father read to her the very story. Princess Rosetta suffered many disasters before she married the King of the Peacocks – including being pursued over land and sea by a wicked witch – but when she was saved by an old fisherman (with the help of her one-eared dog), eight-year-old Rose heaved a very real sigh of relief every time; and when Princess Rosetta made the old fisherman a Knight of the Order of the Dolphin and Vice-Admiral of the Sea, Rose would bury her face in her father's naval jacket in recognition and delight. 'It's me! It's me!' she would cry, for she knew that her name was Rosetta and that her father was an admiral in the navy. So great was her delight to think herself a princess that her father only smiled.

Although there were many big words that defeated her, occasionally her father would read to her from the newspapers and the periodicals that lay on his big desk in Brook Street, next to the maps and the official documents, and the vellum paper and the quill pens and the ink, and the box of cigars, and the clock from Genoa that Rose believed chimed in Italian. Then there would be the rustling of her mother's skirts and more gentlemen from the navy entering the room in their blue jackets (often with confections for the little girl) and Rose would be taken upstairs to the light, airy drawing room where her mother had her own desk, a mahogany desk with quills and inkstands and a secret drawer, a desk that could turn as if by magic into a card table. And there, as the sun shone in through the big windows and the horses trotted past over the cobblestones with their carriages and their carts, and the passing traders with their rumbling barrows shouted to each other and called their wares, Rose held her first quill, and with her mother guiding her hand made the particular, special marks that showed the letter R.

'We are drawing in the drawing room,' said Rose in delight.

'No, this is not drawing,' said her mother, smiling. 'I am teaching you to write. This is writing, making words.'

'Writing, making words,' repeated Rose in awe.

Sometimes, as they bent over the paper, they could hear the sound of a harpsichord, drifting in from the house next door, mixing with the calls and the cries and the horses. So that the sound of the harpsichord mingled in her memory with the adventure of learning to write. Soon the next day could not come quickly enough; it was all so natural, made so easy and enchanting, that it was only later that Rose realised that many people could neither read nor write and that the servants in Brook Street put ink on their thumb, to make their mark. Very soon Rose had the idea of making her own marks, not the R and the O and the S and the E that her mother formed.

'Why cannot I write like this, Mama?' she would ask, drawing a small rose. Her mother looked puzzled. 'It is me! Rose!' said the little girl impatiently, pointing at her drawing, surprised her mother did not at once see. Then she drew a beautiful shape like a star.

'But that is not *writing*, it does not say anything,' her mother protested, laughing, 'though it is indeed very lovely.'

'It does say something!' insisted Rose. 'The star says "my mama" to me. Because you are beautiful, like a star. It is my writing. I am writing my way.'

Beside her sometimes, Mattie the maid, encouraged by Rose's parents, learnt her letters also.

The small girl began writing letters to all sorts of people: to the naval gentlemen at Somerset House who brought her confections, to her cousin Fanny Hall in Baker Street, to Fanny's mother and father; and every time Fanny's mother had another baby girl Rose would write, welcoming the new baby to the world. (And somehow the new babies always wrote back, in her aunt's round and comfortable hand.) Rose asked her mother if they could have some babies too and her mother's face was sad, and said they could not. (Rose and Fanny planned to have many, many babies.) But her mother took her to a bookshop, and Rose at once fell in love with the smell of books and paper and Indian ink and notebooks and ledgers and maps.

Her mother purchased one of the notebooks and showed Rose how to keep a journal: a record of all she was doing, of what she was reading. She sat at her mother's desk and watched the marks emerging from her own quill and on to the pages. Even now she could never quite take the words for granted; she would stare at them, was always amazed that she could, by willing her hand to do something from her head, convey to the journal all she intended. 'We skated in Hyde Park,' she wrote and then stared transfixed at the marks on the paper that made her see the ice again and Fanny's brother and sisters, skidding and flying. She became almost inarticulate trying to tell of her particular amazement and banged her feet on the mahogany desk in her anxiety to express herself clearly. 'How did it happen? How did people think of it – to make marks out of their heads and on to paper? Who thought of it? Who said one mark was to mean something and another was not? It is the most strange thing I have ever had in my head!' and finally Rose had to be taken to lie down because she seemed to be having a small brainstorm.

Next day she was back again, kicking at the desk, trying to express herself. 'Writing is – writing is better than speaking, Mama,' she said, 'for in speaking it is all forgot in a moment but here in my journal, or in my letters to Fanny, it shall always stay for ever.' Her mother smiled, stilling her daughter's small thrashing legs. Rose tried again to express a thought. 'With these special marks in my journal I am writing our own story, Mama.' And then at last the thought became clear. 'I am writing our life!'

And always, when writing of her mother, she wrote a star.

She began to learn French and saw that most of the marks, that is the letters, were the same letters but that they meant different things and made different sounds. Her small brain actually hurt as she pondered for a long time on how this could be.

Her father, intrigued by her odd curiosity, showed her the quite different writing of the Greeks, with different marks that made different letters altogether. She stared, fascinated. He translated some of the words. He talked of foreign lands, as well as foreign languages. He let her try his cigar, he let her taste the coffee he had brought back from Turkey; he brought the world into his study in Brook Street. And one day he brought out a very old book and showed her for the first time the untranslatable hieroglyphs of ancient Egypt. Rose stared at the strange pictures. There were different kinds of birds: one was like an owl, one was like a hawk. There was a bumble bee. There were straight lines and curls. There was a little lion, lying down. One sign looked like a foot, one looked like a dear little duck, one looked like a beetle.

'What is Egypt?' asked Rose, staring at the beautiful pictures.

He thought for what seemed to her a long time. 'Egypt is one of the most ancient civilisations in the history of the world. In Egypt writing can still be found on old stones, and on old Egyptian paper made from reeds. Their writing,' said her father, 'is the olden days, talking to us. But we cannot hear.'

And Rose repeated, fascinated, over and over: 'the olden days, talking to us.' Finally she said: 'I would like to go and see the olden days talking to us; have you actually seen it, Papa? I mean – not just in this book?'

Her father pulled on his cigar for a moment, the fragrance of the tobacco drifting. 'Once upon a time,' he said, 'when I was a young midshipman, I sailed to Egypt,' and he opened a book of maps, and traced the journey across the oceans. Rose's eyes were round with wonder. 'I was new to the navy – it was long before I met your mama. Egypt was a strange and beautiful place but so foreign and – curious. The sky was the bluest blue, quite different from home, and voices called out all day, calling people to their God, who was different from ours. It was very – strange and unsettling. And everywhere there was sand, miles and miles of lonely, unending deserts of sand stretching away to the horizon.' He seemed to Rose quite lost in reverie. 'There was the smell of oranges and – and – I think mint – along the Nile river. A trader took us in a sailboat along the Nile from a beautiful little town called Rosetta.

'*Rosetta?*'

He smiled at her and for a moment looked at his cigar, did not speak.

'It was called Rosetta?' she asked again, puzzled. 'Rosetta?'

At last he said: 'That is where your name comes from after all, my dear. That beautiful town. You were to be our only child, and we wanted to give you a very special name. But you were so entranced with the story of the Princess Rosetta and her King of the Peacocks that we could not bring ourselves to tell you it was another story altogether.'

'Oh Papa,' breathed Rose, almost swooning with delight. 'Tell me about this Rosetta!'

Her father sighed very lightly, as if he did not know he did so. 'Of course it was many, many years ago – not many foreigners travelled there then, we were a curiosity. The Egyptians were friendly, they laughed and shouted and threw their arms about. They were very generous to us. Rosetta was a little port town near the mouth of the river Nile, which is the river that runs right through Egypt and into Africa.' And in his book of maps he pointed out Egypt, and Rosetta, and the path of the Nile. 'I remember that there were fine mosques – that is what they call their churches – and fruit trees grew everywhere and waterwheels took water from the river for the fields. And the women hid their faces in shawls. But not,' he added slowly, 'their beautiful eyes.' He was silent again. Rose wanted to ask a hundred questions but for once she did not say anything: she somehow understood to wait. And her father, staring unseeing out over Brook Street, said, 'In Rosetta, one hot early morning, on a bank by the river, I saw some Arabs, with their long gowns and their turbans, crushing coffee beans in a big stone container, with big stone pestles.'

'What is a pestle?'

'Like a heavy weight, on a long handle. And beside the container of coffee beans an old man was sitting cross-legged, and singing a strange song, something – different – from our music,' and it seemed to Rose that he heard it. 'The Arabs with the pestles were higher up the bank, crushing the coffee beans from above. I stood beside the container, watching. And then suddenly – and it seemed to appear from nowhere – I saw a very small brown arm reaching inside the container through a hole in the side! and of course it seemed about to be crushed by the big pestles descending. But the old Arab man suddenly sang very fast – and the pestles lifted. And the small arm was safe after all. I was never so surprised in my life. The little boy who owned the arm had to reach in to stir and move the crushed coffee, and push the beans about. And when the old singer sang fast, the men above raised the pestles. And when he sang slowly it meant that the little boy's arm was safely pulled away and they could crash down again and crush the coffee beans.'

Rose waited, entranced beyond belief.

'The sound of an Arab voice singing – it gets into your dreams when you are far from home. And the beautiful eyes of the women. And the sound of the wooden waterwheels, the creaking singing sound, as the blindfold buffaloes walk round and round.' He brought himself back at last to Brook Street, and his daughter, Rosetta. 'And I saw this writing, the hieroglyphs, with my own eyes, Rosie. But the ancient Egyptian culture has been lost for thousands of years, and pillars and statues lay crumbling in the sand, forgotten, covered in the writing that nobody, anywhere, any longer knew the meaning of.'

'Is it – the first writing in the whole world?'

'Perhaps it is. Everything, everything we saw was so very old – the way of life, the broken pillars, the land itself. Almost I felt . . .' he searched for the words, 'I felt as if I was – inside the Bible.' But Rose did not understand.

'Why did the ladies hide their faces?'

'It is their custom.'

'Why?'

'Other people live in other ways from us, my dear. We are not the only people in the world.'

'Why were the buffaloes blindfolded? Is that their custom too?'

'The buffaloes were blindfolded to stop them getting giddy. They walked round and round in circles pulling a waterwheel all day long to water the fields, and the wheel creaked, and sang, as it turned.'

'Papa, may we go to Rosetta one day? My place?' She hardly breathed, waiting for his reply.

'Perhaps, dear girl,' he said. 'Perhaps one day.' And he sighed again, but it seemed to come from long ago. 'It is far away, and very, very different from our country. But—' and he smiled at her – 'who knows what is allotted to us? Perhaps we will go to Rosetta one day, if dreams come true.' She was too young to think he meant any dreams but her own. And the Admiral, usually so stern with his navy papers, let her make a tiny picture of a rose on his map, her sign for herself, in Egypt, at the port of Rosetta, where the river met the sea.

'Papa,' said Rose finally, 'a person wrote all the writing down even if it is broken now. On stones and things but writing, just like I write in my journal. They were writing their life.'

'Ah, but the key is lost,' said her father.

Her father and his blue-jacketed colleagues were often away at sea. While he was away, his wife and Fanny's mother took Rose and Fanny, and sometimes Fanny's older brother and younger sisters, to the pleasure gardens and the new galleries and circulating libraries and concert halls that were opening up all over London; once even to a new circus where animals roared and danced and men and women stepped on wires up in the sky. Acrobats were the latest craze. The children's favourite part of all the entertainment at Vauxhall Gardens, among the orchestras and the fireworks and the conjurors, was The Singing Acrobats: beautiful ladies entwined in sparkling scarves who slithered up and down ropes or pillars and sang 'Where'er You Walk' by Mr Handel (the children's favourite, because Mr Handel had lived in Brook Street), or Mr

Schubert's latest songs. Often The Singing Acrobats sang upside down (the children were forbidden to do this at home). Sometimes the family went to Greenwich, to see the Observatory, and the cousins rolled themselves down Greenwich Hill, laughing, covered in grass.

Brook Street fascinated all the children, not just because of Mr Handel. They would, even the littlest cousins, kneel at the big windows of the Admiral's house; they would watch the horses and the carriages and the people going past: businessmen, traders, pedlars. Once they were extremely surprised to see a beggar running away fast, without his crutches. At night they fell asleep to the sound of the night coaches, or the rumbustious singing of the men coming home from the hostelries or the coffee houses, or the cries of the nightwatchmen. Fanny spoke to her dear friend, God, and asked him to look after the beggars and pedlars and find them somewhere to sleep too.

One day they were taken to the docks and actually aboard a ship of the East India Company and saw Fanny's father sign papers. They were awed to take tea from Indian gentlemen with turbans and there was the scent of pepper or cinnamon in the air as well as the smell of the Thames, and they saw large rats and Rose wrote about everything in her new journal.

When Fanny and her brother and her sisters had been taken back to Baker Street Rose felt lonely, and asked her mother again if they could have some babies.

'It is not possible,' said her mother, and her face looked sad.

'I shall have lots of babies anyway,' said Rose, kicking a chair, listening to the empty house. In her mother's room there was a chaise-longue; on the chaise-longue there were four small cushions. Rose stood the cushions underneath the window and read to them of Princess Rosetta and the King of the Peacocks, and Robinson Crusoe. The cushions acquired names: Margaret, Elizabeth, Angel and Montague. Sometimes Angel accompanied Rose and her mother to the wonderful shops in Bond Street, and Rose would whisper secrets.

When the Admiral was back from sea, he and his brother, Fanny's father, took their families abroad: to Germany, to Spain, to Italy. The Admiral felt it was important for children to travel, to understand something about other peoples, and something about Art. (Fanny's father cheerily agreed, as long as there was good food and wine at the end of the day.)

And most of all they went to France. Rose and Fanny loved France best of all, said to each other over and over, *'La belle France'*; told each other excitedly that after three, two, one more sleep they would be going again to *la belle France*, and they would be almost beside themselves when the journey towards the sea began. France meant elegant women and boulevards and the river Seine and the bridge across called the Pont Neuf and the French language all about them. Rose stared in delight at the glorious fashions and the glorious cathedrals indiscriminately, writing it all down in her journal. Fanny, a more serious little girl than her cousin, read almanacks and poetry and thought about the Meaning of Life even in Paris, even with younger sisters clinging to her hands or to her gown. 'Fanny is the thoughtful one,' the grown-ups said. Fanny's stubborn little freckled face was often seen trying to work out life's meaning but thanking God – whom she knew personally – for the world they lived in. Rose on the other hand saw God as a kindly background. When Rose emerged from her *joie de vivre* to think, it was the meaning of words, not the meaning of life, that caught her imagination.

From as early as she could remember Rose's parents were visited in Brook Street by their wide circle of friends. They would sit in the drawing room as the lighted candles threw shadows on to the pale walls and on to the painted portraits of Rose, and her parents, and her parents' parents. And they would talk.

At first it was a babble of voices, grown-ups who smiled at the little girl before she went to sleep; later she (and Angel) would be allowed to stay and listen: naval men, men in waistcoats, old men with short white wigs, younger men with their own hair tied behind, young women with curls, older women with white caps on their hair. Rose always remembered one woman with a white cap who was called Miss Proud. ('Is she proud, Mama, is that why she is called Miss Proud?' Rose whispered, and her mother replied, 'I would be proud if I were her, she has travelled all over the world and she writes books,') and Rose looked at this old lady in the white cap with new interest. Miss Proud read books with such voracity that she seemed almost to eat them as she bent over them. Several times she was escorted out of the closing Hanover Square Circulating Library apologising, the last customer again. Once, one summer evening, she was actually locked in; the librarian was in a hurry to leave and had not checked the map section. (Miss Proud recounted this adventure with pleasure, saying she felt it a privilege to sleep with so many books for company.) Her knowledge became formidable. Young poets and writers often came to see her and talk to her and time was forgotten. One of her brothers and the young William Wordsworth were friends; the brother brought Mr Wordsworth, Mr Wordsworth brought Mr Coleridge and Mr Southey; they spoke of poetry and revolution and government. They would drink tea and talk and argue and suddenly it was two in the morning and the young men would walk out into the night at last, talking still, carrying lanterns to light their ways home.

In the drawing room in Brook Street people talked about everything, the whole exciting, newly expanding world: books, 'the Rights of Man', the new science of electricity, the theatre, the antipodes, women's education, God, the monarchy, the Evangelicals, telescopes, microscopes, balloon travel, Unitarians, astronomy, philosophy, music, reason. Rose knew all these words before she was ten (if not always their meanings). Sometimes they would talk of the avalanche of books beginning to be published and all the frivolous new fiction: would people read only dross and forget the great books that were considered indispensable to education? Could there be women's colleges? Her mother's eyes would be shining as she put Rose to bed: 'My dearest girl, you are so lucky to be growing up into this exciting new world,' and the warm scent she knew as her mother lingered in the room, drifted there with the flickering light from the lamp in the hallway and the sound of the voices from below as Rose finally fell securely asleep.

Fanny and Rose were both shocked and extremely put out when a Revolution struck France and they realised they could no longer go there, but the Admiral explained to them how important it was that all men were free. 'It may curtail our travelling in the mean time but it is nevertheless for the best, it is for freedom and equality and the brotherhood of man,' and Rose swirled the words round and round in her head, 'freedom' and 'equality' and 'the brotherhood of man', and addressed Margaret, Elizabeth, Angel and Montague on these matters.

But soon young girls who could read, like Rose and Fanny, could not miss all the references in the newspapers, not to freedom and equality any longer but to blood and terror and death in their beloved France. There was talk of a mad Frenchman called Napoleon Buonaparte, and War, and Fanny's brother Richard joined His Britannic Majesty's illustrious army and wore a red jacket. Mattie the maid came to live at Brook Street, for her husband, Cornelius Brown, was sent to war. The Admiral was gone to sea; Rose and her mother wept; wept again when he arrived back safely from yet another mission; wept most of all and most joyously when it was decided he should remain in London where his skills and knowledge were needed by the Admiralty. Friends still came, the drawing room was still full of talk. Rose heard many heated discussions about where revolution could lead; how bloody this revolution had turned; whether a republican was a traitor now that France had declared war on England; sometimes there were raised voices that went on, long into the night.

The pages in Rose's journal danced and blurred. A consultation with a doctor evinced the information that she read too much. Small magnifying spectacles could be purchased from Dickens and Smith, said the doctor, but were only to be worn for one hour each day because of the damage they did to eyes. 'One hour's reading per day,' he reiterated sternly. Rose stared up at him, her face blank, as if he was not there. In the first week of the spectacles she set fire first to a blanket, trying to write in her journal in bed by candlelight, and then to a damask tablecloth, trying to read *Robinson Crusoe* secretly under the big table in the dining room.

Mattie's husband, Cornelius Brown, like a number of his fellow sailors, did not come back to England with his ship, nor apparently had he been killed. He had gone off to see the rest of the world. 'What a thing to do to his mum,' said Mattie indignantly.

'What a thing to do to the navy,' said the Admiral most sternly. 'He has deserted his King and his country, Mattie. He now has an

R beside his name, in the records: Run Away. I am sorry, Mattie, but the punishment for all such men is that they are hung for desertion.'

Rosetta gasped, stared at poor Mattie.

'Well,' said Mattie, 'I'm very sorry, sir, I'm sure.' But they could tell she felt that nobody would catch Cornelius Brown and she seemed almost to be smiling. 'You could say he has deserted me as well but I told him I wouldn't have thirteen children like his mother thank you very much! So I hope he finds a suitable girl in a land far away to do her duty,' and she began clearing the table. And then she announced, 'I'll get him for this though, see if I don't!' yet she did not seem, Rose observed, unduly upset; rather, hummed and looked thoughtful.

When the Admiral's wife, Rose's beloved mama, depicted by a star, began to lose weight, she was at first still interested in everything, still waited for the evenings in Brook Street. Mattie tried to feed her up. Then the pain began. It was understood that something inside was eating her and that she was dying: within a year the beautiful woman who Rose had always drawn as a star was as thin as a bird, her face creased in terrible pain. They could not assist, they could not assuage, they could not bear it. Finally, with a wise doctor's assistance they gave her opium. They tried not to hold on, but they could not help it: 'Mama,' wept Rose, 'you cannot leave us.' But one summer night in Brook Street when Rose was fifteen, as nightingales shadowed against the darkening blue sky and flew home to the trees in Hanover Square, the pain and the anguish and the horror were mercifully extinguished and the beautiful woman left them, after all.

The Admiral wept. 'But I have you,' he said to Rose at last, seeing how his weeping distressed his daughter. 'Your mama lost so many children. That is why you were so precious.'

At the funeral Rose and Fanny held each other tightly, tears pouring down their inexperienced cheeks. It had not occurred to them that the people they loved would not live for ever.

It was the first time in her life that Rose had experienced grief and sadness and loss and she drew her very last star, beautiful and shining, to be buried with her mother. She heard the empty house, and vowed to have so many children that she would never, *ever* live in an empty house again.

And then she met Captain Harry Fallon, Viscount Gawkroger, at a ball near Vow Hill, and Fanny met the Reverend Horatio Harbottom in the Hanover Square Circulating Library.

TWO

The two cousins had never before been separated and despite their new and wondrous felicity missed one another most painfully.

The Rectory
Wentwater
May 1796

Dearest Rose,

Six o'clock in the morning, time for me to write before Horatio descends! I look first, always first, for Letters from you – I miss you more than I can say – but of course I do after we have spent so much of our lives Together. I am sorry my Letters are always so short! but the life of Mrs Fanny Harbottom is so busy! Dear Horatio has much work to do with Visiting Clerics, they meet for hours in his Study, so I attend to the hundreds (it seems) of small Matters that People's lives seem to need help with – and I love it, I enjoy it, I share their Lives and their Stories. There is much suffering among the poorer people – we did not know much, Rose, you and I, but I am learning.

And Rose – have you heard? – the East India Company is to send Mama and Papa to India in only a Few Months' Time – India – what an inconceivable Adventure! Papa is to be overseeing the choosing of Cottons in India I believe. Mama is beside herself with Arrangements for four young girls (Richard is to of course stay in the Army). Oh Rose – all my Family suddenly scattered over the Globe. But of course we have our Whole Lives stretching before us and – who Knows? – one day Horatio may be sent by the Church to somewhere Across the Sea also!

But to be suddenly without all my Dear family, that is hard.

But of course I am so busy with my Married Life. It is wonderful to have my own House – already there is the scent of honeysuckle – the Rectory is a lovely rambling place, large rooms (for our children! – oh my dearest Rose, I believe I may already be expecting one – but will not tell my family until I am sure – but Mama will be gone) . . .

I think I am very suited to be a Vicar's wife! for you know I have always loved going to Church, the echoing Peace, and the knowledge that God is there. But I have never visited Church quite so Frequently – Horatio is rather fond, some evenings, of entering the Wentwater Church and lighting several Candles and then Delivering, just to me, his Sermons. (I have learnt to take many shawls for the Church can be very cold in the evenings!) And it is not only Horatio who speaks of God in Wentwater – there are some odd, rather Earnest people who have begun to visit this town on Market Days and they preach in the Town Square – they are I believe Methodists or Evangelicals or even, yesterday, Quakers. And Rose, one of them is a Woman! I never thought to see a Woman Preaching and she is so simple, and people Listen, Amazed. All these visitors Preach on little stools that they carry about with them: they stand on little stools – even if it is raining – talking about God, it is a strange sight, truly. Horatio names all these (uninvited!) visitors Charlatans and Dissenters – he says they cheapen the Great Church of England and are Traitors. He especially

Thunders in Church on Sundays – it is irreligious of me to say so but his wonderful Voice is just made for Thundering and the faint scent of lavender (Horatio has it in a bottle in the Vestry and applies it to himself before he appears!) has now Irrevocably become mixed with the smell of old Pews and Hymnbooks and candles, and my Life . . .

Oh my dearest coz, I miss you. I long to talk to you. There are Strange things in being Married are there not? – (as well as the Strange Things we knew about quite well, I mean!) Remember when we found that copy of *Aristotle's Master-Piece* (that book with Diagrams of the Human Body that young ladies were not meant to read) and hid it behind the curtains in the Library when we heard people coming?! Well, I am not sure, now, that I learnt all I should have, or Understood everything, in that Forbidden Book . . . And Rose, what are you reading? I am Famished for Books. Having, after all, met Horatio in the Circulating Library by Hanover Square, I am somewhat Amazed to understand – of course he is not against Books, that would be Unthinkable – that he does not think Women should read Novels – he is quite Eloquent on the subject, he says they are a danger to Marriage! He says that Books are meant to be read aloud and shared, and he implies that there is something immoral about reading – especially Novels – on one's own! Well, I shall find a new Novel and read it to him aloud if it pleases him. And his dear and very beautiful face when he looks lovingly at me, as he often does, gives me much Happiness and I know how much I will learn from him.

Except that – oh Rose, you of all people know how very much I have always, all my life, talked to God, who I know Watches over us. But – Horatio believes that God has not really Touched me yet, and that I do not have a Mature Vision of God – oh Rose, there is so much I do not know and of course he is very likely right, but it is odd to feel that I have not quite – Understood. But I am sure I will Learn so much from Horatio, who Knows so much. I tell myself over and over that he will be my Education, and my Teacher.

Write soon, dear Rose, you will never give up writing
Letters and your Journal, will you, dear coz? Just because
we are married? My forever picture of you is sitting at your
mama's old desk that could become a card table,
Concentrating absolutely on what you are Writing, as if the
rest of the world does not exist. Dear Rose, I miss you so.

There is Moorland at the back of the town where I
sometimes wander, if there is time. Occasionally now that
the Days are warmer I lie by myself among the Trees and the
Grasses and I look up at the Sky and see the clouds drifting
past and I say Dear God, I know that You are there and I
wait for Your Word if You have not, after all, been Speaking
to me when I thought You were. And the clouds form, and
reform, and seem to be saying, 'We hear you.' Is that
childish, do you think? Yes, I expect it is!

God Bless you, my dearest Rose,
Fanny

Wimpole-street
London
May 1796

Dear, dear Fanny,

You are the wisest person I know, not childish; you are
my own dear cousin, and I miss you terribly. Your dear
mama and papa and all the Girls have just been to call – oh
to travel across the World! India! Who knows what they will
Encounter! Your sisters believe that there are many eligible
young English gentlemen in India just waiting for their
arrival! and they speak of monkeys and snakes and
elephants, and Army Balls and literally shudder in
excitement! and everyone looked Harassed and we wept
and they said they must soon say Goodbye to you – oh
Fanny! when shall we See them again?

They go to India, and we are Married Women in charge of
our own Establishments! (do you sometimes pinch yourself
and remember that you are no longer a 'girl'? – oh Fanny,

how I miss Mama, even now.) Am I really not Rose Hall any more? It seems that I have become Rose Fallon, Viscountess Gawkroger, Hostess and Wife! Oh Fanny, Harry loves me, and makes me so happy. We have an extraordinary life when Harry is ashore: we rise late, we go to bed late, four or five o'clock in the morning is nothing! And Fan, note the new address – Harry and I have at last moved into our own (large!) house in Wimpole-street. (But nothing actually happens in Wimpole-street, fashionable though it may be, and it doesn't lead anywhere – only up to the fields behind Portland Place.)

The best part about our move is the escape from my Mother-in-law! and that cold house in Great Smith-street so pompously named Gawkroger Hall. The Dowager is a terrible Trial as you have had several chances to Observe. I may be considered (as I am told so often) very Lucky to have 'ensnared' a son of such a Family but there is indeed a Price to be paid! Even your dearest Horatio (who we know appreciates Titles!) looked what can only be described as Terrified, as the Dowager Viscountess Gawkroger bore down upon him on my Wedding Day and he perceived there was no escape as the Torrent of Words began. I became more and more Curious about how she was able to talk so long without taking breath and by Serious Observation I have ascertained that she goes on Speaking even when Breathing Inwards, as well as when Breathing Outwards, so that there is no chance at all for Interruption!

In Wimpole-street we entertain in a long blue Drawing Room hung with Fallon Family Portraits: old faces, candlelit, look down on me, some stern, some benevolent. I of course assumed they were Ancient Noblemen until the housekeeper assured me they were mostly 'Businessmen' – with what Disdain she spoke that word! Any Noblemen on the walls are from the Dowager's family: it is she who has apparently brought a little Aristocratic Blood into the Fallon Family veins! My favourite painting is a large one of the present Family Fallon in earlier days – the Late

Viscount Gawkroger in long wig and buckles, Harry a
mischievous-looking boy, his younger brother, George,
looking rather sly. The Family is Most Seriously poised
around a Harpsichord where the Viscountess sits with her
hands upon the Keys. She is in full high wig and Plumes,
young but already Imposing, that long noble nose and
those piercing blue eyes that I have come to know so
unfortunately well. She dominates the Painting but as I
have never seen her play a note, nor heard one word of
interest in Music expressed by any member of this
Illustrious Family, the Painting is obviously more about
their Social Yearnings than their Musical Appreciation!
What we apparently are, dear Fanny, is the 'new'
Aristocracy. (As if I care! I have my darling Harry and that
is all that matters to me, and he himself is so busy enjoying
life I am sure he does not care either!) But the Dowager and
George YEARN to be grander, and not 'new' at all – they
yearn to be part of *le beau monde* – I mean the few,
important, old Established families, Dukes and Earls and
Marquesses, that surround the King and the Prime
Minister and I suppose the Prince of Wales (though it is
known he has some very strange acquaintances). But of
course the *beau monde* cannot be yearned for: the rules are
very strict and unbreakable – you cannot be 'in' unless you
are particularly Noble and of Ancient Lineage – and we are
not 'in'. How could we be? Nevertheless the Dowager and
George seem to spend every waking moment aspiring to
move Upwards and Upwards – everything they do is to
this end and money is no object (for the Fallon Family is
VERY rich: I have only just begun to comprehend this).
And so, much of our life is meeting with the Right People.
In London we are forever visiting Grand Families, or
making up parties for the Theatre, or Ranelagh Gardens, or
Vauxhall – all the entertainments and fireworks and
champagne and suppers (remember how we too used to
go – although less expensively! – and Fanny, our
favourites, The Singing Acrobats, remember them? are still
there!). And we go on Country Visits to elegant houses and

even Castles! where we languish drinking Champagne and dancing – once they made me go Hunting and it was so horrible I refused to go again. They shot a deer; there was a tiny fawn beside it. George, Harry's brother, picked the fawn up and killed it with his bare hands, broke its little neck and threw it among the trees, and then we rode on. George laughed at my face, he said he was being cruel to be kind.

But nobody ever seems to read Books or talk about what they have read, or what they have been thinking as you and I are so used to doing – Harry never reads anything! he says he hasn't time to read. Books seem to make him Impatient and so now I keep all my Books in my own room. I had wanted to share so much with him but the only book he has showed interest in my having read is *Aristotle's Master-Piece* – he laughed when I told him about you and I hiding it behind the Library curtains and said no Respectable girl would know of such a Book, yet he mentions it often and looks knowing! (Do you suppose Horatio has read it also?!) I was so enraged with Boredom one evening lately, at some soirée, that I went and read a book in another room; unfortunately I was followed by an odious large man who breathed upon me so closely that I had to say, 'Desist, Sir' just like the Heroines that we read about!

And of course we entertain. That blue drawing room becomes full of London Society – such gowns, such jewels, such Grecian hair! Such Perfumes and Pomades! People arrive so elegant, so sophisticated, a hand reaches out so languidly for Champagne, sometimes we even have a little Orchestra. Exquisite food is served. Money piles up on card tables in one room, Ladies fan themselves and exchange Gossip in another. But Fan – sometimes a lady or a gentleman disappears. And then another . . . and then they reappear in a way I can only describe as Mysteriously Dishevelled! – but just Slightly, so I wonder if I am only imagining this. (One can hardly of course chase one's guests about one's own staircases to solve the mystery!) Harry only laughs, I smile as a good Hostess should; the Dowager Viscountess holds Court in the middle of the blue drawing room and George (who arranges everything of course) judges the success of his *soirée* (for of course it is really his *soirée*) on the Social Standing of Guests, not their Activities once they are here. This then is Society! And so often, sitting in dark corners, malevolent young gentlemen consuming enormous amounts of Champagne and criticising the Company, or the Host, or the Ladies' Gowns behind their hands, which turns George Puce with rage. I do not see why it should – I have seen him behaving in just that way at other people's Houses! Oh but Fanny, imagine inviting Papa to such an evening . . . His disapproval of my Marriage is my only Sadness. As he foretold there is a lot of Exquisite Fashion and not much Brains – many of the people we meet are so *louche* – as you can guess from this letter. 'Dissipated', Papa warned, and 'Artificial'. All of it is true, I suppose – but not my darling Harry. I wish Papa could see that. Harry is exuberant – but good.

Today after your Mama and Papa and the girls left I sat in the blue drawing room and listened to the silence, just the ticking of the clocks, and I thought of all the empty rooms and closed my eyes and imagined them full of children (which surely cannot be very long in coming, for from your letter you seem to have managed it, dearest Fanny). And the clocks ticked, and I waited for my Life – there, I am as childish as you! We have acquired seven clocks actually! from our wedding, including Papa's old Italian one from Genoa that I always loved, that I insisted chimed in Italian, remember? And, having been examined by a Clockmaker and all given the same time, they all – in the hall, in the blue drawing room, up the staircases – chime, but slightly out of Synchronisation. I like this, I like the different chimes vying with each other, I like the idea of time being not necessarily what we think it is. And – after all – it is still the old clock from Genoa that is the most reliable. Mattie winds them meticulously each day, Mattie came with me of course as my personal maid, and thinks our whole way of living is

Ridiculous, I often hear her mumbling ruderies! Can you believe she is still determined to find that sailor husband of hers, Cornelius Brown? – she threatens to get on a ship disguised as a man and look for him, not to re-acquire him (or so she insists) but to punch him in the eye for his bad behaviour! It is years since he jumped ship and disappeared but she is still serious and I believe she is saving to travel, and I would not be at all surprised if she carried out her threat! But I have made her promise to stay with me at least until I have my first Child. 'Promise me, Mattie!' I say. 'I promise, Miss Rose,' she says. 'I will not leave you until you have your first Child.'

Harry is getting Impatient – he says others in the Navy are already in the Mediterranean: Malta, Italy, Greece – and even Egypt – oh if I could go to Egypt with him and see the things Papa told us of! Napoleon Buonaparte is everywhere and nowhere it seems. Harry wants to be a Hero and feels Others are already getting Chances but he has to wait to obtain a Ship of his own, he says there are too many Captains altogether in the English Navy – well – if only the English Navy could keep their Captains in Town I should be the happiest person alive in this Beautiful World, for you know the fairytale: the Princess Rosetta lived happily ever after once she found the King of the Peacocks (and Harry in his yellow waistcoats and pink jackets is the King of the Peacocks certainly!).

Last week, through the offices of my brother-in-law, who seems to have some dealings with him, I was presented to the Prince of Wales at Carlton House, an extraordinary and Flamboyant Abode – I was received in a room decorated in gold and scarlet! I felt rather apprehensive at the Prince's somewhat oozing, fat flattery – he had taken a good deal of wine I should say – and he was wearing a deeply alarming wig and had Spangles sewn on to his breeches. I almost asked him if he, at least, reads Books! – he must, of course. He spoke of Art very interestingly but rather drunkenly for five minutes and then my 'audience' was over. But I met there the Duchess of Brayfield! You must know who I mean – she is always written about in the newspapers as the power behind the government, behind the Prime Minister, and even Papa spoke of her legendary dinner parties for powerful men. She was very beautiful and very charming, and we spoke together – oh joy! – of the books of Mr Smollett. George bowed very low, meeting such a personage! (Not a person to ever become Mysteriously Dishevelled at his sort of parties – not a person to ever attend his sort of parties, I am sure!) I shall model myself on the Duchess of Brayfield: perhaps, one day, I could become an Interesting Hostess? In the mean time, through the offices of a cousin of the Dowager, the Duchess of Seaforth, I believe I am soon to be presented at Court – and must wear hoops and CORSETS and feathers – just like the olden days!

I am waiting now, in my pink bedroom, at Mama's old desk, for the sound of the carriage, for Harry. For my beloved husband, Harry. (It is still a delight for me to write those words, I write them in my journal nearly every day!) He is at some Club or other, playing cards for money I have no doubt. Harry gambles on absolutely Everything, not just cards: the horse-racing; the Velocity of coaches through Bond Street; dice; the trajectory of these new Balloons that fly above us; even (Harry confided in me) whether it is possible to make love to a woman in a Balloon as it traverses London!! (I think he was teasing about that one, to see if he could Shock me!) And all these antics Harry shares with his brother – who visits us constantly in Wimpole-street. He seems – George – not to be able to live without his older brother. His face lights up when he sees Harry – he does everything Harry wants: spoils him – and rules him. I try to like him, George I mean, but there is something . . . something about him that I cannot like (the memory of that little deer, perhaps). He looks like Harry, but he is not Harry. (He cannot carry off Colours as Harry can, a yellow coat that on Harry looks so wonderful looks, on George, too flamboyant, slightly wrong – as if he were an Actor!) Yet despite myself I cannot help admiring

George for his – what is it? – I suppose it is his Energy. I see
that he makes the 'real' Aristocracy seem lazy and languid.
He is never still. He is always busy with Family Affairs, as
I say he does everything for Harry – and yet, no matter
how busy he is, he is always 'around' – even when you
thought he was not. To tell you the secret Truth he reminds
me of a Snake, poised one day to strike! But of course I
hardly even let myself think of Snakes, for Harry's sake.
And he – George – is always perfectly pleasant. So: I do my
best to be charming for indeed I want to be a Fascinating
addition to this 'illustrious' Family. I actually feel
Illustrious anyway, sitting in my silk nightgown – Harry's
favourite. (Oh, but I have ink on my fingers, some things
never change, Fanny darling! safe here at Mama's desk
with my journal and my quills and my dear old
magnifying spectacles – though Harry insists I must not
wear those where he can see me!)

All I wish now is that I could tell you that I am expecting
a Child also.

When will you come to London to farewell your family?
Let me know at once. Dear girl, dear Fanny, I miss you so.
But let us only think that our world has got larger. We will
learn all sorts of new things in our different lives, and share
them as always – and I know that God will send you lots
and lots of messages, for he was always your dear friend.
Oh Fanny, may Horatio make you as happy as Harry makes
me.

Rose

The Rectory
Wentworth
May 1796

Dear Cousin Rose,

Fanny and I are praying for you Daily, that God will help
you overcome the Frivolousness of your new Life and turn
that Life to Righteousness and His Words. I feel it would not

be Suitable for Fanny to Visit you in London, nor for you to Visit her here now that your Lives are so Different. Please take great care to Write to her in a Proper manner, as befitting the Wife of the Vicar of Wentwater.

May God guide you.

Your cousin,

Horatio Harbottom (Reverend)

Underneath this short missive the following words were very hastily scrawled: *he read your letter.*

THREE

Harry and Rose were considered the Perfect Couple (if not by the bride's father, who deemed the Fallon family 'hangers-on to the real aristocracy and even more immoral'; or by the bridegroom's mother, who had quite seriously wanted her beloved son to marry royalty and heave the family socially upwards). There were many who sought the newlyweds out: they were delightful company and attractive, not to mention very rich. Harry made Rose look at themselves, together, in a large mirror: 'Look, *Rosetta mia*. See how beautiful we are,' and she looked away shyly from their naked bodies. But he forced her to look back, and she agreed. (And so she always saw them: both dark-haired, both with champagne-shining eyes, her own blushing face as Harry held her, and showed her.)

*

They named it the High Heavens Club (HH for short) an innocuous enough title; if required to explain, they spoke of an interest in astronomy: several gentlemen were, anyway, quite informed about constellations (except that actually it was necessary to descend before darkness fell). They would swear that if you ascended on a bright day, sometimes you *could* see the stars, reflected by the sun.

Members of the High Heavens Club carried, on the inside of a particular waistcoat worn for balloon ascents, stars made of real gold. One gold star for each successful endeavour. It was an exclusive club; only those who had achieved their objective were considered members: that of course was why there had to be Observers – the Observers were honour-bound (of course) to at least pretend to watch the scenery. Occasionally the cries of a young woman were piteous: then it was the Observers' task to persuade her, kindly, that as she was here, up in the sky, she may as well enjoy it. Once there was a fire in Captain Ocean's balloon and a young girl was badly burnt, she was not seen again in polite society (but the gentlemen had clubbed together and sent a donation).

Captain Ocean hired out his balloon and his services for one hundred guineas an hour (much more than his coachman could earn in a year): only the financial elite could join the High Heavens Club. Some gentlemen guaranteed an hour was all they needed; bets were laid. The weather had to be right, of course; bets were laid on the weather. Various young ladies were wooed with seeming decorum right under the noses of their ambitious mamas; bets were laid on the success of the wooing (for the gentlemen who could afford one hundred guineas an hour were also the gentlemen that ambitious mamas were trying to ensnare as sons-in-law). Sometimes the mamas even came to see their daughters off, kept waving a handkerchief as the lovely balloon got smaller and smaller.

The married gentlemen had to be just slightly more discreet, but some of the more adventurous and experienced married women were not averse to becoming High Flyers themselves: they laughed at the thrill of it, and reported the adventure behind their fans.

The clubs in St James's provided picnic baskets which contained oysters, truffles, asparagus (and trifle, in case people were hungry afterwards). All picnic baskets of this kind were accompanied by two dozen bottles of champagne: the empty champagne bottles and the crystal glasses were thrown over the side. Once a cow behind Portland Place was killed outright when it was struck by what seemed to be a bolt from the blue; it was actually a full champagne bottle mistakenly dropped from Captain Ocean's balloon.

Captain Harry Fallon had the most stars; when he was away at sea, the High Heavens Club lost its most frequent flyer.

*

Rose hugged her secret. Her eyes shone. Alone in the carriage on the way to Drury Lane, she knew she was smiling, she could not help it (any member of the HH Club, seeing the look in her eyes, would have assumed she was going to meet her lover, and would rather have wished it was him).

She looked out of the carriage window at the squares and the streets; it was just getting dark and the lamps lighting the shops along the Strand glowed, people walked and laughed and called in the dusk: ladies and gentlemen in gloves and hats, street boys in bare feet, businessmen with little cases. Carriages ran alongside each other, just missed each other, the drivers called to each other; there was the smell of onions cooking, and coffee, and fish, and drains: her city.

Fanny already had two children. Rose had lost her first baby, and her second, but this magical time she was past the danger period and she and Mattie had taken every possible care and precaution. No one yet knew, especially not the Dowager Viscountess to whom everything else in the world had become secondary to Rose producing an heir for the Fallon family and fortune. Until Rose was successful the Dowager would follow her daughter-in-law about – especially when Harry was at sea as he was now – joining her dinner parties and her theatre visits uninvited, keeping up her monologues, sometimes boring Rose's new young friends to the point of stupefaction. The Dowager Viscountess was of course guarding her son's wife, keeping her beady eye on her daughter-in-law. When Rose lost her first two babies ('They were not formed babies,' Mattie said firmly, 'you saw it, it was blood, it happens to lots of women'), the Dowager Viscountess blamed her gay life.

This time Rose would not lose her baby. She was even confident enough to write the news in her journal. She was ecstatic. Now she would begin filling empty rooms with many voices the way she had always planned; she saw the children of Harry and Rose running through the rooms of the big house in Wimpole Street. But she knew she could not keep her beautiful secret much longer. Tonight, at the theatre (having miraculously escaped the old lady's clutches), she would announce her news to her friends; tomorrow she would visit her beloved papa, who would be happy in this, she knew, and only then would she inform the Dowager Viscountess. When Harry returned from his adventures with Lord Nelson in the Mediterranean, he would be a father.

She alighted at Drury Lane, hurried into the foyer. She was about to go into the box that Harry kept all year round, to meet her friends, when she suddenly felt sick: for a moment she sat on a chair just outside the red curtains; attendants proffered water. 'Thank you,' she said. 'I am well now, thank you.' She breathed in and out deeply. And heard tinkling laughter from the other side of the red curtains. Somewhere violins were tuning.

'Harry?' A clear, loud voice, one she knew.

'Ssssssh!'

'Well, you little temptress – I thought he was courting Lucinda!'

'Harry, as you very well know from experience, can court more than one!' The laughter again. 'I received a note from the ship vowing eternal devotion and urging me to remember him in Lovers' Lane in Vauxhall Gardens should I happen to be passing!'

'Have you joined the HH?'

'What is the HH?'

There was some whispering and then shrieks of laughter.

'In a *balloon*!'

'My dear, there is something exhilarating—'

'—if surely a little *cold*?'

'—about the wind on one's bare skin up in the sky!' The laughter again. 'But do not tell Rose!'

'Harry says Rose would never think of such a thing! Rose loves Harry!'

'Oh – love! One must never love a Man About Town – one must just enjoy oneself!' The voice lowered. 'And Harry Fallon knows how to assist one to do that!' Peals of laughter.

'Ssssssssssh!' The laughter, containing itself. The red curtains. The piercing, discordant violins.

Rose was shocked beyond words. Harry was indeed correct: nothing in the world had been further from her thoughts. She sent word she was ill, and left the theatre, hearing the laughter still.

In the blue drawing room she tried to pick up the pieces of her heart. *Harry? Her friends?* All those giddy young people who drank champagne with her and laughed until they cried and vied with each other to see who could run up the largest bills? Laughing at her ignorance, behind her back? *But Harry loves me.* Card games, house parties, soirées: had she misunderstood everything? She walked up and down the blue room. Who could she speak to? She could not tell her father, of course. She could not write of this to Fanny in one of the polite, inconsequential letters they now exchanged: she saw the lavender-scented Horatio Harbottom leaning over her letter, checking that she was respectable.

She could not bear being watched by Harry's ancestors; she let herself out of the house and walked in the darkness. She did not consider where she was going, walked all the way down towards Brook Street, as if her mother was still alive. There was music drifting out from the Hanover Square Concert Rooms; quickly she went inside. A harpsichord played and she thought of her mama and the drawing room in Brook Street so long ago, and learning to write, and terrible tears ran down her cheeks.

She came out before the end of the concert. Mattie was waiting.

'What are you doing here?' said Rose angrily.

'What are *you* doing here?' said Mattie calmly. 'You came back from the theatre early enough!'

Together they walked slowly back to the house in Wimpole Street.

Ten days later the excruciating pains began. Doctors were called. Admiral Hall sat, silent, in the blue drawing room below. The Dowager Viscountess walked up and down outside in a rage when they finally insisted she leave the pink bedroom. Mattie brought hot water up the stairs over and over. This time it was not blood. It was a small, dead baby with hands and feet. It was a girl. Never in her life had Rose felt such pain as when she saw the tiny, tiny body. They turned her head away, wrapped it up quickly, took it away.

'I fear,' said the doctor, washing his hands, 'that there are unlikely to be any more babies,' but he was a kind man and did not impart this information to the Dowager Viscountess; said it when only Rose and Mattie could hear him.

*

Harry became a hero at last.

Horatio Nelson defeated the French in the glorious Battle of the Nile and Captain Harry Fallon returned home as one of the heroes, full of stories of the sea outside Alexandria set on fire, the whole French fleet burning in the night, thousands of Frenchmen killed. He was awarded honours: he was painted, newly decorated; the painting was hung in the blue drawing room. Ladies stroked his medals.

'Was Egypt beautiful?' asked Rose. 'My father loved Egypt.'

'Egypt was disgusting and vile!' said Harry. 'A pile of old ruins. But we defeated the French!' When he was not wearing them, his medals were placed on a small table underneath himself and his ancestors in the blue drawing room.

Harry found it difficult to talk about dead babies. Their social whirl began again. At the balls and the parties and the country houses Rose looked about her. Now that she knew, it was easy to see: almost all the men had mistresses, one just had to look for the signs. *How could I have been so stupid!* When she visited her father she smiled and smiled, for she wanted him to believe that she was happy.

'But whatever did you expect!' asked one of the young women in surprise, when she realised that Rose knew. 'This is our life. Produce a son and then find yourself a lover! You must just accept it.'

Finally Rose stopped writing in her journal that she had kept since she was eight. She could not have believed it would be so hard; her fingers literally ached to pick up her quill, she wanted to breathe in the smell of ink as she had always done, to sit at the old desk. 'I am writing our life!' she had said so long ago to her mother. She did not want to write her life, not now. She would rather write of nothing than write the pain in her heart. One day she smashed her old magnifying spectacles into pieces against the mahogany desk.

'You are getting dull, *Rosetta mia*!' said Harry, and came to her less.

And then her father, the Admiral, died. Rose wept and kissed his cold, wise forehead in vain. At his very large naval funeral in

Greenwich, blue uniforms everywhere and grave faces, Rose saw Fanny at last, after all the years. They held each other very tightly, without speaking of anything except the Admiral, for the Reverend Horatio Harbottom oversaw their meeting, holding Fanny's arm. (Harry had held Rose kindly when she received the news, and had comforted her, but he was now in the tent with the brandy and the rum and all the blue uniforms.)

'God bless you, dearest coz,' said Fanny. And actually seeing Fanny at last, not relying on their now inconsequential letters to each other, Rose at once recognised something in her cousin's eyes; perhaps Fanny did the same. They said nothing more to each other, and old naval gentlemen came to Rose, took her hand. Horatio Nelson wished to meet her. But when the cousins parted, each going with her chosen husband, they looked back for a moment, and understood.

Rose had only one ambition now: *I must have a child, there must be someone who belongs to me.* She blocked her ears to the doctor's words.

Harry went to sea.

Rose stayed at home. She was now twenty years old and she was not pregnant.

1801

The intricacies of the human heart are as various, as innumerable, and its feelings, upon all interesting occasions, are so minute and complex as to baffle the power of language.

FANNY BURNEY
(unpublished preface to *Cecilia*, 1782)

FOUR

All the clocks struck midnight, the chiming and the stroke of small bells starting at their own convenience. The last chime of all was from the old clock from Genoa.

Although it was summer, Rose Fallon shivered in the long blue drawing room in Wimpole Street and drew on a small cigar and watched the smoke. In her hand she held a letter.

She walked slowly from one end of the room to the other, past the Fallon family portraits and the sofas and the small tables.

She stared at herself in one of the big mirrors lit with candles at either side: saw a pale, flickering woman standing there, staring back. A draught came from somewhere, the candle flames danced and the cigar smoke drifted upwards; the woman in the mirror became more cloudy, indistinct, as though she might altogether disappear, and Rose looked away, closed her eyes, so strong was the feeling of fog and mist and desolation inside her own head.

She and her father sat together in his study in Brook Street; she could see the vellum paper, the seal on his desk, the clock from Genoa that Rose believed chimed in Italian, the model of a ship made by his sailors, his blue jacket, and his short white wig that often, in impatience, he took off and hooked on to the side of his chair. And she could smell it all: the precious books, the maps, the desk, his quills, the inkstand with the black ink, and wreathed around it all the smoke of her father's exotic cigars, tobacco brought home from the sea. And she had fallen in love with the writing and the books. And then she had fallen in love with Harry Fallon instead.

Rose opened her eyes and the smell of cigar smoke was still there, but it was her own cigar. Slowly she read the letter again, the letter from the Admiralty regarding the Battle of Aboukir. The letter made her a twenty-two-year-old childless widow. *The Battle of Aboukir.* The empty words went round and round her brain.

In a corner of the room a threadbare old cushion lay, called Angel.

FIVE

At the Battle of Aboukir the British were the victors, at last, over the French, in Egypt.

Two years earlier, at the Battle of the Nile, with the huge loss of French life and almost the whole of the French fleet burning outside Alexandria, all the newspapers had accounted Nelson a hero and Captain Harold Fallon, Viscount Gawkroger, had received his victory medals. Rumours had abounded that Napoleon and his remaining army had been hacked to death by Arabs and hopefully eaten by them. But the truth had later emerged somewhat differently: Napoleon had not been defeated. His fleet had indeed been destroyed by Nelson outside Alexandria, but Napoleon Buonaparte and his army had already arrived in, and taken, Cairo. Nelson may have won the Battle of the Nile, but the truth was, the French had stayed in Egypt.

However *this* time the British were ousting the French from Egypt for good. THE GLORIOUS VICTORY OF THE BATTLE OF ABOUKIR shouted the British newspapers. At last the French had been Truly Defeated. But the elusive Napoleon Buonaparte, already back in France, was *still* alive and had proclaimed himself First

Consul. And Lord Abercrombie, the British Commander of the Battle of Aboukir, had himself been killed.

And when Rose Fallon, Viscountess Gawkroger, received the letter of regret from the Admiralty advising her that her husband had also lost his life, it was not stated that Captain Harold Fallon, Viscount Gawkroger, had actually been stabbed in a street in Alexandria by an Arab outraged at the behaviour of the British troops there towards Arab women.

That day in Alexandria, the day of the killing of Harry Fallon, the women – their faces and bodies completely covered – turned away, seemed not to be involved, seemed not to notice. Except that their eyes watched everything carefully from behind their veils, watched the English sailors, whose boots clanked on the broken stones as they passed by towards the harbour with the body of the Englishman, that day. The sailors tried to go down the back streets with the body; found their way barred by angry Arabs with shining eyes and swords. The tension in the air was palpable; anything could have happened. Those hot, sweating sailors, the victors, who had been expecting some days ashore sampling the sweets of the desolate, melancholy port of Alexandria after the battle, were angry also: one of their captains had been killed by a native and they had been given orders to collect the body and leave the streets at once, without any delights at all.

Carrying the body the sailors marched stonily back again to their ships. To be stuck in this dump, without any pleasure, even though they had won. 'Look at those tarts in their nosebags,' they said, as they passed the veiled women.

Months later the infelicitous alien heavens opened, as they sometimes did in Alexandria. It had rained continuously since morning. The narrow alleys were now rivers of slush and mud as huge wild drops of rain smashed down from the foreign grey sky. But the red-coated soldiers with six or seven carts that they were pulling themselves, making their way through the mud and the broken stones lying everywhere, did not complain (any more than usual) even in the rain. They hated Egypt fervently; they had never hated a place so much, had been stuck there for months after the glorious victory at the Battle of Aboukir. Now, however, they were leaving this God-forsaken place: they were to sail home at last! As dusk fell they had been ordered, finally, to collect the spoils of war and were hoping to find something for themselves after miserable months in an alien land. Gold, they had heard, and curious stone statues.

The strange, surly houses seemed to lean towards them malignly from either side of the alleys, darkening the already darkening sky still further. The soldiers marched on stolidly: just the calls of the corporal and the drumming of the rain and the sound of their boots, and the wheels of the carts squeaking and rumbling through mud and stones. Then somewhere a harsh voice called to prayer . . . *Allahu Akbar* . . . *Allahu Akbar* . . . the cry that had become so familiar echoed all around them. The soldiers marched doggedly on, heads down, ears deliberately blocked to the strange, unsettling sound.

Everywhere dark windows were shuttered by something that looked like iron lace. It was not possible to know if inhabitants of the city were there in the houses or not. The soldiers felt uneasy, watched; still the call was heard... *Allahu Akbar* . . . *Allahu Akbar*. But at last, down towards the harbour they saw the large warehouse they had been sent to: flare lamps were already burning outside; inside voices were violently raised.

'*Cette antiquité, c'est à moi!*' shouted the French general for the tenth time. He was trying to put his arms around a large object wrapped in matting. '*C'est à moi, absolument. Je l'avais trouvée, moi!* I found it. It belongs to me, it is mine *absolument.*'

'I am sorry, sir, we have our orders. This object, like the others on the list – but this object particularly – is to be handed over to the British as agreed by the capitulation.'

'*Cochon,*' spat the French general. '*Cochon!*' The British captain and the British official accompanying him were deeply shocked. They would report this, certainly. This was not how an officer and a gentleman behaved. The Treaty of Reparation had been signed, all was agreed.

'Thieves! *Ecoutez-moi!* Thieves!' cried the general. And suddenly he and some of his officers, despite the murmured admonitions of the French scholars standing with them, started tearing at the matting that was so carefully wrapped around their treasure, and after the matting – while the British looked on in incomprehension – soft lengths of bright Egyptian cloth. With an angry energetic shove the agitated Frenchmen had pushed the upright stone violently on to the stone floor: the crash echoed eerily around the warehouse, and as it fell shards of stone flew upwards.

'Now look here, look here,' said the British official angrily, 'this is quite uncalled for. You will damage this valuable antiquity more than it is damaged already.'

'*Bon!*' said the French general. 'It is falling into the hands of the most ignorant race in the world: *nation boutiquiers,* the nation of shopkeepers! Of what use is it to them? Have you lived here, as we have? Studying the antiquities for years, as we have? *Non! Bon,* so let it break then. It is to be taken by savages!'

The hand of the British captain shook upon his sword as he tried to control himself at such insults.

The huge stone lay silent, face down, its secrets intact. It was indeed damaged but mostly before this evening: there were pieces off several of the sides and a huge lump broken from the top corner.

At this point the British soldiers, covered in mud now, arrived at the door, as ordered. Twenty or so of them marched into the warehouse and obeying some terse orders from the captain they heaved and lifted the large damaged stone, carrying it out to one of their carts in the rain. It could now be seen that the stone was covered in strange markings and there were small patches of black ink on some of the lettering, as if someone had been trying to make a copy of it. The French general seemed as if he would weep; the rest of the Frenchmen looked grim. Other British soldiers loaded other antiquities: suddenly a mummy case slipped to the floor and fragmented. A shroud – for a spilt second they saw it was a shroud – fell to dust in front of their eyes; only a part of a skull remained intact, fell towards one corner of the warehouse, bounced slightly, came to rest. For a moment everyone was silent. They were all men of war: they had seen hundreds of dead bodies. But here it was, as was promised: *dust to dust.*

At last, but more sullenly, the British soldiers went back to their work, filling their carts with other items named by their captain.

The French general and his officers began complaining again; one of the French scholars unwillingly identified antiquities; another, a tall man whose whole face was filled with regret at what was happening, grudgingly and yet carefully, almost despite himself, draped some of the Egyptian cloth back over the biggest stone of all as it lay on a cart in the rain, for protection. *'Vous faites l'idiot, Pierre!'* called one of the Frenchmen mockingly, and the tall man shook his head at his own foolishness: the stone had withstood the elements for two thousand years; of what use was a piece of Egyptian cloth now?

French calls and curses followed the carts and the soldiers as they carried the antiquities off into the darkness and through the mud. The fiercest, angriest curses were for the loss by the French of the greatest treasure of all: the broken stone that would unlock the secret of the world.

SIX

It was a small dinner.

The Duke of Hawksfield, adviser to His Majesty King George III, was visiting his family in Berkeley Square to hear at first hand from his nephew of the defeat of the French in Egypt.

The Duke and Duchess of Torrence, long-established members of the best London society, entertained rarely in their magnificent establishment in Berkeley Square since the Duchess, once a forceful and very powerful hostess in London, had become – as they described it around other dining tables – *less herself*. Or, in the privacy of bedrooms, by some who in the past had visited hers, *mad as an Albanian*.

But tonight, in honour of the Duke of Hawksfield, illustrious brother of the Duchess, the whole Torrence family was present: the Duke and Duchess; their son William, Marquess of Allswater; their daughters Ladies Charlotte and Amelia and Emma, who held among them various confusing titles through marriage; and the youngest daughter, Lady Dorothea (known to all as Dolly). They sat with perhaps merely thirty other guests at a small dinner: soup; *le turbot à l'anglaise avec la sauce anguille*; *le sauté de faisons aux truffes*; several turtles had been obtained, as well as veal, tongue, goose, and, of course, English roast beef and large assorted joints of pork. This repast was followed by fruit pies and plum pudding. Footmen in wigs that were much more elaborate than anything supported by the ladies and gentlemen hurried about the huge table where everything was laid out: passing dishes, pouring wine. During dinner there were long gaps in conversational intercourse while food was, extremely noisily, consumed. But there had been much wine, and round about the entry of the fruit pies some loud dialogue began: a conversation about the life of the young Princess Charlotte, whose parents, the Prince and Princess of Wales, lived (everyone knew) in separate establishments; the poor little, dear little princess lived in an establishment of her own. At one stage Dolly's pet peacock found its way into the dining room, and her sisters screamed and the tall feathers (very possibly peacock feathers) that they wore in their hair shook and waved to Dolly's peacock and Dolly dragged the bird away by its little collar, talking to it severely. There were some (very discreet) looks around the table about the young Lady Dorothea. But now, with the serious business of eating over and the large table partly cleared by servants, wine bottles were passed around once more and everyone's attention, including that of the ladies, who had not withdrawn, was properly directed upon the Duke of Hawksfield's nephew William, Marquess of Allswater, recently returned from the Mediterranean and the final routing of the French in Egypt at the glorious Battle of Aboukir.

William would not, of course, speak of death and battles with the widow, Rose Fallon, present. So while the ladies were still at table he began recounting marvellous adventures with Turkomen; then he spoke of antiquities and treasures and jewels and a particular valuable broken stone – all recovered from the defeated French. He had the attention of everyone; the candle-light shone in their eyes, threw shadows, caught the plump white arms of his wife, Ann, caught the highly polished wood of the table and the warm red colour of the wine, and the powdered hair of the older women, and the Duke of Hawksfield's medallions, and the sisters' jewellery and feathers, and the two guests who were dressed in black. Fourteen-year-old Dolly

Torrence, her peacock safely ensconced in the kitchen with the servants, saw that her father the Duke, a shrunken, crumbling man, looked somehow elsewhere and stared into his glass as he listened, or did not listen, to his son. But the Duke of Hawksfield stared only at his nephew, listening intently. And darling William was so handsome in his blue uniform, his gold stripes showing he was a captain now, his fair hair tied behind. *We are somehow like a painting*, thought Dolly, who had artistic leanings. She looked around the table wondering what painting she was reminded of. Some people listened to William without looking at him, some leaned forward, totally intent, staring at her brother. The old, barking gentlemen were quiet, had stopped snuffling and coughing and clearing their throats and blowing their noses the way old gentlemen did. The Duchess, once one of London Society's beauties, wore a white cap with a few curls attached to hide her baldness. She now did not know her brother, but she smiled.

Dolly, watching, suddenly realised which painting she was thinking of: *An Experiment with an Airpump*, which she had visited in a picture gallery. Several people present could have told Dolly that the painting was actually nothing at all like this dinner table, but it was the *light* that made her connect it, the way the shadows fell across the faces as William spoke. Dolly's art education, like all her education, was, to say the least, sparse.

There were still confections of various kinds about the table but people were replete and had mostly forgotten to go on eating, so great now was the concentration in the room (though Dolly reached for several small sweetmeats without taking her eyes off her beloved brother). William stretched back at last in his chair, a glass in his hand, and Dolly smiled at him. How glad, and how lucky, they were, to have him safely back. Poor George Fallon, Viscount Gawkroger himself now, of course, had lost his older brother in the Battle of Aboukir. Poor Rose Fallon, dressed in black, who sat so very still, was a widow now. To Dolly, watching Rose obliquely, Rose had a certain look about her, the look of a Heroine (but then, as her family often remarked, Dolly was somewhat too *romantique* for her own good).

'Soon,' continued William, 'all these antiquities, including this very important broken stone I have mentioned – everything that we recovered from the French – will be where they belong: in Great Britain, yet another proof of our triumph over Napoleon.' The old gentlemen coughed and barked in agreement at this proper turn of events. 'And now a treaty with Napoleon is being negotiated as we speak. I believe peace between our countries will soon be declared – and we are the victors!' and William held out his glass for more wine. 'Although of course, sir,' he added hurriedly, addressing his uncle, 'you would know more of such matters than myself.'

The Duke of Hawksfield, advisor to the King, nodded noncommittally. He did not discuss affairs of state at dinner tables.

The candlelight again caught the bare arms of William's wife Ann, and the diamonds at her neck sparkled and danced as she leaned towards the wine also, held out her glass to be filled again; a footman came forward quickly, although not all ladies drank wine at the dining table. But probably not all of them had toothache.

'And the jewels?' she asked her husband, feeling her throbbing teeth with her tongue.

'Our generals finally allowed the French to keep some of their less interesting finds – but we of course have rescued the most important, and jewels I saw myself.'

'Where is all this treasure now?' All the ladies leaned forward further.

'Making its way on a barge through the Bay of Biscay, I do hope,' said William. 'We left them completing arrangements in Alexandria for the big stone to be transported with the other antiquities.'

'How big is it, this *pièce de résistance*?' Ann regarded her husband, drank more wine quickly.

He shrugged. 'Maybe a yard tall, two foot in width, a foot deep. It is blackish in colour, basalt perhaps.'

'Heavens, how huge!' Dolly saw that with her slightly mocking voice and her slightly mocking smile Ann was perhaps trying to tease dear William, or perhaps entertain him. It wasn't – was it? – an unspeakable thought suddenly flew into Dolly's head – the new Viscount Gawkroger she was trying to entertain? Ann often seemed to smile at the new Viscount. She saw that William looked back at his wife, an unreadable expression on his face. (But then Dolly consumed with delight all the new 'ladies' novels', saw drama everywhere, and hoped for drama in her own life – as long, of course, as she herself turned out to be the heroine and there was a glorious ending.)

The guest of honour at dinner, Dolly's uncle, the Duke of Hawksfield, cleared his throat. 'If I understand things, William my boy,' and the powdered hair of the older guests and the sleek hair of the younger guests turned at once in the Duke's direction, for he was one of the most powerful men, it was said, in England, 'the value of this particular Egyptian stone above all others is that there are three languages upon it, including Greek, which was the language of administration in Egypt after Alexander the Great. Is that correct?'

'Yes, sir,' said William.

'Ancient Greek as we understand it?'

'Yes, sir.'

Dolly saw that Rose Fallon suddenly leaned forward; the folds of her black mourning dress, rustling slightly, touched the table. 'What do the Greek words say?' Rose asked in a low, almost harsh voice. 'Why is it important?' It was the first thing, apart from social pleasantries, that she had said all evening, and Dolly saw that her eyes glittered slightly in the candlelight, and the light caught the tiny frown mark that seemed always to be there, on her brow, like a little question mark. To Dolly, the tiny frown mark was beautiful; it made Rose look as if she had thought about everything in the world, and understood.

William turned to Rose politely. 'Among other things, ma'am – and this is of course the point – I believe the Greek words say that the text on the stone was to be repeated three times: in sacred Egyptian writing, in native Egyptian writing and in Greek. This is common knowledge now – the French had actually made a copy of the stone; they inked it and copied it before we were able to liberate it. So that information at least has always been available in French. And, as I understand it, the sacred language of the Egyptians was, of course . . .' and he could not help pausing for effect, *'the hieroglyphs.'*

There was a gasp in the room: *the ancient hieroglyphs?*

'Hieroglyphs – the writing of God's words,' said Rose wonderingly, and William bowed in agreement and the Duke of Hawksfield looked at Rose speculatively.

'With a large part of the Greek words intact,' William continued, 'it will surely be simple for our scholars to translate them. And the hieroglyphs will say the same as the Greek! That of course is why His Majesty wanted us to be sure of capturing that particular antiquity above all others. Once our scholars translate the hieroglyphs it is possible that we will be able to look again at Egyptian antiquities and then we will understand,' he tried to shrug off the portent in his words, 'everything.'

George Fallon, the new Viscount Gawkroger, put his own glass down on the table. *'Everything?* What an extraordinary thing to say.'

William suddenly leaned forward again. Up to now he had contained himself as he recounted the story; he was able to do so no longer, and his excitement transferred itself to everybody in the room, except to the hostess, who smiled vaguely. William repeated Rose's phrase as he turned again to his uncle. 'You know what they say, sir, about the mysterious hieroglyphs that we have never been able to understand. "The writing of God's words!" It is believed by many scholars all over the world that the Ancient Egyptians *knew the secrets of the universe!'*

'You think we shall find them?' The Duke of Hawksfield betrayed no emotion; perhaps he thought that there were no secrets in the world that he did not already know.

'We will be able to translate any hieroglyph we find and Egypt is sinking under the weight of such examples! It is said that *all knowledge* is hidden in the magic of the hieroglyphs, in the symbolism of the signs. If we can wade through the stinking rubbish of the country,' his face wrinkled in distaste, 'and pick out the best examples, we may perhaps be about to discover . . .' William searched for a word big enough, 'infinities!'

'Perhaps,' said the Duke of Hawksfield drily. He looked unimpressed. 'Still. I would be interested to see the Greek translation alongside the other inscriptions.'

And Rose Fallon could not stop herself. 'Oh, Your Grace, so should I!' and a look passed among the men, Rose saw at once, of indulgent disbelief – none of them however voicing anything impolite to Rose, so becoming in black.

George Fallon had been listening to everything carefully. Now he said, 'Tell me, William, could one find antiquities for oneself, should one perchance find oneself on the banks of the Nile?'

William laughed. 'They are everywhere, George, absolutely everywhere. Egypt is a mass of ruins, nothing more. Stones from old monuments and temples lie around the harbours, in the deserts, along the Nile – and statues are there for the taking, gods and goddesses and eagles and what-have-you. Alexandria is nothing but a city of smashed antiquities! Carved obelisks lie there in the rubble, if you can believe it,' and Dolly saw that now the new Viscount's eyes suddenly glittered in the candlelight.

The Viscount saw Dolly watching him, and raised his glass slightly to acknowledge her. Dolly looked away at once, busied herself helping her mother, who had dropped a great deal of cheese on to the floor; she was not certain what she felt about the Viscount Gawkroger, but she thought she did not much like his smile. The Duke of Hawksfield watched carefully.

Again Ann's voice was mocking; her teeth now throbbed excessively. 'Were the Egyptians not just a *little* sorry to see this stone leave their country, considering it contains the secrets of the universe?'

'My dear,' William answered his wife crisply, 'the modern Egyptians do not understand hieroglyphs or care about them. The modern Egyptians are ignorant and uneducated and lazy, and to them – Mohammetmen now – their pagan past is apparently something to be ashamed of. I tell you again, you would have to see Egypt to believe it: smashed stones everywhere; peasants have even set up house in ancient tombs! Ugh!' He gave a sound of disgust. 'They do not care. This very treasured stone I told you of was itself found by the French in an old army fort. Imagine! A treasure such as this and it was being used to strengthen a wall! But the British will solve the enigma of the hieroglyphs and the Egyptians may even be grateful.'

'Of course, of course they will be grateful!' called the old men, thinking of England, and their short white wigs nodded in agreement, the Egyptians were natives and would be grateful indeed, and the wine bottles went up and down the table and the old men barked loudly and spat into spittoons.

'Are you not interested in the antiquities of your own country, George?' asked one of the sisters.

George looked very surprised. 'Not in the least,' he said. 'There are no ancient secrets for sale here.' The Duke of Hawksfield looked at George, his face quite devoid of expression.

'William,' said Dolly almost severely to her older brother, 'have you *touched* the stone with the secrets? Have you actually touched it?' The others laughed. 'No, no, what I meant to say was, if it was me I should have wanted to actually touch the lettering that is so old and so magical and so full of secrets. To be,' she struggled to find the right words, 'part of history.'

'We *are* part of history,' said William. 'We not only touched it, we wrote upon it!'

'Whatever do you mean by that?' said Rose Fallon, shocked.

'"CAPTURED IN EGYPT BY THE BRITISH ARMY IN 1801." One day, as I say, that stone will stand in its rightful place in the British Museum and you will see on its side a new inscription telling of our triumph!'

'I should like to have an Egyptian obelisk when I build our Gawkroger Hall in the country,' announced Viscount Gawkroger, particularly addressing the Duke of Hawksfield. 'That would be very fine.'

'Where should you place it, sir?' asked a young lady who was paying a little more attention to George Fallon now that he had a title; not that he would do, unless one was desperate.

'I think I should place it in my fine gardens, on a plinth, facing the house. It would be a charming addition to the trees that I shall plant, do you not agree, Dolly?'

William saw that his young sister was unsure whether she was being teased, came to her rescue. 'We brought back some pretty trees, Dolly,' he said to her. 'Mimosa.'

'What is mimosa?'

'A tree with little yellow flowers.' William turned to include his uncle. 'I should like to try and grow them in this country, sir, sweet-smelling, beautiful. And something else. A frankincense tree.' There was a bemused silence round the table.

'Frankincense like in the Bible?' said Dolly, awed.

The Duke of Hawksfield said, 'Yes. I have heard of this. We shall plant them both in the castle grounds and see if they thrive in the climate of this country.'

'What *is* frankincense?' asked Rose, and the Duke turned to her.

'It is a gum that is extracted from this tree of which William speaks. The Ancient Egyptians believed that its healthful properties were extracted by burning it. We shall grow the tree, and see if it is so.' And he smiled at Rose, a powerful old man's wintry smile, a man who could plant forests if he so chose, and Ann's heart contracted, even as her teeth ached.

'William, what do they call it, the special stone?' she asked her husband quickly.

'I understand it was found in a small town between Alexandria and Cairo called – by the natives, or the French, or someone – Rosette. And so they, and we after them, named it from the town – *la pierre de Rosette* I believe the French called it. And it has come by us to be called the Rosetta Stone.'

'*Rosetta?*' Rose Fallon spoke quietly, yet everyone heard her, so astonished, so intense, was her question.

And George laughed. 'Ah, Rose,' he said. 'You shall have fame beyond your wildest dreams!' And then he turned to the others. 'I believe my sister-in-law was herself christened Rosetta.'

Dolly's voice rose in excitement. 'Is that true?' she said.

And Rose smiled at her. 'Yes,' she said. 'My name is Rosetta.'

'You were named after the Princess Rosetta in the fairy tale!' cried Dolly. 'The one who married the King of the Peacocks! Oh how proud I would be if such a stone had been called the Dolly Stone! That there should be a connection to me!' and she actually stood up, she was so overcome (and people saw that the poor girl was extremely tall, taller even than her brother, though she was only fourteen years old). Ann, Marchioness of Allswater (putative Duchess of Torrence), finding Dolly extremely irritating and her own toothache almost unendurable, stood also, knowing her mother-in-law was no longer capable of these things, to indicate that the ladies might perhaps like to follow her into the drawing room. Dolly pulled herself together and helped her mother up, who smiled even more brightly than before. Crumbled cheese fell upon the floor.

'Perhaps we shall be able to go again to the continent,' said Ann over her smooth white shoulder to William and to the men in general, as the ladies were leaving. 'If you will assure us we have defeated France, and that the world is to be safe again, and that we will soon know the secrets of the universe.'

It was the new Viscount Gawkroger who answered her. 'The world, my dear Ann, never mind the secrets of the universe, will never be safe until that madman Napoleon Buonaparte is dead. He is a threat to the civilised world. It is our duty as a nation to destroy him. However, it seems there is to be a truce for the moment. And my mother would like to travel again, and I am sure that, by the spring, my sister-in-law Rose will be living with us once more as is proper,' and he bowed, smiling, to Rose as she turned back sharply, 'and will accompany my mother and myself to Paris.' And George continued to Ann: 'I am sure William will be happy for you to join the party if he is not here to take you himself,' and despite her aching teeth the Marchioness smiled brightly, like her bright diamonds, and the Duke of Hawksfield observed everything.

The voice of Dolly's father, the old Duke of Torrence, who had hardly spoken, echoed out now to the ladies in the drawing room before the doors were closed. How pleased he was that peace was to be concluded and that French wine and French sausage and particular French books and little French milliners would again be available; and the gentlemen sighed in relief at the women's departure and the footmen at once scurried to the cupboards at the bottom of the large sideboard and produced the chamber pots.

'I may go to Egypt.' George Fallon, Viscount Gawkroger, took a large amount of snuff in his corner of the carriage and his several sneezes drifted out into the cold night.

'Whatever for? It is a disgusting place I do assure you, despite the antiquities. Your brother was killed there by savages!'

George brooded in his corner, offered nothing about his brother. 'I am sick of Swiss mountains and Italian lakes,' he said. And then he touched the side of his nose in a knowing manner. 'I see wider horizons, William! There is a great deal of money to be made, I believe, in antiquities – you know very well I have brought many treasures into this country: from Greece, from Italy and – after the anarchy – from France. Treasures were going for a song when the rich in France were desperate only for their lives.'

'And having obtained them for a song, I remember you sold them at very high prices in England!' William, Marquess of Allswater, laughed. 'Well, George, antiquities are lying there in Egypt waiting for you.'

'It could be my contribution to our country! Now that could very well interest the Prince of Wales—'

'You mean you would *give* these treasures to the nation,' interrupted William mockingly.

'Of course not. But by bringing such age-old antiquities to Britain from a place like Egypt,' said George grandly, 'I could improve the taste of the nation!'

William laughed again. 'The natives spit on them as pagan monstrosities, and use them as piss-pots!'

'Hurry up and beget an heir, William,' said George softly in the darkness of the coach, 'for you might think to come with me,' and William was silent.

The dinner was over, carriages had been called and the guests had gone on to further entertainments; the Viscount and the Marquess had left the house in Berkeley Square and were on their way, they said, to the theatre, though it was of course to a gaming house (and possibly elsewhere) in the inclement December weather. The men might have walked, their destination was not far, but apart from the weather London was far from safe as ruffians and wounded soldiers prowled the unlit streets.

George suddenly changed the subject abruptly. 'It is high time Rose moved back to Great Smith Street with my mother and myself. She is, in my opinion, behaving in a ridiculous and unsuitable manner clinging to Wimpole Street as if poor Harry might return. She has given us nothing: no heir to the Fallon family, nothing. She is in our power, of course, and should be dependent on our charity.' He sniffed again at his small gold box. 'If I had ever been in favour of money being settled upon women I would not be in favour now. Her father made a special marriage settlement upon her, and so she has a degree of independence even though my brother is dead, a most unsuitable thing in a woman.' He stared out at lights coming from the big houses in St James's Square. 'She is damaging his reputation,' he added, and was angered by the quizzical look he saw on William's face from the flare of another carriage passing. His own face became red in the darkness. 'You know very well what I am really saying: *her* behaviour must be beyond reproach, so that *his* is not brought into question. Harry's death must be allowed to die down quietly, that is the best we can hope for.' He sighed heavily, tried to loosen the cravat at his neck. Mention of his brother and his brother's death still caused tumultuous emotions inside him. 'It is all very well for you, you know: you are *there*, you are *safe*, part of the *beau monde*; the Duke of Hawksfield is your mother's brother. But we, as yet, are only on the peripheries. Everything must be watched so carefully – you know very well the King and Queen will receive no one with the hint of a scandal touching them.'

William said softly, 'The sooner you are elevated the better, George. There are no rules for us as long as we keep up outward appearances.'

'I know,' said George moodily. 'How *well* I know it!' He regarded the night. 'Rose is a fool. All this pretence of interest in Greek and hieroglyphs! I want her in Great Smith Street as company for my mother and then – well, you know the rest. The Duke of Hawksfield is not stupid, he knows I am a solution to many problems.' Shadows and light reflected across the dark carriage as the horses ran southwards. Suddenly the driver got into competition with another vehicle, they raced wildly towards Piccadilly neck and neck; two crashed coaches just ahead slowed them again. The winter's first flakes of snow drifted downwards, settled on the sleek black coats of the horses.

'I must say I find your sister-in-law a most attractive woman,' said William. 'But it is not surprising perhaps that she is troubled still, becoming a widow at her age!'

George stared out of the window and sneezed again. 'It is snowing,' he said, as if he had not heard William's words. Then suddenly he added, 'How would one know now, with Rose, what she thinks? She is not the innocent young girl we agreed for

Harry's sake to take into the family. She has changed a great deal. She is as still as a snake!'

William was surprised at the venom in the Viscount's voice, and laughed. 'I say, George—' but George leaned forward and ruffled his friend's hair and laughed also.

'Never mind, my dear,' he said.

Home, alone, in Wimpole Street, Rose Fallon gave a huge sigh of relief. She forbade Mattie to wait up for her; she had told the last footman to go to bed, sat now beside the roaring fire, her feet out of her winter boots at last and up on the sofa in the long blue room. She heard the crackle of the fire and occasionally the chiming, out of time, of the clocks in the quiet house. On the table beside her lay the old book that had belonged to her father: she had sought it out as soon as she had come in the door. Now Rose lit a small hand-rolled cigar, lay back on the sofa.

Her brother-in-law had insisted upon her attending dinner with the Torrence family, saying it was high time she began fulfilling her social obligations and this was a very important family connection. She was making an effort to go about; she had agreed – not knowing that the hostess, the Duchess, had somehow left this world, in her mind at least. Rose had met the Torrence family several times, at Berkeley Square, or occasionally some of them had drifted through George's soirées at Wimpole Street: the raddled Duke with his propensity for spending the family fortune on his mistresses and gambling (apparently sometimes he gambled his mistresses); the giggling married daughters – although the older one had a certain languor that Rose now recognised: she was somebody's mistress. But the one who had always held a kind of unpleasant fascination for her (who was never seen at George's soirées, of course) was the old Duke of Hawksfield, and she had been impressed tonight by the way he seemed suddenly to plan to observe if frankincense had medical properties, and to plant fields of mimosa trees. She supposed it was his power that fascinated her: his closeness to King George, his slightly repellent but dominant aura. He was the authority in that family. Everybody became silent when he cleared his throat, and she had seen, tonight, that he watched her. But she was safe, she was not part of his family, *that is a man I would not like to cross.*

William looked like a much younger version of his uncle, but there was something softer about him, less imposing, though he was certainly most handsome. Rose liked the way he seemed protective of his strange youngest sister. She had only, before tonight, observed Dolly as a child flitting about in the background – how very odd she had become. And how very tall she was, and ungainly. *Like a flamingo*, Rose thought suddenly. Cigar smoke drifted. *The Rosetta Stone . . .* how she wished her father was alive to hear this extraordinary news of the town where the old man had sung by the mortar and pestle. Perhaps they would have gone back to Rosetta after all. *If dreams come true*, he had said, and she suddenly wondered if he had meant his own dreams and felt an odd shivery feeling on her neck as if a ghost walked. And then it was gone. She looked down at her father's book about hieroglyphs that she had once known so well.

She had not thought about words, about the act of writing, about the hieroglyphs, for years. She had almost forgotten that she had once loved words more than anything in the world. She remembered again walking with her mother as a child: reading the notices that would hang sometimes at the church in Hanover Square, or the big signs in shop windows in Bond Street, or book titles in bookshops which she painfully spelt out, like ENCYC-LOPAEDIA BRITANNICA. *Why do people take the miracle of writing so for granted? What makes our brains work?* She suddenly thought again of the Duchess of Torrence at the table tonight, crumbling cheese and smiling so tightly and brightly, that hostess's smile, at nothing. Rose Fallon shivered again. What a terrible fate: to sit at your own dinner table seemingly mad, and smiling.

Quickly now she sat up, and placing her cigar in a special jar she kept for the purpose she took up her father's book. There were the painted hieroglyphs: the different birds and beetles, a bee, a lying-down lion – all the beautiful shapes, just like her own star for her mother. She stared and stared as she used to when she was young, as if staring would somehow force the meaning out. Thousands of years ago a Greek scholar had written about them; her father used to read the translated passage to her, and she read it now again, squinting, holding it directly under the candle so that she could see.

> When they would signify *god*, or *height* or *lowness* or *excellence* or *blood* or *victory* they delineate a HAWK. They symbolise by it GOD because the bird is prolific and long-lived, or perhaps rather because it seems to be an image of the sun, being capable of looking more intently towards his rays than any other winged creature . . . and they use it to denote HEIGHT because other birds when they would soar on high move themselves from side to side being incapable of ascending vertically; but the hawk alone soars directly upwards. And they use it as a symbol of LOWNESS because other animals move not in a vertical line, but descend obliquely; the hawk however swoops directly down upon anything beneath it. And they use it to denote EXCELLENCE because it appears to excel all birds – and for BLOOD because they say this animal does not drink water but blood, and for VICTORY because it shows itself capable of overcoming every winged creature; for when pressed by some more powerful bird it directly turns itself in the air upon its back and fights with its claws extended upwards, and its wings below; and its opponent, unable to do the like, is overcome.

But in the end the scholar had not been able to translate the signs after all, and Rose and her father agreed that perhaps he was mistaken, that it would be difficult to have so many meanings for the one symbol – a hawk. Perhaps different races of people *think* differently? They had stared and stared at the bird symbol, fascinated.

And Rose had reminded her parents yet again that she understood hieroglyphs: for to the star denoting her mother and the rose denoting herself she had added a tree denoting her father. 'I understand their thinking,' she had said airily, aged thirteen, 'they write pictures.' Then she became more subtle: because Fanny's father was always laughing, she depicted him with just one simple mark: a smile.

And to think that now, just at the beginning of the new century, the mysterious hieroglyphs were travelling across the sea *at this very moment*: magic markings that would speak to England after thousands of years, and uncover the secrets of antiquity (and the meaning of the hawk), and she and the stone had *the same name*. She saw the Rosetta Stone in her mind: a heroic piece of granite, sailing to England, battling storms.

What would the secrets be? she mused, as she stared just once more at the mysterious signs, at the birds and the shapes and the figures. Would they be secrets of the beginning of the world? Would it be God who would be revealed? (That would be so pleasing to Fanny.) Would she herself be able to believe that her parents still shone somewhere, from secrets learned from the magic signs? Or would there be revealed – and she closed the book at last – secrets of the human heart?

For a moment longer she stayed sitting there as the fire died down, thinking of Harry. Harry Fallon, charming, beautiful, feckless Harry Fallon, had hurt her beyond belief, and when she wept at the news of his death – for she did indeed weep to think her husband had been killed in battle in a strange land – she wept, really, at the knowledge of what damage one human being could do to another.

She was expected, she knew, to give up Wimpole Street very soon. She had such mixed feelings, now, about this house: it contained some of her happiest, and some of her unhappiest, memories. She looked about her in the long blue room: at the businessmen and the noblemen looking down from the walls, at Viscountess Gawkroger with her fingers placed elegantly on the harpsichord, and finally at the portrait of heroic Harry. She looked at the clocks that chimed in disharmony to say that time is not quite as we think of it. She would take the beloved old Italian clock with her, of course. But from George's unwelcome conversation earlier tonight, the next part of the Fallon family plan seemed to be that she move back to Great Smith Street, to be a companion to her mother-in-law.

'Indubitably *not!*' said Rose Fallon aloud, as she picked up the candle-lamp to light her way upstairs to her room. She must be ready with plans of her own when George and the Dowager pounced, as George's comment in the dining room tonight had warned her they would. But her hand trailed on the polished stair rail; she felt as if there was a fog in her brain, preventing her from making real decisions. From her room she looked out at Wimpole Street, saw snow falling.

Still she did not actually go to bed, for that was where the demons waited. Instead she sat in her room at her mother's mahogany table, and for the first time for many months, she very slowly opened it: first into a larger table, then into a card table, and then into the writing desk with the secret compartment. From the secret compartment she gingerly took a particular notebook and stared at it as if she hardly knew it. Very slowly and carefully she made the marks that she had once made so often: *Tonight*, she wrote without any preamble, *I was told of the discovery of an ancient stone that may yield up the secret of the hieroglyphs, in the town of Rosetta where my beloved papa saw coffee being ground and women with hidden faces and where, one day, he and I might have travelled, if dreams came true.* That was all she wrote. Then she put the notebook back into the secret compartment.

After a while she drew a blank sheet of paper towards her.

My dearest Fanny, she wrote.

But they never, now, wrote the secrets of their hearts. For Horatio's presence was always there in the letters, Rose could almost smell the lavender. Hearing of her miscarriages and now the death of her husband, they had advised her, very kindly, to bow to God's will. Sometimes Horatio added a stiff, formal paragraph in his own writing, almost always about their eldest child, a son, who was the most extraordinary human being that had ever been born in the whole history of the world: Rose understood that he would almost certainly be the Archbishop of Canterbury by the time he was ten. Of their second child, a daughter, there was no news (except that Fanny had said she was a cherub), so obviously they were both children sent down straight from heaven to the vicarage at Wentwater. For just a moment Rose saw Fanny and herself again: crossing the Pont Neuf with their families, running ahead, stopping and staring over the parapets at the water of the river Seine, avowing it more *French* than the Thames, running back to report, delighting in the world. That was when they were children; there were other children now and the past was over.

My dearest Fanny, she saw she had written. She knew her dearest Fanny still existed: she had seen her, at last, at her father's funeral. But they had married, and they had lost each other. She put the paper away and undressed.

And then, finally, Rose went to the small cupboard beside her bed. There a bottle of opium waited, to still her dreams.

Lady Dorothea Torrence had locked her peacock in the small room next to her own, after giving it a report of the evening's events. His comment was to shriek in the particular plangent way of peacocks and spread his feathers and peck at the door handle, but she told him he would be cold in the garden and tried to wrap him in a blanket. Small defecations lay all about the room. In the end, cold herself, she left him sulking in a corner. Her sisters and their laughter and their whispering and their clothes and their carriages and their husbands were gone. Now she lay in her bed, her long frame stretched out under all the bedclothes, feeling for the warm stone. The peacock shrieked.

Dolly might have been only fourteen years old, and an uneducated girl, but people would have been surprised by how much she knew. For instance she knew what hieroglyphs were because she had seen pictures of the mystic, untranslatable signs in one of her father's books as she climbed about his library when he was out of town, no doubt cavorting (her mother said) with one of his Jezebels. Dolly had spent many very productive hours in this library. She had read anything that appealed to her. She had found *Pamela* and *Tom Jones* and in particular *Fanny Hill*, which at first she did not understand but from which she now realised she had learned a great deal. She had read lots of books about war in the olden days; about telescopes; she read angry poems by Alexander Pope. She had pored over her father's collection of drawings of nude women doing strange things – to each other sometimes, sometimes to men – having found them behind a false shelf when she was twelve. She studied them often, and nobody knew. Nobody knew the extent of Dolly's knowledge and how familiar she was with *Aristotle's Master-Piece* and *Tableau de l'Amour Conjugal*. And she certainly knew what hieroglyphs were. To think

65

that Rose Fallon was really called Rosetta; how wonderful that was! *If only I could be Rose Fallon instead of myself.* She thought again of the tiny frown on Rose's forehead, and how it was somehow fascinating, as if Rose had pondered the secrets of the world. What *were* the secrets of the world? Might they be discovered from the Rosetta Stone? Could she, Dolly, marry the translator? She felt a tingling in her head as her thoughts spiralled away and she fell asleep.

She dreamed of the stone. In her dream she seemed to float with a black stone which was somehow light and beautiful and shining, and she could read the words easily. The birds and the animals and people of the hieroglyphs spoke to her and the columns yielded up their meanings. In her dream someone else floated, a man wearing a turban of some kind and long, flowing robes. He was, like Dolly, more than ordinarily tall and she moved towards him urgently, in another way altogether.

Ann, Marchioness of Allswater, had watched the carriage go out through the square in the night as the snow began to fall, carrying her husband and his friend. Her husband and *her* friend. George Fallon knew that she needed his help. She stared at the silent, drifting snow. *Make him!* she had whispered to George tonight. *You must make him!* She drank brandy in her room, to dull the pain of the toothache. The pain was in the front of her mouth where everybody could see; she could on no account have teeth removed from *there*, not yet.

As they had been going into dinner, the Duke of Hawksfield, brother to the Duchess of Torrence, had taken her arm for a moment and had said to her quietly, 'Come, my dear. Now that William has been returned to us I urgently want news of an heir. We would be sorry to lose you.' It was said so lightly, but he had smiled so coldly: she knew she had not imagined the threat. The Duke of Torrence, her father-in-law, was a fool, everybody knew that, and the Duchess was mad. But the Duke of Hawksfield, who had much to say about decisions taken in this family, was an extremely powerful man. Was he observing the widow, Rose Fallon, thinking of her as a possible successor to Ann if she failed to produce an heir? And Ann shivered in her room. Despite the fire, her room was cold as it always was in winter, but it was not that. She herself came from a very fine family. All had been pleased at the marriage, including the Duke of Hawksfield. But she knew her position as the next Duchess of Torrence was not safe until she had produced a male child, and until she was pregnant she did not think she should be minus her front teeth.

The brandy dulled the throbbing.

Her maid helped her to remove her jewellery – her own jewellery, family jewellery; she had brought much to the marriage besides herself – and she stared at herself in the mirror. She was pretty, everybody said so. It was not *such* a chore for William, surely, until she was with child. He had come to her less and less since he had been back, yet he too knew the importance of an heir. She looked in the mirror again, turned her head from side to side. Candlelight became her, as it became almost everybody. Then she drifted back to the window: the snow was falling heavily. She had noticed, tonight, the new Viscount Gawkroger smiling at Dolly. And now, her toothache assuaged with the help of the brandy, Ann smiled too, watching the silent snow, how it so softly touched the maple trees in the Square. Viscount Gawkroger would help Ann, the putative Duchess of Torrence. She drank more brandy. And Ann, the putative Duchess of Torrence, would help Viscount Gawkroger. That was their agreement.

SEVEN

On Christmas morning, snow falling all over London, two old gentlemen from the Naval Office in Somerset House – friends and mentors of Rose's late father, men who had watched Rose learning to read long ago in Brook Street, (occasional recipients of childish letters) – called at Wimpole Street. Always, years ago, these two had visited Brook Street on Christmas Day with small gifts for Rose. Rose's mother had given them sugared plum cake and mulled wine; after her death Rose had done the same. Since her marriage Rose had not seen the old gentlemen on Christmas Day; this year they had sent her a message saying they would like to revive the custom if she would allow it. Rose wept when she received their note.

While Mattie was sugaring the cake she said to Rose, casually, 'You know I'm off to see my mum and the mum of Cornelius Brown?'

'Of course,' said Rose. 'Everyone may go today.'

'What will you do?'

'I have for the first time excused myself from Christmas Day at Gawkroger Hall. That is Christmas celebration enough!'

'Well. I won't stay away long. But – I had a message.' Mattie spoke most mysteriously, laying the cake on a plate.

'What was it?'

'Cornelius Brown was seen in Italy; he's a trader now, buys and sells all sorts of things apparently! And he was making plans to go back to Egypt, as soon as the navy left there, he has been living there!'

'Good heavens!'

'Might be just a tale, of course, but it's the first time his mum has heard anything in all these years.'

There was a banging on the door. The old naval gentlemen had brought Rose little gifts, as if she was still seven and not twenty-three. Mattie, smiling to see the gentlemen who she remembered so well, brought in the cake and a jug of mulled wine; the smell of cloves drifted, mixing with the smell of old men's jackets and bodies and old pipes. Snow fell past the long windows; soon they saw a be-hatted Mattie, bundled in shawls, on her way to Ludgate Hill. After many warm words about her father and her mother had been exchanged, the old gentlemen asked with great seriousness if they might give Rose some information about the death of her husband that they thought she should be apprised of.

She looked at them, puzzled.

The two old gentlemen sat in front of the big fire in the long blue room and told Rose that her husband, although given naval honours at his funeral in England – where Rose had stood with the Fallon family, quiet and pale, the widow in black – had actually been killed by an Arab in a brawl over an Egyptian woman. Although Rose turned pale to hear their words, she did not weep or protest.

'I see,' was all she said.

'We thought long about telling you this,' said the old gentlemen. They spoke kindly but not patronisingly. 'Your father would want us to guide you. We know he had' – the old gentlemen cleared their throats, trying to find the right words – 'reservations about the Fallon family. They perhaps do not have the – the moral stature of your own family, and when your father knew he was dying he asked us to keep ourselves informed of your situation.'

'Does the Fallon family have this information?'

The old gentlemen shrugged. 'We assume that they do. They

will have contacts in the navy. Nobody wishes to speak of it, naturally – not just the Fallon family! A great victory had been won at Aboukir, a great general was dead, the capitulation of the French was being negotiated – there were many more important and triumphant things happening there at the time. In the scheme of things an unfortunate incident like that was no more than that – an unfortunate incident that it was hoped would fade away. For that reason – and because you are your father's daughter – we decided that the funeral was to be carried out with all naval dignity. But sailors talk, of course.'

'Of course.'

'The difficulty was that the young woman involved was an Egyptian woman who had been betrothed by her father to some ruling Turkish official, and the shame and anger felt by both the Egyptians and the Turks was very great, just at the moment that our negotiations with them were delicate. In all the circumstances we were anxious there should be no repercussions. She was not' – throats were cleared again – 'one of the girls of the streets, as it were. She was very carefully guarded but she was allowed to walk in the orange groves of her father, it was said, and somehow she was – stolen away. When your husband was killed, the girl, for her own safety, was secretly taken into the house of an English merchant there; she would otherwise certainly have been killed also – it would be a matter of honour. The whole affair has been a great embarrassment.'

'And now?'

'Now most of the British army has left Alexandria – so the traders themselves are in real danger, the whole place is in chaos. We do not know how long we shall even be able to keep a British consul – or any sort of British presence – there. And we have heard rumblings that the Egyptians are demanding that this girl be returned to them, to whom she belongs. It seems, for the sake of peace and avoidance of further – unpleasantness, that that may indeed happen. We do not have much choice, we do not have an army. Poor girl. She will be killed, of course. That is their way.'

'Poor girl,' Rose found herself echoing.

'There is nothing to be done,' they said. 'We will probably not hear the end of this sad story. But your husband's actions have cast long shadows. It is not a story that reflects well on British integrity,' and for just a moment Rose wondered what the scrupulous old naval gentlemen would make of the High Heavens Club.

She was silent for some time, pale. The old men waited, still and serious. The fire spat. At last she spoke, but not of herself. 'The Fallon family is obsessed with elevating itself, and Harry's reputation as a hero is part of that elevation. They would not bother themselves about any of this, unless a further hint of scandal should emerge concerning Harry's death, because of the woman's fate.'

The old gentlemen nodded. 'We understand that. And we do not tell you of the girl, or of her fate, lightly.'

Slowly Rose poured more wine and cut the plum cake, but it lay untouched on all their plates for they thought of an Arab girl in Alexandria. Rose saw they wanted to say something else but were embarrassed. 'I am all right,' she said. 'My husband's – interest in other women was not unknown to me.'

'My dear.' There was again much clearing of throats. 'You may wonder why we have told you all this when it is obviously distressing to you. It is unlikely, as we say, that we shall ever know the end of this affair – we can do nothing more. This is not about that unfortunate girl, but about you. The long and short of it is, dear Rose, that your father *knew*, although you tried to hide it from him, that you were unhappy.' If they noted Rose's intake of breath they did not say. 'And he worried that, at some stage – and here we come to the point of this whole matter – the Fallon family might not treat you as well as their duty prescribes. Your father had a particular aversion to the present Viscount Gawkroger.' There was some shifting about in chairs and more coughing. 'They must treat you, as a widow in their own family, with great care. Especially as you now have no immediate family of your own and your uncle and aunt are in India.'

For another long moment Rose sat in silence but at last she spoke. 'My father has provided for me, as you know,' she said slowly. 'For which I am so eternally grateful. Because of his wisdom I shall be able to look after myself.'

'Nevertheless the Fallon family may have their own ideas about your future. The new Viscount Gawkroger is a ruthless man. It would be to your advantage if the Fallon family were very *clearly* persuaded to treat you with dignity and honour.'

She looked at them in surprise. 'I hope you are misreading the situation. I have lived among this family for some years, I cannot think they would wish me actual physical harm! The worst they have suggested is that I live with them. But I will not agree to that,' she added hurriedly.

'We wished only to empower you should the circumstances arise,' said the old gentlemen doggedly. And then, at last, she realised. They had given her some information with which to fight the Fallon family – who of course spoke of Harry as a hero and (she had heard) were having a huge memorial portrait painted – if she had to. 'And to let you know that certain people in the Admiralty would support the story – should it be necessary. We talked it over very many times before we decided to take this rather unorthodox step, and if your father was wrong about your late husband's family, then we are only glad.'

'It is very kind of you,' said Rose dubiously. 'Thank you.' And she smiled at them and they relaxed at last and cast an eye at the small table. 'Please. Please, eat the plum cake, and have more wine – and know that should there be difficulties I will consult you, as of course my father would wish.'

The old gentlemen, relieved, smiled too, and crumbs fell and more wine was taken and the talk turned to the navy, to the hopes of peace with Napoleon, to people they had all known, to her father again. There was even laughter in the blue room, as they remembered some of his adventures, and the old gentlemen were still smiling, rosy-cheeked now, as they were helped into their coats before they went out again into the snow.

'We, of course, are always glad to be at your service,' they said, and they bowed to her as the door opened and flurries of snow swirled at the doorstep.

She came outside to wave to them. 'Go in, go in, dear girl,' called the old gentlemen, standing in the snow, refusing to leave till they saw that she did as they bid. They made little shooing movements to hurry her inside as if she was a small hen, as the snow fell on their old heads and their thick navy cloaks and the door of the house in Wimpole Street closed.

She listened to the empty house. The servants had gone, Mattie had gone.

In the blue drawing room she lit one of her small cigars, stared at the family portraits. She remembered again the dignified naval funeral for an English captain, the swords and the admirals. Afterwards in the carriage, even the Dowager Viscountess silent, Rose had seen George Fallon cry. She thought of Harry and the Egyptian girl, and heard the sound of silence.

Finally she stubbed out her cigar right in the middle of the portrait of Captain Harold Fallon, be-medalled.

*

When she woke on the day after Christmas, fourteen-year-old Lady Dolly Torrence remembered she had been dreaming about that very tall man in a turban again. She felt her face turn slightly red. When the British were defeating Napoleon in Egypt there were sometimes drawings of fierce Turkomen, with large turbans and large swords, in the newspapers. So if such a man appeared in her dreams it was no fault of hers. She might even write it down, suitably censored. She had never written of dreams in her journal before, only an account of her day-to-day activities, but she had been paying most particular attention to her journal lately. She had noticed several times that the marker in her journal seemed to have been moved. The first time she chided herself for being ridiculous, but nevertheless carefully left the marker in a very specific way. It was clear, later, that it had again been moved. Dolly was at once both flattered and curious, decided to make her journal as interesting as possible. She did hope it was her brother William who was reading it, for the journal had only been interfered with since he returned. To write her journal for dearest William would be a labour of love. (Perhaps, however, she would leave out the Turkoman.)

When she was dressed, Dolly went quickly to her mother's room, for this was when her mother became most distressed, when she came out of the fog of sleep only to find herself in the fog of waking. The Duchess of Torrence was growing more and more confused. In the time he had been back from sea, she had not recognised her son William at all, and although Dolly was only fourteen she saw clearly that it distressed William not to be remembered by his own mother, however much his mother smiled brightly and his wife teased him across the dinner table. So Dolly sat with her mother for at least an hour every morning, coaxing her to drink Indian tea, which some said was good for the brain.

And Dolly would talk. She would talk about William's journeys in the Mediterranean and Malta and Egypt; about cousins and aunts and country visits they had made years ago; even about the balls that her mother had always found more important than her daughter, hoping to give her mother (so Dolly explained it to herself) some feeling of reality. Dolly had never had such attention paid to her in her life; grasping the opportunity with both hands, she talked and talked and talked. When her mother seemed more than ordinarily anxious Dolly would tell her fairy stories, as if her mother was a child; she retold all the stories that she herself had dreamed of having recounted by her illustrious mother (but had always had to make do instead with nurses and maids). All this talking made Dolly, at least, happy, for her mother had found her uninteresting, and tall, in earlier times.

As she went into her mother's room she heard a little scream. 'Who are you?' said the Duchess of Torrence, staring at her daughter.

Dolly's heart jumped. She saw that a new look of puzzlement had come to her mother's eyes, and something else. The old lady looked frightened. Dolly immediately looked frightened also. Quickly she took her mother's hand. 'I am Dolly, you are my mother,' she said. 'I have come to talk to you as I always do.' But her mother looked only confused and smoothed at her balding hair over and over, the way she did when her anxiety was at its worst. Dolly rang for her mother's maid very long and loudly. 'Shall I read to you Mama?' she said quickly and nervously. 'Or shall I tell you a story? You like fairy stories.' The maid came in and they began between them to dress the Duchess, and to hide the baldness with the cap and the curls.

'Once upon a time,' began Dolly, 'there was a beautiful princess, called Princess Rosetta—'

'Who are you all?' asked Lady Torrence in a sudden, loud voice. She pulled her hands away from Dolly and from the maid, and in her eyes fear and panic lurked. And then louder and louder in great distress, 'Who are you all?'

Thoroughly frightened now, Dolly said helplessly, 'You must sit by the fire here, Mama,' but her mother began pulling at her gown and at her hair in that agitated way and seemed as if she would run into the hallway. Dolly signalled to the maid that she would get help. She ran down the staircase calling for her father in a very loud voice. William would no doubt already be gone to the Admiralty, looking for another ship; Ann of course never rose till noon. Servants gathered, but her father did not appear. The Duke of Torrence was in his library, totally immersed in one of his special books: *The School of Venus* (illustrated), translated from the French.

'Father?'

'What is it?' He did not look up from his magnifying glass.

'Father, Father come quickly, quickly, it is Mama. She has become most agitated. She is—' and Dolly burst into loud tears.

'What is it, Dolly?' The Duke closed the book reluctantly, stood in exasperation: the girl was becoming more hysterical than ever, why didn't somebody do something?

'Mama is – she does not recognise me.'

'Surely, Dolly . . .' he demurred, sighing. These were things that the women dealt with.

'Father, she no longer recognises William, and now she does not know me. I am frightened. You must come, Father, for surely she will recognise you and then she will be calm again,' and the Duke reluctantly took his daughter's arm and went slowly upstairs to his wife's room, but his wife saw only an ugly old man.

Within a month, the Duchess of Torrence had died and was buried in Westminster Abbey with others of the great and good of England. Many people attended – the Torrence family had lost a great deal of money (it was well known) but they were still of immense importance in the scheme of things, so much of the land of England had they once owned. The Prince of Wales and the Dukes of Clarence and Kent attended, with their mother, Queen Charlotte. The dead woman's brother, the Duke of Hawksfield, walked just behind them. The husband and the son and the daughters walked in black: people commented on the one extremely tall daughter, whose pale face seemed to poke out over the other heads in a very odd manner. Much farther back in Westminster Abbey, but amongst London society nevertheless, the new Viscount Gawkroger sat with his sister-in-law and his mother.

The tombstone read: HERE LIES LYDIA, LOVED WIFE OF JAMES, DUKE OF TORRENCE, for tombstones do not always say how life has been.

*

The dark winter days continued; February came. Peace negotiations with the French went on. Rose Fallon began reading again, acquired new magnifying spectacles from Dickens and Smith. She arranged for the (slightly damaged) portrait of Captain Harold Fallon to be delivered to Great Smith Street: *You will, of course want to have this last likeness*, said her accompanying letter.

And then, almost imperceptibly, the evenings began to grow just a little lighter, and one day there was a newspaper report: THE ROSETTA STONE CAPTURED BY HIS MAJESTY'S GALLANT SOLDIERS IN EGYPT HAS LANDED AT PORTSMOUTH HARBOUR.

EIGHT

Joy abounded, all over the country.

All the newspapers reported that Napoleon Buonaparte's deranged behaviour had been halted: the war was over! The English began flocking back to their favourite city, Paris, even before the Peace of Amiens was formally signed.

Amid the excitement it was widely predicted – in the newspapers, in the coffee houses – that the British would be translating the hieroglyphs almost immediately. The French, naturally, had failed; the Rosetta Stone was with the Society of Antiquaries; one day it would be on show to the world.

The world waited with bated breath for the secrets of the universe.

Something happened between Rose Fallon and her brother-in-law.

It was not known what exactly, except to themselves, for neither of them told.

He had arrived one evening, unannounced, at the house in Wimpole Street. The new Viscount Gawkroger was more shocked than he supposed himself capable of (being an unshockable man, on the whole) when he came into the long blue downstairs drawing room to which a maid had brought him, where ancestors observed him silently. *Clearly he could smell cigar tobacco.* Somehow this threw him into disarray. Only sailors and thieves smoked anything other than pipes. (And, very occasionally, gentlemen.) Had Rose been entertaining someone before he arrived? Was she planning to marry again, so soon? That was out of the question: she was still in mourning for his brother, she belonged to the Fallon family, she carried its name and he had plans for her. He looked quickly into the mirror, adjusted his stays, walked to the window, seeing with irritation books everywhere: lots of new books, novels he supposed, time-wasting rubbish that women read. Still the tobacco lingered. He contained his shock, and, with care, something else that he had brought with him: his anger. He was furious to have been put in this position, but he *needed* Rose. He walked about the room impatiently.

He took a gold snuffbox out of his pocket as Rose entered the room. He sat, finally, on the sofa by the fire and threw out his legs in front of him almost petulantly, leaning slightly on his swordstick.

'This is a surprise, George,' said Rose. But of course it was not. Since the visit of the old gentlemen she had somehow been expecting him. And she had thought very carefully about what she might discuss with him. Nevertheless her heart was beating fast: she had never before had a confrontation with a member of the Fallon family.

A maid brought coffee. That was another thing that irritated him. Men drank coffee in coffee houses, meeting to talk about politics and war and peace. They did not drink it in ladies' drawing rooms.

Rose busied herself, pouring and serving; the new Viscount, still unusually discomforted, did not speak as the unknown visitor's tobacco hung there in the air.

As Rose handed him his coffee in a gilded cup, and sat on the tall straight chair opposite him, she said, 'Have you seen Dolly, George? I felt very sorry at her mother's funeral, she seemed so distressed.' George sat up, put the ridiculous teacup on a table beside him: men did not drink coffee in *teacups*. He felt ill at ease on this sofa, it was always softer than he expected.

'The Duchess was unkind to Dolly for most of her life and then needed her when she became insane. Dolly, who is a somewhat fanciful child, was grateful to have her to talk to at the last, that is all. She apparently set enormous store by this "talking" to her mother – but of course nobody was listening!'

Rose felt a stab of pity for the ungainly young girl. 'Did she tell you of her feelings?' she asked curiously.

George gave a smile. 'Let us say I am privy to her thoughts,' he said oddly. 'She will, I am sure, recover – and you, Rose, can take the opportunity to help her to do so.' And then he went on abruptly, almost without pause, 'My mother and I, Rose, feel it is time for you to move back to Great Smith Street, to Gawkroger Hall, where you surely belong, as part of the Fallon family. You will not have to stay there long. Heaven be praised, we shall be vacating that house very soon and moving to Berkeley Square.'

'Berkeley Square at last? That is indeed a grand move.'

'Of course. Now, we have been patient with your grief, for we have of course had our own to deal with, but frankly it is bad for Harry's reputation, that you continue to live here alone.'

Rose did not answer him at once; she too put down her cup and then sat very straight again in her chair. She said at last, 'Your brother's reputation, George, is safe with me.'

His snuffbox was halfway to his nose. It hovered there for a few seconds, such was his surprise at her choice of words.

She seemed to change the subject entirely. 'I have been waiting impatiently to see the Rosetta Stone, but I understand that it is not yet on display in the British Museum. You are known to the Museum Trustees, I believe, for your interest in antiquities in general.'

He looked at her most carefully, took a pinch of snuff before speaking. 'I have learned that it is at present with the Society of Antiquaries, where various scholars are giving it their utmost attention.'

'Has a translation of the Greek text been made public? I would give a great deal to see that!'

'I believe the Greek text has been sent to universities and libraries so that the best scholars can make the best translations. After that the real puzzle, the translating of the hieroglyphs, will begin. I am sure it will not take long. Why does it fascinate you so? – apart from carrying your name, of course,' and she heard the mockery in his voice. 'The ancient language of the Pharaohs! It is hardly a suitable interest for a woman.' Then he went on at once, as if it were the same subject: 'I and my mother wish you to come back and live with us, Rose. I require it. *And* it is the law. The law entitles you, as a widow in my family, to live in my house and,' – he smiled grimly – 'have use of my fire. Those are the very words the law uses.'

'But the law does not say I *must* have use of your fire, George! You should marry – you are Viscount Gawkroger now. You need a wife to do the things you seem to require of me.'

He got up abruptly from the soft sofa. 'I shall of course marry when it is necessary, and I have made arrangements accordingly.' And Rose saw that the subject was distasteful to him for some reason. And she saw her own life if he won this battle: George would be free of his imperious, demanding mother; he would probably postpone any marriage; Rose would face endless dull social engagements with old ladies in caps with false curls attached, and with rouged and powdered faces. She would listen to perpetual conversations about the shortcomings of the princes of the Royal Family, and the immorality of the young (and not so young): other people's scandals. And above all, the interminable monologues of his mother. And, always, George Fallon, slithering about in the background like a snake. *I would not be able to bear it.*

So she held his gaze steadily. 'I am mindful of course of the honour that you and your mother do me in asking me to join your household. But I am not a frivolous young girl who needs to be chaperoned, or a spinster who needs to be put up with. I am – or I was – a married woman and my life has changed.' She spoke to him simply. 'I cannot go back, George.'

Still he regarded her. 'I require it, Rose,' he said silkily. 'I require it, and it shall be so. You are not a married woman now, you are a widow. You belong to us and your future is in our hands. I prefer not to marry before I must.' He picked up one of the books, perused the title. '*The Old Manor House* by Mrs Charlotte Smith, indeed.' He looked at her slyly. 'You know what they say about young ladies reading novels alone in their rooms, Rose?'

'But of course. "Reading novels gives untrained minds the wrong impression of life, and leads to great frivolity among women."'

'*Frivolity*, is that what they call it now? We knew another word to describe overexcited young girls alone in their rooms!' And he laughed, and it was an unpleasant laugh.

Rose looked away. How *dare* he speak to her that way? *But how dare I know what he means?* And she knew the answer. *Because I was married to his brother, who taught me very many things.* George picked up the next, very old, book: *The Allegories of the Egyptian Hieroglyphs.* He looked at it without comment. Then he put the two books down impatiently.

'I know your father made a marriage settlement, but it is the Fallon family that owns this house. I intend to sell it. Berkeley Square will be big enough for us all. You have not produced an heir, and your position, apart from the use of my fire, is very dependent upon our goodwill.'

She took courage from the sight of the ridiculous white snuff marks around his nose, and from the information that she had, and she sent up a little prayer of thanks to the old naval gentlemen who had armed her for this encounter. 'I am sorry about the lack of heirs for the Fallon family,' she said coldly. 'It is something you will have to remedy yourself. I have, of course, been sensible that this can no longer be my home, that you will not wish me to live here longer, and I am grateful to have been allowed this period of' – she hesitated before she said the word – 'mourning. I am ready to make other arrangements as soon as you require it.'

But he only smiled. 'The Fallon family is very powerful, *Rosetta mia*, and extremely rich. We have excellent lawyers at our disposal. We are looking very, very carefully at your marriage settlement. I have been advised that they can often be found to be inadequately framed.'

For the first time she was discomposed, and he saw it. Money was the key; money was always the key.

'Harry agreed to the settlement,' said Rose angrily. 'You could not – and should not – interfere with that which he and my father agreed upon.'

'Harry knew how much you loved him. He knew perfectly well

he could persuade you to make everything over to him if we deemed that advisable.' She stared, appalled. 'On the other hand, if you live in our family your personal settlement will of course be considered inviolate. The Fallon family wishes to do the right thing. Of course.' He was standing now against the window, smiling slightly. There was a candle-lamp on a tall chest beside him and he was partly silhouetted against the light; she thought of dioramas and light shows and stories of the Evil King. Who was always, of course, defeated. *How dare he threaten me! How dare he pretend! How right the old gentlemen were, after all.*

She took a deep breath and then spoke calmly, still sitting very upright in her high-backed chair. 'If you dishonour the wishes of my father, George, I will make it known about town that – that your brother is not a hero of the Battle of Aboukir but was killed by an Arab in the streets of Alexandria in a tawdry brawl over a local woman.' She heard his sharp intake of breath. 'It was considered by the Egyptians, I understand, that he, the English lord, had been wildly disrespectful and familiar in a manner quite contrary to the religion and customs in Egypt; it was an incident of great embarrassment to the victorious British Army because the girl was not only Egyptian but betrothed in some way to the ruling Turks. This incident could easily – even now – bring disgrace upon the Fallon family.'

The silhouette against the light had become perfectly still, and because of the way he turned she suddenly could not see his face at all. But the sheer power of anger in the room was electric. One of the clocks chimed nine, and then another. Rose found she was gripping the arms of the chair; she forced herself to let go, and put her hands in her lap.

Only when the clocks were quite silent did he speak, and his voice was low and savage and full of violence. 'The Egyptians are barbarians. The Turks are barbarians. They are all, all of them, barbarians.'

She knew she must never be frightened of him or she was lost. She answered him at once. 'Your brother was, as you know' – she paused for the right word – 'indiscreet.'

Again there was silence. Just for a moment, as he stood there by the window, she was reminded of Harry. She supposed George was good-looking, but – there was something – different. And although he was younger than Harry, he was *much more dangerous*. She saw that he was trying to control himself. Another clock chimed nine.

'Who told you this?'

'Did you know, George?'

He did not answer, and so she understood that he did. But of course William, Dolly's brother, was a naval captain, was in Egypt, could have known. 'My sources, George, were no doubt the same as yours: persons inside the British navy. Lord Nelson and Lord Abercrombie were at my father's funeral – you should never forget that my father was an admiral of great repute.' She saw at once that he was appalled, had not allowed for this. 'Some naval officers came to see me on Christmas Day.'

Silence in the shadowy long blue drawing room as George digested all this and then controlled himself again. She saw the effort required.

'That is a strange Christmas *cadeau,*' he murmured at last.

'Indeed,' said Rose, offering no further elucidation.

He stayed beside the window for a moment, thinking quickly. *Naval officers? How wide is the knowledge of Harry's death? Public knowledge of Harry's foolishness is the kind of scandal that could ruin all our plans. Rose must never, never be allowed to use this information.* He walked very deliberately towards the tall chair and stood right in front of her, nearer than felt comfortable; she could smell the snuff. *At the very least Rose must be persuaded to come to Paris.* He looked down at her. 'I could get you a copy of the Greek translation of the Rosetta Stone, *Rosetta mia,*' he said softly. 'It is within my power to do that,' and he saw the light burst into her eyes for a split second, and then she tried to conceal it.

'I do not wish to live with you and your mother, George.'

'Rose, that apart for the moment, my mother strongly wishes to go to Paris now that the war is over. She is a lonely old woman. She wants your company.' This was a lie. The Dowager Viscountess Gawkroger did not in the least require the company of her daughter-in-law; only required her son. But the powerful old Duke of Hawksfield made many of the Torrence family decisions. The Duke of Hawksfield had decreed that fourteen-year-old Dolly, who had been invited also, was not to go to Paris as part of the Viscount's party unless the widow travelled too; those were his words, *unless the widow travels*. Nobody knew how or why the Duke came to his decisions, but apparently he felt that Rose would be a respectable and intelligent companion for Dolly, who rather lacked such appurtenances. Ann had been furious. She would be there, with Dolly's own brother: what was the old man thinking of? But George wanted Dolly in Paris: she must begin a wider education. The Duke had spoken; therefore Rose had to be persuaded to travel also.

'Does your mother know about Harry?' asked Rose.

'Of course not!' The violence in his voice reared up again. 'It would kill her, you recognise that at least!'

Rose stared at him, said nothing.

'But – as I say – my mother needs you. I want you to travel with us to Paris.'

Rose allowed herself to think of Paris, just for a moment. *Fanny and I running across the Pont Neuf calling, 'La belle France,' Notre Dame Cathedral, the beautiful French women.* But so much, they said, had happened there, so many stories of terror and bloodshed . . . it was not a place yet, perhaps, to travel to alone. *Oh – to travel to Paris again after all these years!*

It was as if he could read her thoughts. 'You know you have dreamed of going back, Rose.' He still stood too close to her; she did not answer. He gave a large sigh and she could smell his breath now, onions perhaps, and wine, and old meat. She forced herself not to turn away from such unpleasantness. He went back at last to the sofa, threw himself down upon it again. For some moments he seemed to be deciding what to say. He fidgeted, rolled his gold snuffbox around his hand. He automatically unscrewed the top of his swordstick, glanced into the small mirror inlaid there, almost as if he had forgotten Rose was sitting there. He screwed the cap back again. Finally he spoke, almost sulkily, for he had not planned to discuss this particular matter with her at all. 'Actually, I am worried about my mother. She is obsessed with the idea of seeing Napoleon. All the grand ladies of London are obsessed with the idea of seeing Napoleon. But my mother wishes to actually speak to him. She blames him for Harry's death and she wants to tell him so.'

And Rose burst out laughing: of all the things she had expected him to say next, she could not have guessed this one. 'Buonaparte should indeed tremble!' she said, still laughing. 'Your mother could delay him for some hours with the torrent of her speech should she get him in her power.' She saw, from the way he stiffened and stood again, that she had gone too far. 'I do beg your pardon, George. But I think the idea that your mother might meet Napoleon is – rather far-fetched.'

'I am afraid it is not. It has come to her knowledge through her cousin the Duchess of Seaforth that Josephine receives English ladies of class at the Tuileries, and that Napoleon sometimes enters the salon also. It is apparently all the rage now, with the English ladies in Paris, to have met the First Consul of France.'

Rose stifled her laughter. 'Really? It seems odd – on both sides – to want, so soon, to meet the enemy!'

'So I should have thought. But there is no accounting for the tastes of *les grandes dames Anglaises*, and apparently that madman Napoleon *enjoys* the whole performance.' He sat down yet again and she saw his face was red, with anger still, and something else. 'Well – you know about Harry's death. So you must see I cannot allow my mother to blame Napoleon, in person.' Rose looked across at him, slightly puzzled. 'For Harry's sake,' he said harshly.

'But surely – Napoleon? George, it is well known Napoleon was in France at the time!'

'The Fallon family cannot be too careful. Unfortunately some of the French were still there when – when Harry was killed. They were preparing to leave Alexandria under the treaty.'

Rose found it hard to believe that George, even in his passionate desperation to avoid scandal, could think that Harry was that important. She wanted to laugh again. 'This is absurd, George.'

'We cannot be sure. I know we can hardly stop my mother travelling to Paris, of course, but she cannot be allowed to embarrass us with Buonaparte. You can assist me in dissuading her.' He saw Rose's lips tighten. 'She made things difficult for you, I know, especially – when you miscarried.' He saw her flinch, but continued. 'Nevertheless you owe this to Harry's memory.'

'I think you take a risk in telling me what I owe to Harry's memory,' she said shortly.

He looked at her carefully for a moment. He thought again of the smell of cigar smoke in the room when he arrived: *what is she planning?*

'Perhaps, George, you should tell your mother the truth.'

Viscount Gawkroger sprang up from the sofa, stalked to the window, then turned to face her, his face still red. 'I wish you could understand what is at stake here, Rose. Our family *cannot have any scandal*! I tell you again, it would kill my mother! We might become a laughing stock! You do not understand, we are on the very cusp; there are some – services – I am able to do the Prince of Wales, and I have very high hopes in other matters – but we are not yet part of *le ton*. I believe we can buy our way further up the aristocratic pole, but all the money in the world would not prevent us falling if we were involved in any scandal. I repeat – we cannot be too careful. And I cannot believe you would want your husband's memory sullied in this way. You loved him.'

She did not speak.

'You loved him,' he repeated. And then more softly and more terribly: '*I know how much you loved him, Rose*,' and she felt the blood rise to her cheeks. Before she could speak, he continued. 'Very well, then. If you will come to Paris with us, for the month of May, I give you my word that on our return I will have a translation of the Greek text on the Rosetta Stone made available to you. And we will say no more, for the moment, about Great Smith Street. But you must see how I need you to be in Paris.' He watched her very carefully. 'So I will indulge your little hobby for antiquities.' He was careful to speak politely, but his words could not have been more contemptuous. And then he actually laughed. 'This is an extraordinary thing with which to be bribing a woman, Rose,' and she heard the mockery in his voice. 'A Greek translation! The Prince of Wales would indeed be ashamed of me. It should be diamonds.'

Rose did not laugh, but she looked at him oddly. 'I have always considered the written language to be the most fascinating thing in the world,' she said.

'I think ladies should remain adherents of the spoken language, where they belong,' said George lightly. But he knew she would come, now. 'William and Ann will join our party,' he added. 'I have suggested that they have some time together in Paris – having been deprived of such a thing at the time of their marriage thanks to Mr

Buonaparte.' He smiled. 'A second honeymoon. And Dolly will come also. A change of air will be good for her, and so would your presence: she has taken to you, and I have persuaded her that having you in the party would be more suitable than her pet peacock.' He flicked a glance at her. 'But most of all you must do this because of your love for my brother – of which I know much.' She looked at him, and understood. Again colour rose in her face, but she did not lower her eyes.

With enormous self-control she stood, and the two of them regarded each other, protagonists of the unspoken. 'I want the translation of the Rosetta Stone before the journey, George,' said Rose.

There was a moment's absolute silence, and then Viscount Gawkroger bowed low, as if to acknowledge that she might, for the moment at least, be more the victor. But it was a mocking bow.

When he had gone, Rose sat very still, alone in the house in Wimpole Street as the clocks ticked time away.

I know how much you loved him, Rose. She heard again his taunting words. And saw the two brothers, the two corrupt – she made herself repeat the word in her head *corrupt, corrupt* – brothers, talking of her, of her most intimate, private moments with her husband. Quite suddenly she made a sound between a gasp and a cry and tears fell down her cheeks just once more for beguiling, betraying, beautiful Harry Fallon. Who kept humiliating her, even in death.

At last, much later, she picked up a lamp and went slowly upstairs. For some time she wandered about, opening her desk and closing it, picking up books and putting them down again. It was time to prepare for bed.

But this was always the hardest part. Harry Fallon had done her much damage, but the greatest was this one, the one that came up the stairs with her: the one he had obviously shared with his brother. *The secret.* Again she felt her cheeks redden, just to think of such a betrayal: *the corrupt Fallon brothers.* For Harry Fallon had awoken in Rose feelings and sensations for which she was utterly, totally unprepared: her delighted shock filled her nights and wished the days over; she waited in almost indecent haste for his arrival into her room. It was *this*: *this* was what had made everything else seem irrelevant, those things that might otherwise have dismayed her in her new life. *This* she had not learnt from all the conversations in her parents' house. *She was intoxicated by what he taught her.* And it had made her blind.

When he came less, when he often came home not at all, when she realised he loved other women, her torment began. Perhaps that was lucky, for when he was killed in Egypt and she knew he would never come again, she had already suffered so much that it was almost a relief that at least she would not be listening, every part of her body taut like a bow, for carriage wheels, for steps coming upstairs, for the moment when she would understand if her door would softly open. Or not.

Rose put the lamp on the table beside her romantic pink bed with its curtained canopy. She did not allow Mattie to attend her when she was going to bed: *you must not always be waiting up for me*: at first because she wanted to be alone, waiting for Harry; now because she was afraid Mattie would see into her heart. And so tonight, as on so many other nights, she slowly put on her nightgown. And then, as always now, she reached for the opium, for opium dulled the passionate longing that Harry had awakened in her.

And then shared with his brother.

NINE

Spring arrived; the world had been secured, they said, against Buonaparte's excesses; and Rose Fallon suddenly cut her hair.

Short hair and very simple gowns *without petticoats* were all the fashion from France (some said the aristocracy wanted to portray simplicity itself in their attire, just to be on the safe side), and the old men with telescopes at Vow Hill no longer had to jostle for space above the bathing huts: there was more than enough to excite them just walking through the streets of town. Young girls with short hair wearing not nearly enough clothes (thin white lawn, or high-waisted silk dresses) walked through parks and thoroughfares and gardens with elderly corseted ladies in wider skirts who hid, under small caps, the sad remains of their once powdered and be-wigged hair. High waists had been worn by young girls before, but sleeves had been long, and *definitely* there had been petticoats. Now even these decorums were sometimes forgone. Rose loved the fashions but was almost always cold.

The translation of the Greek inscription of the Rosetta Stone into

English was, as promised by George, delivered to Wimpole Street one evening in April. It arrived with a note.

This, so far, is all that is available. It was read to the Society of Antiquaries this week, and is not, I think, great literature! but will give you some idea. Alas the secrets of the world will not be discovered here.
We leave for Paris on 2 May.
Gawkroger

Rose was so overcome she could hardly open the parcel. George Fallon would not know great literature if it hit him in the face: this was the key to the secrets of the world, *and she held it in her hands*. She dropped her magnifying spectacles twice. At last, sitting by the fire on her straight-backed chair, she smoothed the pages of the translation which had been written in elegant handwriting, and began reading, trembling with excitement.

In the reign of the young one who is King in place of his Father Lord of Crowns, great of glory, who has Established Egypt, causing it to prosper, and is pious towards the gods, triumphant over his enemies, who has restored the civilised life of Mankind, Lord of the Thirty Years Festivals, even as Hephaistos the Great, a King like the Sun, great King of the Upper and Lower parts, offspring of the gods Philopatores, one whom Hephaistos has approved, to whom the sun has given Victory, the living image of Zeus, son of the Sun, King Ptolemy, the ever-living, the Beloved of Ptah, the god Epiphanes Eucharistos ...

Although Rose had always understood perfectly well that her stone was only a *key* to translating the magic, not the magic itself, she began after some time to feel she could tear her short hair with disappointment. She tried to keep feeling excited that she was reading something from the far, far distant past; she ended at last yawning over details. On the Rosetta Stone KING PTOLEMY, THE EVER-LIVING, THE BELOVED OF PTAH, THE GOD EPIPHANES EUCHARISTOS seemed to be a young boy to whom great and extremely long-winded homage was being paid. His long name was repeated over and over again. KING PTOLEMY, THE EVER-LIVING, THE BELOVED OF PTAH, THE GOD EPIPHANES EUCHARISTOS had dammed up the river Nile at some stage. He had it seemed also provided infantry and cavalry and ships to be sent out against those who invaded Egypt; he had avenged and punished rebels who had risen against his father. But not a sign of magic. No enigmatic secrets of the universe. Heroically she finished it, then let the English translation of the Greek fall to the floor, the papers scattered and drifted from the draughts coming in under the doors. On the last page she read:

> And this decree shall be inscribed on a stela of hard stone in sacred writing and native writing and Greek writing and set up in the first- and second- and third-ranking temples next to the image of the King. And live for ever.

I used to say that to Mama, that writing will live for ever. She was out of mourning, days went by now without her even thinking of Harry at all, but the thought of her own naïve writing in her journal about their married 'happiness' sometimes made tears well up in her eyes still. *Some writing should not live for ever* she thought wryly, *but be consigned to the fire!* She opened her father's book about hieroglyphs. *But is this all the hieroglyphs are ever going to mean? Battles and armies and kings? As usual? What about the mysteries of the universe?* She stared again at the pictures in her father's book: at the owl, the hawk, the bee, the elegant swirls. Finally she lit a cigar and watched the smoke and thought once more about the act of writing: the act of making marks – on stone, or on paper, or on anything at all – to make contact with other people. *By writing we preserve ourselves – we cannot know who shall read the words we write.* But how could she know the Ancient Egyptians through this boring document?

At last she put down her cigar and stood up. It was one o'clock in the morning. She opened the shutters and stood at the window. It was not exactly quiet; even Wimpole Street was never quite deserted; the census had told that there were one million people in London now. In the darkness she thought she saw several people moving together, parting again, further down the street: a romance? a fight? Rose pulled her shawl tightly about her. *The Stone is a key, that is its importance.* She picked up the scattered papers. No answers, then, to the mysteries of the world from King Ptolemy the ever-living, the Beloved of Ptah, the God Epiphanes Eucharistos. She moved about the blue room, using the silver candle-snuffer to put out the candles except for one, to take upstairs. *A few more sleeps,* as she and Fanny used to say, and she would be leaving for Paris. It must be nearly fifteen years since she had been there; who was to say how they would find Paris now? George Fallon had kept his side of the bargain and she would keep hers, but it was – she glanced at the papers in her hand – a disappointing bargain. She would make no more bargains with George. She knew she had been in some way paralysed after Harry's death, unable to make decisions. But she was recovered. She knew she would soon decide about the next part of her life. When she came back from Paris she would move house. She was sure her wise father had left her safe, that George's talk of lawyers was only threats, and that soon she would be relieved of the Fallon family for ever.

She closed the shutters and picked up the lamp and went upstairs, carrying the papers containing the translation, pondering the words. *I wish I knew more about languages. As the words 'King Ptolemy the ever-living, the Beloved of Ptah, the God Epiphanes Eucharistos' appear many times in the Greek translation, perhaps they could find that same repetition in the hieroglyphs? And so begin to find the key to the mysteries of the world?* She knew that if she had thought of this, so had all the scholars.

At her desk she took up her quill, dipped it in the ink and wrote quickly.

Dearest Fanny,

   I am to go to Paris at their Insistence, with members of Harry's Family. Who knows how our beloved belle France *will have Changed? I will think of you, and our days there long ago.*
                    Your loving cousin,
                    Rose

Horatio surely could not find much immoral subversion there.

*

In the pretty little market town of Wentwater Mrs Fanny Harbottom, the vicar's wife, did not use the vicar's small trap as much as the vicar did, although the farmers noted she handled the horse well when she occasionally drove by. The vicar's wife liked walking. The vicar's wife was an enigma in the town and much talked of by the townsmen. Nothing you could put your finger on: she visited the sick and infirm as expected, she was always at church on Sunday, of course, but there were (they noted) odd little eccentricities. You could not help but notice her because of her rather short rounded figure and her wild red hair, even though she always wore a hat. Allowing for exaggeration (as the wiser townspeople did), there was still something odd about the way (for instance) she would stop and listen to the people on little stools who spoke sometimes in the market square, next to the nervous bleating sheep and the cabbages and the hen's eggs. The vicar's wife was sometimes seen, stock still, listening to them speaking of God. It was known that the vicar denounced the 'charlatans', as he called them, from the pulpit. The townspeople talked among themselves: some said she was probably out spying for the vicar, who could hardly be seen listening to the charlatans himself. On Sundays she would be in church as usual and the Reverend Horatio Harbottom would thunder from the pulpit in his flamboyant robes about sin and retribution; his beautiful voice echoed to the rafters and the faint scent of lavender wafted down the aisles.

Another story about her was told by a local poacher: he had been out laying his traps one night, he said, in the moorlands beyond the fields, and he'd heard the sound of screaming. He went to investigate, of course, he said, and swore that he'd seen the Reverend's wife standing at the end of the fields all by herself and screaming loudly. Quite shaken he was, admitted the poacher. After a while she stopped screaming and walked, very firmly, he said, back through the fields. He followed her and saw that she came to the vicarage, and as she was going inside she turned to speak to a passing neighbour woman and something was said and they both laughed – he saw the Reverend's wife laugh, just after she'd been screaming her head off! This story was treated with a grain of salt, as all the poacher's stories were.

In April in Wentwater, even though the lightness in the evenings could now be clearly observed, heavy snow had suddenly fallen one late afternoon and people hurried by, wanting to get home to their fires. But then some of them saw that the Quaker Lady was in the square. The Quaker Lady came seldom, she was not a young woman, but when she did come she always got a crowd because she was the first woman on a stool the people of Wentwater had ever seen, and even in the snow, reluctantly but curiously, they now gathered near her. People nudged each other to see the vicar's wife there also, the hood of her cloak covering her red hair. Fanny, perhaps oblivious, perhaps not, stood in the crowd and listened. Inside her glove she could feel Rose's letter about travelling to Paris; she held it to her. The Quaker Lady, seeming not to notice the weather, stood on her stool in her grey Quaker dress and bonnet, and spoke of love.

'You should be home cooking the cabbage and potaters for your family's dinner,' one woman called, 'and then scrubbing the floor and sewing the clothes,' and she hustled and bustled in her shawl, 'that's what love is!' and the crowd laughed, but not unkindly. 'Ain't you ever found out what love is?' called the woman in the shawl angrily. 'Making do, making do is what love is, and God protect us all from its pestilence.'

The Quaker Lady said that God was Love and he loved every one of them equally. And as the snow began to fall again and white flakes drifted on to her grey bonnet and her little stool she spoke of waiting, waiting for God to speak, for he would come. Somehow, despite the weather, the people still stayed, listening in some amazement to the word of God being expounded in the snow from such an unlikely source.

God bless thee, said the Quaker Lady to the woman who spoke of potaters.

*

Just a few days before the Fallon family left for Paris, the Peace of Amiens was finally officially proclaimed in London, a treaty between the French and the British. The long wars that had been waging for nearly ten years had, it seemed, truly come to an end.

The old gentlemen, smart in their dark blue naval jackets and their golden stripes, came for Rose at dusk.

'Come,' they said, 'you must see history in the making and as your father is not here to escort you we shall do so ourselves.'

'But', Rose was puzzled, 'we have known of the peace for weeks – many people have already left for France!'

'The British always do things best!' they cried. 'This is the Official Proclamation, the Mayor of London will present it to the people. It is a most historical moment, it is Peace, and you must be there!'

The celebrations were held around Portman Square, behind Oxford Street, for Portman Square was where many diplomatic houses were, and the ambassadors who had arranged the peace. Hundreds of thousands of people milled about London. The old gentlemen realised they should have left the carriage at Wimpole Street; they got the driver to turn right away from the crush, walked back through St James's, pushed by the excited, singing crowds, passing the gentlemen's clubs that still made up the High Heavens Club's picnic baskets. Young dandies fell out of doors calling, *Boney is gone*; in one of the clubs candles spelt out PEACE and several aristocratic gentlemen staggered. The two old naval gentlemen each held one of Rose's arms and pushed her on through the night-river of laughing, shouting Londoners. Traders sold gingerbread soldiers and small flags. Every house in the streets that led to Portman Square had candles in its windows and the lights shone out brightly on to the crowds and the trumpeters and the Mayor.

'Oh!' cried Rose suddenly, seeing that Portman Square was ablaze with light also. 'Oh, how I love London!' Hundreds of candles shone from all the big windows, and from somewhere fireworks flashed into the sky and people cheered. The old gentlemen laughed to see the coaches and the horses all jammed in the middle of the square unable to move, and congratulated themselves on their forethought. And Rose suddenly stopped her involuntary moving and turned to the old gentlemen in amazement. 'But *of course*! Of course I know what I want! When I come back from Paris, I would like to find a small place near Brook Street, and live as I used to! I want to be myself again!'

'My dear.' In the candlelight and the noise the old gentlemen perhaps looked at her with something like pity. 'My dear,' they said again, and for just a moment the three of them stood almost still in the jostling crowd. 'One can never live as one used to, and the self changes. That is how we know time is passing. But,' and their kindly eyes smiled at her as they were swept along once more so that they had to shout above the cheering, 'when you return to London we will see what we can find!' and the crowds roared and all the fireworks and the candlelights shone like a million stars, because peace had come at last.

TEN

'Should I see Mr Buonaparte, and it is most likely that I shall, I shall tell him that he killed my son – I shall say what I think of his war and his terror and his "democratic" ideas – we care nothing for that, he need not think a lady of England fears a peasant from Corsica! He may be a tyrant, he may have tyrannised the Mediterranean, but he shall not tyrannise me! I have met enough effeminate French men – all those *be-sparkled* creatures who come over here and weaken the resolve of Englishmen with their foppery – it is a wonder that there are English fighting men left to us.' The Dowager Viscountess Gawkroger lurched forwards as the carriage took a bend sharply and her wide skirt covered them all, but her flow was not terminated. 'I have spoken at length to my dear cousin, the Duchess of Seaforth, about the suitability of meeting Josephine – so many stories abound about her – if Dolly was here in this carriage I would not repeat them. The Duchess told me that it is a well-known fact that when these new fashions' – she looked at Rose most disapprovingly, although Rose was wearing a respectable olive-green dress with long sleeves, and petticoats certainly – 'when these new so-called fashions began to emerge, Josephine used to immerse herself in water *while dressed*, and the flimsy gown would *cling* to her body in the most inappropriate manner as it dried so that Buonaparte would be – that is, would notice her.' The Dowager noticed not at all that George Fallon actually laughed and Rose blushed slightly. 'At least we are armoured by such information against being anything but particularly reserved when we meet such a person, although it will be Josephine herself I suppose who will introduce us to Buonaparte, but we must always remember that Napoleon is a common little man and short of stature, and he is responsible for the death of my son and he shall hear it from me!'

George interrupted his mother's flow rather wearily as he had done from time to time: 'As I said, Mama, we won the Battle of Aboukir; the Mediterranean is ours, a treaty is signed. We are at peace now.'

'We are at peace with beloved France, *pas Buonaparte, pas du tout*. We are not at peace with him. He murdered my son.'

'As I have said, very many times, Mama, Buonaparte was already back in France when Harry was killed in Egypt.'

She seemed not to hear him and raised her voice even more to be heard over the coach wheels as they approached the sea. 'For years now we have had to do without our European jaunt; I have felt it quite personally, as a great upheaval. I hope he has left the Hotel de l'Empire untouched at least, and the *boulevards* and the *opéra*. Josephine is holding *salons* for the ladies of England and several times Napoleon has been present – the Duchess of Seaforth shall arrange for me to attend and I *shall* attend, for I feel that it is my duty to tell him what I think of him, but I will not bow down – he need not think we honour *him*!'

They were almost at Dover and night was falling; Rose Fallon and her brother-in-law had endured many, many hours of the Dowager. Rose had a sudden desire to inform her mother-in-law that she too (directed by her husband) had stepped, dressed in a muslin dress somehow obtained from France, into a bath ordered up to the bedroom for the purpose.

The Dowager, as she had always done, spoke almost without taking breath from the moment anyone entered her presence; she had begun at dawn as they rolled away from London. Although it had been a beautiful spring early morning, she had complained at once of the cold; her maid wrapped her around with shawls and before long Rose wished that some brave servant would place one of the shawls over the old lady's head. (George distrusted Mattie – but not as much as she distrusted him – and had insisted that her presence was not necessary for Rose's comfort: 'Good,' said Mattie, 'I'll help the old gentlemen find another house.') The Duchess possessed a loud voice that pierced the ear all the way along the slow road to Dover: as they traversed up and down the hills, when they stopped to give the horses water, when they stopped briefly at Sittingbourne for refreshment. The Dowager, if she had her way, would not stop at all: she had recently been told that someone had ridden from London to Paris in twenty-two hours and did not see why travellers should take days and days as they always did, especially as terrorists and highwaymen (it was well known) haunted the roads in both countries.

Now, after blaming Buonaparte roundly over and over again, often in French, a language she had always, as many noble people had, scattered throughout her conversation (and from which she saw no reason to desist even though her country had been at war with France), the Dowager changed the subject and began talking – again – about the Royal Family. Through her late husband she had had some social intercourse with King George III and felt she knew him. She was, quite literally, outraged at the level royal matters had descended to with the antics of the sons; had stated many times that it would be best if the Prince of Wales would die and his daughter, Princess Charlotte (aged six) take the throne. She repeated facts she knew from her many contacts and acquaintances or had read in the newspaper, over and over again like an outraged litany. As the carriage rolled on she ran another interminable time through the affairs of the Prince of Wales (back with Mrs Fitzherbert even though he was married to Princess Caroline); the Duke of Clarence (and Mrs Jordan, all those illegitimate children); not to mention the Duke of Cumberland, whose sins she refused to name. George's contribution to the conversation was to report that Napoleon Buonaparte had described the extremely corpulent husband of one of the royal princesses as 'an experiment to show how far human skin could stretch without breaking'. Rose, despite herself, laughed; the Dowager recoiled in horror and did not stop her remonstrances for some time. Rose reminded herself it was only for a month, but at the moment a month seemed an eternity and she envied the carriage behind them, where Dolly sat pale and quiet between her brother and his wife.

The winds and the tides allowed them to take the early packet next morning across the Channel – although the sea was not exactly calm. The Dowager was prostrate as soon as they set sail, and Ann beside her. George and William sat in the saloon but Rose and Dolly, their long cloaks and their fur muffs and their Indian shawls held tightly about them, stood on deck, clutching their bonnets and breathing the salty air as the boat ploughed across the Channel, flinging spray into their faces. Rose stared at the sea and remembered other journeys long ago.

'We are already wearing French fashion, are we not, Rose?' asked Dolly, staring out at the appearing and disappearing misty horizon, leaning her cheeks into her fur muff, trying to see France. 'Our fashions are French, simplicity after the Revolution and so on, and Marie-Antoinette dressing as a shepherdess before she went to the *guillotine*, but shall we see other fashions do you think, new to us?'

Rose recovered from hearing *fashion* and *guillotine* in the same sentence. But then Dolly had never been to France and had been a baby at the time of *guillotines*. 'It is so long since English people travelled there freely,' she answered. 'No doubt it will be different.'

'Will the women still be *fashionable*?' asked Dolly anxiously. 'Will France be completely changed?' Rose looked at Dolly's rather pale, intense face, staring ahead; thought again of ungainly flamingos.

'I expect it will be changed,' she answered. 'I was only a child, but I loved Paris. There were real streetlights along the main *boulevard*, and the light came from burning animal fat and so there was a special smell in the nights as well as all the other smells – everything tied up with our excitement. And I have never forgotten – and the elegance and style of most of the French women was wonderful – that there were still ladies of the court wearing high wigs and much powder and rouge – these things had not yet gone quite out of fashion in France before the Revolution. My cousin Fanny and I couldn't take our eyes off them! We begged my mother over and over to recount stories of an old aunt of hers, unfortunately deceased, who spent much time in Paris, and had tubes of water pushed into the stiff curls of her wig so that she could wear flowers in her hair and they would stay fresh all evening. Fanny and I used to run about curtseying and pretending to pour water over Mama!'

Dolly gave a small smile. 'I suppose I will not see such things,' she said wistfully. 'That was the olden days.' Rose suddenly realised that Dolly thought of her as old. *I suppose, now, I am.*

'There have been so many stories of *le temps de terreur,* as they call it,' said Rose, 'and if even half of them are true, there will have been much upheaval.' Looking again at Dolly's rather wistful face, Rose had an idea to cheer her. 'You must help me, Dolly; we will need your help.'

Dolly turned and looked at Rose, surprised. 'Of course I shall help you, Rose,' she said politely, her teeth chattering slightly in the cold. 'What shall I do?'

'We must keep the Dowager Viscountess Gawkroger from meeting Josephine and Napoleon.'

Dolly's eyes widened, and then she looked puzzled. 'But I understand that to be her greatest desire!'

'Indeed! But – Viscount Gawkroger does not really think the sight and sound of his mother berating Napoleon about her son's death will do much for relations between the two countries.'

'Poor Dowager. She doted on her son, they say. No wonder she wishes to say something to the man who – oh—' Dolly suddenly caught herself. 'Forgive me, Rose, for you it must have been so terrible – of course it would not be suitable.'

'Indeed,' said Rose wryly, 'it would not.'

'What are we to do?'

'The Dowager advises us – daily – that she has been in correspondence with the Duchess of Seaforth who is at present in Paris. I think I must suggest that we intercept her mail,' and catching Dolly's surprised look Rose had the grace to look a little guilty. 'Well, there cannot be very many *soirées chez Josephine,*' she continued, shrugging. 'Perhaps it will not be too difficult. We must interest the Dowager in the opera and the theatre.'

'Oh. Yes.' Dolly stared out. 'I too shall, of course, be interested in the opera and the theatre. And Notre Dame de Paris. And the famous gallery of the Louvre. I am sure there are very many beautiful paintings there. I have educated myself, you know, I am aware of all these things.' She sounded a little pompous; Rose stifled an instinct to smile.

'Did you go to a school?'

Dolly looked surprised. 'No. Of course not. William was sent to school. My sisters and I had a governess but she was extremely stupid. She made sure I could read and write at least but I was the youngest and when I was the only one at home I asked for her to be sent away.' Rose had a vision of some poor little governess, dismissed, struggling with her battered luggage along the square. 'I educated myself in my father's library.'

'And he helped you and advised you?'

'Of course not. I just went through the shelves.' She did not tell Rose what she had found. But tiring of education she said to Rose rather beseechingly, 'So I know that we must see culture, but Rose, what I should really enjoy would be to see the new fashions. But of course I am so tall.' She looked downcast again.

'Dear Dolly, you are' – Rose searched for words – 'you are going to become *elegant* because you are tall. You must not be sad any more. You did everything possible to help your mama before she died – but Dolly, she would want you to be happy! And surely we will attend a ball – the Dowager has many acquaintances – and then we will see the latest fashions,' and Rose suddenly, impulsively, hugged the girl who did, indeed, tower over her.

Dolly was so surprised to be hugged that colour came to her cheeks at last. 'Oh!' she said rather breathlessly. 'Oh.' And then she suddenly began talking fast. 'I did not mind being tall, looking after my mother. She seemed not to notice any more and we had many happy times together, I talked to her so much, and she listened to me after all, she did, really. But you see that I am much taller than most girls and my mother often said – before she was ill, I mean – that I should not be proposed to, being tall. She said I would be an old maid. So now I just sit in the house in Berkeley Square. But I should love to see the new French fashions,' she ended somewhat inconsequentially, peering forward again at the coast of the country that seemed to decree what fashion should be.

'You most certainly, in your position in society, will soon have many suitors,' said Rose. 'Ann and William will see to that. And,' trying not to smile, 'it is not quite the end of the world, surely, to be tall!'

'Oh yes,' said Dolly very seriously, 'it *is* the end of the world.'

'Well, we shall have to find you a tall husband then,' said Rose, laughing, 'although fourteen is perhaps a little young to be contemplating marriage.'

'I am fifteen! I was fifteen the day before we left!'

'Well then – you will help me plot to keep the Dowager and Napoleon apart and I will plot to find you a tall husband when you are older, if that is your heart's desire.'

'Of course it is my heart's desire!' said Dolly in excitement. 'Oh, Rose, thank you. I should like to recount this conversation in my journal – and by the way, I do not wish to wait until I am older. I was old when I was fourteen, I am a *very grown-up* fifteen, I know everything that happens when you get married. Actually, Rose, like the Dowager I should adore to meet Josephine and Napoleon: that would be touching history, would it not? What would Josephine be wearing, do you think? But no – I will help you instead, and write about everything. You see, somebody reads my journal – I think it is my brother, I do hope it is him, dear William, he has always been good to me – and I like to make it as interesting as possible, for I am sure my activities are often rather tedious.'

'William reads your journal?' Rose was somewhat taken aback by this change of subject. 'Do you share it with him, you mean?'

'No. It just gets read.'

'But why?'

'I do not know,' said Dolly, suddenly rather glum again. 'But who else would be at all interested? No one else is interested in me. William was very kind at listening to my stories when I was young. So I write to interest him, even if it is not always *entirely* true.'

'Could it be one of the servants?'

'Servants cannot read, Rose, surely you know that?'

The wind blew from the coast of France and caught their shawls and their cloaks and tugged at their hair under the bonnets as they watched the land coming nearer.

'Perhaps you should not write of our plans for the Dowager,' said Rose, finally taking her bonnet off entirely. 'I do not think that would be wise.'

'Oh, but Rose, I want to make my journal interesting for William!'

'But Dolly, I think that no honourable person would read your journal without asking your permission first: I am certain William would not.' And suddenly Rose remembered George Fallon himself saying, *I am privy to her thoughts*. But it would be impossible, surely, for George to have access to Dolly's journal. And why would he want it? Surely he could not . . . Suddenly Rose's mind jolted. Dolly's family was part of *le beau monde*. Everybody knew that the Duke of Torrence and his father and grandfather before him were old land-owning Englishmen (despite their impecunity) of ancient stock. But surely George would not . . . Dolly? Who had just turned fifteen?

'I could pretend, then, in my journal, to have an admirer! That would make it interesting!'

'Why not?' said Rose, still trying to put the thought of George Fallon reading Dolly's innocent journal out of her mind. 'As long as you are absolutely certain that William is used to your made-up stories. Just make sure the admirer is someone of great importance! It will be a diversion on this rather long journey, from our problems with the Dowager!'

'I will start tonight!' Dolly said. 'I know how to do it – secret admirers appear in all the new novels. I shall call him . . .' She paused and looked at the spring sky, at the white clouds that seemed to race to France ahead of them. 'I shall call him Monsieur X, to be mysterious!'

'The young, very tall, very handsome Monsieur X,' said Rose.

'Or perhaps le Marquis d'X,' said Dolly. 'A French nobleman who – who is a hero of the Revolution! That would be very exciting. I shall say I met him on this packet, and he bowed very low to me, and yes, of course, he is extremely tall and handsome and told me that he too was to stay in Paris, although he must be careful of the *guillotine*!' and her eyes sparkled for the first time in many weeks as Calais port came into view in the distance.

There were officials and passports and papers, and matters to be declared or stamped or permitted. The Dowager Viscountess Gawkroger kept up a steady flow of conversation in her French (which nevertheless was perhaps not quite as fluent as she imagined), but at last a man bowed and said, *Bienvenue à la France*, and they left on the long journey to Paris with two nights in doubtful hostelries.

After some time even the Dowager was, almost, quiet. Perhaps it was because very soon they passed damaged churches and destroyed buildings and were forced to think of the Revolution as something real. Rose remembered the exotic-looking, rich formal *châteaux* scattered about the countryside that they had passed when she was a girl. But now windows had been smashed, doors battered down, torn fragments of cloth hung, caught. However, neat rows of trees were planted in very many places and from small, tidy farms children sometimes waved. Then another bleak, empty *château*. Every now and then they passed what the coachman informed them was *un bois de liberté*, trees that had been planted in village squares to celebrate the Revolution; sometimes one of the trees, behind a small white fence, looked bedraggled, as if the celebration had failed.

On the second night a bright yellow moon rose over Amiens, and from the window of her room in the inn Rose saw moonlight catch the broken beams of a church with no roof. Shadows fell everywhere across long grass. She brought out a small cigar from a box in her bag, lit it slowly, breathed in the tobacco. Suddenly she pulled out her old journal that she had packed at the last minute: she felt again, in the town where peace between countries had been negotiated, the urge to make the kind of magical marks that transferred what was in her mind on to paper, so that her description of France, one night in the moonlight after the Revolution, would last for ever.

And fifteen-year-old Dolly wrote in her journal also. She wrote of her sudden passion for the tall, handsome Marquis d'X, who had helped many people of noble blood to escape from the *guillotine* and who had bowed so low and kissed her hand so romantically. She thought of dear William, enjoying her stories.

In the Hotel de l'Empire in Paris, with its heavy dark furniture and extremely expensive suites, the party of Viscount Gawkroger was settled in very large rooms. Dolly looked around immediately for French fashions, and found to her disappointment that most of the guests were English. The Dowager immediately sent messages to the Duchess of Seaforth, which were intercepted unwillingly by Rose under George's instruction, and spirited away by him. Rose found the whole activity melodramatic in the extreme; it made her want to laugh in a rather guilty manner, and she reminded herself that this was positively her last entanglement with the Fallon family.

This business attended to, the party at once took a *chariot-fiacre* to look at this new, different Paris. Some buildings, damaged in these long years of turmoil, had already been rebuilt; also completely new buildings had begun to appear. But many parts of the city still lay in ruins. Landmarks were gone, the names of buildings had been changed, even the streets were often nothing but broken cobblestones and mud churned up by the horses. To Rose's dismay many of the statues on the façade of the big Notre Dame Cathedral that she remembered clearly had been broken: the Virgin still stood above one of the porticoes but she no longer had a baby in her arms, and the cathedral had a hurt, damaged look about it. However the Louvre Palace had been opened to the public. And the public, including Viscount Gawkroger's party, flocked inside the magnificent building in wonder: the space and the staircases and the long, long gallery and the sculptures and the paintings: Italian, Flemish, Dutch, French. It was spectacular.

'Almost worth a revolution,' murmured George.

'They should have English paintings,' said Dolly patriotically. 'Our paintings are just as good, there are many art rooms in London now.'

'I think you misunderstand, Dolly,' said George drily. 'Many of these paintings are from certain countries that France has defeated. They have not defeated England!'

'Oh,' said Dolly. 'Oh, I see. Then I am glad at the lack of English art.' She had been given permission by Ann that they should not wear mourning in Paris, and wore white again. She was deeply disappointed in the French fashions, for most of the women were dressed something like her, if somewhat flimsier. Dolly wanted drama.

'Perhaps,' said Rose, 'people feel it is as well not to dress too noticeably. This is a new society.'

'Nonsense,' said the Dowager. 'The old society will come back – and I will live to see it. There has been no revolution in England; here they will call again for royalty, mark my words! Apart from anything else, I cannot imagine anyone wishing to live in a society where it is impossible to judge people by their appearance!'

Later they went to the opera, once the prerogative of the rich; now it appeared anybody could attend and they were amazed, all of them, at the vulgarity of some of the audience who took the best seats that were once reserved for the aristocracy. The Dowager was loudly apoplectic.

'Oh look!' cried Dolly, enchanted, on their way back. One of the public squares was open and people were dancing in the lamplight. 'There is an orchestra under the trees!'

'Good heavens,' said Ann. 'There has certainly been a revolution if ordinary people are dancing in the streets of Paris!' and the Dowager again spoke at length and disapprovingly.

'And I have always said I do not like eating at this hour,' she said, as they finally sat down to dinner. 'And all this' – she waved at the meal laid out in a private dining room they had reserved at the Hotel de l'Empire 'all this *French* food. However, you will all be glad to know that the Duchess of Seaforth has left a message. The day after tomorrow there is to be a parade – Buonaparte and all his armies – and we are to be given places where we shall have good vantage.'

Dolly saw that Rose and Viscount Gawkroger exchanged glances as the Dowager carried on in her loud, incessant voice.

'The Duchess never received the letters I sent this morning but of course I did not trust the French servants: I sent my own maid, with a message in person. We do not know if there will be further *soirées chez Josephine*, and if I am unable to stop the whole parade I intend to go the palace at the Tuileries immediately afterwards and leave my card – who knows, he may recognise our illustrious name and remember Harry as a worthy opponent; and – *par parenthèse* – the Duchess has informed me' – here she lowered her voice and looked at Dolly: 'My dear, please fetch my fan from my room,' and when Dolly had obeyed, the Dowager continued – 'the Duchess has informed me that she was – imagine! – shown over their *appartements* in the Tuileries Palace by a *very well-placed* acquaintance, and that Buonaparte and Josephine *sleep in a double bed in the same room*! Even the Prince of Wales, *louche* though he is, is probably not that disgusting! Nothing really surprises me, of course, now that France is in the hands of ignorant Corsican peasants!'

Rose at last escaped, exhausted, before George could delay her with discussions of what damage the Dowager could wreak at a military parade; felt her head full of everything she had seen. She wrote at once to her dearest Fanny, to say that she was now in Paris, a city so changed and yet so much the same, and how she remembered their time here together when they were young and had run across the Pont Neuf and stared at palaces from the outside. *You would love the Louvre Palace, Fanny,* she wrote. *Now anybody can go through the doors and stare up at the Decorated Ceilings and walk up the extraordinary Staircases – and there is a wonderful long Gallery with pictures covering the walls, the longest Gallery I am sure in the World! It is all absolutely, absolutely Magnificent!* Impulsively she signed the letter not with her name but with a rose, her own childish hieroglyph.

Dolly, in her room, too excited to sleep, wrote at length in her journal about the glories of this beautiful city, Paris. But she knew that this would not be very interesting for William, as he was seeing it too. So she dipped her quill into the ink again and, bringing into her mind all the novels she had read, confessed to her journal that the tall, handsome French *marquis* had declared his passion and begged for her hand in marriage. *I told him that he must wait until I talk to Papa,* wrote Dolly, *but I encouraged him to hope, for I said I was sure my father would be glad for me to be a French* marquise. *It is all the rage, I am told.*

ELEVEN

Dolly, passionately, wanted to see new French fashions. She had voiced her admiration of the thin, rather rude muslin dresses on young girls like herself, but did so hope for something a little more exotic.

So as the sun shone next morning, the young ladies of the party (William and George off somewhere to find a particular snuff shop; the Dowager plotting in her room) went again to the Tuileries, walked in the beautifully manicured gardens past statues and fountains, with Dolly commenting, rather disappointedly, on what people were wearing; past the very apartments in the palace where they had been told Napoleon and Josephine now lived; along the neat paths and out on to the square where the King and Queen had been guillotined: it had been renamed, they were told, the people wanting to forget those horrors, the Place de la Concorde.

'I want to see somebody looking like Madame de Pompadour or Madame du Barry,' said Dolly sulkily. 'Something exciting!'

'I rather think people take great care *not* to look like Madame du Barry,' said Rose wryly, 'for I believe it was here,' and she looked about her, 'that Madame du Barry was guillotined and they say her screams as she was brought to the people could be heard all along there,' and she pointed to the rue St Honoré which ran along beside the gardens. Dolly and Ann looked at Rose in amazement; Rose still looked about her carefully. 'My father told me,' she said, frowning at the sun or at her story, 'that there were so many executions and other killings in this very square that a herd of animals – oxen I think – that were being encouraged to cross it could not, or would not, move – so strong to them was the smell of blood and death embedded in the paving stones.' Dolly stared, horrified; Ann gave a little scream and refused to cross the square also, so they abandoned their idea of walking down the Champs-Elysées, which anyway looked extremely muddy, and turned back into the gardens, where they settled themselves on small, provided chairs under the shade of a large tree.

'There would never be a revolution in England. Would there?' said Dolly, and her voice sounded nervous. 'Would there?'

'Really, Dolly!' said Ann and she looked angry: her front teeth throbbed. 'Those things could not happen to *us*, and I wish, Rose, you would keep your horror stories to yourself.' The sun gleamed across the shining roofs of the palaces and birds sang in the trees above them.

They sat in silence for a while, dreaming in the spring sunshine.

I am travelling again at last, thought Rose, hearing the French language all around her, and feeling again the foreignness that she had been so aware of when she was young. *If it is so easy to come to Paris, perhaps I could travel to Egypt and solve the hieroglyphs?* But she suddenly thought of the young woman in Egypt: perhaps she had already been killed for Harry's recklessness. Rose Fallon shut her eyes.

Ann's dreams were quite hidden but they were actually, as they often were, about her teeth. A doctor had told her that there were now excellent porcelain paste false teeth available: her own front ones, he said, were definitely not to be saved. Yet still she dared not have them removed, and suffered terribly. But surely here in Paris, with George's encouragement of William, she would be with child at last.

Dolly stared about her. 'Oh look! *Look!*' And she stood in excitement, pointing. 'Look at those two old ladies! They are still wearing high wigs as you remembered, Rose! They look so *funny!*' Dolly's voice had become loud and piercing in her excitement. 'I expect they're bald. Is the Dowager Viscountess Gawkroger bald?'

'The Dowager takes great care with her *toilette*,' Rose answered firmly.

'Oh,' said Dolly. And then, after a pause, 'Might we go to look at the shops? To see the silks and the laces and the gowns? I should like anyhow to acquire a muslin dress with the split down the sides as all the French girls are wearing.'

'Absolutely not!' said Ann. 'Muslin is indecent!'

'It is the fashion,' said Dolly. '*Everybody* is wearing it.'

'You, Dolly, are not everybody,' said Ann tartly. 'You are part of the English *beau monde*.'

The sun went behind a cloud and the three young women wandered into the alleys of the notorious Palais Royale, where rather vulgar-looking Parisian women wearing much jewellery gesticulated loudly over Sèvres china and old lace.

'They are the *nouveaux riches*,' shuddered Ann.

Later they went down to the river and amused themselves poking through the things in the *brocante* shops, handling old books and pieces of china that had once belonged to the deposed aristocracy and were now for sale very cheaply. Ann mocked the cracks and the unfashionable designs and reiterated that the world might end, but Torrence family china would *never* be found for sale in a second-hand pigsty.

To Dolly's delight the Dowager had arranged for them to go to a ball that evening. But to her disappointment William and George said there was no point in arriving until after midnight.

'However,' said George jovially, smiling at Dolly, 'William and I have not been idle and we have found a place that it may amuse you to visit, to fill an hour before one needs to change into more salubrious attire – not you, Mama, of course, you must conserve yourself for the ball.'

'Where will you go?' asked the Dowager plaintively. 'I do not intend to be excluded from any place of interest.' She looked at her son suspiciously.

'I do not believe a public room, open for dancing, would amuse you, Mama,' said George. 'You do not care for the less affluent people of Paris.'

'Indeed I do not,' said the Dowager firmly. 'And I cannot imagine why they should interest you: we have seen the behaviour—'

'These new halls for public dancing,' George interrupted smoothly, 'are one of the ideas, apparently, of the new regime and it would be good for Dolly to see such places.'

'You would not, of course, dance, Dolly,' William added kindly, 'but you could promenade.'

'I should be interested indeed!' said Dolly quickly, smiling at her beloved brother.

'And I,' said Rose.

'I suppose so,' said Ann languidly, who was consuming brandy for her teeth.

Dolly was first up the stairs, hoping for fashion and romance at last. Her heart sank. The large uninteresting room was very brightly lit with many lamps, no romantic corners of darkness. People in clothes less elegant than hers danced sedately.

'This is the latest dance,' William explained to her. 'It is called the *waltz*.' But Dolly could not hide her disappointment: the waltz seemed very unexciting and the equally unexciting accompaniment was provided by three elderly violinists in shabby black jackets. As always a room full of dancing people smelt overpoweringly of bodies. Dolly sighed. Somehow Viscount Gawkroger and William had implied that there were secrets here, that the less affluent people of Paris would be making assignations. But she could see no secrets, although she looked hard.

George spoke to Rose in a mutter over the violins. She had to strain to hear him. 'Do you suppose there is a possibility at all of my mother interrupting the military parade tomorrow?'

'I feel that not even your mother, George,' she said carefully, trying not to laugh at the idea of the Dowager brandishing her fan at the combined French forces, 'could interfere with a large military spectacle. Her consciousness of her position would not allow her to do such a thing,' and she saw his brow clear.

'Those are of course my thoughts on the matter,' he said.

Respectable couples waltzed by. 'Shall we promenade?' said Rose to Dolly. She felt uncomfortable, standing and staring.

'Yes,' said Dolly, longing to find better entertainment.

'Accept no invitations of any kind,' said William.

The two women, arm in arm, strolled slowly along the length of the room. Couples danced, changed partners, women sat on chairs, men lounged against the walls, the three violins played. Suddenly, but discreetly, Rose motioned towards a woman talking and laughing in a bright gown and much powder and rouge. Dolly looked, and then looked again. Her mouth fell open and she stared at Rose.

'Is that – is that a *man*?' She spoke loudly, out of shock.

'Sssssh.' They kept walking and passed a woman with extremely short hair, wearing trousers.

'Heavens,' said Dolly. Her face was very red and then she started to laugh. 'Such assignations, after all,' she said, with great aplomb in her childish voice. Her face was still red when George came to say it was time to dress for their own ball; she looked back over her shoulder as she went reluctantly with her brother. The waltzing violins followed them downstairs and out into the night.

In the carriage Dolly asked her brother about the men and women dressed as each other.

'Ah, this is Paris,' said William, and he and George, in high good humour, laughed, and even Ann smiled knowingly, and George took Dolly's hand to her great surprise and embarrassment and said she had a lot to learn and he would be glad to teach her.

The Dowager delayed their arrival at the ball by complaining that the young women of her party looked *ill*; she herself had rouged her cheeks and would not be satisfied that a pale pallor was the fashion. But all the arguing and waiting and rubbing of cheeks was worth it when Dolly saw that she was in the presence of French fashion at last.

'I can see that woman's whole back!' she whispered loudly to Rose behind her fan as women, seemingly half undressed, waltzed in men's arms around the room. 'A man is holding her *bare back*!'

George, hovering near, overheard her. 'Those are the *nouveaux riches*,' he said lightly. 'But you will also see some members of the traditional aristocracy here. You will recognise them at once – you are unlikely to see *their* bare backs, little Dolly. I cannot myself see how these two societies can ever come together as one – and indeed it would not be acceptable in England.' Rose looked at him in surprise – surely he was not so far removed from *nouveau riche* himself – but she said nothing and he added firmly, 'These new *faux-aristocrates* have no style.'

Suddenly Rose was almost sure she saw some hieroglyphs dancing past on a large medallion; she blinked in surprise and the hieroglyphs had whirled away into the crowd of dancing couples. Even some of the young men looked extraordinary: colourful high-necked jackets and striped stockings, and many men and women had short wild hair. A large orchestra played much more exuberant waltzes than had been played in the public dance hall, and to Dolly's delight and loud and rather pointed exclamations, one of the violinists was a black man. As George had said, some members of the *ancien régime* were present – Dolly and William were soon claimed by some remote cousin – but the aristocracy did not dance, only stared in disapproval. Rose saw that the Dowager Viscountess Gawkroger also stared avidly from behind her fan, no doubt storing scandalous stories for her friends: *Nude! Nothing but a ribbon over their shoulders!* And everywhere that same overpowering scent of perfumes and bodies and powder and teeth and breath and peppermint pastilles and sweat and cloves, and as Rose watched, an old aristocratic gentleman shook his head vigorously in disapproval at something and immense quantities of powder drifted from his wig through the odorous air.

At one point it seemed that Dolly had disappeared completely, to the immediate disturbance of Ann, William and George.

'Where is she, Rose?' said George hurriedly but almost accusingly. 'You were walking about with her.'

'Indeed I was. But another of her family's acquaintances had asked to meet her, and somebody took her away.'

'She must never be left alone, never!' Rose saw that George looked truly alarmed. 'She must stay with us at all times!'

'A ball is not a prison, George,' she said, surprised. 'Perhaps she needed some air, it is extremely close in here,' and she looked on in amazement as Ann, George and William searched the ballroom with some urgency. Ann in particular looked quite pale. *What is the matter with them?*

Dolly was finally found hemmed most uncomfortably against a wall by a fat old French friend of her father's who greeted William with enthusiasm and started telling him, as he had been telling Dolly, about the exigencies of the lives of the aristocrats under the new regime. He had a red face and was very angry. Ann placed herself close to Dolly, held her arm tightly.

Of course, it is Ann.

Rose drifted away, reluctantly put all the connections together in the hot, crowded ballroom. *Ann has been reading Dolly's diary. They are making fools of themselves because they have been reading her diary and Dolly has been writing about her tall French* marquis. *Surely they know all young girls dramatise their lives. She said herself William was used to her stories!*

Dolly herself, much excited by her wonderful evening, wrote in her journal at some length before she slept of all that had happened, especially the public dance hall. The only untrue bit (but she got quite carried away) concerned the French *marquis*, who tonight had, against all the rules, kissed her gently *on the lips*, she wrote, *under the trees of Paris in the moonlight.*

TWELVE

The spring sunshine shone only weakly on Paris the day of Napoleon's parade and there was rain in the air but the crowds turned out in full to see their hero. Bells pealed and cannons fired and George and Rose knew that the Dowager Viscountess Gawkroger could do no damage here, being many yards away from the man of her intent, and a lot of French soldiers between. Dolly whispered to Rose in some disappointment: 'It is just a small man on a horse.' He was too far away for them to see clearly. It was a disappointment. 'And the troops are rather untidy!' added Dolly. Rose thought of Harry's oft-repeated stories of the glorious Battle of the Nile with Lord Nelson: of the sea on fire; of Napoleon nowhere to be found; of the thousands of Frenchmen who never returned. Josephine was pointed out, at a window in the Tuileries Palace, wearing a magnificent shawl; it was whispered around them that Napoleon and his men had brought many such things back from Egypt. Rose also noticed that George and William and Ann conversed urgently while watching the troops, after which Ann and William escorted Dolly closely in a most unusual display of family affection, and George kept a wary eye, just in case, on his mother.

They were hardly arrived back at the hotel, hardly sat in the *salon de thé* (Ann had not yet had time to find brandy for her toothache), when a carriage and a commotion were heard outside and the Duchess of Seaforth swept in, brushing aside French servants with her fan as if they were flies.

'Henrietta!' she was calling, and all realised with a start that this was of course the Dowager's name.

'Henrietta!' She sat down, fanning her large self, breathing loudly, calling to the servants, now, for tea. Like the Dowager she wore many curls attached to her cap and one of them had come a little unpinned, such was her agitation. 'Henrietta, you have only one hour to prepare yourself – I was misinformed – Josephine is receiving today, and Napoleon is leaving Paris tomorrow so may very well attend, I should suppose; this anyway will be your only chance to see him – I have acquired an invitation for yourself and Viscount Gawkroger and of course dear Rose – you must change at once and come with me.' George had stood in alarm and so had Dolly.

'Oh!' said Ann, piqued. She was connected to a very much finer family than the Fallon family, after all, and her teeth were throbbing.

'I must come too, I must come too!' Dolly cried, looking at Rose.

William remonstrated but Rose said firmly, 'Let Dolly come, she may perhaps be given entry. She is fifteen years old, it is a chance for her to actually see history in the making. I shall say she is my cousin,' and Dolly blushed with pleasure.

'Then we shall attend too, William,' said Ann firmly also. 'You can most easily get us tickets – you have only to mention the name of Torrence. And I suppose it will be *chic* to say one has met Napoleon.'

William raised his eyebrows resignedly to George, but Viscount Gawkroger was walking about most agitatedly and did not notice. 'You are too tired, Mama,' he said urgently. 'You have been overdoing things in Paris. I do request that you do not go!' but the Dowager was already repairing to her room at remarkable speed, calling for her maid, and crying, 'Paris is so *dirty*, I must prepare myself to face Buonaparte at last.' Her cap was literally shaking in excitement as she hurried from the room. The Duchess followed her emotionally.

'We must stop her,' hissed George, taking an enormous pinch of snuff from his gold box and sneezing rather many times, then wiping his nose with his usual large white handkerchief and sitting down again most suddenly.

'There *is* no stopping her,' said Rose wryly, deciding that she would enjoy an altercation between the famous small leader of France and the Dowager Viscountess Gawkroger. She observed George's ridiculous pale face and ridiculous fast-emptying snuff box. 'George,' she said firmly, 'it is so unlikely that Napoleon would know anything of your family! I am sure you flatter yourself to think he will know who we are. And I believe that it is highly unlikely that your mother would in the end behave in public in any manner other than that of a lady.'

William reluctantly went to arrange further tickets; the women dressed hastily and returned; George continued to walk about the *salon de thé* in a most agitated manner, worrying deeply about the honour of the great family Fallon. Ann engaged him, Rose noticed, in private conversation every now and then, after which he seemed to look more worried than ever.

'Where is Dolly?' he said several times, distractedly.

'I am here!' said Dolly impatiently. 'In my prettiest white gown, waiting to be taken to meet Napoleon Buonaparte!'

Within the hour, despite George's protests, William and Ann had already left and the great family Fallon, with Dolly, were seated in the Duchess of Seaforth's large coach and hurrying towards the Tuileries.

'We are at peace with Napoleon,' Viscount Gawkroger insisted, trying to remain controlled.

'*I* am not at peace with Napoleon,' retorted the Dowager Viscountess. Her maid had pinned extra curls for the occasion so that her white cap rose on her head slightly to accommodate them.

At an inner door Dolly gave her first gasp of the afternoon. A tall man in a turban and pantaloons and wearing a sword, like the one in her dream, stood guard.

'He is like the man that I – that I dreamed of – he is—'

'He is a Mameluk Bey, brought back from Egypt,' said another woman knowingly in heavily accented English – she was, it tran-spired, the wife of the Italian Foreign Minister. As they came through the door and into the salon, Dolly was not the only one to gasp. The room was magnificent, shining almost. It was decorated in bright yellow, with dark embellished furniture and tapestried chairs. Chandeliers glittered with thousands of candles. Mirrors reflected the flickering lights of the chandeliers; the mirrors were draped elegantly with long brown fringed shawls, a fashion note quite unknown in England. Ormulu clocks and Sèvres-designed vases stood proudly on marble tables. There was high-pitched, for-eign chattering and the Fallon family realised that, although they could see William and Ann further down the line of people, the English contingent was not the only one: there were also foreigners. Rose could see that the Dowager was put out by this discovery, sniffed in distaste, stared about her with her piercing blue eyes. And the male contingent was small: apart from a few Frenchmen in some sort of odd uniform, standing separately, who were perhaps Napoleon's officers, George and William were two of only a dozen men, perhaps, in a room that contained sixty or seventy delighted women from all over Europe who sounded like excited birds.

'I have not forgotten about the Dowager, but do you think we shall see Josephine's bare back, her *whole* back?' whispered Dolly, bursting with excitement.

But suddenly the chattering fell silent: the double doors at the end of the salon had been opened by two small black boys in blue livery with silver lace collars. Josephine appeared: Josephine alone; smiling, decorous, beautiful (her back entirely covered), dressed in a gown of bright primrose silk that had obviously *not* been placed in any bath beforehand, and a small primrose hat. She greeted the guests and spoke in a pleasant but abstracted manner, presumably having no idea who they were. As she came nearer to the Fallon family down the line of people Rose saw in excitement that the jewellery round her neck was a beautiful – she leaned forward to better investigate – gold medallion covered in hieroglyphs. *Napoleon must have brought it for her, from Egypt.* She felt George beside her relax very slightly and give a small grunt: Napoleon, after all, would not come.

But Napoleon came.

The doors were opened again by the ebony children and Napoleon Buonaparte, First Consul of France, appeared in the doorway, accompanied by two (no doubt specially chosen for their size) very short *préfets du palais* in scarlet and silver dress uniforms, who made even Napoleon seem almost tall. For a moment there was an awed silence: Josephine heard it, turned, bowed slightly to her husband. Then Napoleon walked to the beginning of the line. One of his short but splendid *préfets* (who had a surprisingly loud voice) had a list of names, and, conferring occasionally with the guests themselves, announced each person and to which country they belonged. *Italie,* came the booming voice from the man in scarlet, *la Bavière,* and very occasionally *Grande Bretagne.*

The Fallon party was greatly taken aback. The Dowager had prepared herself for condescension, but this was definitely no short Corsican peasant. He seemed taller and more dignified than some of his more elaborate guests, with his short hair and his simple consul's clothes and his somewhat regal bearing. His shoulders were broad and he held himself as a man who knew very well his destiny, his place in history. He spoke in French, seeming to be actually interested in his guests; he appeared not to mind making small talk to the ladies, asking them if they had been to *l'opéra,* how they found Paris, how long they intended to stay. When he came level with the Duchess of Seaforth he smiled and said, *'Ah,* milady, *je suis enchanté de vous voir encore,'* which caused the Duchess to blush with pleasure and look about her proudly. When he reached the wife of the Italian Foreign Minister he took her hand, bowed over it and spoke Italian. Then Napoleon came towards the Fallon family; beside her Rose saw that the Dowager was shaking in anticipation or anger or fear. George kept trying to restrain his mother slightly by unobtrusively holding one of her elbows extremely tightly. Dolly, staring at Napoleon, was very red in the face.

Just as the man with the list approached them, just as he introduced in his booming voice *la famille Fallon de Grande Bretagne,* Dolly fainted, right at the feet of Napoleon Buonaparte.

Afterwards Rose wondered if she had dreamed.

She had quickly, instinctively knelt to Dolly, as people moved and murmured to give the girl air, and as she bent over her Dolly opened one eye, smiled broadly, closed it again. There was a smell of perfume or oil: Rose was aware that someone else had knelt to Dolly also and would have seen Dolly's smile. She raised her eyes and realised that it was the First Consul of France, Napoleon Buonaparte. Grey eyes of great intelligence looked at her in amusement, then he stood and gave a command in French. Servants at once appeared and Dolly was lifted gently and whisked away. Rose made to follow, found her way was blocked, she could not definitely say deliberately, by one of the scarlet-coated *préfets*.

'*Tout va bien, madame*,' said this gentleman, 'she will be well attended. It is not the first time a young lady has been overcome in the presence of the Consul.'

Napoleon had turned to the Dowager Viscountess Gawkroger and before she could speak had with courtesy taken her hand, over which he bowed. '*Tout va bien*, milady,' he said, and then began to speak in rapid French of the joys of Paris. The Dowager, although she towered over Napoleon (especially with the extra hair pinned under her cap for the occasion), was nevertheless stunned into silence; finally, by nodding faintly, she seemed to acquiesce that she must, indeed, attend *l'opéra* once more. Viscount Gawkroger bowed, flushed, but said nothing. And Napoleon Buonaparte ended the audience in heavily accented English: '*Adieu*, milady. It seems an enchantment to meet one of your stature.' His eye caught Rose's again with the same amused look, then he bowed to them all and was gone with his scarlet-coated attendants and the list of names, and they heard his voice speaking politely to the next group: '*Vous rendez-vous souvent à l'Opéra, madame?*' The meeting of the Fallon family with Napoleon Buonaparte, First Consul of France, had taken less than a minute and a half.

The Dowager Viscountess Gawkroger, who had not said a word, was ushered by her son to a tapestry-covered chair and sat fanning herself, overcome.

For some moments Rose watched the First Consul. She suddenly thought of how the English newspapers mocked this man, called him mad, ignorant; laughed with glee when they discovered that Josephine had been unfaithful. He moved so confidently down the room among the grand ladies of Europe. So this was Napoleon

Buonaparte. And she had seen him, quite particularly! Then her eyes took in the little group of French officers. They were laughing at something now and at once they reminded Rose of a confident group of English officers talking together, like Harry and his friends, laughing in the same belonging way, handsome in their uniforms, their world defined. She looked away quickly, looked back at Napoleon Buonaparte. He was 'the enemy' and all the ladies were charmed. How odd it all was. A tall French officer, one of the group, moved to her side.

'You have been interested to meet the First Consul, *madame*?'

The first thing she noticed was the smiling kindness of his eyes; immediately she felt at ease with him even though he was a Frenchman, the 'enemy' also.

'It is just that in England, for so long he has been – you must excuse me, *monsieur* – a monster! Something to frighten children with if they were naughty – *Napoleon will get you!* – and I see that he is not a monster at all – and – and that he has a sense of humour! We do not expect monsters to have a sense of humour!'

He laughed down at her. 'He is, indeed, a most interesting and complicated man. I am very, very proud to work with him.' And for a moment they both watched the First Consul as he moved further down the magnificent room.

'You are one of his officers, *monsieur*?'

'Not exactly, *madame*. We were meeting with him this afternoon – he has a large study upstairs, a magnificent – palatial indeed – room,' and the Frenchman raised his eyebrows very slightly, 'well, we are after all in a palace! and our meeting was interrupted for this *soirée*. My colleagues and I are some of the *savants*, the scholars you would perhaps say, who were on his expedition to Egypt. We are the last to return, have only recently arrived home.'

Rose felt a pang of excitement. '*Egypt*! You were actually there with him in Egypt? You have seen the hieroglyphs and the treasures – perhaps you have even seen the Rosetta Stone?'

The smile went a little from the Frenchman's pleasant face. 'It is perhaps not wise, *madame*, if you will forgive me, to mention *la pierre de Rosette* to a French scholar who has spent so much time gathering information about the lost civilisation of Egypt. We very much regret that your country felt it necessary to deprive us of our greatest treasure. For it is ours indeed, discovered by us, and rescued by us from obscurity. It does not belong to your country.' He might perhaps have bowed and left her: she instinctively put out a hand and touched his arm.

'Oh, *monsieur*, forgive me. I have heard the story – the taking of such a treasure from those who had found it was perhaps – unreasonable – but – but the stone may open the secrets of the ancient world to us, its knowledge and its history; we must not quarrel over it, but share the knowledge, surely?'

'So far, *madame*, the knowledge remains impenetrable – to the French, to the English, to anybody. It is over two years since we originally found that stone in the old fort in Rosette, and the Greek was translated into French at once, but we have made no further progress. It will be a scholar indeed who solves the mystery for, so far, the hieroglyphs and the other markings retain their secrets absolutely.'

'It was disappointing was it not, the Greek text?'

He looked astounded. 'You have *read* the Greek, *madame*?'

'Oh – an English translation of course! I was – lucky enough to be given a copy. But I was so hoping for revelations and magic and I found merely obeisances and inordinate praise for a very young man indeed!'

His face regarded her with open delight, as if he was a very young man himself, which he was not. 'Madame, I wish to introduce myself. My name is Pierre Montand and you are the first woman I have met who has read the Greek translation of the Rosetta Stone.'

Rose broke in excitedly. '*Monsieur – pardonnez-moi* – is it perhaps thought that the frequency of the name of the young King Ptolemy in the Greek may correspond with a frequency in the hieroglyphs and so begin at least to give us some information?'

'I wish it were that easy, *madame*. That frequency has of course been noticed. But the hieroglyphs, until now at least, have always been regarded as a picture language, a mystical language carrying secrets perhaps – rather than sounds or letters that might lead us to a simple translation,' *and Rose saw the star that she drew as a child to indicate her mother, her own picture language.* 'There is a great deal of rethinking to be done,' he went on. 'We feel that the clues perhaps will be found in the middle of the three texts, the text that is in the language of the common people but must nevertheless be surely related to the hieroglyphs. We do hope that a scholar of languages will eventually make a connection between the two. Until then we can only surmise, and it is a disappointingly slow matter.'

'Oh,' breathed Rose, listening intently.

'And *madame*, I have indeed seen this stone, I have examined this stone, and the most damaged part is at the top where the hieroglyphs are written and there is much missing. But the middle part, the common language, is the most complete.'

'Oh,' breathed Rose again, and he was enchanted.

'We – the French *savants* I do mean – are working on the publication of a number of volumes; it is to be called *Description de l'Egypte* and will contain many wonderful details of what we saw there.'

'You are not then a soldier at all, *monsieur*?'

'*Non, madame*. Napoleon, he understood there was much knowledge to be found in Egypt; he took with him on that expedition with the army very many scholars.'

'What sort of scholars – do you mean historians?'

'Practical scholars, *madame*: artists, mathematicians, linguists, chemists, writers, architects – archaeologists like myself. We spent some years there, studying the culture and the monuments but also building roads and hospitals and windmills.'

'Oh. No wonder then you are so angry about the Rosetta Stone.'

'Napoleon Buonaparte loved Egypt. I think you could not say the same of the English generals, if you will forgive me for saying so. And so we resent the stealing of *la pierre de Rosette* from us. However we have acquired nevertheless much information.' He smiled down at her so that she would understand his words were not now meant as rudeness to her. 'The Commission de l'Egypte is very near to here; perhaps, *madame*, as you have a special interest, you and your family would be interested in seeing some of the paintings and drawings of things *égyptien*, including hieroglyphs, that we intend to publish?'

Rose's face lit up. '*Monsieur*, that would be quite the most wonderful thing. You cannot believe how much this interests me. I have loved the hieroglyphs since I was a child, and my father was in

Rosetta, as the English call it, when he was a very young man, long before I was born, and he named me after that beautiful town,' and she saw interest and delight cross his face as he listened.

'*Quelle chance extraordinaire!*' he said.

And then she remembered herself. 'Oh, forgive me, *monsieur*, my name is Rose Fallon. I am visiting Paris with my late husband's mother and his brother, the new Viscount Gawkroger, and some other acquaintances, and we are residing at the Hotel de l'Empire. My husband was a captain with the British navy in Egypt.'

For just a moment he seemed to regard her with shocked surprise. 'Ah,' he said finally, 'the Viscountess.' And she was struck at once by his tone of voice and did not know if he meant her mother-in-law or herself.

'Rose! Rose!!'

Rose turned quickly: Dolly was returned, looking excited and not at all pale.

'Oh Rose, I have seen their *rooms!*'

Rose immediately indicated Pierre Montand before Dolly could let fall any piece of indiscreet information. 'Dolly, this is one of Monsieur Buonaparte's scholars. He has been to Egypt and seen many hieroglyphs, not copies in books but real ones. Monsieur Montand, this is Lady Dolly Torrence.'

Dolly's face was a picture. For a moment, in her excitement at her adventures, she had not seen the French officer. *A tall Frenchman!! Good-looking!! Who was a scholar!!* Had she not swooned before, she might have swooned at that moment.

'Oh! Oh! *Enchantée*, Monsieur Montand. Have you solved the beautiful hieroglyphs?'

'Not yet, *mademoiselle*. But I am glad to find so many English ladies with such an interest in them! Have you too read the Greek translation of the Rosetta Stone?' He was smiling at her enthusiasm.

'No, *monsieur*, of course not, but I heard about it from William, my brother, who rescued it.'

Without noticing Rose's embarrassment or the look on the Frenchman's face, Dolly would have continued but Rose said firmly, 'William was in Alexandria at the time, that is all.'

'Oh yes, that is what I meant,' said Dolly and continued with the utmost fervour, 'Monsieur Montand you are so handsome and so tall! Are you married?'

'Dolly!'

He laughed, unable then to be angry. 'I am not married, *mademoiselle*. I spent some years in Egypt and all the beautiful ladies were married on my return.'

'Oh,' sighed Dolly, looking up at him.

There was a stir at the end of the room and then Napoleon, with Josephine now on his arm, walked slowly back past the groups of people. He nodded very slightly to Pierre Montand, standing with Rose and Dolly, then the doors closed, the little black boys in their blue uniforms disappeared inside, and the *soirée* was over.

The French scholar was immediately called away by his colleagues.

'Oh no!' said Dolly, deeply disappointed.

'*A bientôt*,' he said. 'We need to finish our meeting with the First Consul. I shall call at the Hotel de l'Empire tomorrow afternoon,' and he gave one more bow to the ladies and then the scholars too disappeared behind the closed doors.

Dolly looked after the tall Frenchman longingly. Her face was glowing.

'I believe – oh Rose, I believe you have found me my tall husband!' she said. 'I misunderstood my dream: the tall Turkoman was *leading* me to my tall husband – for of course a Turkoman could not be my husband! Oh Rose! And was my fainting useful?'

'It was' – Rose laughed – 'so extremely useful. Thank you, Dolly, for being so – distracting. The Dowager said not a word and all is well and war has not been redeclared between the two countries, for which I believe you must take some credit!' But still she heard the Frenchman's voice: *Ah, the Viscountess*.

Dolly glowed. 'Oh, I am so glad! I only opened my eyes for the briefest moment! Now, when shall we meet Monsieur Montand again? Oh Rose! Napoleon and Josephine sleep in the *same bed*, can you imagine it? I saw it, it was under draped curtains – the bed was covered in blue silk and I contrived to sit right beside it while they gave me some *cognac*!' And Dolly laughed excitedly. 'I looked all around, it was very beautiful and I thought it might be interesting to sleep in one bed all night long with a man: I had never thought such a thing. I am sure Mama and Papa never did so, nor William and Ann, but I should think of it for Monsieur Montand! And all the French servants were kind and patted my head and said I was *très jolie*, and even the little black boys smiled finally when I teased them. Oh Rose, I have touched history, have I not? This is better than *any* novel I have *ever* read. To think I have been in the rooms of the great Napoleon Buonaparte – and to have sat beside his bed! And now – oh Rose,' and Dolly stared again at the closed doors that might lead to paradise, 'I never thought so many wonderful things could happen in one wonderful day. I have found my tall husband, Monsieur Montand, and you must help me; now I shall be able to write in my diary of a *real* admirer!' And in the magnificent yellow room beside one of the shawl-draped ornate mirrors Dolly threw her arms round Rose in her excitement. 'I do love you, Rose,' said Dolly, just before they were hurried away by George. His mother, walking slowly back to the carriage, waiting for her son's arm, spoke not at all.

The Dowager spoke very little also on the way back to the Hotel de l'Empire. She obviously could not believe that her moment had come and she had not mentioned her beloved son. She could not understand herself. She was pale under the rouge her maid had so artfully applied and she stared out at Paris with its broken cobblestones and newly mended churches. But George was extremely jovial now that the crisis had passed: he kept saying how *immaculate* his mother's behaviour had been, he made Dolly sit beside him in the carriage, and he had his arm loosely about her shoulders although such was her suppressed excitement she did not notice. The Duchess of Seaforth kept up a commentary about the salon, the clothes, Buonaparte's rather *too* simple attire – but his charm – *oh là là* he was a charming man.

'And you, Lady Dolly,' she said archly, 'how could you faint in that manner, at that exact moment – what were you thinking of?'

'I was overcome,' said Dolly dramatically, 'at the sight of History, of a Man who has featured for so long in our Consciousness!' and Viscount Gawkroger patted her hand rather kindly and smiled once more.

'Sweet little Dolly,' he said, 'I do long to introduce you to my friend the Prince of Wales who will one day, long after Napoleon's star has waned, be King George IV of the greatest nation in the world. And one day I shall do so. And eventually you will meet the King and Queen themselves.'

'I have met them,' said Dolly, off-handedly, thinking of other things. 'Papa and Mama took William and my sisters and me to the Palace several times; once we got lost in some dark corridors that had nothing to do with us – remember, William? – and they were disgusting, I slipped on some rotten fruit – at least that's what I thought it was – but it turned out to be a turd.'

'Ah.' George flinched (either at his faux pas, or Dolly's words); recovered, took charge of the conversation in the suddenly silent carriage. 'But now you will be going not as a child but as a young lady about town. And you must not be overcome, as you were today. In fact I see that there are many things I need to train you for,' and he smiled again. Dolly was still oblivious, full of her own exciting thoughts. The Duchess of Seaforth nodded benignly, but Rose looked at her brother-in-law sharply.

'I do not think, George, that an introduction to the Prince of Wales is necessary for Dolly's education,' she said, watching him. But George just kept on smiling.

'Neither Napoleon nor the Prince of Wales is *tall* ,' said Dolly, and she looked happily at Rose and then out of the carriage window where evidence of Napoleon's power was all around them as they drove through the rutted and dangerous streets: sticks of barley sugar with his head on them being offered to them through the windows, and indolent Parisians who did not immediately step obsequiously aside as they once had done, when the Duchess of Seaforth's carriage rolled imperiously by.

THIRTEEN

The *salon de thé* of the Hotel de l'Empire was crowded with visitors who had seen Napoleon ride before his army earlier in the day, and were still speaking of it. Dolly heard them, looked at them pityingly. They knew nothing: she had seen his *bed*.

William and Ann were already returned, and were waiting to exchange opinions of the French First Consul. Dolly, her eyes shining, immediately gave them a full account of his private rooms; she could have been the Dowager the way she gave no one else a chance to speak. 'And I saw a gown of Josephine's with jewels sewn all round the hem, it was thrown over a chair, oh and Rose, I forgot to say, I believe there was a *bath* in the room behind, I could not be sure, it was disguised as a sofa and covered in crimson cushions, but I believe I saw one of the legs!'

Ann's eyes had grown wider and wider. 'Did the Dowager speak to him?' she interrupted imperiously at last. 'You were invited to meet him privately?'

'No, no!' Dolly was jubilant. 'I fainted at his feet!'

'Was that you? I saw someone behaving ridiculously.' Ann was immediately cross. 'Well then, I am glad I was at the other end of the room. Torrence women do not faint.'

George Fallon loomed up behind them, relaxed, benign. 'Nor do Fallon women,' he said cheerfully. 'Mama is resting. She was charmed by Napoleon and behaved with great dignity, as I knew she would. And I have told little Dolly here' (as if Dolly was not taller than he) 'that she needs to be trained not to be overcome by such occasions because I wish to present her to the Prince of Wales. I shall have to give you lessons, Dolly,' and to Dolly's enormous surprise George, Viscount Gawkroger, took her hand and actually kissed it; she felt the whiskers of his chin. 'And who,' he added, turning to Rose, who was receiving the tea from the servants, 'was that Frenchman you were cavorting with at the *soirée*?'

Dolly looked absolutely outraged. 'She was not cavorting!' she protested loudly, so that her voice could be heard clearly by those around them in the *salon de thé*. 'She was finding me a husband.' Then, seeing that she had everybody's attention, she said loudly and dramatically in her young girl's voice: 'I believe I have met the man I am going to marry!' She looked to Rose for confirmation. George and Ann exchanged shocked glances, and then both of them looked at William.

Ann spoke first. 'It is for your family to find you a husband, Dolly, not Rose,' she said, and her voice was like ice. William, looking first at George, then at his wife, got up rather regretfully (for he had not had his tea) and said to Dolly, 'Come, Dolly, I wish to speak with you.'

Dolly was delighted and took her beloved brother's arm. 'Dear William,' she said, and smiled at him as they disappeared arm in arm through the big door, Dolly the taller.

'Then I think I must' – George Fallon glanced at Ann for confirmation – 'go to my mother.' Rose noted that he too was going without his tea. Ann and Rose were left alone together; for a moment neither of them spoke.

'I think,' said Rose at last, carefully, unable to believe what was happening, 'that Dolly is too young to be contemplating marriage with anyone.'

Ann's long earrings flashed in the late-afternoon light which filtered through the large windows and into the *salon*. 'It is never too soon to think of the future of a young girl in Dolly's social position,' she said. 'She is of a very fine family, but she is an extremely impressionable young girl, we cannot have her throwing herself at unsuitable people.' She had acquired a glass of brandy for her teeth, downed it quickly. She looked at Rose speculatively. 'Well, my dear, I suppose there is no reason why you should not now know. We realise that Dolly is ready to marry. If George should do her the honour of asking for her hand it would add greatly to the closeness of our two families.'

Rose at once sat up very straight. 'George is *twice* her age, more. He does not intend to marry yet, he has told me so himself. It would be ridiculous and I am sure it is not at all Dolly's desire.'

'We happen to know a great deal of Dolly's desires.'

'Ann!' Suddenly Rose was aware of, and indicated to Ann, the people nearby, who seemed to have been greatly enjoying the conversation of the English family.

Ann had nothing to hide and like the Dowager she seldom lowered her voice. Other people did not exist. 'She wishes to be married, she has apparently been indiscreet enough to speak of marriage with a French *marquis*, which is of course out of the question, but the Frenchman has been behaving with unbelievable indiscretion. George and William have agreed this long ago, they have only been waiting until she is old enough, and they have decided to move now and avoid any further – difficulties. After all, *you* did not supply an heir to the Fallon family and one is urgently needed.'

Rose saw again the interested spectators. She stood, took Ann's arm forcefully, and literally marched her, protesting, to the courtyard outside where *fiacres* stood and horses stamped on the cobblestones and Rose felt drops of rain on her short hair. 'The French *marquis. It is only a fairy story!*'

'*Vous désirez un fiacre, mesdames*?' A servant bowed low.

'*Non, non,* go away!' Rose pulled Ann to one side. 'You have been reading her journal and passing on the information to George. That is despicable!'

Ann looked only very slightly disconcerted, shook Rose's arm off calmly. 'George and I are old friends. We understand one another. This marriage has been arranged for years. And journals are certainly not private, whatever gave you that idea? Journals are public records. Especially the journals of fifteen-year-old girls!'

'Ann, we must stop this at once. Dolly is a child. She was writing these stories in her journal because she thought William was reading it and she wanted to keep his interest.'

'Nonsense!' said Ann dismissively. 'Where do you think she disappeared to at the ball last night? She has just announced she has met the man she wishes to marry. For all we know this Frenchman is stalking the hotel at this very moment, knowing the illustrious family she comes from, wanting to – to kidnap her!'

'This is ridiculous, she is . . .' Rose looked for words, 'she is not grown up enough. She is still recovering from her mother's death. She has just turned fifteen – surely William could not agree to this, she is his sister, she is devoted to him, and he is kind to her. He could not agree!'

'William is very much guided by George.'

'Then surely her father will never allow it. You cannot do this to her simply because you require it! You cannot!' Now Rose's voice was raised despite herself.

'We can,' said Ann, 'and we shall.' And she smiled. 'You were a child yourself when you married Harry Fallon, and he also was a deal older than you.'

'I was seventeen! And I was wildly in love.'

Ann had turned to go inside; she turned back, smiling still. 'You are very foolish, Rose, if you think love has anything to do with things like this. Why do you think the Prince of Wales married Princess Caroline? It was not love, I assure you – he had to take brandy when he first saw her! You are not from the same part of society, you do not understand these things. Dolly is already part of *le ton* and George will become more so, and that is what we all want. Fifteen is not young for girls of our class to be betrothed.'

'Why does the Torrence family agree?' Rose asked suddenly, sharply. 'The Duke of Hawksfield would surely not be a party to this – for Dolly would be marrying beneath her in the eyes of your society.'

Ann did not even show embarrassment. 'We badly need the Fallon money,' she said simply. Rose stared. 'Oh Rose, you are not of our class. Once she has borne him a son Dolly can have her own life, love whom she pleases. That is how it is with us. Dolly will have a perfectly pleasant life and I hope you would not think of standing in the way of a young girl's happiness and good fortune.' And Ann walked back up the steps and disappeared inside.

For a moment Rose was speechless. Poor, poor Dolly: a pawn to be sold; it had been arranged long ago. The Duke of Hawksfield must know of the plan, or they would not dare. She thought of Dolly eagerly taking her brother's arm not fifteen minutes ago.

As she went slowly inside she saw that Ann was sitting now with George and his mother. The Dowager was obviously extremely pleased about something. She had put a little more rouge on her face.

In the middle of the *salon de thé* the old lady began at once in her loud voice. 'Where is dear Dolly? I wish to speak to her – we shall move to Rome at the end of the week – I have done what I came to do and there is now no need to linger in Paris. I know Buonaparte knew Harry was a hero and knew my displeasure, that is why he spoke to me so – kindly – and indeed he dealt with the matter very charmingly – although I could never be charmed by him of course.' George smirked beside the window. 'The Duchess has advised me that the Pope is also receiving ladies of the English society, even those who are not of his faith, and in good society I do not see what faith has to do with it and so I have asked George to make the necessary arrangements for us all – I do not feel that there is the same – atmosphere – in Paris as we have been accustomed to expect – oh! the *rude* behaviour of all those Parisians sitting in the best seats in the theatre in their unclean clothes while we were forced to sit further back, for all the world as if they owned the place, I found that most distasteful – now *where* is dear Dolly? I do so wish to speak to her, and Rose, who was that French officer to whom you were paying *far* too much attention this afternoon? I believe I saw you holding his arm, we do not expect such behaviour from the women in our family. Your conduct was displeasing to me.' Rose looked at her mother-in-law, now so full of her meeting with Napoleon, in disbelief.

'He was not an officer,' she said coldly. 'And I was certainly not holding his arm.' *What bullies this family are, all of them – yes, yes, Harry too. And she saw her husband hold her face, make her look at their bodies in the mirror, making her watch him touch her: aren't we beautiful?*

133

'Then who was he – if I may be permitted to enquire of the widow of my son?'

'He was one of Napoleon's *savants*, one of the French scholars who had been with Napoleon in Egypt. He knows all about the Rosetta Stone and many other antiquities.'

George's face lit up and he reached inside his jacket for his snuff-box. 'Does he, by Jove – then you must flirt for us more often!' And he laughed. 'Perhaps you can be of value to the Fallon family after all! I must meet him. What was his name?'

'Monsieur Pierre Montand.'

'More. I want to know more.'

Rose bit her lip. She heard again the Frenchman's voice: *Ah, the Viscountess.* 'They are working on a many-volumed book about their studies and discoveries in Egypt.'

'In that case, I absolutely must see him before we leave Paris. Anything about the hieroglyphs?'

'They know no more than your colleagues, I should think.'

George took a large pinch of snuff. 'It will be a race then,' he said excitedly, 'which of course the English will win.'

At that moment Dolly and William returned. They both had red faces and it was obvious that Dolly had been crying. And Rose saw that though Dolly had so eagerly taken William's arm when they left, he was now holding her arm tightly, as if to stop her from running.

Nobody made any comment on their appearance at all. 'Now we shall go to the *opéra*, as suggested by Monsieur Buonaparte,' announced the Dowager. 'Dolly dear, come and sit beside me at once.'

Late that night (after the opera, after another huge, late dinner during which nobody had mentioned anything about plans for Dolly and during which Dolly, placed between the Dowager and George, had looked more and more distraught), Rose went quickly to Dolly's room. Dolly was lying clenched in misery on her large four-poster bed.

'William says I must marry Viscount Gawkroger on my sixteenth birthday. He says Papa will agree. But more than that he says the

Duke of Hawksfield will agree and he is the one who makes decisions for us. He says they know I wish to marry *someone* because they have read it in my journal! I tried to tell him it was a story to entertain him but I do not think he believed me. He says I was talking about you finding me a husband only this afternoon, which is why they decided to tell me now. William told me I am very, very lucky, that not everybody would marry a tall girl – oh Rose! Viscount Gawkroger is *much* shorter than me and I dislike him and he keeps kissing my hand.' And she could not suppress her sobs: 'He makes my hand smell of *snuff*.'

'Dearest Dolly.' Rose put her arms around the girl. This made Dolly cry harder.

'It was my journal. They have all, *all of them*, been reading my journal! I only wrote it for William, to entertain him!'

'Yes,' said Rose. 'I know. I told Ann it was not true.'

Dolly continued to sob for some time. Rose despaired, stroked her hair. Then the sobs suddenly stopped and Dolly sat up. 'I want to marry Monsieur Montand. He is tall and kind. Viscount Gawkroger is short and, I believe, unkind or he would never make me do this. Rose, you must speak to him, to Monsieur Montand, and tell him that I love him desperately.' Strange agitated breathing accompanied the words.

'Dolly, I think perhaps you are very overwrought. We do not know anything about Monsieur Montand, nothing at all – we met him for five minutes.'

'But we will see him again! He said so! His eyes are kind.' Her voice sounded almost hysterical and Rose felt deeply uneasy.

She said reluctantly, 'He is working on some books about Egypt and knows we would be interested in them and has invited us to the Commission de l'Egypte.'

Dolly face completely changed: she quickly smoothed back her hair, wiped her eyes, the tears were gone. 'Then we must tell him.'

'But Dolly – I think – we cannot suppose he might care to marry a fifteen-year-old English girl whom he barely knows.'

'I will persuade him. As long as I can see him I will persuade him. I would be everything to him, everything he wanted. I know what happens in marriages, I can do it. I will love him so much that he will have to love me.'

'All this because he is *tall*?' Rose could not help smiling slightly.

Dolly looked at her angrily. 'You have never been tall, you do not know what happens to tall girls. Men do not dance with them. They only talk to them when they must, or if they are extremely rich. Our family is *not* extremely rich, my father and my grandfather have spent our fortune and our estates on their gambling and their mistresses as everybody knows and never mentions. We have to sell our paintings, we owe money everywhere. The Duke of Hawksfield even pays for our carriage! Love is something I haven't had yet and I know I can find it with Monsieur Montand. My mother did not love me until' – Dolly's voice broke again – 'until she was mad. Viscount Gawkroger does not love me. He wants me to bear him a son. That is what William said.'

'Heirs are very important, Dolly, in the society you move in.'

'Let him find someone his own age! He seems a hundred years old to me! Will you speak to Monsieur Montand for me?'

Rose was silent. *How can I speak of this to a man I have hardly met?*

'Please, Rose,' Dolly insisted. 'Please, please, Rose, I beg you.' When Rose did not speak Dolly said suddenly, 'You mean to keep him for yourself!'

Rose looked at Dolly's desperate young face and remembered that, not so much older than Dolly, safe and secure in her innocence, she herself had been determined to have her way.

'I will do what I can,' she said, and she kissed the girl and turned to go. 'Whatever happens,' she promised, 'I will try and help you *not* to marry George Fallon!'

FOURTEEN

The next afternoon Monsieur Pierre Montand appeared at the Hotel de l'Empire, presented his compliments to the Fallon family and enquired whether they had any interest in seeing the preparations for the volumes of *Description de l'Egypte*.

George was extremely pleased, shook the Frenchman heartily by the hand. Dolly was stricken with excitement and anticipation and hysteria and agreed with George, very loudly.

'Very well,' said the Dowager grandly, 'I see my son and dear Dolly have some shared interest.'

None of them, not even George, who was a collector of antiquities, was prepared for what they saw. Once they had entered the main doors it was as if a bright light had suddenly illuminated everything. Yet it was not light. It was the colours that shone. In room after room – on all the walls, on tables, on chairs, on the floor, on plinths – were statues of lions with human faces, pieces of opulent jewellery, coloured boxes, an old wooden harp, a beautiful sculptured head with only one eye, a huge granite foot. There were pieces of stone and pieces of paper covered with writing. There were sections of carved walls that had been removed from tombs and temples depicting life in ancient Egypt in red and blue and gold and white and green and brown: wonderfully painted musicians playing instruments like small harps; scribes writing, gods receiving gifts, boats, brightly coloured ducks. And cats, cats everywhere: statues of cats, carved cats, painted cats and – it was explained – mummified cats. And even more: paintings by Napoleon's French observers of what they had seen: huge, brightly coloured paintings of temples and tombs and tall obelisks and large beautiful figures of people, or perhaps gods. A mother and child, as if they were Christians thousands of years before Christianity. Birds and scorpions and fish, and creatures half-animal, half-man. Paintings of the river Nile, lush palm trees, small sailboats, farmers, blindfolded buffaloes, fishermen. Painting after painting of the Pyramids and a mysterious figure called a *sphinx*. And everywhere the beautiful lettering, the tantalising Egyptian writing: carved into all sorts of pieces of pottery or stone, written on torn pieces of something that looked half like paper and half like cloth, or painstakingly copied into the paintings.

'Ohhhhh,' breathed Dolly, so close beside Pierre Montand that he could feel her breath and smell her pastilles. Frenchmen crossed the long hall quietly, their eyes hardly rising from piles of papers and files and paintings and objects they were carrying from place to place.

'This is papyrus,' said Pierre to Rose, seeing her looking so concentratedly at a scroll of writing. 'It is their paper, made from reeds. All these things we sent to France. Before your – Treaty.'

'I presume you have repainted everything,' said the Dowager. Pierre looked shocked.

'Of course not, *madame*. This is what we found.'

'Then I presume your artists have exaggerated the beauty and the colours in their paintings,' said the Dowager, but somewhat uncertainly because what she saw simply stunned her.

'I assure you, *madame*,' said Pierre. 'Our artists were meticulous, they made many sketches and drawings before they began painting, and checked colours over and over. You can see these things with your own eyes. *I have seen them*, I have travelled up the Nile with weary uneducated soldiers who nevertheless sometimes cheered at what they saw. Despite all the battles and the dangers it seemed as if their – their hearts or their spirits, something inside them – somehow suddenly responded to what they found.'

'These treasures were not in Alexandria,' said William, aggrieved. 'I would have brought some home, of course.'

George was ecstatic. 'And you have actually seen the Pyramids, *monsieur*?'

'I have seen the Pyramids. We approached them at dawn and they seemed to be massive shapes floating in the morning light. I am an archaeologist and have seen many signs of old civilisations but I account the day I saw the Pyramids as one of the most' –he did not notice that he turned back to French in his excitement – *'des jours les plus extraordinaires de ma vie!'*

'There must be some way to transport those pyramids to England!' said George.

Pierre smiled slightly.

'Perhaps it is best they are left in the desert, *monsieur*, where they belong.'

'The sky was blue like this in Egypt,' said William, slowly, remembering. 'I had forgotten.' And he stared at the paintings by the French artists again, surprised.

For a while they were all silent, almost as if they were in a church. Dolly stood beside Pierre at all times, moved where he moved. Ann, quite trembling with lack of brandy for her toothache, nevertheless could not tear herself away from the jewellery: much bright gold, amethyst, the most unusual stones of bright blue, pendants, necklaces, crowns, and an extraordinary jewelled blue ring, encased in gold. Rose was almost mesmerised by the writing that she had come to know: the same birds and shapes and animals and figures; she could not help herself, she knelt down, looked closely at the markings on a piece of stone, ran her fingers over the lettering. She hastily opened her reticule and took out her magnifying spectacles. Now she leant nearer, saw the hawk, saw the beetle clearly, bent over the stone in concentration (did not know she looked a little like the old lady Miss Constantia Proud, who had seemed to devour books). Pierre Montand watched, fascinated, heard her say to herself: *They have written their lives. They are trying to tell us.* He knelt beside her: showed her the hieroglyphs carved in stone and then the seemingly different writing made with some kind of quill and ink, on some of the papyrus.

'It was when they started writing with a quill of some kind, and ink of some kind, that the writing probably changed,' he said, 'and eventually, perhaps, became the native writing; it is called the *demotic*, the middle section of the Rosetta Stone.'

'Like joined-up writing?' she said, and he looked at her and smiled. 'Something like that,' he said, 'joined-up hieroglyphs perhaps, simplified hieroglyphs. But too many thousands of years have gone by since hieroglyphs were used, and the connection of the common writing to hieroglyphs is not understood at all. Look at this piece.' In his hand he held a small stone statuette of a seated scribe with a tablet on his knee, writing.

'Monsieur Montand?' said Dolly, and he stood courteously to answer her question about the animals.

Rose turned the little statuette over and over, *the olden days talking to us*; she felt extraordinary, as if she wanted to kiss it. Finally, very reluctantly, she placed it back on a table. Her head ached. She put away her spectacles slowly, closed her eyes. *If I could go to Egypt and find the missing parts of the Rosetta Stone . . .* As she stood up her eye caught that of a broken stone face on a shelf: an enigmatic eye seemed to stare right at her from an odd egg-shaped head; the other eye and part of the nose were missing but, nevertheless, the statue seemed to regard her with a strange expression. She walked slowly towards it, as if drawn. She put her face very near to the broken one, leaned into it, and seemed, Pierre saw, to sigh. Always, afterwards, he held that picture of her.

George began interrogating the French scholar, rapping out questions, demanding answers, asking again and again about the places Pierre had been to. 'Are you telling me they are still *there*, somewhere in Egypt, all these antiquities that you either have here' – he was now looking very keenly at the jewellery with Ann – 'or that have been painted in these wonderful pictures?'

'You would be able to help yourself, *monsieur*,' said Pierre wryly. 'But we travelled many miles, with much difficulty, over many months and years to find such things. And you cannot remove whole temples. But the things we saw – it was – *incroyable*! *Magnifique*! We saw statues many, many times bigger than ourselves. And tombs of the ancient Pharaohs deep under the ground where our artists sat for days and nights on end. Much of the work we had to do at once, in the sand and the terrible heat of the sun and sometimes sandstorms – and of course the continual battles with the Arabs and the Turks and the Mameluk Beys, for we travelled with the army.'

'I know what a Mameluk Bey is,' cried Dolly in excitement. 'There was one at Napoleon's palace!'

Pierre smiled at her but George said, 'Sssssh, little Dolly,' and indicated to Pierre to continue.

'We had to work very fast under appalling conditions, but very carefully nonetheless, as you can see. It has been a long and meticulous exercise,' he stressed again, 'we were there for three years. Almost everything we were able to remove is at the moment stored here, or has been seen and copied by our artists. Or now resides in England,' he added, his face darkening, 'as you are aware, *monsieur*, *la pierre de Rosette* in particular.' He stopped speaking for a moment, so painful was this to him, but then his enthusiasm got the better of him. 'We, the *savants* of Napoleon, his scholars – we live and eat and sleep Egyptian antiquities, the things we have seen and known. We are – what is your English word? – bewitched! However, many, many things remain and it is my opinion that many more treasures are as yet unrecovered.'

'I must go to Egypt,' muttered George, half to himself.

'But to *understand* what we have discovered we need to find the key to the hieroglyphs,' continued Pierre, 'the writing of Ancient Egypt. And *our* finding of *la pierre de Rosette*' (he stressed the word most firmly) 'has meant that we have, for the first time, hope. I was very impressed,' and Dolly watched as he bowed towards Rose in a wonderfully foreign way, 'that your sister-in-law has read the Greek translation. I cannot believe that half a dozen Frenchwomen will have done the same.'

'*Monsieur, monsieur, I* would read it! I would adore to read it, I would adore everything if you would show me!' Dolly was shameless, but desperate. She still stood very close to Pierre Montand and the two of them towered rather over Viscount Gawkroger of Great Smith Street. George was aware of it.

'Dolly!' he said sharply, but Dolly could not, or would not, hear him.

'Shall you return to Egypt, Monsieur Montand?' she said. 'For surely it must be the most beautiful country in the world, is that your opinion?'

Pierre laughed. 'Parts of it are so beautiful that one can hardly take in all one has seen, Mademoiselle Dolly. If I could tell you of the river Nile and the orange groves and the extravagant gardens and the wheat fields and the beautiful mosques!' Rose was mesmerised, remembered her father's stories, saw herself walking in orange groves, eating fresh dates. 'But the cities are crowded and there is much *malaise* – plague, the Nile itself carries death in some parts, blindness – many French soldiers as well as Egyptians died of such things while I was there. And – I think that the people are not very happy to have us there, I do not believe they think of us as friends – although such was Napoleon's intention. On the way through the Mediterranean to Egypt on board *l'Orient*' – he flashed a look at George and William: everyone knew of the sinking of Napoleon's flagship *l'Orient* by Nelson at the Battle of the Nile – 'Napoleon read the Koran. That is something like the Arab Bible,' he explained to Dolly. 'He admired it tremendously and in the evenings we would sit on deck under the stars and discuss religions.' Pierre stared at one of the paintings, lost; then he pulled himself together again. 'He even obtained, rather forcefully, a printing press with Arabic letters from the Vatican so that he could print an Arabic newspaper! They could not believe their eyes in Cairo!' He ended briskly: 'But nevertheless, they do not like us. They are very religious and their religion is very different to ours.'

William interrupted. 'Indeed you may say so, *monsieur*! I too was in Egypt. All that eerie sound from the mosques and the ridiculous kneeling down and praying a hundred times a day just when we were trying to get the lazy fellows to work!'

'As I say, *monsieur*,' repeated Pierre, and Rose heard something cold in his tone, 'the people are not happy to have us there. And perhaps they have reason. Some of the soldiers in Egypt – from several countries – did not behave well. Behaved very much against the Egyptian ways, in fact.'

Rose saw George flush; he caught her eye and she looked away quickly. *It can only be a coincidence, of course.* But again she heard Pierre's voice at the Tuileries, the odd way he had looked at her: *Ah, the Viscountess . . .*

'So, Mademoiselle Dolly, it is a beautiful place in many ways. But – there were terrible battles on our way across the desert to Cairo, and I regret to say that many bones of my countrymen lie buried in the sand of that great and terrible expanse.' He wanted to add *and in the waters round Alexandria* for Nelson had destroyed almost the whole French fleet there, not just *l'Orient*, with the loss of so many young Frenchmen's lives. Pierre's face was grave and nobody spoke; they looked rather with sudden unease at the treasures that had cost so much.

'Come, Dolly,' said the Dowager suddenly, loudly, breaking the odd atmosphere among the priceless antiquities. 'Now we must go. I need you to take my arm.' Rose could have sworn she caught a glimpse of something blue and bright in one of the Dowager's hands: *I must be mistaken, surely.*

Dolly looked at the Dowager astounded, almost as if she was in a dream. '*Go?*' she said disbelievingly.

The Dowager turned to the Frenchman. 'Thank you, Mr Montand, for showing us your little treasures, and even if they are somewhat exaggerated they are nevertheless interesting. Come, Dolly,' she said more firmly. Expression after expression passed swiftly over Dolly's face.

William said, 'Come along, Dolly.' And then Dolly's shoulders seemed to fall and she left the side of Monsieur Montand at last, looking back at him as she did so.

As the group moved down the street to the waiting carriage, their feet clattering on the broken cobblestones, still exclaiming at what they had seen, Pierre managed to intercept Rose, to waylay her almost. '*Madame*, forgive my haste. It is my great desire to see more of you. I – I have things I wish to say to you. Do you remain in Paris?'

'We go to Rome,' said Rose wryly. 'My mother-in-law wishes to be presented to the Pope, although we were all of course christened in the Church of England. I think it is not to do with faith, but with society.'

'I see,' he said doubtfully, perhaps not quite understanding. 'But will you return here?' From the carriage now Rose could see Dolly, who was already being wedged between the Dowager and George, looking anxiously back at them, willing Rose, almost, to put her suit.

Rose turned back to Pierre Montand, looked up for a moment at his kind face. '*Monsieur*, I have enjoyed meeting you more than I can say. I shall never forget seeing these marvellous treasures, and the wonderful hieroglyphs that – you cannot imagine how much I have thought of them in my life – that I should like so much to understand. But we leave tomorrow and I – I expect it would be best that we do not meet again.'

He was so dismayed he slipped back into French. '*Mais pourquoi, madame? Je desire de vous voir encore une fois!*'

She again looked back at the carriage, saw the pale face of Dolly gazing out in anguish. Rose took a deep breath. 'The situation is, *monsieur*, that Mademoiselle Dolly has – has taken a very great delight in meeting you.'

He looked puzzled, glanced at the carriage and saw Dolly's stare, looked back to Rose. 'She is a child, of course.'

'Of course. But that makes no difference. She – she wishes you to save her from a marriage that is unwelcome to her.'

'But – *mon Dieu* – it is you, *madame*, whom I wish to see again, it was of course for you that I entertained your family. It is you to whom I wish to speak. You have such a sad face – until you smile. I think you have encountered much sorrow.'

To her horror (she had not cried for months), Rose's eyes instantly filled with tears. She looked away quickly. 'I am quite well, *monsieur*, thank you.'

'Rose!' called George. 'We are waiting!'

She turned to go but Pierre caught her arm. She was aware of the whole carriage watching: in front of everyone he picked up her hand and pressed it to his lips. She was horrified. This was outrageous. She knew how closely Dolly was watching and waiting, not to mention the Dowager; she tried to snatch her hand away but could not.

'Mademoiselle Dolly must, for her own sake, understand where my interest lies,' he said, and very deliberately he kissed her hand again. 'You can find me here. I almost live here. I must talk to you again for I think I understand something of your sadness.' Still he held her hand gently. '*Ecoutez-moi,*' he said to her. 'A few of us stayed in Alexandria longer than we were expecting – we have only just returned as I have told you. I – I was therefore present when your husband was – when your husband died.' She understood *Ah, the Viscountess* at last.

'It is all right, Monsieur Montand, you do not have to choose your words. I – I am aware that he did not die a hero.'

He breathed out and she could tell that he was relieved. '*Bon.* You should not have expected us to know, of course, but gossip moves so fast in a garrison town. I would not of course have had the discourtesy to mention this to you, not at all, except—'

'Rose! Rose!' called George, and now his voice was angry. He looked as if he would dismount from the carriage.

'Except?' said Rose. She did not hurry. *George may come and hear this if he wishes.* 'You should perhaps be speaking about this to my brother-in-law, not myself. He also knows, but nevertheless keeps a be-medalled painting of his brother to show to visitors.' She even allowed herself a little laugh. 'His mother, you understand, has *not* been advised. But George will no doubt be extremely interested to hear details.'

'You do not care for your brother-in-law?'

'I do not.'

'I am glad. I do not care for him either. But *madame* – I left very recently. The child was born.'

'What child?' She looked at him, puzzled.

He understood at once that she did not know, tried to backtrack: she saw his face. She stared. 'What do you mean? What child?'

'Ah – forgive me, *madame* – for some reason I had assumed . . .'

'*What child?*' Something so terrible clutched at her heart that she could hardly breathe. Suddenly she had to hold on to him, his arm, his shoulder; he saw that she would fall, held her, put his arms around her.

'*What child?*' cried Rose. *She saw the little hands and feet of her own dead baby.* She tried to beat at his shoulders with her fists as if it was his fault and tears ran down her face. 'What child?' she whispered.

Pierre heard rather than saw George dismounting from the carriage. He took a deep breath and spoke quickly and quietly. 'I am so sorry. I just assumed that you must know about the child, if you knew of the fate of your husband. It was a baby girl – if she is not already dead now also. An English merchant had managed to hide the mother until the baby was born but – ah, *mon Dieu*, it was terrible – there is no law in Alexandria with the military gone from there. We could not stop it, they were determined – both the Turkish and the Egyptian families took the mother from the house of the English and we saw her dragged past, she was screaming for someone to help her – we think they did not know at this time about – about *l'enfant*. Ah – *pardonnez-moi* – you should not have to hear of this from me. It was terrible – the poor woman – the stoning and the screaming and the ugliness – and we could do nothing.'

George strode angrily towards them. Before he could speak, Pierre Montand raised his voice. 'And so I thought you should know that I was in Alexandria the day your husband died.'

George stopped in his tracks, stunned. His face turned red again. He was unable to speak. Very gently Pierre let go of Rose's arms, kept one hand under her elbow in case she should fall. He said nothing more and nor did Rose. The three of them looked away from one another but could not move. Tears dried on Rose's stunned face. The silence extended until it was a terrible embarrassment: three people standing outside the Commission de l'Egypte saying nothing (as if retrieval was impossible), being watched closely by four people in a waiting carriage.

They were saved by a mad dog. (Much later, weeks later, remembering this, Rose rocked with silent, almost hysterical laughter.) The dog came snarling round the side of a small building. It ran towards the horses of the carriage. The horses reared, the carriage looked as if it would turn over; they could hear screams, and Dolly emerged, wildly jumping, then William. People ran: George and Pierre ran towards the tottering carriage. A soldier suddenly appeared from a doorway with a battle-weapon: a musket with a bayonet at the top for close encounters. He hurled himself towards the carriage and thrust at the dog. The enraged animal jumped up, snarling at the soldier's face, at the musket. The hero was William. Somehow he grabbed the dog from the back and twisted its neck violently, holding its mouth away from him. People were crying, *Shoot! Don't shoot! Shoot!* The soldier, despite screams of warning from Ann, managed finally to plunge the blade on his gun into the dog's heart, as far away from William's hands as possible: William nevertheless had bits of the mad dog over himself and was taken by Pierre Montand to a *pissoir* at the back of the Commission de l'Egypte.

This event gave the Gawkroger carriage much conversation on the way back to the hotel: Rose's ashen face was unnoticed. When the Dowager, recovered from her brush with death, at one point remembered to rebuke Rose, George of all people came to her rescue. 'Monsieur Montand knew Harry in Egypt,' he said. 'He wished to speak of that to Rose and give her his condolences. It was upsetting for her.' They returned to the subject of the mad dog; later, as they approached the courtyard, the Dowager Viscountess Gawkroger suddenly said very bitterly, 'He should have given condolences to *me*.'

Dolly, for the whole of the journey, looked down at her hands and did not speak.

Over dinner in the private dining room, plans for the journey to Italy were finalised: details were discussed, footmen and maids were packing belongings. To Rose's horror and embarrassment the Dowager was, quite shamelessly, wearing upon one of her wrinkled fingers the extraordinary blue and gold Egyptian ring. Dolly was silent, refused to look at Rose; George, on the other hand caught Rose's eye all the time: it was clear he wanted to speak to her. And Rose herself, trying to control the thoughts that were screeching inside her head, attempted to dwell on the bright paintings and the treasures and hieroglyphs that she had at last seen for herself. But the screeching went on: *an Egyptian girl having Harry's child and not me*. She did not mean to think of the stones killing the mother along dark alleyways, the screaming and the death. She tried at least to get up, to leave the table: she could not move.

Finally the Dowager went to her room; Ann followed her, looking back at her husband. Dolly at once left the table also and went away quickly and quietly, along the long candlelit hall. George, signalling something to William as William too left the dining room, moved quickly so that he was beside Rose before she too could leave; actually held her wrist with his hand, across the table. The hard, painful grip of his hand suddenly brought her to her senses, as if someone had slapped her.

She looked at him coldly, pulled her arm away at once, and said: 'You should control your mother, George. Of course Monsieur Montand will miss that priceless ring.'

George simply brushed the matter aside. 'My mother owns very much jewellery, Rose. Now, what did the fellow know?'

'What do you mean?' *Did George hear?*

'Why were you so upset, clinging to him so inappropriately like a sad flower! After all, you knew!'

'What do you mean?' she said stupidly again.

'You knew how he died. You had been told.' *He does not know.* She did not know why this was important, but instinctively she kept the information to herself. George looked at her carefully. 'There is – no other scandal?'

'What do you mean?' she said again.

'He did not kill someone else?'

'Monsieur Montand did not say so.'

'This – story – *must* die away. There is to be nothing – *nothing* – but a memory of Harry as a hero.'

'I – knew Harry was killed by an Arab but – I had not heard it first hand. Monsieur Montand was in Alexandria that day.'

Even George looked disturbed. 'He actually saw Harry killed?'

Words came out. 'He did – yes, yes, he saw the Arab.' *She saw the mad dog, leaping upward.* 'And – and the knife. It had a silver blade and went into his heart.'

George stood abruptly, called at once for a servant; more wine arrived immediately. George emptied his glass, held it out to be filled again, then took the bottle. '*Va t'en!*' he said sharply to the servant. 'Go away!' He filled his glass again, drank it. Still he could not speak. She saw that he was actually trembling. He could not bear this. At last he sat back slightly, and she saw that with an enormous effort he was pulling himself together. He closed his eyes for a moment. Then opened them. And then spoke calmly. 'The antiquities were astounding, simply astounding. William and I feel we should travel to Egypt. William has decided there is more to the country than he realised. Life was more interesting, he says, when we were at war with Napoleon – it is rather tame to meet him on his wife's arm! He will extricate himself from the navy and we will travel to Egypt. Ah – how I would love to get my hands on some of those treasures.'

Rose did not speak.

George filled his own glass again and slid the bottle across the table to Rose. She saw his absent-minded surprise as she poured some into her glass and drank it quickly. 'It does *not* matter,' said George. 'It does not matter if a French adventurer knows.' He was completely in control of himself again. He raised his glass to Rose. 'I like your short hair, Rose. Dolly shall be shorn too. Drink my health, *Rosetta mia*! I am soon to be led to the wedding altar. Like a lamb to the slaughter. Ah – we could be friends, you and I, if you would only try to see my good points. And,' anticipating her, 'do not lecture me about Dolly – you always wanted me to marry.' Rose understood that he had heard nothing of Pierre's conversation; like him she made a tremendous effort to control herself. She tried to speak slowly.

'George – if you have any feelings at all, you cannot do this to Dolly. You will break her heart – surely even you can see how unhappy she looks now that she has been told of the plans for her future.'

'Dolly is an actress, Rose, as you must have noticed. If it suits her to look unhappy, she will look unhappy.'

Rose ignored his words. 'I cannot imagine what William is thinking of, to even consider such a thing. Surely her family will not give permission.'

George looked amused. He was completely recovered. He emptied his glass, slightly tipped the chair back that he was sitting on and regarded her, feeling for his snuffbox. 'It is of immense importance that I marry into such a family. The Fallon family has worked for many generations for this. Only then, at last – with this marriage – will our name begin to be honoured, will our behaviour begin to be our own business; we will I believe have begun to slip in through the back door and we will be part of the *beau monde* that my father aspired to and that I shall at last enter. My mother was his stepping-stone; Dolly shall be mine. Never mind Monsieur Montand. Harry will be remembered for the charmer he was – and that at least you will attest to! As for the Duke of Torrence, he will do what William suggests. William will do what I suggest: you could say, then, that *I* am the Duke of Torrence! Part of *le beau monde*, the cream of English society!' and he laughed. Rose was silent. He shook his head, looking at her. 'How little you understand the times, *Rosetta mia*. What you do not understand is that things have changed. The Duke of Hawksfield may patronise me, but he himself knows the Torrence family *needs* me. Look at the Duke of Torrence – lazy, only ever interested in women and cards, most of his ancient family fortune lost by him and his father before him. Now look at the Fallon family – my father and my grandfather were meanwhile men of industry and energy and *money* – and so am I. The Torrence family needs new blood, they need my expertise and business knowledge or they will go under for good in one more generation. The Duke of Hawksfield knows this and William knows this. They need me, or perhaps I should more accurately say – being a realistic man as you know, Rose – they need my money and the bank that I am part of.

'Look at poor stupid Dolly, filling her mind with these new, ridiculous novels obtained from any circulation library or book-shop. She has a totally unrealistic view of the world – romancing, I hear, in her diary, if indeed it was romance, which I wonder. She needs me too – to prepare her for the world as it really is.' He became exasperated by her silence. 'Is it marrying you disapprove of for Dolly at her age, or marrying me? She will only be a year younger than you were when you married Harry, and you were a very, very happy little bride, I well remember you.'

'This is not the olden days, George, this is the new century. If Dolly had had the benefit even of the kind of education my parents arranged for me, she would be a very different girl, so you should not patronise her. And she is still a child, and she does not love you. And you know you do not love her. It is cruel.'

'Don't be ridiculous, Rose. Your parents were very eccentric if I may say so, for, tell me honestly, what good did your so-called education do you – once you had met Harry?' He grinned. She looked down at her glass. And then she filled it again. 'And love has very little to do with marriage in the circle I am aspiring to. Dolly can find all the love she likes once she has given the Fallon family an heir: she will be very rich, thanks to me, she will be honoured, and I will be a most complaisant husband, I do assure you.' And then just for a moment his smiling mask slipped and he leaned towards her and she saw the naked, angry ambition that she knew. 'You know nothing, Rose. You should understand that I will eventually become part of *le beau monde*, no matter what the price is. You are from a different class entirely, and the morals of your class are not the morals of Dolly's family, or of mine. This is how things are arranged in the society that I am *utterly determined* to be part of, *will* soon be part of: nothing is going to stop me, certainly not you and your talk of either education or love.'

'I believe – Harry married me for love.' Her voice shook slightly. *An Egyptian girl with a child and not me*. George grunted. He drank from the bottle.

'Rose, for once and for all: Harry was charming. Harry got his way. We all loved Harry – yes, even including me, who disbelieves the word: he could wrap me around his little finger and he knew it. But Harry would not be serious about society at all, he was too busy enjoying himself. It was always I, the younger son, who had the energy and the understanding of what was required – you must have known after all that *your* antecedents could add nothing to the Fallon family, and so, of course, did Harry. But Harry got his way – and I knew long ago that if Harry married you, I would have to marry Dolly as soon as she was old enough. It is as if our positions in the family were reversed by mistake. Of course my mother disapproved of you but she could never refuse Harry anything. Harry married you because he always got what he wanted, and if you wish to call it love you may do so. Harry was intrigued by you certainly: your father was a naval hero, and you were seventeen, and there was something about you that he wanted, your – innocence and your *joie de vivre*, I think. It is a pity you lost them.' George emptied the wine bottle. 'So Harry got you, and you got us, and I – we – get Dolly. You should be realistic about this. Who would marry Dolly if not for her position in society? Who wants his wife to tower over him unless she has a great deal of money, which Dolly has not? And she is prone to hysteria, as we all know. But – she is young, and she is of Torrence stock. And she knows I will not beat her – unless she asks me to! – or leave her penniless. She is very lucky!'

Rose stood abruptly from the dining table. 'I will come to Rome with you, George, only because I gave my word and I was taught as a child never to break my word. But I will not be joining any more of the plans of the Fallon family.' She at once left the dining room and hurried along the wide, shadowy hall, passing only English people, but they nevertheless addressed each other in French – *bonsoir, bonsoir* – the words echoed into the distance. She quickly entered her room and closed the door.

By the window there was an elegant blue-covered chair that matched the blue-covered bed and canopy. She sat there, closed her eyes, then opened them and stared down at the flares illuminating the courtyard below: the uniformed *portiers* and the *fiacres* and the drivers all flickered and shadowed in the burning light. Everyone looked cold. Guests in expensive fur coats called to one another in English; horses trotted out over the cobblestones, she thought she saw rain falling past the flares *I simply must not think about what Monsieur Montand has told me* but now that she was alone her thoughts were tumbling and whirling and muddled with each other. People passed her door, there were bursts of loud laughter in the distance and she saw sand and turbans and mosques and anger and bright colours in the sunlight and a child and stones being thrown over and over at something unmoving in the dust *O dear God!* Rose quickly took her Indian shawl and the candle-lamp from beside her bed, and slipped back along the dim corridor; another lamp flickered going into another room, she heard a woman's low voice and laughter. Dolly's room was nearby. She knew Dolly would not be sixteen for almost a year; they would think of something. *She cannot be made to marry George Fallon with all his tawdry ambition and plans.* Rose pushed the door and quickly went inside. The room was in darkness.

'Dolly?' But Dolly was asleep.

Rose turned to go, relieved; then something about the bed caught her attention in the flickering light. Dolly lay so that she looked very small. Rose moved closer, held up her lamp. The bed had been turned down and a pillow protruded from the covers.

'Dolly?' The light from the lamp caught other shadows, the big rosewood wardrobe, the heavy curtains, the washstand and jug. But Dolly was not there.

For a moment Rose stood quite still. Again she saw Dolly's face: in the carriage, at dinner. *I have not paid her enough attention – of course she saw me with Pierre, she will think I am a rival, I should have come to her at once!* Quickly she turned with her lamp in her hand and hurried, her breath coming quickly, along the wide, dim hall to George's room. She did not stop to knock, opened the door and hurried in, her lamp held ahead of her, calling George's name urgently. And then suddenly she was motionless.

At first Rose thought that Dolly was with George on the wide canopied bed: certainly there were two people there in the darkness.

But with her lamp held up she saw that the other person on George's bed was William.

The two men were conjoined in such a manner that, disturbed thus, it was difficult just for a moment for them to spring apart. And then at last the room was silent, except for the sound of three people all breathing heavily and an Admiral's daughter knowing that this was what King George III named 'the infamous act', punishable by hanging.

George broke the silence. 'Well Rose?' He was still panting.

At last she made a sound. 'Dolly.'

'What?'

'Dolly,' repeated Rose stupidly.

'What of Dolly?'

But Rose could not speak. Quickly she turned to leave the room, the image of the two men's bodies whirling about in front of her eyes. Then with a supreme effort she turned back. 'Dolly is gone,' she said. And then she ran, ran with her candle-lamp flickering, finally going out, and her shawl falling, so that anyone who passed her might have concluded that a madwoman was running that night along the vast dim corridors of the Hotel de l'Empire in Paris. In her room she wildly pulled the blue cover off the bed and put it over her head, as if she could somehow leave this world and go elsewhere.

Very soon there were more people running along wide corridors. Doors were knocked upon, voices were raised: *la jeune anglaise* had disappeared. Rose at last lit another candle and walked quite slowly into the *salon de thé*: there were George and William, dressed now, and Ann and the Dowager. They were all in loud, agitated conversation with the manager. Paris streets in the night were not a place where young English ladies would be safe, any more than London.

'Find her!' cried the Dowager Viscountess Gawkroger imperiously. 'My son's betrothed would never have left the hotel of her own volition. We are continually told how unsafe the streets of this damnable city have become.' The manager looked most startled. 'Damnable, I said. Damned. We believe she has been abducted by a Frenchman. I will advise the King of England!'

'*Mother!*' hissed George. But he was looking at Ann. 'So the story in her diary was true, then?' But Ann was literally holding her face, so bad suddenly was the toothache. She called wretchedly for *cognac* but the manager did not hear: he was waving his arms about and giving voluble reply to all accusations against his country.

George was trying to speak quietly. 'There is a French *marquis* who has been pursuing her,' he whispered hoarsely. 'She must be found, before . . .' His face expressed the inexpressible.

Nobody, in the consternation, saw Rose leave. Outside the rain was falling heavily now and the flares in the courtyard were flickering and hissing, casting fast-moving shadows. The straggling line of *fiacres* was still drawn up: Rose hailed one, she hardly thought what she was doing, only allowed herself to say, '*La Commission de l'Egypte*', to the driver, who answered not a word but whipped his horse away into the darkness *if he is a terroriste and will drive me to the guillotine so be it*. But they travelled towards the river, the horse running through mud, the water battering on the roof of the cab and dripping on to the seat. Rose did not notice. Lights moved mistily in the rain, French voices laughed and called in the darkness, and at the entrance to the Commission de l'Egypte a brazier flared and leapt as the dark rain fell on the cobblestones where Pierre had told her about the baby girl whose mother was stoned to death. Her heart beat very fast.

'Wait here!' cried Rose to the driver. '*Attendez-moi ici!*' as she alighted from the *fiacre*. She took a deep breath and then ran in the rain to pound on the door of the Commission, from wherein, to her relief, lights shone. A French *portier* unlocked the door, surprised to see yet another hysterical Englishwoman asking for Monsieur Montand.

'Is Dolly here?' asked Rose stupidly, the rain pouring down, but the *portier* understood no word of English.

'*Etes-vous une amie de la jeune anglaise?*'

'Yes,' said Rose in relief. '*Oui!* Where is she? *Est-ce-qu'elle est toujours là?*'

'*Oui, oui, madame,*' and as if he did this every midnight he let her in, bolted the door carefully and escorted the next distressed lady along the hall of antiquities, past the shadowy forms of Egypt, including many Egyptian cats who looked at Rose with antique eyes.

She heard Dolly's voice coming from a closed room. She was weeping, pleading. 'Please, Pierre, you must listen to me, and help me. They will force me to marry him, my life will be ruined. I love you, I will do anything, anything you want, my family is one of the finest families in England.' Rose could not hear Pierre's reply in the room, just the sound of his voice, low and rumbling.

'Do you love Rose?' cried Dolly, her voice rising, hysterical. 'I saw you kiss her hand, I saw you holding her in public! You cannot marry her, she is an old widow! She promised she would speak to you of me. She promised she would ask you. *Did she ask you?*'

Rose opened the door and walked inside and the candles in the room shivered in the sudden draught and showed paintings and papyrus. There were artists' easels, small obelisks and a large broken arm from a statue. And colour and stones, and everywhere the hieroglyphs, the hidden language.

Pierre Montand was standing by the window, looking embarrassed and sad. Dolly, her eyes red from crying, taller than the small obelisks as she stood very close to him, saw Rose at once.

'Why did *you* have to come?' she cried wildly.

'Dearest Dolly,' Rose leaned on the door as she closed it, adjusting her wet shawl, trying to calm her pounding heart, 'dearest Dolly, you must come back quickly to the Hotel de l'Empire. Everybody is looking for you, they are most frantic, worrying that you have been abducted by a French *marquis*. There are soldiers out searching for you. You must come back at once.'

But Dolly simply sat down on one of the small tables covered with antiquities and burst again into tears, crying loudly with her head thrown back, like a *diva*. Pierre, observing that she was sitting on a piece of papyrus, moved towards her; she thought he had come to comfort her and wept louder. Rose suddenly wished she could sit down and weep too, but pushed away all the day's events that threatened to overwhelm her as Dolly's cries filled the room. She said incoherently to Pierre, 'I have too many things inside my head,' and then she walked quickly across the room to where Dolly sat and slapped her face. Dolly stopped crying immediately, her head jerked up and she looked at Rose in astonishment.

'We must go back, Dolly, everyone is looking for you! You must return with me at once. Somehow we must stop this marriage to George but we cannot involve Monsieur Montand, whom we hardly know, in our troubles; one does not do this. I do beg your pardon, *monsieur*, I assure you we will not return.'

He began to speak but she brushed him aside. She had Dolly's arm: Dolly was rising, still shocked into silence. 'I am deeply humiliated at all that has happened,' Rose continued over her shoulder, leading Dolly across the room, stepping past pillars and papyrus, 'and I would be very grateful if you would put this whole day – *everything* – out of your mind entirely.'

Pierre stared at Rose but she did not return his look. As the ladies moved to the door he said, 'Mademoiselle Dolly.' Dolly turned quickly back from the doorway. 'I am so very sorry, *mademoiselle*, that you have been made so – *triste*, so unhappy. Madame Rose did tell me of your – offer to me. You are a very lovely and intelligent young girl, and a brave one, and a man will be very fortunate one day to have you as his wife. But it is true that my heart is elsewhere. If there is anything, however, that I can do to assist you . . .' But his voice now followed disappearing, rustling women. Rose was herding Dolly down the long corridor past the treasures and the cats, and out into the rain and the waiting *fiacre*.

As it clattered off the *portier* turned to Pierre, chuckling. '*Quelle chance pour vous, Monsieur Montand – elles sont belles!*' but Pierre strode back to his office where he so often worked late, and closed the door.

At the Hotel de l'Empire, soldiers were standing about in the rain, only half sheltered by the portico, muttering together at the weather and the late hour and making ribald bitter jokes in French about *la jeune anglaise*. As she alighted, Rose said firmly, *'La jeune Anglaise est ici,'* and hurried Dolly up the steps and into the entrance hall, where the first person they saw was a distraught William who had just returned from searching for Dolly in the Paris streets. He looked quickly, embarrassedly, away from Rose and took Dolly's arm at once, just as George loomed up towards them. George took Dolly's other arm: 'Where have you been?' he hissed as they marched her inside. Rose looked after them: William and George with their plans and their schemes, and Dolly, taller than either of them, held firmly between them. Rose turned quickly, moved outside, and in the anonymity of the dark cobblestones did something she had never before done in her life: she took a small cigar, in public, from her bag; before she had a moment to think of lighting it a soldier was at her side with a burning light: she was aware without caring that he was whispering to her in his language of unmentionable things.

So great, for various reasons, was the derangement of the Fallon and Torrence party that they returned to London at once: the trip to Rome was abandoned. Unfortunately they all had to travel to Calais together in one large public *chaise*: nothing else could be arranged in this new France at such short notice, but the Dowager would not stay one second longer. Throughout the uncomfortable, crowded journey all the way back to the coast, through day and night – past again the churches with no roofs and the looted villas, the neat farms, the staring children – only once did the Dowager Viscountess Gawkroger speak. In terrible tones (and forgetting, presumably, that Dolly had once stood upon a turd in a dark corner of Windsor Castle) she said to the assembled travellers: 'No member of a family touched by scandal and disgrace is received at the court of His Majesty King George the Third.' Otherwise, not once did the Dowager address Dolly or Rose, not once did Rose address George or William, not once did Dolly speak to anyone at all. Ann spent the journey trying to find ways to drink brandy in public, for her toothache. Rose, (controlling herself from the wild horrible laughter that kept threatening to bubble up as the Dowager spoke of 'disgrace' *shall I take this moment to tell her of her Egyptian grandchild?*), stared out on to the French countryside as the carriage sickeningly bounced and swayed towards Calais. Her mind was agitated almost beyond bearing, she longed to light a cigar: she saw in her head the haunting Egyptian paintings: they turned into George and William, a gold and blue ring, a child, Pierre Montand, Dolly, a dead woman in the sand as the coach rattled and swerved. And then, at last, she actually laughed out loud and then by way of explanation, as everybody in the post chaise stared at her, she heard herself speak.

'Paris in the springtime is *so* enchanting,' said Rose Fallon.

FIFTEEN

Rose set fire to her pink-curtained bed in Wimpole Street.

She had woken with a start: she had been dreaming of a child, or was it Dolly? or was it the figures of her brother-in-law and William entwined? Her heart beat so oddly that she jumped out of bed, opium wafted about her brain. Slowly she lit a cigar, slowly she waited for the strange heartbeats to stop, slowly she climbed back in among the pink curtains. Beside her bed was one of her father's old books of maps: she opened it again and traced the journey across the land and across the sea. She only did this in the privacy of her bedroom where nobody, not even the omniscient Mattie, would see. Cigar smoke drifted. She understood her own foolishness. She had wanted a child so much: the Frenchman's information had filled her mind full of folly, and dreaming, and the romance of her father's stories. She dreamed of palm trees and roses and a child and the river Nile, she dreamed of Rosetta . . .

Next Mattie was pulling her out of bed, flapping at smoke with wet towels. The canopy curtains were badly singed, pink had turned to brown. Mattie flapped the towels further, poured water.

'We could go, of course,' she said. 'Cornelius Brown is there somewhere.'

'Where?'

'Egypt,' said Mattie. 'I know what you're thinking.'

'That is ridiculous,' said Rose.

'Very well,' said Mattie, picking up the book of maps. 'Ignite yourself if you want, but kindly do not set fire to the Viscount's house while I am asleep in it.'

Rose received a letter from France:

Madame la Viscountess,

I am most regretful of the shock I gave you in Paris, and I must write to apologise both for my stupidity, and for my misunderstanding of your own knowledge of the situation.

I can only explain myself in this way. As I told you, we had just arrived back from Alexandria. I have seen many men killed, *madame*, in my travels, things that all soldiers must deal with as best they can. But to see a young woman stoned to death in front of my eyes by her own people – and to be able to do nothing – that, I found very difficult to deal with. This however was not enough of a reason to distress you with the whole story, *madame*.

I hope that we will meet again, and that I may know that you have understood.

I also hope the difficulties of Mademoiselle Dolly have been resolved.

A bientôt, Viscountess.

Pierre Montand

Rose replied:

Dear Monsieur Montand,

The events you recounted to me were not, after all, your fault. I realise one cannot blame the bearer for the news. Thank you for your letter, *monsieur*.

Rose Fallon

The Torrence family, Viscount Gawkroger – indeed, all London society – had been away from London, for nobody of consequence (it was well known) stayed in London over the summer. Rose Fallon had stayed in London over the summer nevertheless, for she was moving from Wimpole Street: Mattie and the old naval gentlemen had found the top half of a house to rent in South Molton Street, just off Brook Street where she had grown up. The old naval gentlemen were satisfied because Miss Constantia Proud, the house's owner, was known to both of them (being the sister of several naval captains), and was very happy to let half of her house to the daughter, whom she believed she knew, of the late Admiral Hall.

'Miss Proud? Miss Constantia Proud? But of course I know her, she was locked in Hanover Square Circulating Library because she was reading and forgot the time!'

'Then it is settled,' said the old naval gentlemen, delighted. 'She is a wonderful woman. And a brave one. She lost her betrothed when she was young. A sad affair.' But they imparted no more.

Rose went to see Miss Constantia Proud. She crossed Oxford Street, walked through her dear Hanover Square where the leaves were turning colour: there was the old bakery, there was the Circulating Library where Fanny had met Horatio Harbottom, there was the house Mr Handel used to live in. Rose heard the streets of her childhood, as cacophonous as ever they had been, the cries of the pedlars and the knife sharpeners, the rumble of the coaches and the shouts of the coachmen. She passed her parents' old house with a pang; walked firmly on; from a cart along the street she caught the bright, warm smell of oranges before being assailed by the smell of rotting fish mixed with horse dung. Somewhere a man was singing, horribly off-key; somewhere again, the sound of a harpsichord. Rose observed everything with delight.

Miss Proud served tea, talked of Rose's parents, declared her pleasure that Rose was to be her tenant. Miss Proud wore the white cap of older or unmarried ladies but she seemed the same age as years ago, and all her rooms burst with books and newspapers and periodicals as if she herself had become a library. Four pairs of magnifying spectacles lay about her drawing room. In the top part of the house autumn sunshine came in the windows, and the scent of fresh bread wafting up from along South Molton Street more than made up for the smell of effluent and other unmentionable things rising from the gutters.

There was room for fifteen-year-old Dolly in South Molton Street. Rose thought of Dolly's face in Paris, hearing her fate. She wrote to her, innocuous letters, saying she hoped they would meet soon. There was no reply but still Rose planned: South Molton Street could be a sanctuary for Dolly. Nervous thoughts flitted about her mind: *I wonder if I could blackmail George into letting her go?* She tried, she even (she would have died rather than admit this to anyone) walked up and down her pink bedroom in the evenings, planning a momentous speech . . . *George, I have something I must say to you . . . George, I wish to bring up a subject that it is most difficult for me to introduce . . . it is not for me to judge, George . . .* and often her cheeks were hot with embarrassment even in the privacy of her own room, such was her distaste for such a role. She could try *George, Harry has a child in Egypt* – but perhaps he would not even care. But something must be done, for Dolly.

Rose and Mattie were packing the last of the clothes when the footman announced that Viscount Gawkroger was waiting in the blue drawing room (where the furniture was already covered in white sheets prior to removal the next day). She thought how odd it was that George always suddenly arrived, uninvited, at night, as if he was the kind of man who walked in darkness.

There was nothing Mattie did not know. 'Take care, Miss Rose,' said Mattie, with pursed lips.

Rose came slowly downstairs, ordered coffee; as she caught sight of George her stomach gave an unpleasant lurch. Although it was many weeks since their hasty departure from Paris, he had, indeed, been in her dreams.

'Good evening, George.'

'Good evening, Rose.'

'Your mother is well?'

'Very well, thank you. A *most* interesting summer in the country.' She regarded him silently. He looked about the room. 'So, Rose, you leave Wimpole Street at last.'

'As you see. I am grateful for the time you have given me to make my plans. Will you sit down?' and she removed the white drapes from the sofa and the high-backed chair.

'Where are you going?'

'Near to my family home in Brook Street.'

'Somewhat down in the world then.' He sniffed, just the way the Dowager did when she disapproved. 'This does not reflect well on the Fallon family. It will be thought we are lacking in solicitude. You still carry our name.'

'I hope you will never have cause to think that I will not do credit to the family name,' she said, and if he heard the irony in her voice he made no comment. Neither of them sat and neither of them spoke. *I will have to do it then!* Rose felt her heart beating fast; before she had time to think about it she took a deep breath. 'George, I am removing myself from both the support and the influence of the Fallon family. I do not wish for any financial arrangement whatsoever, I have no wish to have anything to do with, or to interfere with, or to make a judgement about, your life in any way in the future, and I hope you will feel the same towards me. Harry's death has severed the ties that bound us together.' She heard her own breathing, saw George's inscrutable face. 'However.' She took another deep breath as if she had been underwater. 'I have just one thing to say before we part. If you proceed with this monstrous plan of forcing a fifteen-year-old girl who does not love you to marry you, I will prevent you' – two spots of colour stood in her cheeks – 'in any way I am able.' She stood with her head held very high looking at him, knowing she was blushing.

'Really, *Rosetta mia*?' And she saw that he was smiling. 'And how, exactly, would you prevent me?'

The coffee arrived. Rose saw that Mattie had, unusually, taken that duty upon herself and that she scowled at George. George strolled to the window, looked out at the darkness. Neither of them spoke until Mattie had gone, but then he turned.

'Well, *Rosetta mia*?'

She poured the coffee into the gilt cups; he took a cup from her, and sat on the sofa at last, forgetting again that it was softer than it looked. The coffee spilt. He put his cup down, brushed at his clothes in annoyance. 'Really, my dear! You should leave the coffee to the men. It is somehow unbecoming in a lady's drawing room.'

Still she looked at him steadily. For Dolly's sake she had to call his bluff. She swallowed and began again, jumping at once into deep waters. 'This matter could be very difficult for William,' she said doggedly. 'I am the daughter of an admiral. It is, as I know, in His Majesty's Navy in particular that this – matter – is regarded with such – opprobrium.'

George meant to stand up powerfully and calmly; the soft couch, however, made him look slightly ungainly instead and he knew it. He walked in silence along the procession of his ancestors on the walls. With his back to her he said: 'Never, *never*, presume to meddle with me, Rose, for I am, and will always be, the more powerful.' And then he turned. 'I am afraid you are too late. You should have whisked her away as soon as we returned to London, if that was your heart's desire. Dolly and I were married in a private ceremony two days after we arrived back from Paris. William, Ann, my mother, and the Duke of Hawksfield were present. My mother and I have already moved to Berkeley Square. The house in Berkeley Square belonged to the late Lady Torrence, and with the Duke of Hawksfield's support it became part of Dolly's dowry, so now it is mine. The others stay, of course, but it is mine!' He grinned: he could not hide his triumph. 'You must call, my dear! I am having a complete renovation! And we are already building our country home on land I have acquired from the Torrence estate, and *that* shall become Gawkroger Hall, not a merchant's house in Great Smith Street.' She heard clearly the naked satisfaction in his voice. 'Have you anything to say?'

And then he stepped very close to her. He was not smiling now, not at all: menace emanated from him. 'Listen, Rose, listen to me very carefully,' he said quietly. 'As you seem determined to interfere with my life without invitation, there are several things you should know, for I have told you many times that I shall allow absolutely *nothing* to come between me and my plans. First, I believe you will find these little matters are of no accord in France, which is a much more sophisticated country than our own and where laws were changed some time ago as the result of the Revolution. Second, there are far too many naval captains and not enough ships: William has dispensed with the navy. He and I are making plans to travel to Egypt – that is as soon as both Dolly and

Ann are' – he paused delicately – *'enceinte* – a matter to which I am now giving my full attention, I do assure you, for we can hardly leave without ensuring a brace of heirs!' And all the time he spoke it was the same ominous tone, something still to come. 'And at the moment, *Rosetta mia*, we while away the time more happily than I could have imagined – for I have made it quite clear to William that he must spend time on the same activity, for which Ann is very grateful. We shall then leave them to the good offices of my mother for the duration of their confinements and the production of heirs for the Fallon and Torrence families, and William and I will commence our adventures in search of antiquities. To this end I have contacted your admirer, Monsieur Montand, who I am sure will give us further information.

'Third . . .' and he stopped for a moment and regarded her carefully; she braced herself for whatever was coming 'third, your extraordinary conversation with me this afternoon has led me to believe, *Rosetta mia*, that you are unwell. Widowed women are often unwell when their' – he paused subtly, 'their domestic happiness, shall we call it that? is so sadly snatched from them. They cannot bear other people's domestic happiness and I have much domestic happiness, Rose, which may surprise you, but will surely be of interest to you.' And he put his face close to hers, almost as if he would kiss her; she smelt his breath, forced herself not to turn away. 'Yes, this will certainly interest you. Your innocent little Dolly had spent a quite amazing amount of time among Lord Torrence's books, many of which are of – shall we say – an unusual nature. And she knew a great deal more about "domestic happiness" than I expected, a great deal more,' and he suddenly ran his tongue over his lips. 'I am sure I do not need to elaborate: you of course *know* what you are missing – my brother reported to me of the many things that he taught you, the delights you shared. And it is the loss of that, of course, that makes you ill. The "spinster's hysteria" is the name for it, for of course you are really nothing now but a spinster – a spinster however with memories that no doubt haunt her. So should there be any repeat of your conversation – anywhere – I will arrange for my physician to examine you carefully, as a member of my family. I will tell him you are having feverish dreams; I will also tell him that you have always had a –

what should I call it? – a heightened imagination. And in particular I will inform him – for I must reiterate once more that I was always my brother's confidant – that for a woman you have a morbid interest in' – and he smiled again at last – 'matters of a – physical – nature. Apparently, it seems now, other people's affairs as well as your own!'

If Rose was red-cheeked before, she was scarlet now.

'I believe there are several women like you held in' – he paused delicately – 'suitable places. It is an illness, you know. I have heard – from one of the superintendents at Bethlem as it happens – that passion in a woman is dangerous, and *unsatisfied* passion a lamentable state of affairs which can lead to madness. Have you ever been to Bedlam? No, perhaps not. Well you should, Rose – you would find it instructive. There are many women like you: they beat at their bodies and at their private parts in desperation so that their private parts become public for any visitor to observe.'

And George Fallon, Viscount Gawkroger, bowed to his sister-in-law and left the long blue room where his ancestors, as well as Rose, had listened to him with appalled incredulity. Or perhaps, on the portraits' part, as they were ancestors of George Fallon, with prurient fascination: who can say?

Less than fifteen minutes later the sound of the bell outside echoed again through the house in Wimpole Street. Rose's muffled voice came from the other side of the locked door of her room to where Mattie stood in the hall.

'I am not at home. Tell the servants I am not at home to anyone, anyone at all.' Some time later Mattie knocked again.

'Go away.'

'There is somebody waiting, Miss Rose.'

'It is late. I am not at home, I told you.'

'I think you will be at home for this one,' called Mattie firmly, and Rose heard her footsteps go back along the hall.

It must be Dolly! Of course, it would be Dolly. Rose quickly bathed her face, brushed her hair, tried to put George and his shocking words out of her mind. She walked slowly down the stairs, *poor, poor Dolly, married to George already* and opened the door to the long blue room. She saw the hair first: a red-haired woman was perusing the portraits on the wall.

She stood stock still, could not believe her eyes. 'Fanny?' she whispered.

Her cousin heard her and turned.

'Fanny!' cried Rose and threw herself headlong into her cousin's arms. For some moments they stood there, holding each other, Rose unbelieving: half-laughing, half-crying. At last she pulled away but kept hold of Fanny's arms, looked into her face.

'Ah – Fanny!' was all she could manage.

It was only then that she heard another sound. A small voice stirred, wakened. 'Mama,' said the sleepy voice, 'did my aunt come yet?'

On the sofa that George Fallon found too soft, a little girl was slowly sitting up, pulling at her red hair. She saw Rose. She frowned to herself for a moment, remembering the words she had been practising, and then said formally: 'I am very pleased to meet you, my Aunt Rose.'

Rose stared at the little red-haired girl. '*Oh,*' she said. Then she walked slowly towards the sofa, still staring; she sat in the straight-backed chair. 'I thought your mama had turned back into a child again.' For a moment still she stared, knew of her own empty arms. 'What is your name?' she asked gently at last.

'Jane,' said the child shyly.

'I am so very pleased to meet you, Jane,' said Rose. 'How old are you?'

The little girl did not answer. She looked at her shoes.

'You should tell your Aunt Rose that you are nearly five years old and that you have a brother, Janey,' said Fanny from across the room, 'who is five and three-quarters.'

'Nearly five and I have a brother,' mumbled Jane, not looking at Rose.

'What is his name?'

'Horatio.'

'Like your papa?'

'Yes.' She examined a little bow on her small shoe.

'Oh, Fanny!' said Rose, looking back at her cousin. 'I cannot think of anyone in the whole world I would rather have seen when I walked into this room than you. And this small version of you!'

'You are moving house, Mattie said – she has told me much news. We decided to let you – rest for a while.'

Rose made a small sound: anger, embarrassment, shame? Fanny could not tell. 'I am so sorry, dearest Fanny. I had just had a – most unpleasant interview with my terrible brother-in-law.'

'Mattie entertained me. We had much to remember, we spoke of Brook Street and *la belle France* and Hanover Square and all sorts of things – including her husband, whom she still wishes to find!' And both the women said together: 'Cornelius Brown!' Jane stared.

'She has heard he may have gone to Egypt!' said Rose. 'Yet she still seems not to wish to have him back at all. She just wants to punch him in the face for behaving badly!' and the cousins laughed as if they had never been apart. 'And she will have told you – we have a wonderful new abode – oh, Fanny – in South Molton Street, just beside Brook Street!' And the shock of George's visit faded: it seemed only like one of her disturbed dreams.

'I have had to come to London to manage some pressing business for Papa,' said Fanny. 'We have only just arrived at this late hour. Even Horatio had to agree that I must travel to the den of iniquity that is London because it concerns finances – Papa implied to Horatio there may be some gain for him! So here I am! There was no time to write, but may we come with you to South Molton Street for a few days?'

'*Of course!*' said Rose, smiling and smiling at both of them.

All night the cousins talked, literally all night, they did not go to bed. They tried to put Jane to sleep in Rose's singed bed. 'It is burning!' Jane cried and flung herself at her mother.

'I had a slight accident,' said Rose in embarrassment, 'it is not burning now,' and Fanny rocked her daughter, and spoke to Rose about her family in India. At last Jane Harbottom, aged nearly five, fell asleep among the singed pink drapery to the sound of soft laughter: her mother and her aunt recalling the days of their youth. Rose stared at the girl, Fanny's daughter. Her heart beat strangely.

'She will sleep through the night now,' said Fanny softly, smoothing her daughter's hair back from her face. 'She is,' and Fanny sighed, 'a nervous child. She is frightened of her father, so she thinks the world is full of men – and boys – who shout, and I think she only feels safe when she is asleep.'

'Small Horatio shouts also?'

Fanny was still looking down at her daughter. 'Small Horatio, who of course is Janey's hero, is the image of his father. He walks like him, talks like him, and takes his cue on how to treat people from him. I love small Horatio very much, and it is not his fault, but' – and Fanny put her hand across her eyes for just a moment – 'I sometimes dislike him very much also.' The two cousins made their way downstairs in silence. Mattie stoked up the fire, brought them hot chocolate, just as she used to so long ago.

All night they talked, laughter and tears all mixed together. They talked as if they had had no one to talk to for years. Fanny spoke of Horatio's shock at the contents of Rose's long-ago uncensored letter and his adamant refusal then to let Fanny visit London. *A vicar's wife must be at his side*, he wrote to Fanny's family to their bemusement. *She is necessary at all times. It is a sacrifice made for the Lord.* The whole large family travelled to Wentwater before they went to India, anxious about Horatio's strange intransigence. Fanny's mother wanted to stay in England for the birth of her first grandchild, to postpone the journey, but all had been arranged for such a momentous change. Tearfully they bade farewell to Fanny at the Wentwater Vicarage gate, where honeysuckle bushes twined; they looked back to see Fanny waving, until the vicarage was out of sight. She had her first pregnancy alone, and was pregnant again extremely shortly afterwards. When Rose spoke of her own lost pregnancies (and her secret knowledge that there might be no more), Fanny held her, and did not say it was God's will.

I saw her, wept Rose as if her heart would break still. *I saw her little hands.* Fanny's tears fell softly on Rose's hair.

The fire burned down, they stoked it up again; at last they let it go out, pulled their shawls tightly about them, huddled into the sofa. Candles burnt down, new ones were lit; finally they went on talking in the darkness, their voices a small ongoing sound in one corner of the large room. Clocks chimed somewhat irregularly all about the house, including the old Italian one from Genoa that Fanny remembered.

Grey light slipped in around the sides of the shutters and into the room and still they went on talking. Rose told Fanny of hearing her husband spoken of at the theatre: the red plush curtains and the tinkling laughter of women; then she told of the truth about Harry's death in Egypt, heard Fanny gasp. And finally Rose told of the woman in Alexandria being stoned to death and of a Frenchman telling her of a child. Fanny listened, shocked, but not once, by any word, by any intimation, did she imply that she had once laughed behind her fan to see the smooth-talking, hand-kissing Captain Harry Fallon. Rose told of George's hasty marriage, and of George and William together in Paris, and her own ridiculous attempts at blackmail. Fanny said that such a matter had emerged in Wentwater and Horatio had thundered so loudly that parishioners had looked nervously up at the church roof. Rose told of the coach journey from Paris wherein nobody looked at each other, and of setting fire to her bed. Fanny told of Horatio's uncle, the bishop, who expected her to cut his toenails. The cousins laughed, but in a weary kind of way, as if the tales of the night had taken away laughter at last. For a long time then they were silent. They sat back into the corners of the soft sofa. All the clocks ticked loudly. It was almost as if they slept as morning came, but their eyes were open.

'Dear Rose.' At last Fanny spoke again. 'When I received your letter from Paris – signed with your own dear hieroglyph just as you used to so long ago – I suddenly felt – overwhelmed by *the change in my life*. We were so very sure that marriage would be a positive thing! I had thought Horatio would enlarge my world further and extend my knowledge. But he didn't like *my* knowledge, Rose, and in the end I actually had to pretend not to know about something, to keep the peace. Imagine marriage doing that to us – making us *smaller*! – although it is true he knows the Greek language,' and in the grey dawn the cousins suddenly burst into peals of laughter again, as if perhaps the years in between had taught them well that the Greek language could not help them.

'But it may help us to discover the secrets of the world,' said Rose, and she told Fanny of the Rosetta Stone with the three languages, and the marvellous coincidence of its name, and all the treasure they had been shown in Paris, and in the first morning light Fanny pondered the papers Rose showed her with the paeans of praise to KING PTOLEMY, THE EVER-LIVING, THE BELOVED OF PTAH, THE GOD EPIPHANES EUCHARISTOS.

At last Rose opened the shutters and let the morning in. Blackbirds from the Marylebone Gardens sang in Wimpole Street, a cart rattled along to the fields beyond Portland Place, an early coach clattered past the windows.

'Oh Rose!' sighed Fanny, still holding the translation of the hieroglyphs, listening to the coach. 'How we change! Do you still write in your journal?'

'I do,' said Rose, 'sometimes.'

'Of your life?'

'I found I could not write of the painful things.'

'I scream,' said Fanny.

'What?' Rose thought she had misheard.

And Fanny told Rose how she would walk to the furthest field and scream because it made her feel better. Rose had a vision of her beloved cousin with her red hair and her freckles screaming alone in a field, and something caught at her throat.

'Does screaming really help?' she asked finally.

'I was told that Maria Rienzi makes very loud noises every morning in preparation for her opera roles, so if anybody had ever questioned me I had decided to tell them that I was training my voice!' Fanny laughed but her laughter faded. 'I was screaming at my life.' She saw Rose's appalled face. 'Rose, Horatio speaks always of "duty". But his idea of duty is something that happens to equate with his own desires. Often he does *not* properly carry out his duties in the poorer parts of his parish; he is more often to be found immersed in "business" in his study. Sometimes if he is busy and I hear someone is ill or dying and I manage to walk over to visit them I find – can you believe the sadness of this? – they are spending their last breath in some miserable hovel worrying about hellfire and damnation and brimstone and salt! Is that all they have received from the Church? So,' and Fanny's red hair shook defiantly, 'I tell them there is no Hell. I say there is only a calm place, and that God is Love, not hellfire. I assure them that I know!' And Rose saw Fanny holding someone's hand in a dark, dirty room, like some sort of red-haired angel.

Then Fanny suddenly jumped up, walked in some agitation

about the room. 'Do you know what I have come to believe? *I have decided that many churchmen are not actually religious at all!*'

'Fanny!'

'*They are not!* I hear all those vicars and curates and the occasional bishop who pass through the vicarage and lock themselves with Horatio in his study and exchange church gossip and whisky. I hear them! And even those new people, the Evangelicals, who write in the newspapers about "a new morality" – I have read what they say so carefully but I notice it is not a new morality that will apply to *churchmen*! All I find so often is a kind of fear. Almost nobody – except perhaps the Quaker lady in the town square and one or two genuine dissenters – seems to care about the actual lives of the people, that somehow there must be a way to ameliorate them. I believe that all the churchmen really care about is the safety of the Church, that it will survive.'

'Whatever do you mean?' Rose, surprised, half laughed. 'Of course the Church will survive, Fan, it is part of our life! Christenings and funerals and Sundays and church bells – the Church is part of England, like the King!'

'*Exactly!*' Fanny pushed at her wild red hair. 'And I assure you they want to keep it that way: I have heard them talk! Do you not realise how the Revolution in France has terrified the Royal Family – they say that the fat, indulgent Prince of Wales is now so unpopular that he hides inside his coach when he is going through town! – all his mistresses and extravagances. Well, the Church of England is terrified too! You wrote to me from France of churches desecrated and ordinary people walking the corridors of the Louvre Palace to look at those long-hidden paintings – well I think the English Church is in dread of such a thing happening here. Imagine *anybody* being free to walk about Windsor Castle criticising what is on the walls, or Westminster Abbey with all its windows smashed – Heaven forfend!' Again Rose could not help it, she began to laugh, but Fanny went on. 'If there should be an uprising here against royalty, then the Church here too will be swept away in a revolution! That is what they are afraid of, all of them: High Church bishops and young curates and Evangelicals and missionaries and vicars, all of them – that they will lose their *power*! And for the poor people in their parishes who really need them, they care not at all.' And she threw herself down on the sofa again beside Rose.

'Heavens!' said Rose, looking at her cousin in a mixture of consternation and admiration. 'You have become a wild revolutionary yourself!' A terrible idea struck her. 'All this – it has not shaken your belief in God?'

Fanny did not look at her. 'You remember how I always thought I had conversations with God when I was young? – it was part of my life. But Horatio told me I was childish and He had not spoken to me at all.' She gave a small sigh. 'Of course I knew that Horatio was right in a way, my conversations with God *were* childish – they were probably conversations with myself.' She stared at the rug on the floor. 'The Quaker woman in the square says that one must wait quietly and listen, and God will be there. Well – I have waited and waited, and nobody came.' She sounded so bleak that Rose wanted to put out her arms, yet something about Fanny's face stopped her. 'What I am saying, dear coz, is that after six years of living with servants of God – and seeing poor people whose very last thought in the world is of hellfire – I do not believe a word of it!'

'*Fanny!*' Rose could not have been more shaken. Fanny's faith had been part of her.

'However!' And Rose saw that her cousin could not talk of it more. 'However,' and Fanny's voice shook very slightly, 'if He does exist, I would be glad of His advice in my present life!'

They heard the servants stirring, coming downstairs. 'Fanny dearest,' said Rose, 'you have your children, and Horatio supports you and, I am sure, loves you, even if he has faults – we were mad to think that men were perfect beings!' Never by word or intonation did she imply that she had once laughed behind her glove at the handsome, pompous clergyman with the beautiful voice. 'Is there nothing good about him? He is wonderfully handsome, certainly!'

Fanny was silent. A blackbird sang so sweetly on the railings just outside.

'I am very fond of him when he is *gardening*,' said Fanny, and suddenly the cousins broke into peals of laughter again: release, or sadness, or just the relief of being able to talk to one another after so long. 'It is true!' exclaimed Fanny. 'He would have made a wonderful gardener – a much better gardener than vicar. He spends hours outside sometimes and I have heard him talking to flowers in a gentle, friendly way he never uses with people. And he is handsome, certainly,' and she gave a sombre smile. 'His uncle the bishop with the toenails is a bully, and Horatio has copied him, just as young Horatio copies his father.' And Fanny sighed. 'Perhaps human love is elusive, just like God's love. Perhaps we only read about it in the new novels. I cannot ever remember my parents speaking of love – though I am sure they love each other and their children, of course. But it was not spoken of. I do not believe that I even know what it means. Do you, Rose?'

Rose tried to form the right words. 'I had strong feelings for Harry, certainly,' she said slowly. She took a deep breath. 'Physical feelings,' she said firmly, and she saw Fanny's startled look and felt the colour come to her own cheeks. But she determined to go on. 'I used to call those feelings "love" – I thought that was the word to use,' and she shook her head. 'Do you remember Mattie telling us to *like* our husbands, as well as love them?'

'She was a wise woman,' said Fanny drily.

Suddenly George's visit and his terrible words came back to Rose clearly and she felt her face reddening even further. 'Oh, how should I know what love is!' she said angrily. 'My *brother-in-law*,' and she gave a bitter little half-laugh, 'says my – wild feelings – love? – for Harry were an illness in a woman, and perhaps he is right, as you too seem to be shocked by my words!' and she heard again George's hateful words whispered into her ear. 'Let us say then that love made me ill! I am ill!' and she, like Fanny earlier, jumped up and began walking about the room.

'Rose,' said Fanny quietly. 'Stop it.' And Rose did stop, leaned against the window, looking out. 'I know now how much Harry hurt you, and what a demon your brother-in-law is – a snake you used to call him. 'But – I think it would be possible perhaps to see things in a different way.' Fanny paused, bit her lip. She spoke even more softly so that Rose had to turn and move back towards her to hear. 'Rose, if I understand what you mean about your feelings for Harry, then Harry taught you something that – that I imagine is probably very important in a marriage. That Horatio never taught me.'

They spoke as if it were in a coded manner, yet they both understood. Rose sat down again on the sofa.

'Never?' whispered Rose.

'Never,' said Fanny.

A maid opened the door, yawning, nearly dropped the ashes bucket seeing the two women in the room. 'Beg pardon, ma'am,' she said.

All day carts and carriers went from Wimpole Street to South Molton Street. Men shouted at furniture, jugs broke; Jane Harbottom, aged four, who usually ran a mile from shouting men, saw that they were not *angry*, that they were laughing as well as shouting: she had never had such an exciting day in her life, especially when a cart got stuck on the corner of South Molton Street and the horse broke loose and stood right in a trader's cabbages, who hit the horse, who bit a woman.

The servants, except of course Mattie, were dispensed with in great relief, part of the Fallon family that they were leaving behind. Rose and Fanny and Mattie and Jane carefully carried the old wheezing clock from Genoa with them in a carriage supplied by the Fallon family for the last time. Mattie did not say aloud what she was thinking (which was *good riddance*). Rose did not look back but thought with pleasure of the burnt pink curtains. She had left her mark. The clock chimed four in its Italian way as they crossed Oxford Street.

Miss Constantia Proud made many cups of tea and gave them fresh-baked bread and cold lamb chops and Rose and Fanny exchanged envious looks at the shelves and shelves of books.

'I believe she is a blue-stocking!' whispered Fanny in delight.

'*Of course* she is a blue-stocking!' said Rose.

Fanny and Jane were to sleep in the top room with windows that opened high above the street. Fanny and Rose, both pale with exhaustion, put Jane to bed there. They held their shawls about them and spoke softly as she drifted into sleep talking of cabbages; as a thin moon rose they stared out over the rooftops into the darkness, saw the shape of the spire of St George's Church by Hanover Square.

'Never?' asked Rose again at last, as if their conversation had never stopped.

'Never,' answered Fanny.

The nightingales had long settled in the trees in the square, but coaches still passed and people still called and the city lived and breathed beneath them and the smell of the gutters was just as they remembered it from long ago. 'If I did not understand it from your conversation about Harry,' continued Fanny, 'and I do believe that some hint was given to us in *Aristotle's Master-Piece*,' and both women gave a small smile in the half-dark, 'I would not have known what you were talking about.'

Reluctantly Rose said: 'He taught me of that part of love, yes. And of course it seemed wonderful, and made our life exciting. But' – she stumbled – 'but Harry found such love anywhere.'

'Rose,' said Fanny, 'Horatio has – taken me – every night of our life together. Every single night except for a few nights when the children were born. I am never away from him. At first I was glad to – to join to this man who had changed my life and seemed to set such store by this – thing that seemed to be loving. But now . . .' She stopped for a moment. 'Now when Horatio says those familiar, dreaded words: *'Come, Fanny'*, I feel my heart close. I have come to *hate* the nights of my life.'

Rose was speechless, looked at her cousin, appalled. It was hard to think that Fanny had been expounding so eloquently on the Church and revolution not so long ago: she looked suddenly small and vulnerable.

'So thank Harry for that,' said Fanny, 'for such care I think is at least a kind of love.' And she stared out at the moon.

There was a long, long silence.

'Thank you, dearest Fanny,' said Rose at last. She kissed her cousin goodnight and went to her own, new room. There her beloved mahogany desk that could become a card table sat by the window: continuity. And there, despite her exhaustion, Rose Fallon lay awake for many hours.

'All's well!' cried the nightwatchmen calling the hours in the darkness.

SIXTEEN

Early next morning a message was delivered to South Molton Street, requiring Rose to attend a small dinner that afternoon at Berkeley Square. The Fallon and Torrence families were expecting a guest who had asked that Rose be present, the note from Ann mysteriously stated.

Rose was outraged. 'Never! Never, ever! I moved from Wimpole Street, I have been gone one day, they still pursue me: *why*? They no more wish to see me than I do them.' (She was indeed correct: once again George Fallon was forced to ask something of Rose to get his own way in another matter entirely.) 'Never! Never will I speak to him again, after the terrible, unforgivable things he said to me. I could not bear it!' And two spots of red stood on her cheeks as she remembered his offensive, loathsome words. 'At least now I shall not have to witness poor Dolly's unhappiness. For I will not go!'

'But it is surely important to see Dolly,' Fanny observed mildly, 'and perhaps see what is to be done, if anything. She may be less unhappy now.'

'Perhaps.' Rose thought of George's words . . . *your innocent little Dolly had spent a quite amazing amount of time among Lord Torrence's books, many of which are of – shall we say – an unusual nature.* 'What he has done to Dolly I cannot begin to imagine.' Her eyes flashed. 'I sometimes think that that man is some sort of devil incarnate! His behaviour towards me was outrageous. The things he said to me were appalling!'

'*Rose!*' Rose looked in surprise at her cousin's tone, saw Fanny's laughing eyes. 'You must understand, dear Rose, that all this is very far removed from the vicarage of Wentwater! I may be eloquent about the secrets of the Church of England but my life is not, on the whole, full of quite such extraordinary events as you describe. I should like, once at least, to experience them as a bystander!'

Rose was silent for a moment, remembering once more the conversation with George; again she felt colour come to her face, spoke almost to herself. 'He need not think I am afraid of him. I shall not let myself be bullied by such an evil man!' She turned back to Fanny. 'Do you know he threatened me with *Bedlam*! But,' and she shook her head slightly, 'I know George: he had to have some sort of revenge of course for what I discovered in Paris. Perhaps we are equal now.' Fanny waited; at last Rose gave an odd little grimace. 'Well, we shall go together then, if you would like to,' she said, and saw the pleasure on Fanny's face. And suddenly Rose said fiercely, 'I am so glad you are here, Fanny.'

As they made plans about what to wear – 'If we are going to do this, we are going to do it with style!' insisted Rose – they discussed Miss Constantia Proud again. Rose said, 'I remember her from my childhood – she was a writer and she seemed to me to *eat* books, she was so passionate about them!'

'She looks so respectable in her black dress and her white cap, but did you see all her books?' said Fanny. 'Lots of unrespectable ones! She had Thomas Paine, and all the new poets – she had two copies of the *Lyrical Ballads* of Mr Coleridge and Mr Wordsworth, and all the new novels, and philosophy and politics and Mary Wollstonecraft, books that many people – I am thinking of Horatio! – would find quite shocking.'

'He may have reason to be even more shocked, for I believe Miss Proud actually knows Mr Coleridge and Mr Paine and she has travelled further than we have dreamed!'

'Maybe she has an exotic past!'

'The old naval gentlemen told me her betrothed died – at sea perhaps, I do not know. "A sad affair," they said. Let us ask her to take tea with us before we go, to thank her for her kindness to us,' and Miss Proud, in her starched white old lady's cap climbed the stairs and brought small sweetmeats and entertained the two young women and the small girl with stories of her naval brothers, and her journeys and the sea.

'And you have written books?'

'Pamphlets, more. About travelling.'

'How lucky you were,' said Fanny admiringly. 'And brave! What an amazing life you must have had.'

'I hope it is not yet quite over!' said Miss Proud, laughing at them. 'But it is true I have been very lucky – in many ways.' And a kind of silence fell – although noise came up from the street – and neither of the young women dared ask about her betrothed. And although her voice did not falter in the least as they went on talking, Miss Proud stared at the leaves of the tea, and moved them about with her spoon, and soon thanked them very charmingly and made her farewells, and left them.

'How old do you suppose she is?' Rose wondered in a quiet voice, but they could not guess.

There was no such thing as a 'small' dinner party now that George Fallon owned the house in Berkeley Square. Inside, the house appeared rather bizarrely to have taken on the accoutrements of a palace: the austere architecture was gone, and it was already decorated as if George saw himself like the Prince of Wales at Carlton House: scarlet and gold rooms; swathes of material hung to make other rooms look like Roman tents; oriental ornaments; and Grecian columns with the Dowager Viscountess much in evidence beside them. And – in the centre of the entrance hall where it could not be missed – an extremely large painting of the late Viscount Gawkroger, Harry Fallon. Rose stared, realised at once that this was an enlarged and embellished copy of the one she had stabbed with her cigar. It was indeed Harry, but Harry as a minor god. Winged chariots approached from the distance (to take him to a better place?) and the blue of his naval uniform and the gold of his captain's braid shone. Harry's face shone too: he looked forward at his Noble Destiny with such enthusiasm that it may possibly have been the High Heavens Club or the card tables in St James's that he was gazing towards. Below the painting, specially mounted, were Harry's medals from the Battle of the Nile (looking carefully, Rose saw that one or two extra had been appended).

A little ripple of appreciation passed round some of the visiting gentlemen when the two young ladies from South Molton Street, both dressed in white, were announced. They looked so fresh. (As well as wearing white, they had, remembering the old aunt in France with the vases in her wig, both attached flowers to their hair.) This offended the Dowager Viscountess and George, who both felt keenly that the one thing missing from the atmosphere of Harry's portrait was a shadowy, adoring widow still in mourning, and they looked with disapproval at the women in white, wearing flowers and smiling.

Rose bowed once to the Viscount in his new role of host, and then did not acknowledge him again. The house was crowded. Card tables were set, footmen glided, guests mingled among drifting draperies where members of the High Heavens Club twirled young ladies, and people sometimes became indecorously entwined amid much excited laughter. Suddenly Lady Dolly, Viscountess Gawkroger, fifteen years old, appeared through curtains. Rose stared in disbelief. Dolly's scarlet and white gown was split at the sides (as she had observed in the Tuileries Gardens), low at the back (as she had observed at the Paris ball) and low at the front (because she had insisted). The new Viscountess Gawkroger was, indeed, dressed in the very latest French fashions. She bowed at Rose and Fanny from behind her fan and turned immediately away, disappearing and reappearing among draperies and guests. It occurred to Fanny, seeing her for the first time, that anything less like a sacrificial lamb could not be imagined; Rose had to shake herself slightly, to accept the transformation.

Ann greeted Rose and Fanny coldly, as did the Dowager Viscountess, although she managed to talk volubly at them at the same time; Rose noticed at once that she was wearing the blue and gold Egyptian ring from the French collection: *how can she be so brazen!* If Dolly's father was present he did not show himself, but the Duke of Hawksfield came forward and bowed to the cousins. What he thought of the new decor was not divulged, but when it transpired that Fanny's father was involved with the East India Company the Duke spoke about the importance of Trade (although the Dowager would not have let such a rude word pass her lips). As the voices and laughter got louder and the champagne went swirling round the rooms, he also questioned Rose closely about her trip to France and her present lodgings, and Rose again could not escape the feeling that the Duke of Hawksfield was very like his name and was watching her like an angular bird of prey. But she could no longer respect him: he might be powerful, but he had sold Dolly like property, and Rose looked at him coldly and answered his questions shortly and felt the feeling again, something like revulsion. And a memory of the hieroglyphs came to her . . . *other animals move not in a vertical line, but descend obliquely; the hawk however swoops directly down upon anything beneath it.* And in the crowded heat of the summer drawing room, speaking politely to the Duke, just for a moment Rose Fallon shivered. Nearby Ann, the putative Duchess of Torrence, shivered also, and wished she could get at the brandy, for her toothache.

William avoided Rose's eye at all times; Rose presumed they would never look at each other again. George greeted his guests, watched the Duke of Hawksfield, attended to Dolly rather (Rose thought) as if he was acting the part of The Husband. Dolly was extraordinary, seemingly in total command. She stood tall (somehow even taller than her new husband than one had remembered); with her hair swept upwards and her eyes glittering she fingered expensive jewellery at her bosom and spoke condescendingly to everyone. Rose noted that the glittering eyes kept flicking towards the entrance. Dolly laughed a great deal, flirted outrageously with old men, leaning over so that her small bosom was near their eyes. George watched Rose, watching Dolly.

And then Monsieur Pierre Montand was announced.

Rose, incredulous, saw the tall Frenchman appear in the doorway and felt colour rush to her cheeks as she remembered the encounters in Paris. But then, as Dolly ran to greet the Frenchman with a little scream of delight, Rose thought of his letter, and calmed her heart: *the news he gave was not his fault.*

Dolly put out her hand to be kissed and welcomed Monsieur Montand like an old friend, as if the midnight scene in the Commission de l'Egypt had never taken place. She moved with him, introducing him in the crowded room; laughing; leaning, as if by chance, against his arm; trying to bypass Rose and Fanny. Pierre Montand saw them, stopped at once. 'Viscountess,' he said.

'Rose is the Viscountess no longer!' said Dolly, laughing. 'I am!' But he took Rose's hand, just looked at her. Rose was calm, smiled back at him.

'I am glad to see you again,' she said, and saw his face relax.

Dolly took the Frenchman's arm, trying to lead him away. But for a moment, without seeming impolite, he did not go. 'I said I would attend only if you were here, Madame Rose,' he murmured, 'when the Viscount asked me to come,' and he smiled at Fanny as Rose introduced them. Only then, all the time with impeccable politeness, did he allow himself to be led away by the tall young lady at his side, who again leant into him slightly in her flimsy dress.

'Good heavens,' said Fanny, very quietly.

A group of the men present were antique collectors: they gathered round Pierre Montand and fired questions at him. Dolly did not leave his side.

As they sat for dinner Fanny literally paled at the amount of food: dish after silver dish appeared in the arms of bewigged footmen, people leaned forward, took enormous platefuls, stopped talking, ate extremely loudly – coughing and spitting and hawking – took more food, piled it up. Trying not to seem impolite by eating what seemed so little compared to many of those around her, Fanny observed the guests, saw that the French *savant* looked intently at her cousin while listening to Dolly, next to whom he had been placed.

And Ann Torrence, drinking wine quickly, watched the Duke of Hawksfield watch Rose Fallon and fear clenched her like ice. For despite William's now regular appearances in her bedroom (sometimes very much the worse for wear, stinking, so that she had to turn her head away and pray for fertility), she was not pregnant. To her dismay she heard the Duke inviting Rose and Fanny to visit Hawksfield Castle in the country. What were his plans for Rose?

Why was he so interested in her? Why did William never look at Rose? Was she, Ann, to be supplanted? How could she, when things were so uncertain, remove her aching front teeth?

At last the dinner slowed down to the dessert stage and talking once more took place; Pierre Montand was again plied with questions.

'Egyptian antiques are going to be the next fashion,' said George, and some of the gentlemen about him howled in agreement. 'I am certain of it. One must get at them urgently. What is the quickest route, now that war is over?'

'I imagine, *monsieur*, that the Mediterranean is perhaps even less safe now that the naval fleets are gone. I have heard many stories of pirates and buccaneers. Some missionaries and traders have lately decided it would be quicker to go to India via Egypt but many of them, I have heard, never arrived at their destination. I feel that anyone who goes to the chaos that is Egypt at the moment takes his life in his hands; for myself I would never again attempt to cross the desert, we lost too many men that way.' Fanny saw that Rose listened as if hypnotised, wondered if her cousin had found a new *beau*.

Dolly's still child-like voice suddenly piped up and she laid her hand on the arm of the tall man sitting beside her. 'Surely, Monsieur Montand, if one obtained the best guides, the best service?'

'I can only say, Lady Dolly, that the best guides may also be the most dangerous for all that we know of them.'

'The hieroglyphs, Monsieur Montand,' said the Duke of Hawksfield without preamble. 'Has there been any progress on your side of the Channel? For here, stalemate seems to have been reached already.'

'There is great interest, *monsieur*,' said Pierre, 'but no progress,' and he spread his hands and shrugged his shoulders, and it was clear that his brief answer disappointed his listeners who, to a man, suspected that the wily French were keeping secrets.

'And tell me, Monsieur Montand,' and the Dowager's voice now came loudly across the table, 'is that pretty Egyptian jewellery going to be for sale soon? Some of it was very sweet. We saw everything in Paris, you know,' she advised the fascinated guests, 'very primitive stones and rubble, you understand, but some nice little paintings and jewellery that interested one,' and as she spoke the beautiful blue and gold Egyptian ring sparkled shamelessly under the chandeliers full of candles in Berkeley Square. Suddenly George, William, Dolly and Rose were riveted; even Ann, reaching for brandy, froze, her arm outstretched. For they saw that the Frenchman had seen the ring.

Pierre Montand made a very small sound, regarded the Dowager and the ring, his face and body absolutely motionless, as if he had turned into one of his own stones. Rose felt herself holding her breath. Did Pierre Montand know about English duels? George looked deeply shocked at the Frenchman's expression; his face was red as he stared at his mother's hand. Impervious she continued, 'Shall there be a sale?'

When at last Pierre spoke, his voice and his eyes were very calm and very cold. 'You are very lucky indeed, *madame*,' he said gravely, 'to have already acquired such a treasure as that Egyptian ring you are wearing, which, of course, I recognise most particularly.' He stood abruptly and would clearly say more. Rose actually closed her eyes in unbearable embarrassment (then opened one eye very slightly). George stood at once also, as did the Duke of Hawksfield.

'You are receiving our hospitality, *monsieur*,' the Duke said quietly in his gravelly, imperious voice. 'We shall discuss this matter later if you would be so kind.' And Pierre was quite still for a moment, then bowed coldly to the Duke, and sat, and the moment had passed without most of the other guests properly understanding what had happened.

But still the Dowager was not to be deflected. 'I am indeed lucky!' she said as she saw others staring at her hand. 'Of course you know that my son collects antiques like this, he has much knowledge of antiques, no doubt a great deal more than yourself, *monsieur*,' but slowly, as the Duke of Hawksfield stared at her silently, and she saw his anger, her voice faltered slightly, and she held her napkin to her mouth and then suggested to Ann that the ladies move to the new conservatory.

Rose, safe now from the ridiculous Fallon family, found it extremely difficult not to laugh. And then, there in the roomful of chattering society women, seeing Dolly's glittering eyes and sighing bosom as she suddenly now looked bored, and fanned herself in a corner of the conservatory, waiting for the gentlemen, Rose almost wanted to cry also, for she saw that Dolly was lost to her. *I cannot help her.* The young girl who had talked so longingly to her mother, and wrote make-believe stories in her diary to please her brother, seemed no longer to exist.

When carriages were called and the two ladies in white prepared to leave, Monsieur Montand prepared to leave also, could not be dissuaded. The Duke calmly arranged a further appointment with himself and George the following morning; Dolly looked ostentatiously away from Rose and Fanny and Pierre as they said goodbye.

'You must travel in our carriage,' said Rose politely.

In the carriage she apologised for her mother-in-law.

'It will be resolved, *bien sûr!*' said Pierre so gallantly that both the women smiled at his wonderful French *politesse*, for his dismay and anger at the dinner table had been palpable and the Egyptian ring beyond price. 'We knew it had disappeared but I had not thought to find it in London!'

'Monsieur Montand,' said Rose suddenly as the women alighted in the dusk, 'would you take tea with us tomorrow afternoon? You could advise us of a happy conclusion to this unfortunate matter and' – the words rushed out – 'and you could tell us a little more about Egypt.' He said he would be enchanted and kissed their hands.

In the drawing room Fanny collapsed on to the soft sofa in disbelieving laughter. 'What an extraordinary house, Rose! If that was your life, dearest coz, however could you have borne it? Everybody secretly staring at everybody else, and caught in flowing tents, and all that eating and spitting and shouting and lying and subterranean activities – the Dowager is nothing but a common thief, it seems! It makes our early lives in Brook Street and Baker Street seem positively mundane!'

Rose hugged herself, laughing also. Fanny saw that her cousin's eyes were shining. 'I do not have to do that any more!'

'And your *protégée* Dolly seemed not to be unhappy in the way that you feared.'

Rose's face changed. 'She has found a way, it seems, of – dealing with the situation she was forced into. Can you believe that she is still fifteen! Perhaps, after all, she will survive,' but her voice sounded doubtful.

'Survive? I think she will *reign*!' said Fanny. 'But what drama! I would not like to get on the wrong side of that presiding Duke!' And she shook her head, although still smiling. 'You know, Rose, I felt also that – you should perhaps be careful.'

'Whatever do you mean?'

'Dolly seems certainly not to wish you well. And you and George were like two snakes, poised to strike across the room – and yet you never said a single thing to each other all evening. I believe you actually hate each other!'

'I do not have to spend time with them any more! It is *over*, all that life!'

'The Church is right to be afraid, you know – perhaps there ought to be a revolution here. What sort of world is Berkeley Square? I felt I had strayed into a madhouse! Like a shocked country vicar's wife! Which of course,' and Fanny sighed suddenly and began taking the flowers out of her hair, 'is what I am.' And as she undid the flowers one by one: a rose, a peony, she added, 'But I liked Monsieur Montand. He seemed interested in you, Rose. Do you think you could care for him? Is that why you asked him to tea?' She saw that Rose's eyes suddenly shone again.

'I asked him to tea because – can you not see? – I want to hear more about *Egypt*! George talks about going. Why should I not go?'

'To Egypt?'

'Yes!'

'Why?'

'To find Harry's child maybe.'

'*Rose!*'

'Fanny, let me at least say all these words *out loud*! I will never have children of my own. I know it. And this – yearning – I do not want it to be part of me for the rest of my life!' And then she laughed, as if at her own dramatic tone. 'If I could find the child I would be able to give her part of her history at least, I could help her to know who she is. You told me I had something to thank Harry for, after all, so maybe I will thank him this way.' She spoke almost flippantly.

Fanny's face was a picture of incredulity. Was her cousin merely joking? 'Dearest Rose, you know how much I want you to be happy, you are the dearest person to me in the world. But *think*! How would you even *begin* in a strange country? And you know the law – you would not have any rights over this child. *George* would be the person to whom this child would belong should you – by some miracle – find her. Rose, listen, I will help you find a child. There are thousands of children all over England who would be so lucky to be chosen by you.'

'No,' said Rose.

'But Rose – *Egypt*! We know nothing!'

'Pierre knows something! And Mattie thinks Cornelius Brown may be there. George need never know anything about this – our paths are not going to cross ever again. And Fanny – Egypt has always been the dream of my heart, you know that more than anyone!' At last Fanny gave a small, reluctant nod: she too had been entranced many times by the story of the old Arab man singing in the sunshine and the little boy's arm and the coffee beans on the bank of the river Nile. 'So, at least, hear with me what Monsieur Montand has to say. Nothing more than that.'

'Very well,' said Fanny, slowly. Suddenly she desperately wanted to see her daughter, to make her real: her own little girl who she would give the world for; suddenly she wanted to get back to Wentwater to see her son, knew how lucky she was, felt suddenly infinite pity for her cousin and her dreams. 'Dearest coz, of course we will listen to Monsieur Montand together.' She stood, with the flowers in her hand. 'But first tomorrow you know I must see Papa's lawyer, and then, perforce, we must plan to return to Wentwater. But,' and she bent to kiss her cousin goodnight, 'I am so glad to be here.' And she turned to go upstairs.

'Fanny,' said Rose, and Fanny turned back and saw that Rose looked at her with love. 'I have thought a great deal of all you have said – about your own life with Horatio, about mine with Harry.'

Fanny stood with her wilted flowers, waited. Her red hair framed her face in the shadows, like a halo.

'I have been so angry, and – perhaps I will always feel something of that. But something has – has lifted off my shoulders – since we talked. Harry and I *were* happy I think, for a time, and I *did* love him, whatever love means! But I had pushed all that away from my heart and only remembered the bad things.' Rose's peonies came out easily from her short hair; petals lay in her hands. 'What I did not understand when I became so unhappy was that I had anything at all to be grateful to Harry for, whatever else has happened. Fanny, it is *such a relief* not to feel such anger towards him. And it is only your own honesty that has made me see.'

Fanny smiled down at Rose and Rose saw real sadness in her smile. 'I am glad. But I could have told you without mentioning my own life. I have lost count of the number of women in Wentwater who have come to see me and asked if there was some way they did not have to carry out their – *duty*, they call it – to their husbands.'

'Whatever do you say to them?'

'What can I say? I am the vicar's wife. I tell them,' and she half laughed, 'to pray. As I do. But – they taught me something all the same, these women. Have you never considered why I have only two children?'

Rose stumbled slightly. 'Until you came here, I – I thought that perhaps you and Horatio had decided that between you. But you have said—'

'Indeed,' said Fanny drily. 'But you cannot know some of the women of Wentwater as intimately as I have known them and not know about a vinegared sponge. And, truly, Horatio would never know the difference.' Rose looked at her cousin wide-eyed. 'Rose, you cannot imagine what it feels like to – to always dread going to bed. Thank Harry, at least, for that.' And Fanny took up a candle and climbed to the top room where her beloved four-year-old daughter was dreaming of driving pedlars' carts across the heavens, wherein God smelt of lavender and shouted.

Next day when Fanny arrived back from the lawyer almost exploding with her unbelievable, extraordinary news, she found Rose and Jane in the overly hot kitchen with Mattie, trying somewhat unsuccessfully to make a cake for Monsieur Montand. Nobody noticed Fanny's flushed cheeks for they were flushed themselves and the kitchen basement was full of smoke.

'Look, Mama, look!' cried Jane with flour all over her face. 'We are to eat it as soon as it is cooked, look at it cooking! Is it cooking?'

'Look, Fanny, look!' cried Rose. 'I haven't had flour on my hands for such a long time!' Mattie had sweat running down her face: she still hadn't properly mastered the cooking fire. Fanny saw that her news would have to wait. She joined in, tried to help; when Pierre Montand rang the bell outside and was shown downstairs by the landlady, making his way over unpacked boxes and pieces of furniture, he found four females – one of them a small girl – in an extremely smoky kitchen that was filled with a burning smell, looking in some surprise at a very scorched plum cake. Once Miss Proud – wearing her spectacles and carrying her books, completely oblivious to the chaos – had ascertained casually that her house was not actually on fire, she left them all most amiably, as if such things happened daily. Mattie shooed them away, told them to go and take the air in the square.

'It is windy but it is healthy, don't come back for an hour!' ordered Mattie. 'You can have tea, but not for an hour!'

'Forgive us, Monsieur Montand' said Rose, as they picked up their bonnets and made their way out into South Molton Street. 'We failed!' and she and Pierre and Fanny and Jane crossed Bond Street, laughing, and walked into Hanover Square and began to promenade around the neat gravel path beneath the trees (the women hoping the wind would take from their clothes and their hair the smell of burning). Dry leaves blew along the paths. Many others promenaded too: they passed several groups of demure-looking young women and the cousins caught each other's eye and smiled, and knew both were remembering the days when they too perambulated decorously in this square, looking at gentlemen. When Monsieur Montand found some French barley sugar in his jacket pocket Jane looked at him in astonishment and gave him a small, shy smile.

'May we ask,' said Rose, 'what happened at Berkeley Square this morning? I have tried to imagine a scene where George and the Duke of Hawksfield somehow excuse the Dowager, but I have failed!'

Pierre laughed. 'The Duke of Hawksfield is not a man, I think, to accept excuses. The Egyptian ring is – what shall I say – rescued,

Dieu merci! It resides with the French Ambassador in Portman Square until I return to Paris. It was a most interesting morning, for I saw the Dowager Viscountess Gawkroger being – I believe your English word is "bullied". For that is also her own *style*, I think! The Duke of Hawksfield – understanding international diplomacy – had insisted she admit to me her "absent-mindedness in picking up the ring", and I could see that the words stuck in her throat. And then when she had finished her apology, and we took English tea politely as if nothing had occurred, Mademoiselle Dolly suddenly had a large and hysterical attack, for she has set her heart on travelling to Egypt and her husband is not, I believe, of that mind. He is correct in that I do think: I would not want any woman I know to suffer such hardship.'

'I should be glad to suffer it,' said Rose rather tartly, 'if I could go.'

'But Madame Rose – or perhaps,' and his eyes smiled, 'as you were so named, I could call you *Rosette*, for that is the French name for the town.' Rose's cheeks became slightly pink but she nodded. He went on: 'I spoke a little, yesterday, of the dangers. We can walk here in this elegant English square and talk of such a journey, as a dream. It would be difficult enough for Viscount Gawkroger and his brother-in-law to travel there. But Egypt is certainly no place for a foreign woman, it would be an extremely dangerous journey for Lady Dolly to undertake.'

'They are not going – immediately?'

'Perhaps they only dream. It is difficult to tell with the Viscount.'

'Do foreign women ever go to Egypt?'

'Wives of travellers; wives of traders: eccentrics.'

'Please may we sit down,' said Jane, noticing an iron seat, and the three grown-ups did so, though not ceasing their conversation, for Rose asked eagerly about the progression of the translation of the hieroglyphs. Jane banged her heels against the iron seat but they did not notice. *When can I tell of my news?* thought Fanny impatiently.

Pierre sighed heavily. 'We seem to be stuck. We need other keys like *la pierre de Rosette*, for as a key it is very flawed, with so many of the hieroglyphs broken off at the top. We would be so glad to find the rest of the stone. The feeling among our linguists is that the

Coptic language – which is all that seems to remain that perhaps has any connections at all with Egypt's ancient language – is our best clue, yet in the end even that may be too far removed now from the original hieroglyphs.'

'The Copts are the remains of the original Egyptian Christians, I think,' said Fanny.

'*Oui*, Madame Fanny. Once, I believe, all Egyptians were called Copts by the Greek invaders. But the Coptic language, which must, once, have been spoken all over Egypt, is itself no longer a living language, apart from its formal use in the Coptic churches – everybody in Egypt speaks Arabic now. And just to add to our frustration, when the Coptic language was written down it used mostly Greek letters!'

'And my idea of the repetition of the name: of King Ptolemy?' said Rose shyly.

'Yes, of course, I think it is understood that well-known names should help us eventually. The linguists believe that a *cartouche*, a box, seems to surround royal names in the hieroglyphs. We have other hieroglyphs to study of course from other antiquities – but no other treasure so far has a Greek translation.'

'It seems to me,' said Rose, 'for of course this has been consuming my thoughts, that if you wanted to ask someone to a ball, or say you were coming to stay, it would take too long to carve it on a stone,' and they laughed, 'so of course there would be a faster, simpler way with something like a quill and something like ink: you would write a kind of short-hand of the hieroglyphs. And surely that might be, as you said in Paris, what the middle language is on the stone.'

'There must *be* a connection, but it is in no way obvious.' Pierre was frowning.

'And maybe,' Rose sat dreaming, 'if the Greek translation of the Rosetta Stone is anything to go by, we would learn much more *interesting* things from the middle language,' and she gave a little sigh of longing, 'you know what I mean – all that writing you showed me on the papyrus might be full of gossip, and romantic *rendezvous*, and how their hearts were feeling.'

'Indeed,' said Pierre. 'But before any gossip, *s'il vous plait*, I would give a great deal to know what we have found, what our treasures could tell us about ancient Egypt! We speculate endlessly, of course, in *le Commission*, but we *do not know* and there are many madmen all over the world with theories. I read recently the thoughts of a Swedish scholar. He insisted that we only need translate the Psalms of David into Chinese, and write them in the ancient characters of *that* language, and we will find it corresponds exactly! Ah – it would have been so marvellous to publish *Description de l'Egypte* with full explanations of all our treasures!'

'When shall your first volume be ready for publication?'

'We had hoped this would all happen quickly. But there is so much to do, so much careful copying and annotating, and without the written knowledge that we so desire we still actually understand very little. We work as fast as we can but it is a long project.' He shook his head, and added, as if talking to himself, 'I do wonder if the later Egyptians decoded the hieroglyphs themselves, before the invasions of the Mohammetmen? They had so much knowledge, and they were nearer in time, and in language. What if their key is even now still in Egypt somewhere, locked away from Western scholars like us?'

'Could you kindly take me for a small walk,' said Jane to the French visitor, her patience for further barley sugar exhausted.

'Jane!' said Fanny, reprimanding her daughter in some amazement. 'Monsieur Montand is speaking. You know you must not speak when someone else is doing so.' And she stared, bemused, at the child. 'Forgive me, Monsieur Montand. My daughter is usually extremely shy.' But Fanny could not help, also, smiling. 'I believe,' she said, 'that that is the first time she has asked such a favour of a gentleman!'

'Then I shall be pleased to accept,' said Pierre, and he stood, and bowed to Jane, and took her hand, and the two of them set off on the path around the circumference of the square. They saw he was telling Jane something; she stood beside him fascinated, as he pointed at the drifts of cloud above them. Fanny turned at once to Rose.

'Listen, Rose, *listen*! I thought I would never get a chance to tell you! I have already written to Horatio, from the lawyer's office, the letter has gone, but I need to speak to him as soon as possible, I must return to Wentwater tomorrow.'

'Oh *no*!' The dismay in Rose's face was comical and Fanny laughed.

'Well, I have been *waiting* to tell you! You might ask me what the business turned out to be, the matter that was so important that I had to leave Wentwater and come to London for the first time since I was married.'

'Oh Fanny, of course – oh, the burning kitchen, the ring, the hieroglyphs. Tell me! *What?*'

'My father has made a very large sum of money available to me, deposited with the lawyer. Papa wants the family to *go to India*!'

'*What?* All of you? The children? Horatio too?'

'All of us. He and Mama cannot get home. He says business is excellent. He says they miss us terribly – oh Rose, we have been apart for nearly *six* years – they of course wish to meet their grandchildren – and he suggests we all go for a year and the children can meet their cousins, Richard's children. Richard is now so tied to Lord Wellesley and the British Army in India that his wife and children are living with Papa. Papa says that it will be good for our children to see the world, that they will be safe, and well looked after. And that there are many heathens for Horatio to convert!'

'Whatever will Horatio say?'

Fanny pulled her shawl about her and stared at the large London houses near the square, and at the spire of the church where Rose had been married. 'I am not sure. Horatio does not actually believe in the rest of the world but – but surely,' and Rose saw Fanny was trying to convince herself, 'surely even he would be excited by such an adventure!'

'Would you like to go?'

Fanny leaned forward and grabbed Rose's face with both her hands. 'Rose! Of course I would! But look at me, dear girl, I have not finished. Papa is now a very rich man, much richer than I understood. He knows you are alone, and he has provided for, and insists, that you should come too!'

'*What?*'

Pierre Montand and Jane appeared behind them, running. Pierre sat down and wiped his kind face with his handkerchief. Jane fell upon her mother, panting and giggling. Fanny laughed to see her sombre daughter happy, and thanked the Frenchman and suggested it was time for tea. And just for a moment nobody noticed that Rose's eyes glittered, just like the eyes of the antique cats of Egypt.

Fanny and Rose only managed to keep the information to themselves for about eleven minutes. They drank tea; Jane had at once fallen asleep on the soft sofa; Fanny and Rose sat either side of her and Pierre sat on Rose's straight-backed chair, looking taller than ever. Outside tradesmen called and horses trotted past and the knife sharpener yelled – for it was never quiet in South Molton Street. Pierre could see that the women were suddenly almost breathless with excitement; they reminded him of his younger sisters keeping information to themselves when they all lived at home in Nantes; usually such excitement was about a man. So although he had the strongest feeling that he would like to pick up Rose Fallon in his arms and take her anywhere where they could at last be alone, he waited somewhat stoically, rather unlike himself, in case his fate was already sealed by another. He already loved the tiny frown mark on her forehead. The beautiful forehead she had rested against a damaged Egyptian statue.

Rose in particular seemed as if she would explode. At last she said to Fanny, and the words literally burst out of her: 'Please may we discuss this matter with Monsieur Montand, who will have much information about many things we need to know?'

'Yes!' said Fanny. 'I was waiting for you!' And both women started laughing excitedly.

'Whatever this piece of news is that has been shining out of your faces, I would be *enchanté* if you would address me as Pierre!'

'Tell Pierre, Fanny!' Rose's eyes sparkled. And Fanny Harbottom, wife of the Vicar of Wentwater, looked at her daughter who was fast asleep with her mouth open, and then explained what the lawyer had said. When she had finished the women were dismayed to see that Pierre did not seem to share their wild excitement. He regarded them gravely.

'That would be a very long and perilous journey,' said Pierre at last. 'India is very far away and there are many dangers on that long sea journey. Do you think your husband will agree to such a plan?'

He saw their uncertain faces. Fanny had been over it ten times in her head on the way back to South Molton Street from the lawyer. Would the rest of the world exist for Horatio if he was given such a chance to see it for himself? Would he think it hindered his career or helped it? She could not tell.

'I cannot tell,' she said.

'Please,' said Rose. 'Listen to me. Both of you.' And her mouth was suddenly quite dry. She swallowed and licked her lips nervously. She finished her tea. She got up from the soft sofa, and then sat down again: *had not Pierre said only yesterday that India could be reached through Egypt?* Finally the words came out in a rush. 'If I am to go to India, why could I not go by way of Egypt and find Harry's daughter? If it were possible. If she is alive,' she added, throwing a nervous glance at Pierre. 'I know she may not be.'

Neither of them said anything for a moment. They could hear Rose's breathing.

'And then?' said Fanny quietly. 'Rose, dearest, *what then*?'

Rose frowned in concentration. 'She comes into my dreams no matter how hard I try to stop her. I have thought and thought about it. I realise,' and she looked at Pierre uneasily again, 'that – should I find her – I might not help her by appearing, I may even make it more difficult for her. But I could, at least, investigate – see if – see if she needs – my assistance.' She knew how weak such words sounded when they were said aloud: in her head they felt strong. 'Oh God – I have this – no doubt self-inflicted – feeling that I *must* find her.'

As if at the sound of the name of her father's employer Jane opened her eyes. They did not notice.

'Rose,' said Fanny gently, 'surely, as I said to you last night, you understand the law. If the child is alive, and if you find her, she would belong to George. Not to you.'

'But George knows *nothing* of a child; I do.'

'You would have no rights. None at all.'

'He need never, never know! My life is – from this moment –

completely severed from the Fallon family. I need never see them again. And what would George want with an Egyptian child? A girl in particular? He is busy begetting his own!'

'I am very hungry,' said Jane. 'What is begetting?'

Pierre Montand had not spoken at all.

Late into the night, Jane asleep upstairs, the three of them still sat at the small table in the lamplight, talking. Mattie bustled about, bringing food, taking plates, listening, stoking up the fire, making the mixture of red wine and hot water that she knew Rose and Fanny enjoyed. Pierre still did not offer an opinion, only information: he told them the routes to India, how most people took the very long route by ship round the Cape of Good Hope. It was shorter in time, but much more dangerous, to cross Europe and then sail, probably from Italy, through the Mediterranean to Alexandria. Then they would have to cross Egypt, either through the desert or by small boat down the Nile, to Cairo; then again through desert to the Red Sea and so to India. 'I am sure your husband,' he said to Fanny, 'will understand the dangers and the difficulties.' And then he could not help himself. 'It would be *ludicrous* to do this, to think of going through Egypt! The children would not survive – *you* would not survive. It is a ridiculous idea!' He heard his own angry tone. 'Of course – this is not my business, *pardonnez-moi.*' But, then, speaking about Egypt, he quite unconsciously got caught up in his own memories; talked of the desert sand and the swaying camels and the ruins and the boats on the Nile with their sails, and the Arab traders who had already begun to realise that antiquities could be sold and offered things they had found in the rubble to any passing foreigner: hieroglyphs or skulls or jewellery. And of Bedouin horsemen who would either kill them, or meet them in the desert with dates and hard-boiled eggs.

The women looked at him in surprise. '*Hard-boiled* eggs?'

'I expect they keep better in the heat when they have been cooked!' *and the women saw men in turbans and flying cloaks on horseback raising the yellow desert sand as they galloped away.* 'They were rogues, of course, many of the people we had dealings with, but I met some of their scholars too, especially in Cairo where we opened the first Institute de l'Egypte. I am not sure that they were very interested in the ancient things we found, but they were wise, wise men, and most intriguing to talk to.'

'And women?'

'A foreign man does not meet Egyptian women, Rose' – he saw her face – 'other that is than women of a certain class – forgive me. Once I was asked to the house of a scholar, but the food was served by manservants. I believe the women were upstairs in what they call the *haramlek*. There are so many rules regarding women. One must not even ask of a man if his wife is in good health – I learned that one only must say, for instance, "I hope the mother of your children is well." That time at the house of the scholar, I felt conscious of eyes looking down from a grille above. But I may have been mistaken.' They stared at him.

'A grille? Is it a *prison*?'

'I am sure it is not exactly that.'

He still had said nothing at all about the child in Alexandria. Rose showed them her father's old maps: they saw his old sea routes marked. At the mouth of the Nile, at Rosetta, a small flower faded: 'I drew that when I was about eight,' said Rose, 'when Papa told me where my name came from. It was my hieroglyph.'

Pierre looked at the childish drawing. 'You have made a picture language, a picture to remind us of you, and it would encapsulate all we knew of you, Fanny and I , when we saw that: your eyes for instance' (*I must leave them together*, thought Fanny) 'and your face and your hair and . . .'

And the women saw him catch himself, go back to the subject that haunted him. 'What I am really trying to say is: for hundreds of years people have talked of the hieroglyphs as pictures like your picture, and dreams and mystery, and I suppose that may yet turn out to be partly true. I am sure the hieroglyphs *began* as a picture language. But – although I am *un archéologue*, not a linguist, I believe it has to be a hundred times more sophisticated than that. I see that there is too much information to be expressed in *pictures*. But of course we can only wait for the real scholars, and sometimes it makes me, as I work with the treasures and the markings, so often in the dark, feel crazy!' And they saw how obsessively he spoke, how he could not leave the subject, how he rubbed his eyes and frowned.

Fanny picked up her shawl. 'Forgive me,' she said. 'I leave for home early in the morning – to find out our fate! But you must promise not to forget us, Pierre,' she added as she said goodnight, 'for whatever we decide we will need you to advise us.'

'I will, of course, be at your service,' said Pierre gravely, and he kissed her hand. 'I will be most interested to hear the decision of your husband, who I am sure is a wise man.'

When Fanny had gone he closed the maps slowly. They sat in silence for a moment, and it was as if Rose's wild cry in Paris: *what child?* echoed there in the room now, where the candles flickered (and perhaps the silent house listened). The knife grinder was still calling along South Molton Street, as if darkness was a good time for sharpening steel; two horses trotted by over the cobblestones; they heard a woman laughing.

'*Ecoute-moi*,' said Pierre at last. 'Listen.'

Rose was suddenly frightened she would lose his friendship because he thought her so foolish. 'Please, Pierre,' she said quickly, 'promise me you will remain our friend whatever happens. We shall need your advice, you will be the person who can help us most on this magical adventure. Please, Pierre,' as she saw his face.

'I will be your friend, whatever happens,' said Pierre gravely. 'But, Rosette, *it will not be a magical adventure*. Forgive me, but you have absolutely no idea what you are proposing. You could so easily – I am in no way exaggerating – *lose your life*, and I curse the day I ever spoke of the child to you. How could I have imagined for a moment that it would affect you this way?'

'I will read every book that has ever been written about Egypt before I go,' she said stubbornly.

'No book can tell you of that place.' He sat back in his chair and his shadow was tall and strange on the wall behind him. 'You feel that it is your duty to look for the child for your husband's sake?'

'No,' said Rose, and she bit her lip, 'not duty.' The shadow was very still. 'The Egyptian girl was one among many women, and I found that out long before my husband died. He made love to many of my friends; he did not' – she gave a small laugh – 'discern for my sake. I assure you I do not carry a flame in my heart!'

Quietly he said: 'So why – *really* – is this so important to you?'

She looked across the table, but she could not speak to him of a tiny dead baby, of the small, perfectly formed fingers and toes. She could not tell him she might not have another chance. 'You told me of her: now I must look for her.'

Very gently he leaned across the table and took her hand as he had taken it in a street in Paris. 'I was foolish,' he said. He looked at her with such tenderness that her heart jolted with shock. '*Ma chérie*, it is impossible for me to leave the Commission at this moment, we are trying so hard to prepare for publication and I am too much required and preoccupied. But perhaps, one day, I could take you there, to Egypt, if this is so important to you. I would comprehend, at least, as you do not, the difficulties, and I could protect you in some ways.' Still he held her hand in his. 'Would you, *Rosette*' – and his kind face smiled at her – 'I never thought to say these words in English – think to become my wife?' Although he held her hand so gently she somehow could not withdraw it. She was completely taken aback. Suddenly she saw Harry, on his knees, refusing to be denied and then sweeping her into his arms, the passion and the laughter. She looked at this different kind of man altogether, at his kind and loving face. 'I like you so much,' she said. 'But . . .'

'But?'

She could not speak.

'But?' he said again.

'Pierre – we know nothing of each other – we have met so seldom.'

'I understand that we would have a lot to learn! And yet it would seem that Fate has decreed that I know a great deal about your life, more than many.'

'In a way that is true, but—'

'And it seems also,' and he was smiling, 'that I have been struck by an arrow from the bow of Cupid. That ancient broken stone seems to have brought us together – and I expect we could find out more of each other, if we so desire.'

'But – but we live in different countries!'

He said nothing, simply held her hand, and waited.

'I think I – I cannot,' said Rose at last, and she looked away from his gaze.

Fanny and Miss Proud and Mattie heard the front door close.

Fanny came downstairs in her nightgown, her red hair standing up around her face; Rose, seeing her at any other time, might have laughed. But Rose was sitting on the sofa with her arms about herself as if she was cold, and beside her, sending smoke into the air, one of her little cigars.

'Dear Rose.' Fanny sat beside her cousin. 'Is it – is something settled between you? What does he say about Egypt?'

It took a long time for Rose to answer. 'He is – I know it – an extremely kind man. I like him so much – I could never forget how he behaved with such chivalry towards Dolly when she went to him in the middle of the night, as I told you. I do like him very much. But – he has asked me to marry him.'

'Dearest Rose! Oh my darling that is wonderful!'

'But . . .'

'But?'

Rose was silent.

'Would he help us travel through Egypt?'

'He thinks we are mad.'

'But he wants to marry you – madness notwithstanding!' Rose said nothing. Fanny waited.

'Oh Fanny, I do not know what to think or feel! I was not in the least prepared. I just – I do not feel – oh Fanny, *I don't know!* You know George says I am ill and should be taken to Bedlam! Perhaps I am scared. Anyway – the truth of the matter is that – *he does not make my heart beat.* There!' And Rose blushed slightly and stood, the cigar in her hand. 'I must go to bed.'

'But . . .' Fanny looked puzzled, stared up at her cousin for a moment. 'I hope – I hope that you are not, after all this, looking for another Harry?'

'What do you mean?' Something uneasy brushed at Rose. 'What do you mean?' she said again.

Something bitter in Fanny's eyes. 'I think one ought to have learned that there are other ways of choosing a husband than the things we thought at seventeen. And *then* the heart would beat. From – something deeper.'

Rose stared at her. 'What do you mean?' she said again.

Fanny looked again at her cousin, and then looked embarrassed suddenly herself. She too stood. 'It is nothing,' she said. 'I am probably not experienced enough to talk of such things. Goodnight, dear Rose,' and she kissed her cousin and Rose heard her footsteps, up the stairs to the attic room.

In the night Rose suddenly sat bolt upright in her bed, her heart beating very fast: she had dreamed of Pierre, smiling down at her with his wonderful, wise, kind eyes: why should she not tell him of her fears, of how much she had wanted a child, *that* child, having lost one half like it? Somebody like Pierre would *understand* that: he was not Harry, to whom she could not talk of her heart. She at once remembered Fanny's puzzled, puzzling words, *I hope you are not looking for another Harry*, and knew – at last – that she was not. *Because I could not* endure *life with another Harry!* She actually put her hand over her mouth to stop herself crying out at her own foolishness *I have made such a terrible mistake! Mattie tried to tell us, all those years ago: we must* like *our husbands also. Such a man as Pierre is – the opposite of what Harry was.* She was being offered another, *different* chance, a chance of happiness, and her heart that she had said did not beat for him was beating wildly *how could I have been so stupid! Have I learnt nothing from the past?*

Next morning at dawn, as soon as she had waved goodbye to Fanny and Jane, saying she would be waiting every day for the letter and then they would make plans at once, Rose ran. She ran to the French Ambassador's house in Portman Square: she cared not at all what they might think of the mud and dust and horse muck on her gown, the early hour *let me not be too late*; she asked for Monsieur Montand.

A footman with an elaborate powdered wig bowed and informed her that Monsieur Montand had left last night, for France.

*

The skies became heavier, and greyer, and the days were cold. Women put more shawls and cloaks around their flimsy dresses and caught colds and suffered terribly with rheumatics, because the houses were never warm. Soon it would be winter: soon it would be December and then Christmas Day and then a new year. *Where is Fanny's letter? Surely Pierre cannot have stopped caring for me already?* She wrote at least ten letters to him and tore them up, they sounded so feeble: *Dear Pierre, I made a mistake.* As soon as she heard from Fanny she would start planning to travel and she would go to Paris. On one of those cold, grey days Rose came slowly up the stairs to the top part of the house in South Molton Street, having hoped, again in vain, for a letter from Fanny, from Pierre. Mattie was cleaning the drawing room. Rose started to go to her room, then turned back

'Mattie,' said Rose.

'Yes, Miss Rose?' Mattie was getting out the furniture polish.

'Mattie,' Rose said again. She spoke casually, but her cheeks were pink. 'When we were young, you told us to make sure we *liked* our husbands. Papa did not like Harry, for all his charm.'

'Hmmmm,' said Mattie polishing noncommittally.

'Did you like Harry?'

'Good heavens,' said Mattie. She was leaning over the big table; she suddenly polished harder. 'What's it got to do with me?'

'But – I thought everybody liked him. He *was* charming!'

Mattie polished so hard that her breathing became heavier. 'If you're really asking me, we had boys exactly like that down Ludgate Hill. I gave them cheek but I wouldn't have touched them with a bargepole.' Rose's face became redder. Mattie stopped for a moment, looked at her. 'I knew there was a problem when he made you put all your books away in your room and you didn't even protest, you were that ensnared.' She pushed the hair out of her eyes. 'You couldn't see what kind of man he really was!' Rose could do nothing about her red cheeks. *How could I have let Pierre go?* 'Listen, Miss Rose, when Cornelius Brown knew your parents were helping me to learn to read, do you know, he would help me too on my day off, even though he might have rather been doing something else! He knew it was important to me.'

The table was now so polished Rose could see her own, red face clearly.

'Oh where are the *letters*?' she cried passionately.

Fanny at last sent the shortest of notes to Rose in London.

He says we may not go was all it said.

Pierre Montand also wrote a short note, from Paris. He addressed it to both Rose and Fanny, told them that the priceless blue and gold Egyptian ring was replaced on its shelf at the Commission de l'Egypt and how all the *savants* had given a sigh of relief. He made no more mention of marriage, nor of anything personal at all. He did not mention journeys. He sent his best wishes.

Rose sat in her small drawing room, the two short letters in her hand.

She lit a small cigar. The smoke drifted.

It would not have been for Harry. It was for myself. I have never wanted anything as much as I want this child, who would be partly at least like the one I lost. The one I saw.

Then a thought exploded inside her head like a firework, stars cascading.

Why am I waiting for someone else to make the decision?

SEVENTEEN

'*No!*' said Fanny. 'No, Horatio, please, I will not!' Horatio had once again caught her unawares: the maid was buying salt, it was the middle of the day, Fanny was making dinner in her kitchen: she did not have her sponge and her vinegar. So many times since she had returned to Wentwater had this happened.

'Do you say *no* to your husband?'

'Horatio, the children are playing only in the hall, wait until later, I beg you.' The pots were boiling, sweat ran down her freckled cheeks, her red hair flew about her.

'Do you say *no* to your husband?' He was unbuttoning himself, panting and pushing. 'We shall have more children. You will perform your wifely duties. St Paul said: *woman was created for the sake of man.* You shall never go near London again. Your cousin' – he pulled up her dress – 'always fills your head' – he pushed – 'with her immoral ideas.' She tried to thrust him away; he knocked the side of her face with his elbow in his frustration but did not notice. 'Do you say no to your husband who is God's representative on earth?' He was beside himself, the hot kitchen was filled with the smell of mutton and lavender and suet and sweat and, suddenly, sex, as his impulse overpowered him. He breathed heavily for a moment, leaning against her. A stain seeped across the skirt of her gown.

'Mama?' Jane's small voice came uncertainly from somewhere near.

'Get out!' her father roared, rebuttoning hastily, and Jane bolted back into the hall like a frightened rabbit, just as the bell was pulled outside the vicarage front door.

Fanny, her hand to the side of her face, looked once at her husband, turned, and walked upstairs; pots boiled over and hissed, unheeded.

So Horatio was still slightly breathless and still slightly dishevelled as the visitors were shown into the vicarage by a maid carrying salt who at once ran into the kitchen to the boiling pots; his demeanour was not helped by the fact that the visitors were his wife's cousin, Rose, and her maid.

'Good afternoon, Horatio,' said Rose, holding out her hand to him. 'What a very long time since we have met.'

He bowed but his words were unwelcoming. 'We were not, I think, expecting you,' he said.

'I know,' she answered. 'But I have been visiting some family friends in Birmingham and as we were almost passing your door, and as I have had the very great pleasure of meeting your daughter, I feel it is my duty to meet your son also about whom I have heard so much. But I shall only stay a very short time – just tonight if it is suitable – for I must urgently return to London.'

Conflicting emotions chased across his face. He did not want this immoral woman having the slightest influence over his son – on the other hand, his son was a spectacular success to be shown to everybody.

Jane who had, unbelieving, heard the voice of her aunt, hovered fearfully just beyond, further down the hall. 'Aunt Rose?' she said in a small voice, looking around the door.

'Janey!' And Jane sidled towards her, her eyes looking anxiously at her father; her brother had disappeared.

Rose hugged her, seeing the anxious little freckled face, feeling how cold Jane's arms and hands were. 'I have missed you so much that I came to see you!' she said to the small girl. 'And I hope' – she looked up at Horatio – 'that I might meet your brother at last.' Jane would have told her aunt that her brother still pinched her every time the adults were not observing, but she could not, in front of her father.

'Call your brother,' said Horatio, and Jane at once, obediently and carefully, walked through the hallway to rooms at the back.

'Now listen to me, Rose,' said Horatio and at that moment his wife flew into the room. 'Rose! I *knew* I heard your voice!' was all she said, and she held her cousin tightly, then looked at her anxiously. 'Is everything all right?'

'Of course!' said Rose. 'I did not mean to frighten you. I am only passing, just tonight. I have been to Birmingham and as I was so near I wanted to meet your son,' and she smiled at Horatio, 'of whom I have heard so much.'

Fanny looked at her cousin, smiling with pleasure but with a hundred questions in her very intelligent eyes. 'Birmingham indeed?' she said. 'In this cold weather?'

'It is spring!' said Rose. 'The days are getting longer. The roads are hard and fine now that the rain has stopped.'

'Now look here, Rose,' said Horatio. He was thrown by this contained, sophisticated person who stood in his kitchen; this was not the skittish girl he remembered. She was different. 'What are you doing?'

'I had hoped I might go to India with you and your family,' said Rose demurely. 'It would have been such a marvellous adventure. But – it was not to be.'

'It was a ludicrous idea, that a minister of the Church might uproot himself for a year to satisfy the whims of an old man.'

'So I understand,' said Rose. 'Perhaps one day I will get up the courage to go alone.'

'Heavens!' said Fanny, staring at her cousin. 'The dinner!' and she bustled to the stove.

'You are ludicrous, Rose!' said Horatio, and his voice boomed.

The young Horatio appeared in the doorway, with Jane just behind him.

'Good afternoon, Aunt,' he said politely but with little enthusiasm (he had heard of this aunt from his father). He bowed slightly and went at once to stand by his father. He was six years old and he looked like the man whom he stood beside: Rose hoped that he did not yet smell of lavender.

'Recite the Ten Commandments to your aunt.'

The boy began immediately. 'Thou shalt have no other gods before me. Thou shalt not make for thyself a graven image. Thou shalt not take the name of the Lord thy God in vain. Thou shalt observe the Sabbath day. Thou shalt honour thy father and mother.' When he got to adultery he stumbled over the word, obviously in some doubt of its meaning but aware of its sinfulness. As soon as he had finished his task he turned to his father. 'Father, I saw a deer in the last field. May we go and shoot it?' Horatio was loath to leave the two women together, but very keen to teach his son to shoot a deer.

'I will expect you at church tonight,' he said to Rose as he put his boots on.

'Tonight?' She looked puzzled. 'Of course, if you wish – but it is Tuesday.'

'It is the night Fanny needs to hear my sermon.'

'Oh, of course. I should enjoy that very much.' And not by so much as a flicker did she seem anything but utterly delighted.

When at last they were alone, Mattie keeping Fanny's maid occupied in the kitchen, Jane fast asleep on a couch, safe among the women, Rose grabbed Fanny by both arms. 'Fanny! Of course I have not been to Birmingham! I have come to see you, for I could not write everything! Fanny, I am leaving this very week for Egypt. I have planned everything! I am going through Paris, of course, to ask further advice of Pierre – he may not approve but I am sure he will help me when he sees I must go! But I could not leave without seeing you.'

Fanny's unbelieving face. 'You cannot be thinking of going alone. Is it Pierre? Is he to take you?'

'I can go alone, Fanny. Since the autumn I have read every single book about Egypt that exists. I am not afraid.'

'Would Pierre not escort you? Are you friends?'

'I – I am sure we will be friends when we meet again. But of course – I could not ask him – not that.' She stumbled slightly, as small Horatio had stumbled over 'adultery'.

'You simply cannot make a journey like that alone, I am sure

Pierre will say the same. It is impossible, he has told us it is far too dangerous!'

'*I am going, Fanny!* Women have done it. Pierre *admitted* to us in London that it has been done by women, even if they were eccentrics accompanying their husbands. There will be other travellers, there are always other travellers. I do not believe that even strangers would let me be eaten by wild animals or slaughtered by an infidel's sword! And I am not going completely alone, of course I am not. Mattie is coming with me most cheerfully. In fact she is absolutely delighted! She will tell you – she feels she is quite likely to find her long-lost husband!' But Fanny's serious eyes still stared out from the frame of red hair, disapproving. 'Fanny, darling, listen. I am cured of Harry. I no longer miss him in the slightest way. But it was you who made me understand that I had things to thank Harry for after all. If I do this I will feel I have acted honourably on his behalf.'

'Why ever should you do something on his behalf?'

'Oh Fanny, that is an excuse if you like! Just so that I do not sound completely deranged! I want desperately to find this strange child if it is possible, and you know perfectly well that I am *dying* to go to Egypt! Always, always I wanted to go there. Truly, I have been planning for months; planning as Papa would have planned, not letting myself travel until I was sure I understood the journey. I have worked so hard. I have read *everything* available. I have taught myself to greet people in Arabic. I have stopped taking opium for I know my mind must remain clear! I know we do not even know that the child is alive but I will do my best to find her and I am sure Pierre will help. There is nothing to keep me in England! I am a widow! I am free!' They heard a shot in the distance.

'Another dead deer,' said Fanny with distaste as the shot echoed.

Rose could not stop. 'Mattie and I leave for Paris in a few days. We will make our way across to Italy or Greece to board a ship.' Her cousin still stared at her, disbelieving. 'Fanny darling, it is not as if I have never been anywhere! I have travelled a great deal as you know. I will take advice from other travellers, and journey in company with them if possible.'

'You think you will find the child – just like that?'

'At least I can try! The English trader who sheltered the mother may know.'

Fanny looked uncomprehending. 'I believe you are completely serious.'

'I am completely serious. I am almost on my way!'

'*Oh, Rose!*' Fanny gave a laugh, or a cry, put her arms around her cousin and they stood there for a moment. 'Let me at least make you some tea!'

Rose hardly heard. 'Pierre was full of so much information that night, and I wrote many things down after he had gone. And – I will see him in Paris – I am sure he will give me any assistance that I need.'

'Does he not know already, about your journey?'

'Not – not that I am travelling without you and Horatio, no.'

'Does he know at least you are coming to Paris?' But Rose avoided Fanny's gaze, looked down at her hands.

'I – have tried to write many times but – that is – it will be better if I contact him when I get to Paris, for I will need his kind advice I am sure.' And then suddenly her voice was almost inaudible. 'I want to find the child, Fanny. Not for Harry's sake. For my own. I want it so much it hurts me.'

Then Fanny understood. 'Yes,' she said.

Horatio said a long grace and dinner began silently in the cold afternoon. Thin chilly rays of something like sunshine came into the room and across the table. Rose understood a little why Fanny had such trouble warming to her own son. He was a beautiful child but he copied every mannerism and movement of his father. He was pompous, if it is possible for a six-year-old to be pompous; he was rude to his adoring sister in a way that crushed her over and over again; and he flicked little curious glances at his aunt as the meal proceeded in almost complete silence, just the sound of eating. And Rose also noticed that something cold moved between Fanny and her husband. What Fanny saw was that Rose's eyes, the decision made, shone.

The kitchen clock struck four. Rose turned to Jane. 'Do you remember my clock, Janey? The special Italian one that I showed you?'

'Yes,' said Fanny, smiling, 'the famous clock your papa brought from Genoa so many years ago.'

'It still keeps absolutely perfect time. Its age does not matter.'

'I saw it, I saw the Illtalin clock,' cried Jane.

'Be quiet, Jane,' said her father, and her brother kicked her under the table, but not very hard because he was so astounded they should be talking in such a manner. Nobody had ever talked about something as interesting as clocks at the dinner table in his whole life: the dinner table, he had been told, was for eating and contemplating the Lord, or his father talking.

'Can you tell the time, Horatio?'

'Of course I can.'

'We understand from Greek writing,' Rose said to him, 'that it was the ancient Egyptians who first divided the day into hours, and so the first timepieces were invented by them thousands of years ago. I believe there is actually such a thing as a water-clock: it is a bowl with an exact hole somewhere in it – the bowl was filled with water every morning and it emptied when twelve hours was finished: the last drop showed that exactly twelve hours had passed.'

Horatio's small face was rapt with attention.

'Do you remember, Rose, your papa telling us,' and Fanny began to laugh, 'that soon after the museum was opened in Montague House a weight fell off an old clock inside and crashed out through the floor and somehow hit a gentleman's carriage in the courtyard!'

'It was a stone vase!'

'No, it was part of a clock!' And the children saw to their astonishment their aunt and their mother, sitting at dinner, and laughing.

'Perhaps a gentleman was hurt,' said the Reverend Horatio Harbottom severely.

'My father always assured us,' said Rose, smiling at him like an angel, 'for of course we too worried at the damage, that no gentleman was in the carriage at the time.'

'It was a French clock, of course,' said Fanny demurely.

Small Horatio was beside himself. 'Do you mean to say,' he said, as if taking meticulous notes on the subject, 'that Italian clocks and English clocks and French clocks are different? Do they chime in different languages, is that what you are saying?'

His shining aunt laughed again and he saw her hair dance as she threw back her head. 'I used to think exactly that, Horatio,' she said, 'and it is true the chimes do sound differently. One day when you visit me in London—'

'—in London?'

'—in London, I will show you the difference between the Italian clock and the English clocks for yourself.'

'We have plain English clocks that keep perfect time,' said her cousin-in-law. 'Do not feed the boy's head with women's whimsy. The dinner table is for eating.' But he could not help adding: 'I shall certainly keep him from London as long as possible.'

'The Archbishop of Canterbury resides in London, does he not?' asked Rose very sensibly.

'My living will be world enough for my son – and the sons that I pray for hereafter' – a significant glance at Fanny – 'for a long time to come.' And dinner was over, and the horse was fed, and darkness began to fall and the children were sent to bed.

On their way to the church Horatio held up his lantern, showed them the dead deer with its dark, glassy eyes where it hung upside down from a hook in the barn; blood ran from it, congealing now, down its thighs and across the mud floor. Rose looked away, remembered suddenly another dead deer, and George killing its fawn with his hands.

In the church they lit three candles. Shadows were thrown about the pulpit, darkness stretched back behind them. Rose and Fanny sat in one of the pews; it had grown even colder and they had wrapped their cloaks and shawls tightly about them. There was the smell of dust and hymnbooks and lilies that were past their best and – Rose could catch it in the air – lavender. She could not shake the idea from her head that Horatio, up in his box, lit by candlelight, looked like one of the actors she and her friends had so enjoyed on their visits to the Drury Lane Theatre.

Horatio began by quoting from the Bible. *'Lest there be any among you – man, woman or family or tribe whose heart turneth away this day from the Lord our God, the Lord will not spare him!'* He leaned forward. Lavender drifted. 'I wish to speak,' he said, 'of those who criticise the Church, of those who seem to seek to overthrow God's will, and God's history. How wrong they are!' and his voice thundered to the rafters of the empty church. 'How wrong they are, for he who criticises the Church is criticising God: he who criticises me is criticising God, for I am God's representative on earth! The Bible says' – here he held the large copy of the Bible up towards the rafters and shook it – *'the Lord will not spare him! the anger of the Lord and his jealousy shall smite against that man, and all the curses that are written in this book shall lie upon him and the Lord shall blot out his name from under Heaven and the whole land shall be brimstone and salt and burning . . . your feet will stumble upon dark mountains. And while ye look for light, he will turn it into the shadow of death and make it gross darkness.'*

He thundered on in this vein, warning how God saw into men's hearts, and Rose saw Fanny's face in the candlelight as she listened, inscrutable. Rose remembered her cousin's words in Wimpole Street: *all the churchmen* really *care about is the safety of the Church, that it will survive.*

Afterwards the three of them walked the short distance to the vicarage through the darkness of Wentwater in the chill evening. Horatio spoke of his sermon, the two women listened in silence, somewhere a dog barked. It was eight o'clock. Wentwater was asleep.

'Come, Fanny,' said Horatio, as soon as they entered the house.

Rose was asleep when she felt someone pull gently at her shoulder. She sat up quickly, saw her cousin crouched by the bed with a candle. 'Fanny?' she said loudly: alarmed, disoriented.

'Ssshh.' And in the light of the candle Rose saw tears running down her cousin's face.

'My darling, what is it?' Rose whispered, shocked.

'It is nothing – nothing. But – Rose, I am going to come with you.'

'You are going to come with me? Back to London?'

'I am going to come with you. To Egypt. To India.'

'Fanny! Do you mean he has agreed after all?' Rose forgot to whisper. 'Oh Fanny, how *wonderful!*'

'Ssshh! He has not agreed. I have decided.'

'Fanny!' Then Rose began to whisper again too. 'You cannot leave Horatio, he is your husband!'

'I can. He has used me *terribly* this night.'

'But—'

'Rose, I have decided.' And there was her cousin's obstinate little face, tear-stained and defiant. 'We shall plan everything in the morning, before you leave, and we shall meet in Paris. You must not by a hint show Horatio or the children what we are planning. I just wanted to tell you.'

And the candlelight moved away from the bed to the door and Fanny was gone.

But Rose was cold, lay awake; heard the horse pawing and whinnying as dawn came. She wanted Fanny to come with her more than anything else in the world. But the law was excruciatingly clear. Fanny could not do this. A woman might not leave her husband. A woman who did so immediately forfeited all rights over her children. Fanny could not be so cruel.

The next morning Rose wondered if it had been a dream. They sat at breakfast, Fanny poured tea and spoke to the maid about dinner, the chickens outside squawked to be fed, Horatio spoke again of all the work of the parish. Little Horatio veered between imitating his father and staring surreptitiously at his interesting aunt. Jane said, 'Aunt Rose?' and was silenced by her father. Horatio disappeared into his study to read the newspapers. Fanny asked Rose to read to the children and check their letters: she had things she must attend to. People came and went to and from the vicarage door; a woman brought butter. Horatio and Jane laboured over the alphabet; each made words in a small notebook. Later another woman came weeping for the vicar: her husband had been killed by a horse. Outside flies buzzed at the congealed blood on the deer carcass and rats ran under the house. But in the garden there were masses of tiny yellow and purple crocus flowers sprouting among the daffodils and the honeysuckle bushes, well-pruned rose bushes waited for summer, small pansies already frowned: Rose saw someone had worked here with love, remembered Fanny's description of Horatio gardening and talking to the flowers.

When Horatio had gone and the children were feeding the chickens Fanny began to make bread, as if this was an ordinary day; Mattie, her sleeves rolled up, was helping her; Fanny's maid had her half-day off. Rose and Fanny always spoke completely openly in front of Mattie; still Rose thought she might have dreamed. At last Fanny said very fiercely, banging at the bread: 'We will meet at the Pont Neuf.'

'Fanny! You will lose the children. There is no law in the world that will allow you to have them if you once leave.'

'I will only lose them if Horatio finds me. As long as I can reach my father I am safe.'

'But *you will never see them again*!'

Fanny looked at her cousin, open-mouthed. 'What do you mean? They will be with me!'

'You are leaving *with the children*?'

'Of course! Whatever did you think?' She put the bread in the oven; Mattie worked on imperturbably, as if the discussion was about dinner.

'You mean to take the children *to India* without their father? You mean to take them through *Egypt*? You cannot mean this! You heard what Pierre said!'

Fanny went outside, pumped water, came back, went out again for potatoes; the smell of fresh bread drifted about the kitchen. Rose trailed behind her cousin wheresoever she went and the conversation continued. 'But of course I would take the children – that was always the plan, you have always known that! I could not dream of going anywhere without the children! I will tell them first that we are going to see you – for I see my son has been bewitched by you and your talk of clocks – you will be good for him, Rose, and he will have other influences – oh, it will be *wonderful* for the children. They speak of the dangers of travelling, but there are dangers in *not* travelling also. And of course I want to assist you in your quest. I do understand what this means to you. I have planned everything. I know you are anxious to leave London but I must ask one favour of you. This morning I sent a letter to my father's lawyer to expect me, to have everything organised and the finances ready. He is to send a letter to my father immediately, to apprise him of my plans. But I will not stay in

South Molton Street or indeed anywhere in London, I will depart immediately for Paris and wait for you there. But Horatio will no doubt come to you at once for I will of course have left him a letter telling him I have gone to India.'

'Now it is my turn to say to you, you cannot, you *must* not be so foolhardy, Fanny. Of course Horatio will come for you at once. He will never let the children make such a journey. And I think for once I would agree with him, dear coz. You cannot do this!' But it was as if Fanny had not heard her.

'He will come to London, but I will already have gone. He will look for you, but I will not be there. But – Rose – and this is the favour I need to ask you – I need you to stay in London till he comes, to tell me what – what attitude he will take to all this. I will be prepared for the worst. I doubt that he will cross the English Channel – he does not believe in the rest of the world, as I have told you. But perhaps he will surprise us – and I need you to be there to tell me what he is going to do. Let him divorce me, marry another woman if he wishes, the children will be with me.'

'Fanny!'

Fanny suddenly took Rose by the arm, drew her into the wide vicarage hall. 'Look, Rose.' Fanny quite unembarrassedly lifted her gown and the petticoat. Congealed blood lay around her buttocks and down the back of her legs, and for a split second Rose saw the dead deer.

'Oh God in Heaven, Fanny,' she whispered.

'Indeed.' Fanny let her skirts go. And for a moment both women stood quite still and stared at each other.

'Will you help me?' said Fanny. 'Shall we meet in Paris? And travel onwards? Pierre will advise us, as you say.' She looked sternly at her cousin. 'Or am I to travel alone?'

'I will meet you on the Pont Neuf,' said Rose.

In the early afternoon the carriage containing Rose and Mattie was waved off by the whole family. It rattled away and disappeared along the rutted road to London; one night not long after another coach travelled the same rutted road: two bemused young children falling asleep at last on either side of their mother, little bodies bumping against the uncomfortable upholstery, small mouths open with half-formed questions that would have to be answered in some way, eventually.

EIGHTEEN

Rose and Mattie were completely ready to leave, waited impatiently. But they had hidden their luggage away, for they had received the message that Fanny had left for France; they awaited the appearance of the Reverend Horatio Harbottom before their own departure; all the books about Egypt that Rose had studied long into the night were carefully put away also. She looked for her embroidery: Mattie thought this was going too far, but Rose laughed and said: 'It will make Horatio feel safe, women's work.' Then they suddenly heard the old naval gentlemen talking to Miss Proud downstairs. Rose's heart sank guiltily as she heard them ascending the stairs: she had told no one in London of her plans except Miss Proud, who had nodded noncommittally and said no more. She had tried so often to write to Pierre Montand, but finally knew she could only tell him everything in person. He came into her dreams, looked at her with love.

Outside, cart drivers and traders yelled and swore at the old naval gentlemen's carriage as it partly blocked the street; small, cold children teased the horses. One boy pulled a horse's tail, the coachman reached for the culprit with his whip and the children ran down through the horse muck and the fish-heads and the wet newspapers full of the turds of South Molton Street, laughing.

The old gentlemen saw how well Rose looked, how pink her cheeks were, and understood that she had indeed become herself again at last. 'We have read in the *Gentleman's Magazine* that the Egyptian treasures have finally arrived at the museum. Should you enjoy visiting them? We have acquired some tickets for Miss Proud and yourself.' Rose's eyes lit up like stars; she looked at Mattie, and Mattie nodded.

'I am expecting my cousin's husband,' Rose said. 'But – an hour – oh, I would love to come!' She threw on her hat and her fur-lined cloak and her muff and the carriage set off through mud and dirt; as they left, a rotten orange was thrown at them and the old gentlemen gestured back in apology and threw out some coins through the grey afternoon. They looked at the lowering sky and clicked their tongues. 'We should have waited for a better day,' they said.

'*No!*' said Rose and her eyes shone. As the coach made its way through the Oxford Street traffic it began to rain, light at first and then heavier; as wind blew the rain across their path they could hear the coachman swearing.

'We should turn back,' said the old gentlemen.

'*No!*' said Rose, and still her eyes were shining. Miss Proud looked at her. *You will have to tell them, my dear*, said her eyes, and Rose looked at the dear, concerned faces: they had treated her like their own daughter. She would have to tell them of course: she should have done so already but knew they would object, and she nodded imperceptibly to Miss Proud.

Along Great Russell Street carriages were caught by a particularly grand coach coming the other way; uniformed horsemen tried to clear the traffic, everything was blocked and jumbled and moved very slowly, drivers shouted. Heads appeared out of carriage windows even though it now rained heavily: *royalty*, they opined: was it the King or the fat Prince of Wales? Might they get a glimpse of the poor little Princess Charlotte? Horses flicked their tails and manure steamed on to cobblestones; filthy children ran to warm their feet for a moment. The royal coach finally passed, whoever was inside did not look out, and people jeered and someone called

Vive la République! and Miss Proud looked back with interest to where the voice had come from. The old gentlemen spoke of Napoleon, shaking their heads. 'We think the peace very precarious,' they said.

'Does that mean Paris may be closed to us again?' asked Rose, anxiously.

'Not just that, he may attack our own country at last. Everyone knows he is regrouping, and restoring; he is a madman, he could do anything. There is even,' they gestured back at the crowds who had called and jeered, 'support for him here in some quarters,' *and Rose Fallon saw the grey, intelligent eyes bending to the floor, amused, when Dolly fainted.*

At the museum they were informed that the Egyptian antiquities were in the outer court of the building.

'But perhaps we should come another day,' they said again, 'You will get so wet,' and they looked at old Miss Proud dubiously. But she took no notice, and Rose did not even hear them: the women peered through the rain, would not be dissuaded. So the little group hurried towards a wooden edifice that temporarily housed the pile of treasures.

For a moment Rose was taken with a huge clenched fist, bigger than herself: broken grey stone and yet – a strange effect – mocking. A small obelisk stood beside it like the ones she had seen in Paris with Pierre, covered in the ancient writing. Miss Proud investigated an urn, a sarcophagus shaped like a large bath; part of it poked out from underneath the roof and rain fell into it, making a drumming sound.

And then Rose saw it, recognised it at once just standing quietly there: black, inkstained, covered in strange lettering: the *pierre de Rosette*, the Rosetta Stone. She saw where the hieroglyphs broke off at the top, cutting off the path to the ancient world. The London rain fell, she did not notice. Underneath were quite different markings, almost entirely intact: that would be the common script; underneath again she recognised lines of Greek lettering, broken off at the bottom.

'Oh,' she said, and tears actually sprang into her eyes. '*The key.*'

She moved forward and ran her fingers over the stone, feeling the mysterious indentations. She bent even closer, looking for the *cartouches* Pierre had described that seemed to enclose royal names: in the hieroglyphic section she saw them clearly with her own eyes. Walking around the stone she saw the painted words that William had described: CAPTURED IN EGYPT BY THE BRITISH ARMY IN 1801. And now further words had been painted on the other side: PRESENTED BY KING GEORGE III. She was glad Pierre Montand was not here to read the words with her, but she wished that he could know she was here: standing with the Rosetta Stone as the rain fell.

Again she touched the lettering, feeling the knowledge with strange concentration, and then, fingers still on the stone, she turned to the old gentlemen. 'I am going to Egypt,' she said calmly in the wet grey afternoon, and they smiled, thinking that she meant: one day. But when they tried to hurry her in out of the rain she stood her ground. 'I am,' she said.

'She is going tomorrow,' said Miss Proud.

The kind old gentlemen were disbelieving; when they saw it was so, they were appalled. The four of them stood in the courtyard in the rain beside the Rosetta Stone. Nobody even thought of moving.

'You cannot,' said the old naval gentlemen.

'Women have travelled to Egypt,' said Rose stubbornly.

'With the army, or the navy. As traders' wives. *Never alone!*' Rain fell on their naval hats, on the women's bonnets. 'We have *been there*, we know the dangers! Not women alone by themselves, it is absolutely out of the question!'

'But I shall not be alone. Mattie will be with me, of course, and I feel I will be safer with her than many men I know.' She swallowed rather nervously before adding the next bit, for Miss Proud did not know of this either. 'And my cousin Fanny and her two children are to travel to India to visit her father, my uncle – I also have been invited by him – and so they, too, will be my travelling companions.'

Miss Proud regarded her carefully; if the old gentlemen were appalled before, they were horrified now. 'They are travelling to India *through Egypt*? They plan to travel *over the desert* from Cairo to the Red Sea? *Children?* You plan to take *children*? Your cousin cannot be so foolhardy.' The rain drummed into the sarcophagus.

The old gentlemen quickly conferred in low voices and then spoke again vigorously. 'Quickly,' they said, and firmly forced the two women back into the carriage, which set off at once for South Molton Street. And then they said: 'Rose, we see that we must tell you. We believe there will be war. The government does not want to frighten people, or to advise them that this well-enjoyed peace with France may soon be over. But every sign points to further war with Napoleon. He is involved in Italy, he has troops in Holland. He is mad, he is trouble, we need to be rid of him, to make the world safe.'

'When? When will there be war?' Mud spattered the carriage and the horses and the windows.

'We cannot say when.'

'But we might wait for months and there might not be war at all!' (There could not be war again so soon! It was after all, she thought, not so many months since Napoleon had walked through Josephine's *salon* asking British society ladies if they enjoyed *l'opéra*.)

Miss Proud had taken off her wet bonnet. Her respectable but sodden old lady's cap dripped water slightly as she turned to follow each speaker. With a small, impatient sound she pulled off the cap also, shaking her white hair free. The old gentlemen went on talking anxiously but Rose stared for a moment at the way the hair fell across Miss Proud's face: suddenly she saw her not as an old lady but as a woman named Constantia. Suddenly it was obvious that she must once have been very pretty: a young girl, a young girl who in some way or other lost her beloved. In a small moment the hair was gathered and pinned back: she looked like Miss Proud again.

'I think Rose should go,' said Miss Proud calmly, 'if that is her desire. I believe I would go, if I were in her place. Sooner rather than later, if your intimations about imminent war are correct.' The old naval gentlemen looked at her as if they had seen a ghost, but Miss Proud continued imperturbably, 'She is not foolhardy. I know very well that she has read of nothing but Egypt for months. She is travelling with Mattie to whom I too would trust my life. There will always be other travellers, as there were when I made my journeys.'

Rose stared. 'You have travelled to Egypt, Miss Proud?'

'No, my dear, but I have been as far as Greece. And I am sure in another generation women will be travelling alone to the ends of the earth.' She regarded the old gentlemen. 'Why should not Rose be in the vanguard and at least go to Egypt? She could write a book, for other women to be encouraged! And why on earth should she travel in fear? I cannot believe that – wherever they live, in the antipodes or on the moon, and whatever their religion – most people do not have hearts.'

In the carriage the old naval gentlemen exchanged agitated glances: *Women do not understand anything of the world.*

Rose and Miss Proud exchanged calmer glances: *We can do things men think us incapable of. We have much more common sense than they.* And again Rose caught the surprising glimpse of another, younger woman.

'But,' added Miss Proud firmly, nodding at the old gentlemen, knowing their thoughts exactly, 'I do think you are right to say that Fanny and the children should not go. We do not have the right to hazard our children, even if we are prepared to bravely face danger ourselves. You should persuade your cousin, Rose, not to do this.'

'They are already gone,' said Rose in a small voice just as they arrived back at South Molton Street. Mattie pretended she did not observe the distress of the visitors: made Indian tea, for the nerves.

The old gentlemen had only just departed, still deeply upset, coughing anxiously down the stairs, when Horatio arrived from Wentwater. He had come at once to South Molton Street, he roared and thundered into Rose's drawing room, extremely distraught, waving Fanny's letter in the air and speaking of the law.

Rose asked him to sit down, embroidered neatly. But he strode about in a tall manner, shouting, actually looking into rooms as though his family was secreted somewhere. Rose and Mattie exchanged glances, hoped he would not look into the cupboards and discover trunks. Miss Proud, alarmed by the sounds of his wild behaviour, came upstairs, seating herself discreetly beside Rose in case protection should be required.

'This is your fault! You have arranged this,' Horatio said to Rose. 'Fanny would never have gone off, completely disappeared, without your influence! First you come, then she goes!'

'She has not "gone off" or "completely disappeared", as you put it, Horatio,' said Rose calmly. 'She has gone to India with the children to visit her parents as you must know – you yourself were invited also.'

'It was a ludicrous idea. I cannot leave my flock. I have my duty towards them, as she has her duty towards me,' and Rose remembered Fanny's words: *his idea of duty is something that happens to equate with his own desires*. 'She cannot go without my permission,' thundered Horatio, 'and I withheld it. This is the influence of you!' he cried, rather in the tone he had used from the pulpit to decry the critics of the Church, 'the immoral cousin!'

Miss Proud stood at once, an old lady to her fingertips; her fresh white cap shook. 'I am afraid, sir, that I cannot have you speaking of my valued and respected tenant in such a manner. I shall have to ask you to leave my house if you continue!'

She sounded magnificently stern. Horatio was quelled somewhat, mainly because it was a very long time since anybody had spoken to him in that way. He was, after all, a vicar and received due respect at all times. 'I do beg your pardon, madam,' he said, slightly flustered, and he had the grace to bow slightly. 'You perhaps do not understand the terrible thing that has befallen me. My wife has disappeared and taken my beloved children from me, and I believe this young lady has been of influence.'

'The truth is, Horatio,' said Rose, her needle going in and out of emerging pale pink peonies, 'it has been the other way round. Fanny influenced me. She has very much helped me to come to terms with the death of my late husband, and I feel much gratitude to her.'

'Yes, yes, that is the job of a vicar's wife, I could easily have done the same for you myself.' He spoke impatiently. 'I shall go to the lawyer. She cannot do this. I shall see to that.'

'I am sure the lawyer will have all the facts. But she did not *disappear*, Horatio, you cannot say that. You saw her father's letter, and you have a letter from her in your hand telling you of her plans.'

'Without my permission,' roared Horatio, and Mattie brought more tea as a calming influence. He departed to his uncle, the Bishop.

Rose felt she could not leave London until Horatio had made some decision. She was in a paroxysm of impatience and exasperation.

He came again early the next day. 'She has really gone to India,' he cried dramatically.

'But you *know* she has gone to India, Horatio. She left a letter, telling you.'

'The lawyer told me it is true. She has left me wifeless and child-less, against my wishes. I will take the children from her. I have such plans for Horatio, he will rise in the Church of England like a new Messiah! I wish him to attend a special church school next year – I have influence.'

'Perhaps you should go to India also,' suggested Rose. He ignored this but stayed so long he needs must be invited to dinner.

'What am I to say to my parishioners? Where is my wife to arrange everything? What shall I say?'

'The truth, of course. That she has taken the children to see their grandparents.'

'My parishioners will pity me,' he said.

'Your parishioners are very fond of Fanny. They will see what a generous man you were to let them go.'

'No man would do such a thing!'

Why does he not go home? Miss Proud and Rose and Mattie said to each other anxiously, thinking of Fanny waiting on the Pont Neuf. *Or decide to travel too, and make the best of it.*

On the third day, when he came back early and stayed to dinner again, it emerged that Horatio had had a thought (perhaps suggested by his uncle the bishop): that it was Rose's duty to accompany him back to Wentwater, to cook his meals at least and arrange his comforts. For she had nothing else to do, sitting here in London.

And at that precise moment in the conversation, before Rose could recover from receiving his plans, Lady Dolly, Viscountess Gawkroger, was brought into the room by Mattie. Low-cut gown, fur-lined cloak, flowers in her hair: she looked extraordinary, partly because of her clothes, partly because she was so tall, partly the look in her eyes. She looked much older than she was. Horatio's look of amazement was wondrous to Rose.

'Dolly, this is my cousin Fanny's husband, the Reverend Horatio Harbottom. Horatio, this is Viscountess Gawkroger.'

'Oh!' said Horatio. *A title!* His face was suffused in smiles. 'I am delighted,' he said, bowing very, very low.

'Oh, a curate with the name of a hero, how *sweet*,' said Dolly, automatically smiling up at the handsome Horatio Harbottom, who was taller even than herself.

'I am not a curate, your ladyship, I am a vicar.' But, handsome as he was, Dolly brushed him away.

'I need to talk to you urgently, Rose,' she said, adding significantly, '*confidentially*.'

'Ah – perhaps it is something a vicar can assist with,' said Horatio hopefully.

'Definitely not!' Then Dolly recovered herself and turned her society manners upon Horatio. 'Could you excuse us? I promise not to be long – my carriage I believe is blocking the whole of South Molton Street and riot may ensue if I stay too long!'

'I shall wait in the next room, your ladyship. I myself am not in any hurry and I have not finished my conversation with my wife's cousin. You may of course call upon me if there is any service I can render.' Among such pleasantries a small dance of room-changing began; tea was offered to all but both Dolly and Horatio preferred a little wine.

Dolly leaned back into the soft sofa, and Rose sat on her hard-backed chair.

'How are you, Dolly?' said Rose politely.

'I am *ill*,' said Dolly at once. 'Well – I suspect I am with child, which as far as I am concerned amounts to the same thing. And I cannot possibly be, for I am going next week to Egypt with William and George.'

'Egypt? When? When are you going?'

'Next week.'

'*Next week?*' Rose felt as if she was suddenly swallowing air. '*Next week?*'

'I told you! Next week!'

'Why are you going next week?'

'You know they want to find treasures! So I cannot possibly be *enceinte* because I am not letting them go without me. Let Ann have the heir, not me!'

Oh God! Rose tried to recover. 'Is Ann to have a baby?'

'You would think that she had walked to Scotland to hear her crow. But the Duke of Hawksfield is not as pleased as she had anticipated. Ann believes the Duke had hopes that William would leave her because she gave him no heir, and marry you.'

'What?'

'So I understand. And he does seem very interested in you.'

'Who does?'

'The Duke of Hawksfield.' Dolly gave no other opinion one way or another. 'My last pregnancy miscarried easily, without George even knowing, but this seems to wish to continue. You must help me.'

'What do you mean?'

'Help me to get rid of it. You never had any children and you were married for at least five years. Surely you know the way?'

Rose felt pain in her heart: old pain, new pain, forced herself to think only of Dolly at this moment. 'Dolly, dear Dolly,' she said slowly. 'Come back. I know you must be there somewhere.'

'I do not understand you.' Dolly stood, walked about the room inspecting things. 'You have indeed come a long way from Wimpole Street,' she said critically. And then she added in a low, almost inaudible voice, 'Have you seen Pierre Montand?'

'Not since his return to Paris when his – business was completed.'

'With my mother-in-law's ring?'

'With the Egyptian ring, yes.'

Dolly suddenly sat down again and she giggled, and for just a moment she seemed like the old Dolly, like a young girl who had dressed up in somebody else's clothes. 'You should see the old Dowager in disgrace, Rose! If I still kept a journal I would have much to write there! The Duke of Hawksfield is so angry with her, and he still has to be with us a great deal – he and George and the bankers are locked away every week. So he and the Dowager cannot hope *not* to see each other. They are both going quite mad with the strain! I do believe he would have stopped the marriage if he had known about the ring, no matter how desperately we need the Fallon money. I never saw him so angry.'

'You should still keep a journal, Dolly, to document the interesting things that you do.'

Dolly looked at her. 'I could not write of my experiences,' she said quite simply in her young girl's voice. 'I think the pages would burn.' And for a moment they sat in silence. 'Will you help me?'

Rose stared down at her hands. 'I lost my babies, Dolly. I didn't get rid of them. I wanted children very much. And then my husband – was killed.'

'Oh,' said Dolly, thrown. Then, after a moment, 'I didn't know.'

'George can tell you.'

'I am not going to discuss this with *George*!'

They sat in silence, but Dolly could not be still for long. 'Well I do *not* want this baby. I have been taking precautions, I know all about that: I cannot believe I have got caught again. I must get rid of it. I want to go to Egypt and see the treasures and ride camels as Pierre told us. I know plenty of people who could help me, *of course*, but they are all friends of George, and they would tell him.'

'Dolly – I have heard that – sometimes – doing this prevents you from having a child one day when you might wish to.'

'I do not care,' said Dolly, rising. 'And if you cannot assist me you had better return to your curate and I needs must rely on gin! I trust you not to discuss any of this conversation with George.' She turned back again. 'Are you going to marry Pierre Montand?'

'No,' said Rose, 'I am not.' And she stood also and her heart was aching and she did not know if she was lying. She saw Dolly's young-old face; she felt helpless. 'Take great care, dear Dolly,' she said at last. 'I hope you will not do anything dangerous, or that you will one day regret.'

Dolly began a sharp, angry retort. And then she stopped herself as if, just for a moment, she recognised that Rose cared about her.

'Goodbye, Rose,' she said bleakly, still not quite sixteen. 'Thank you.' And to Horatio's regret, when he hurried out of the next room, hearing voices, she was gone.

Horatio went back to the soft sofa. The wine had emboldened him. He leaned back. He imagined Rose there, in Wentwater. It was not, after all, an unpleasant picture: there was something about her that made him shift slightly in his seat. 'As I was saying, Rose, I think it would be best if you came back with me to Wentwater. I simply cannot manage, and you do nothing.' He did not notice Rose's pale face. She was panicking: *George is on his way to Egypt.* She rang the bell for Mattie. 'Go back to Wentwater, or go to India, but please, Horatio, leave me out of your plans. I have my own life to live.'

He looked at her, truly astonished, stood. 'What does that mean – your "own life to live" – what do you mean by that? You are a woman,' and he grasped her arm. And was then even more astonished to find Mattie beside him, with his coat. He was not ready to leave yet.

'Go away, Horatio,' said Rose. 'Go home.'

*

When Rose saw Fanny and small Horatio and Jane standing in the spring dusk, a rather forlorn group, at the end of the Pont Neuf on the right bank, she ran. She ran across the bridge, holding up her long gown slightly; carts passed, Frenchmen called and the fetid smell of the Seine hit her nostrils, but she paid no heed, ran on, across the Pont Neuf towards her cousin as she had done so long ago.

'I am here!' she cried. 'I am here!' wanting also to cry, 'George is just behind me!'

They hugged and cried, she took small hands, everybody talking at once; soon they were in her rooms in an eccentric small hotel in the rue Mazarine on the left bank, drinking hot chocolate with cream. Mattie's fire sent the chill away from the evening, soon the children were revived, stood staring at the lights in the street as it became dark, pointed out to Mattie how the lights were lit by a man with a flare; smelled the oil. They peered over the window ledge observing the funny French people and saying *bonjour* and *bon soir* to Mattie over and over like loud little parrots.

'What *happened*?' said Fanny at last, laughing now, but not far from tears also, and her face was creased with anxiety. 'I almost lost belief in our plan! What has he said?'

'I am so sorry! We only arrived this afternoon.' Rose lowered her voice. 'We were detained for some days after Horatio arrived.'

But she had not lowered her voice enough. Small Horatio turned instantly from the window. 'Is my papa coming?' he asked eagerly, and he, followed by his little sister, came at once to sit by his aunt, his little eyes shining. 'Is my papa coming?' he asked again, more urgently, and Janey looked up at her aunt with big eyes that might, or might not, have been asking the same question.

Rose looked at small Horatio's shining face: of course he loved his father.

'He seems not to be coming,' she said to them all. 'Not just now,' and she saw that the little boy's face seemed to crumple. 'You all know how hard he works. But he is – most anxious – that you continue learning everything you can, Horatio, that will make you – a son to be proud of.'

'And me, and me?' cried Jane.

'And you, of course,' answered their aunt, realising that Horatio had never mentioned his daughter once and any mention of his son was not of a beloved child snatched from him, but of his importance to his father's ambitions.

'And me,' said Fanny, smiling slightly, but still anxious.

'He has gone back to Wentwater,' said Rose, and she saw the relief flash across Fanny's face, which she immediately tried to hide.

'He should be here with us,' said small Horatio, and he kicked Jane viciously and began to cry and Jane screamed and their mother remonstrated with them both.

'And the other thing your father asked me to say,' said Rose, raising her voice over the noise, 'was for you, Horatio, to remember that you are the man of the party now and we will need a lot of help from you.'

'I want to go home!' wept Horatio.

'He kicked me!' wept Jane.

Within five minutes they were both asleep on a sofa by the fire, tears drying on their faces, and the room was silent, just the fire clicking and sparking. Jane was sucking the ribbons on her dress and Horatio was holding a cushion to him.

'It has been like this since we got here,' said Fanny grimly. 'I was so sure it would be good for them, but they have become almost uncontrollable, especially Horatio. Perhaps I should have left him in Wentwater. I have never seen them like this – my son is very angry with me, I think.' And she began to laugh, yet it was near to a sob. 'So Horatio has let us go?'

'I – I think so.'

'He will not take the children from me?'

Rose did not know what to answer. 'He – he will become calm I think. I do not know what he will do.'

'I see.' And Rose, seeing the disturbed face of her cousin, wondered if they were after all quite mad, herself included. 'We are only in France!' said Fanny. 'Do you think we will ever get to India?'

'Fanny, Fanny, listen! George and William and Dolly are on their way also!'

'*What?*'

Rose explained about Dolly's visit. 'We left the moment we knew, we left that night. But they cannot be far behind us.'

'But – he does not know about Harry's child?'

'Of course not!'

'Then it does not matter, Rose. You can just pretend to be interested in hieroglyphs!'

'It *always* matters when George is around! I cannot believe they should be travelling *now*!'

'So we must leave Paris at once!'

'But we must see Pierre Montand. *I have to see him.*'

Fanny again caught the odd tone in her cousin's voice when she spoke of the Frenchman. 'But of course, I meant after we have done that. I am sure he will help us.'

'I sent him a note as soon as we arrived here,' said Rose. 'I said we would go to the Commission tomorrow morning, I told him we were anxious to set off as soon as possible. I also told him Horatio had decided not to accompany us. I do not know what he will have to say about that – a lot of things about women travelling on their own, I should think.'

Rose was breathing oddly. Fanny saw, made no comment except to say, 'I expect we should leave the children with Mattie while we speak to him. They will only cause us trouble!'

'Oh Fanny – let them come to the Commission. Even small children I think will be astonished.'

'We have already seen the Louvre. They were not astonished. I wanted to admire that wonderful long gallery but Horatio started chasing Janey all along it, knocking into statues and shouting – it was a nightmare, we were more or less removed!' They both started to laugh. 'Horatio has never been away from his father before,' said Fanny. 'And I think the Hotel de l'Empire was a bit of a shock for him!'

'Heavens, are you staying there?'

'You said it was a safe hotel. I never thought I cared about safety, but with my children I suddenly do. And it is a vast apartment but we all sleep in the same bed – and I do not even care that it is full of the most awful English travellers!'

'But it is so expensive!'

'I have a great deal of money.'

Now it was Rose's turn to be anxious. 'George will stay at the Hotel de l'Empire, of course. I came to the left bank so that I would not by any chance meet them. We must leave at once. As soon as we have talked to Pierre.'

Mattie brought red wine and hot water. 'I'd like to go out tomorrow while you're visiting Monsieur Montand, Miss Rose. I shall go down to them boats on the river. I bet I find someone who knows of Cornelius Brown.' And she pottered about, humming.

And Rose and Fanny drank the red wine with hot water in the rue Mazarine in Paris. And the warm fire glowed and their cheeks glowed and they forgot their anxieties and drew word pictures for each other of all that might happen now that they had embarked upon their adventure. And the strained look lessened on both their faces at last. Frenchmen called from the street: *allons* or *au revoir, mon ami*, and women cried *que voulez-vous, monsieur?* and a voice sang under their window, and then fainter, French words drifting in the night. And it seemed perhaps at last that their intrepid journey had begun.

That night Rose dreamed the kind of dream that heroines dreamed in the new novels. She dreamed that Pierre Montand would still love her, and that they would find the child, and that they would all live happily ever after.

NINETEEN

Rose's heart was beating so fast that she thought she could clearly hear it, as if to rebuke her again for the careless words to Fanny: *he does not make my heart beat.* She knew she was shaking slightly; she held her hands together so that it would not show. She would tell him. He would see.

The *fiacre* set them down outside the Commission de l'Egypte where the sun shone and people whistled along the street. Jane saw him and she tried to run, little legs in tiny shoes and a long skirt, staggering almost up to the door where he waited to meet them.

It was something about the way he bent down to greet Jane, something about his easiness and his openness, there on the Paris springtime street; then someone called a greeting to him and he called back, laughing, *Attendez, mon ami!* and Rose felt her face suddenly flush: this seemed not a man with an anxious heart loving and beating, as hers was, and looking for her. He was not looking for her at all. Her face was not a becoming, pretty pink, but a bright flush of panic: *am I too late? have I lost him?* She turned quickly, instinctively, to Fanny, but Fanny was watching her daughter's delight as Pierre listened to her excited recounting of the journey. Then Pierre Montand greeted the ladies pleasantly, kissed their hands. But there was something closed in his face and it came again to her like a blow: *I have lost him*. She felt something cold around her heart as he leaned over her hand impersonally.

Horatio stood back shyly. 'Good morning, young man,' Pierre said, seeing the boy. 'You must be Horatio.'

'How do you know of me?' he said very stiffly.

'I told him,' said Jane. Horatio would have pinched her but these were not favourable circumstances.

'I believe you pinch your sister?' said Pierre Montand.

Horatio blushed to the roots of his hair and he pulled himself up to his full six-year-old height and stood with his hands behind his back. He looked beautiful, embarrassed and pompous; Fanny had to turn away not to laugh or to hug him.

However, for these small children to see statues of lions' bodies with men's faces; to run their fingers down polished heads of tiny cats; to see bright, bright paintings as big as a wall; to see a concrete foot a hundred times bigger than their own: these things were so amazing as to shut out, for the moment at least, anything else: they become unable to speak, so overcome were they with wonder. They came through the corridors of treasures, past so many strange paintings and artefacts that they could not think where they were; Wentwater became a dream, their lives became a dream: finally they began to cry. But Pierre Montand gave them French barley sugar and they revived, walked again among amazing things. Fanny was speechless. Rose had told her, but that had not prepared her for the extraordinary paintings or the intricacies of the writing or the broken statues or the colours, or the queerness of seeing the blue Egyptian ring here in Paris that she had first seen on the wrinkled finger of the Dowager Viscountess in Berkeley Square. Daylight shone through windows, lamps burned everywhere, yet to Fanny the treasures were dark, dark with age and secret meanings, for those were surely gods she stared at: calm, beautiful.

'How bewitching their gods are,' said Rose, standing behind her cousin for a moment. 'Beautiful, and attractive, and they seem almost to smile.' Neither of them broached the subject of their own God. Suddenly Rose caught sight of the same small stone scribe, writing. She moved towards it; once again she lifted it into her hands, saw again the intent look on his face. It was the nearest thing she had ever seen to her father's words: *the olden days talking to us*. Pierre saw her rapt concentration, looked away quickly.

Fanny stared about her in wonder. 'Nothing could have prepared me for this,' she said to Pierre. 'If I see nothing else, I will have seen these things.'

'If you go to Egypt,' he said to her, and to the children now standing beside her, 'this is what is hidden there, among the ruins and the dead bodies and the rats,' and the children exchanged nervous glances. Fanny looked at them, and then at him, in some dismay. She supposed he was severe because Rose had turned down his proposal of marriage.

Rose was lost to them for a moment: she had bent down to some of the writing on a piece of stone, staring hard. 'I see the *cartouche*!' her voice suddenly cried, as if she was a seer looking into the future. 'I see the *cartouche*, just as I saw it on the Rosetta Stone –' she popped up again, '– I saw the Rosetta Stone in London, Pierre!' And Pierre Montand again quickly looked away from the shining eyes that loved the hieroglyphs.

At last they all settled in Pierre's office where once Dolly had wept so bitterly. Jane sat on her mother's knee and looked at Pierre with round eyes; Horatio sat on the floor, near his aunt. She stroked his hair, just once.

'Now,' said Pierre. And he stared for a moment at a piece of bright blue stone, lapis lazuli, that he used as a paperweight. Then he looked at them across his untidy desk. '*Ecoutez-moi*,' he said firmly. 'Listen to me. I was shocked to know yesterday you were already in France, without the Reverend Harbottom, and planned to go to Egypt. Egypt is not a place for women, and it is emphatically not a place for children.' As Rose began to interrupt him at once he said, 'I cannot physically stop you from embarking on this foolish quest, but you must at least hear me, *s'il vous plaît*. Egypt – as I told you in London – is not a place for foreigners at all, who at all times are in danger of their lives. You cannot in your minds, in your wildest dreams, have any picture of what it will be like, of how cruel life can be there. Let me tell you a little about what I remember. I will start with the easy things. Egypt is a dirty place, a filthy place. The river Nile in its inundation spills disease as well as waters all over the country. People become blind in Egypt, from the river and the sun and the sand and the flies. You will be greeted not by friendly Arabs but by hostile people with diseased eyes, or no eyes, or blind. I myself caught the disease while I was there – oph-thalmia – and it is so painful I would not wish it on my worst enemy.'

His audience seemed to stir, disturbed.

'*Ecoutez-moi,*' he said again. 'Waves of plague attack the cities. In summer, in Cairo, the flies are so thick they land in their hundreds on arms and faces, anything uncovered, so that people seem black. I have seen a man in the street try to drink something: he tried to cover the container with his hand, which was black; he raised the container, which was black, to his mouth, which was black, and tried to pour liquid into his mouth. I cannot imagine how many flies he drank. Alexandria runs wild with rats which come in off the ships at the port, and cockroaches that hide in the beams and the rafters, three-inch-long, red-looking cockroaches with long waving horns.'

Jane began to scream. Fanny stood angrily. 'How dare you frighten the children like this!'

'Do you think the children should know nothing of their ports of call?'

Rose stood also, holding Horatio's hand, but Pierre spoke first.

'I have a meeting I must attend. I will come to your hotel in a few hours to discuss this with you further. Please in the meantime think of what I have told you,' and they were ushered out of the building (Jane crying almost as terribly as Dolly had, the last weeping female to be escorted from Pierre's presence), leaving behind the paintings and the statues and the cats that stared so knowingly.

Mattie was in great excitement when they returned: she had met a sailor who knew her husband, Cornelius Brown, and who had told her that, yes, last seen, he worked on trading ships around the Mediterranean and had planned to go to Egypt. 'I believe it is ordained that I shall find him and give him a piece of my mind.'

'By God?' enquired Rose distractedly.

'By Fate,' said Mattie darkly. 'It is *his* fate that I shall have the satisfaction of showing him my disapproval! The sailors talk though of war, Miss Rose, we must get on our way,' but Mattie added this casually as if it was simply another matter to be dealt with. 'Now, shall I take the children for a *glace* downstairs? For those two young people are in a terrible state, if I may say so. Then I will try and put them to sleep for an hour or two even if it is only three o'clock in the afternoon.'

'Please, Mattie,' said Fanny, and somehow Mattie, describing French ice-cream, took the pale and anxious-looking children away.

'What are we to do?' said Fanny, pale herself. 'I should have thought much more about what I was doing. All I could think of was to get away from Wentwater.'

'He was *trying* to frighten us,' said Rose. 'He was using the children to frighten us. Women have been to Egypt, he told us so in London.' *I left it too long. I have lost him.*

'But not with their children, and not without their husbands.'

'I know. But – he is an adventurer, he should at least recognise and salute that quality in us even if we are women.'

'Perhaps I am not really an adventurer. I cannot knowingly endanger my children's lives, I cannot, Rose.'

'I know, Fanny dearest, I know.'

'Papa of course assumed we should come to India the long way round, by boat.'

'I know.'

'I do not know what I should do.'

Thus the Frenchman found them. He refused tea: '*Pardon*, I have to meet with somebody,' *and Rose saw in her head a beautiful young woman, twining her hair with flowers, to meet Pierre Montand.* 'I have just been accosted outside the Commission by the Viscount Gawkroger and his wife and his brother-in-law.'

'They are here? *Already?*' He heard the dismay in Rose's voice.

'They required to see the Egyptian treasures once again. I told them that these things were unfortunately no longer open to the public. They had the grace to look admonished.' He paused. 'They seem not to know of any journey of yours, Rose: they did not mention such a thing.'

'*Of course not.* And you did not advise them?' He looked at her. She was not sure what she could read in his face.

'I blame myself, of course,' he said, 'telling you of the glories of Egypt, showing them to you. We were with an army, with Buonaparte himself: we had provisions and built proper quarters and had the power of France behind us. And – *excusez-moi* –we were men. And yet we lost tens of thousands of other men. It is not a romantic society with a language that will shatter the world with its knowledge and its beauty and its secrets – the Egyptians lost interest in their own civilisation centuries ago. Egyptian society is a *mélange* of Turks and Mameluks and Arabs and Greeks and Jews. Foreigners like ourselves must live in special areas for *franks* – as they call us all – where the gates are closed at dusk by inhabitants who live in fear – for they are only there on sufferance because they are traders, and the soldiers who might have protected them are long gone. I hope you do not think you will find a pleasant hotel!'

'No,' said Rose gravely. 'I know there are no hotels. I have read everything that I could find.'

He laughed angrily. 'Then you will know that you would take lodgings with a trader or a merchant in the *frank* quarters and you will find your brother-in-law in the same house, or the house next door. How would you begin to look for a child? Where would you start? You would be locked in a compound and all around you you would hear the call of the *muezzin* – calling the native population to prayer to an alien God whose adherents hate you.

'Take your children back, Madame Fanny, and if you are to go to India, take the ship, go round Africa. *L'Egypte, ce n'est pas l'Inde!* In India the British, thanks perhaps to your East India Company, have established a little world there for themselves. But Egypt is cruel to those who try to live there, it is a civilisation too broken, too wild, too – *étrange*. There is no rule of law, for although the Turkish Pasha sits in his palace in Cairo, places like Alexandria are really ruled by the Mameluk Beys – madmen, savages: foreigners themselves – who hate each other, as well as the Turks and the Egyptians. The Beys came generations ago from the Caucasus or Georgia – they came as slaves, ended up as wild rulers – they carry scimitars and pistols and wear big bright turbans and they attack anybody they wish to attack – on sight. It is total *chaos*! You would, to be brutally honest, very likely die: women and children, unaccompanied, on

their own, in a city that has no soul. And the foreigners themselves – traders – they are *les vagabonds*, rogues, sailors on the run,
untrustworthy.'

'One of them took in the woman,' said Rose tartly, 'so we must
suppose that even *les vagabonds* have hearts!'

'Perhaps, perhaps! But you will almost certainly find that always
it is a financial transaction. And it may still be summer when you
arrive – *mon Dieu*, the children would never be able to bear the
heat. All this I should have said in London when you told me of
your plans, but I did not know the Reverend Harbottom – I thought
he might have knowledge of these things, and I did not feel I had' –
he looked quickly at Rose and then away again – 'the right to interfere.'

The two women sat before him in silence. Fanny spoke at last.
'You told us in London of the Coptic language that is used still in
their Christian churches. Surely the Christians would befriend us,
help us?'

'Oh, Madame Fanny.' He sighed. 'Egypt had, I like to believe, a
long tradition of the Copts and the Jews and the Mohammetmen
living together in some kind of *harmonie*; once upon a time their
religions seemed to link with each other, their history in Egypt
coming together in all sorts of ancient ways. But the Copts are these
days mostly unsafe like the *franks*. Also, if you will forgive me,
Madame Fanny, the Coptic religion is not celebrated in ways that
you would recognise – a Coptic church would not I feel remind you
of your husband's church in Wentwater. They say the Copts are the
true Egyptians, descended from the Pharaohs themselves; it
seemed to me in my observations that they were nevertheless more
like their fellow Mohammetmen than like any Christians I know,
and anyway' – and he seemed to sigh again – 'although I was
brought up as a Catholic I am now without such certainties. For
many – for me at least – you cannot study old civilisations as I
have and believe that Christianity is the only right.'

'But there are' – Rose struggled to find the words – '*civilised*
Egyptians – I mean, educated Egyptians. I have read of them and
you told us in London that you had met them, and been taken to
their houses. It is not true that all Mohammetans are wild. My
father told me it was an old and honourable religion, like our own.

And he made Egypt sound, and you have made Egypt sound, like the most fascinating place he had ever seen. Are Fanny and I not to be fascinated too?'

'We are *men*, Rose, how many times do I have to emphasise this? *It is a world of men.* As a woman on your own you could never be safe. And it was probably safer in your father's time than it is now.' He got up at last, walked to the window, looked out over the rue Mazarine. 'We are partly to blame,' he said. 'I believe that the influence of foreigners in this part of the world – Napoleon's influence too, I do accept that – disturbed an ancient, primitive land. And now it is so unstable, so unsure of its path – the waters of the Nile will rise as usual, and from the fertile land the peasants will reap as usual, and others will take their profit: Turks, English, French, German, Portuguese, Greek – everyone except the Egyptians themselves. It seems to have been ever so.'

The three sat in silence in the little sitting room as dusk fell over the *quartier*.

'I must go,' he said, but made no move from the window. 'As for the child.' Pierre looked carefully at Rose at last. 'Your brother-in-law will no doubt instantly acquire what knowledge you have the moment he gets to Alexandria and his name is heard among the foreigners.'

'*No!*' cried Rose. 'He cannot!'

'He *will*, Rose! All the *franks* know each other, there are so few of them left. Everyone will know the story of Captain Fallon, the Viscount Gawkroger, and how he died – there is no way you can keep George from hearing about the child once he arrives.' Rose was so pale that he had to stop. '*Pardonnez-moi.* I know you had the finest of ideas, and I accept my own part in all this and regret it very much. But, forgive me, it is not a well-thought-out plan – it is a romantic notion and it can only end in tragedy. And should you by chance find her – should she not have been stoned to death like her mother—'

'*Stop it!*'

'You cannot be squeamish in Egypt, Rose! As I say – should you find her, the English law will give her to Viscount Gawkroger – *et c'est fini!*'

And they saw that Pierre, despite his Gallic good manners, was very, very angry. 'I was wrong to first speak to you about the child, but I did not recognise your' – he said the word that hurt her most, for George had said it too – '*madness*. I must say what I think: it seems to me that you are two *imbéciles irresponsables*, looking for some kind of adventure. To fulfil this you seem to be willing to risk the lives of these children. You will set them down in the ruins and chaos that is Alexandria? You will take them on some sort of wild *caravan* through dangerous deserts on your way to India, Madame Fanny? You will expose them to the plagues that haunt the cities?'

'I thought – I thought such an opening of minds would be an indelible experience that would change their lives for ever.' Fanny's voice tried to be strong but faded away at the end of her sentence.

'It would be *unforgivable*!' Then suddenly Pierre heard his own raised voice. '*Pardonnez-moi*. It is not my business what you decide to do. I have overrun my mark.' He began to do up the buttons on his jacket.

Rose looked at him for several moments in silence. *He does not love me. He thinks I am mad.* She made an enormous effort, folded her hands tightly together and spoke carefully. 'Pierre, I think you do us an injustice to call us *imbéciles irresponsables* looking for some kind of adventure. I have prepared myself for this journey. I believe I have read almost everything that has been written.'

'And very little has been written so far, as I well know!' For just a moment his eyes became gentle. 'You cannot prepare yourself for Egypt, *Rosette*.'

And she saw them, standing in Josephine's yellow drawing room in the Tuileries, the way the Frenchmen *belonged* to each other in public as women never did, and how he had come to her and spoken, and so this story began. She bit her lip and lowered her head. 'Dear Pierre,' she said, but she did not look at him. 'Forgive me.' There was a strange silence in the room in the rue Mazarine, for her words meant many things and each of them knew it. But Pierre did not speak, and Fanny knew she must not. At last Rose gave a small, trembling sigh and then she said, 'I must try to find this child. Do not blame us for having dreams also.'

Pierre stared at her, his face unreadable. After a moment he said in a very quiet voice, 'I cannot argue with you further. I have tried to speak of the dangers awaiting you in Egypt. I cannot tell you more.' He rubbed his hand across his face and then suddenly seemed to come to some sort of decision. 'There is one more matter of which I see I have to inform you. You must all leave Paris. You must leave France – as soon as possible.'

Rose at once remembered the words of the old naval gentlemen. 'Is there to be war again so soon?' she said, but he did not answer. And she understood that – of course – he could not answer. He was a Frenchman. And he was part of the government of Napoleon Buonaparte. She felt her face turning red again, with embarrassment.

Fanny at once understood also. 'You are in an impossible position, Pierre,' she said. 'Please forgive us.' And her strong little face was suddenly set in the way that Rose knew so well. And Rose knew that Fanny had decided.

'It is your own country, and your own king, who have put me in this impossible position! Do you think we wish for more war? Your government has not adhered to the treaty, they refuse to leave Malta, they publish scurrilous lies about the French and about Napoleon in the newspapers – and then say they can do nothing to right such lies because of your "freedom of the press". I think it is your government that will declare war, and so there will be war, yes.' There was silence. After a moment Fanny spoke.

'You are right, of course. If there is any chance of war I cannot place my children in the kind of dangers you describe.' And she looked at Rose. 'I am so sorry, dearest Rose, it is my fault: you know how much I wanted to come with you, but I cannot risk the lives of my children.'

'I know.' Rose placed her hand over Fanny's. 'I know, dear coz, I know,' and both women saw the sudden relief on Pierre's anxious face.

'You will all return to England then?' he said, the strain in his voice and his face suddenly less, and he came back to sit beside them. 'Ah – I am so very glad. But you must leave Paris at once. I will assist you in any way I can. I could not have borne the thought of you all undertaking such a journey – at such a time.' And was amazed to see that both women turned to him in surprise.

'No,' they said in unison.

'What do you mean, *no*?'

'*I* shall go on,' said Rose. 'I thought that was understood.'

'Of course she will go,' said Fanny. 'Rose, and Mattie with her. They must leave France as soon as possible, as you so generously have advised. Thank you, Pierre. You have indeed remained our true friend. I will leave Paris for England tomorrow morning, I will take the children on this long journey by ship, as you suggest, for their better safety. And then – of course' – and her loving look to Rose was sorrowful but sure – 'we will meet in India.'

TWENTY

Some weeks later, in the fine building in Leadenhall Street known as East India House, turbanned Indians served tea in proud Wedgwood china: this was one of the delights, the bishop remembered, of visiting the East India Company's premises. Behind closed doors gentlemen's voices murmured. The Reverend Horatio Harbottom and his uncle (the bishop), and a lawyer, and the directors of the Company shook their heads over and over (although one of the younger directors looked at his own manicured nails and thought that if he had to suffer the bishop and his nephew for long he, too, might fly to India – although the vicar was indeed a handsome fellow). But mostly the assembled gentlemen spoke a good deal of Duty. Not, in fact (the young director noticed), the duty of the East India Company, or of the Church, or of the legal profession, or even the duty of the Reverend Horatio Harbottom and his uncle the bishop; but all were in agreement about the duty of Mrs Fanny Harbottom. And apart from duty, they spoke of the law. Letters were duly dispatched (alas not from the young director, who would, at least, have made Fanny laugh) but from the Law of England, and the Church of England, and the East India Company of

England: they were sternly addressed to Fanny's father. Duty was expected of him also.

But Mrs Fanny Harbottom was already far away and woke now to the sound of wind in the sails and the sound of the sea, and, just faintly, the murmur of a Quaker meeting being held on the deck of the *Treasure* in the dawn light.

'*God is Love,*' said the Quakers.

The *Treasure* was a small barque, and when (after surviving storms in the Bay of Biscay which made anything but lying prostrate inconceivable) the Quakers aboard began holding prayer meetings on deck, the Church of England missionaries going to Africa and the Church of England curate going to India made formal complaints in writing to the captain about Dissidents Disturbing the Peace (although in fact the Quakers at their meetings often sat for long periods simply in silence).

The captain did not terribly care either way, but an Important Personage on board seemed to support the Quakers so a compromise was reached whereby the Quakers' meetings could be held on deck but it would be most kind if they were completed before breakfast.

So as the *Treasure* approached the tropics the Quakers met at dawn while flying fish played around the bow of the small brave vessel. Fanny, curious, had begun to join them in the early mornings as her children slept on; at first on the periphery, then, as they welcomed her day after day, almost as part of the group. The Quakers marvelled at the beauty and vastness of their surroundings. They sat in silence or spoke of God, and to God, as the spirit moved. Both men and women spoke: there seemed no inequity. *God is love,* they often said. They were a fascinating assemblage: not all of them wore grey; the distinction between 'gay' and 'plain' Quakers was explained to Fanny. The 'gay' Quakers seemed to laugh more, and often sang: one evening a short gentlemen named Mr August who was not dressed in grey sang to the passengers of the *Treasure* in a fine tenor voice of the troubles of 'Barbara Allen', and next morning he spoke to his Quaker companions of God's grace.

The curate travelling to India acquired the knowledge that Fanny's husband was a vicar in the Church of England; he cornered her one afternoon beneath the sails, spoke to her about her Duty to God and the Impertinence of Dissidents. Fanny smiled, and thanked him, and removed herself with some difficulty.

At last, one morning, to her own surprise she herself spoke out of the silence. Very diffidently at first, but with growing confidence. 'My name is Fanny Hall Harbottom,' she said. She spoke of her childhood when she had felt near to God, how she used to hold conversations with him. There were nods of recognition. A few mornings later, emboldened, she spoke of her later life when she had difficulty in communicating with Him although she listened so carefully. (She did not mention that this had happened while she lived with a servant of God.) 'Be patient,' said the Quakers, 'He will speak.' Somehow she felt comforted.

Later that day a woman sought her out; Fanny was enormously surprised to find herself talking to the Duchess of Brayfield, of whom of course everybody had heard: she was close both to the Royal Family and to certain powerful members of Parliament; an influential hostess at political dinners. And Fanny remembered: years ago Rose had met her when she was presented to the Prince of Wales and had said she would like to model herself on this woman. The Duchess of Brayfield was extraordinarily beautiful. Fanny had read about her in the newspapers, had even seen cartoons of the Duchess campaigning for an election: cartoons were a sign of enormous fame. The Duchess complimented Fanny on the way she had spoken.

'Are *you* a Quaker, Your Grace?'

'I am a very gay Quaker,' said the Duchess with great charm, 'but I am here under false pretences! The *Treasure* is set to drop me on to another of the fleet shortly, to meet my husband. The vessels are owned by my family; we are hoping to connect with my husband's ship – although it is always a possibility rather than a probability at sea, I am afraid! But I did want to say to you that you have a gift, a very simple and direct way of speaking to a group of people. It comes to you naturally. I wondered – I hope you will not mind me suggesting this to you, and please disregard what I have to say if it is an impertinence – but I wondered if perhaps you had considered joining us?'

'Becoming a *Quaker*?' Fanny could not have been more surprised.

'Re-finding God through us, perhaps?'

'It is my own journey, Your Grace,' said Fanny quietly.

'Of course.' The Duchess looked at Fanny appreciatively. 'Of course. But if I might say so, I believe you would make a wonderful preacher.'

'A *preacher*!' Fanny laughed, completely astonished, and her red hair danced. 'My husband is a vicar in the Church of England!'

It was the Duchess's turn to look surprised, and then she smiled. 'Quakers believe that by faith in Jesus Christ, where there is neither male nor female, we are all one.'

'That is not a belief of my husband,' said Fanny drily.

They were leaning over the rail of the barque, heard the wind in the sails, saw the sea running beneath them The children played together at the other end of the boat, supervised by some of the sailors.

'How did this come about?' asked the Duchess quietly. Fanny looked at her in surprise. 'You are married to a vicar yet you have said that you found it harder to hear God now than you used to.'

'Oh,' said Fanny, looking at the sea. The Duchess did not press her, seemed immersed in the horizon. They both stared at the emptiness: nothing anywhere but the blue-grey water. To her own surprise Fanny found herself talking to this stranger, telling her why she was aboard the *Treasure*. The Duchess listened carefully, sometimes asked a question, made no comment. Fanny left out some things, the worst things.

Horatio suddenly appeared from the other end of the boat in great indignation.

'Jane *bit* me!' he reported in outrage. 'I have been waiting and waiting to tell you but you were speaking and you say I must not interrupt when you are speaking and it started to fade. So – look – I have bitten it again, where she bit me, so you can see what she did!' His face was red with indignation; he put out his arm so that they could see the bite-mark. Both women understood of course that they must on no account laugh. Fanny took Horatio's hand.

'First you must say good afternoon to the Duchess of Brayfield, Horatio,' she said. 'Then Jane must apologise.'

Horatio withdrew his hand from his mother's, stood straight, his hands behind him. 'Good Afternoon, Your Grace,' he said, as taught by his father. 'Very pleased to make your acquaintance.' And then he gave her a confiding smile. 'My father likes dukes and duchesses. He wishes there were some in Wentwater for him to mix with. He told me so.'

'Is that so?' said the Duchess of Brayfield thoughtfully. 'Is that so, young man?'

Next morning another boat hove into view in the distance. All the passengers on the *Treasure* cheered at the thought of seeing other human beings; as they got nearer several from both vessels called loudly, 'GOD SAVE THE KING!' although their words could not carry, drifted up into the sky. A small boat was being prepared, to take the Duchess of Brayfield across. The Duchess, in an enormous hat ('If I drown, I want people to see me clearly!'), sought out Fanny as all the cheering and yelling continued, drew her to the rail on the other side of the ship.

'Listen, Fanny,' she said. 'I want to say something to you before we must part. I have been thinking a great deal about your situation. First of all, you and I can of course both demur if it is ever, *ever* suggested that we have had any such shocking conversation as this in the middle of the ocean!' Fanny looked bemused. 'But I like you very much, and see your talents clearly.' Fanny again could not hide her look of surprise. No one had ever spoken to her of *talents* in her life. The Duchess smiled enigmatically, held her hat.

'My dear, I have found that when there are few choices – and I see that you have very few choices when you love your children so much – sometimes one must seize the weapons of the opposition, in this case the established Church in the parish of Wentwater. I want to suggest something very odd perhaps, and I do hope' (she briefly lifted her eyes to heaven) 'that God in his ultimate wisdom does not in consequence strike me down, as I descend into His ocean.'

TWENTY-ONE

First, in the late afternoon, along the endless, bleak coast they saw the remains of an old tower.

Then the desolate stone ruins of an old, old city came into view. Rose clenched the ship's rail so hard that a splinter of worn wood went into her hand.

Egypt.

The ship prepared to pass a causeway and enter into the 'new' harbour of Alexandria where foreigners and Christians were forced to land. They were not permitted to dock in the other nearby harbour: that belonged to the Mohammetans only.

'But,' said a British trader's wife who was on board, Mrs Venetzia Alabaster (*née* Venetzia Dawkins, of The Singing Acrobats), 'calling this disgraceful wreck of a harbour "new" is a mockery. I reckon that it was on this very shore we approach that Cleopatra built her palace; we are probably sailing over her ruins right this minute.' At the end of the causeway a shabby-looking structure stood, a fort perhaps. 'Where the great Pharos Lighthouse once stood, one of the seven wonders of the world,' said Mrs Venetzia Alabaster. 'It fell into the sea and now look at the rubbish, crumbling old stone, like everywhere.' She suddenly pulled her shawl about her face, not – they felt – to hide herself, but to hide the bleak grey ruins from her view.

When Rose and Mattie had first met Mrs Alabaster embarking in Leghorn she was dressed as they, her gown high-waisted and low-cut; her yellow hair had been done in a slightly old-fashioned style that would no longer have been in vogue in England. In the evenings as they sailed across the Mediterranean Sea they stood on deck when the wild winds allowed, not quite stating their business: Mrs Alabaster implied she was dealing with transactions for her trader husband; Rose implied that Egypt had interested her all her life. And as they talked Mrs Alabaster would sometimes click her bones, the way other people cleared their throats or tapped their fingers. Now she was dressed as an Arab woman, her yellow hair hidden under a long black robe.

The bar was broached, the Swedish trading ship came safely in, the captain and the pilot could be seen negotiating the barque through huge blocks of broken stone and piles of detritus as they made their way inwards. Rose stood at the rail and stared about her in disbelief. *This is the country of the magical writing?*

Then a tall obelisk on the shore made her suddenly catch her breath. 'Those things are called Cleopatra's Needles,' said Mrs Alabaster. 'There is another lying beside that one, though you can't see it from here. They are not of course connected to Cleopatra even remotely! Welcome to Egypt.'

Scattered minarets pierced the low, hot sky between mournful grey edifices. Mattie stood regarding everything with great interest as if she saw some sign. 'I've got a feeling inside me, Miss Rose,' she said, 'that I shall find my husband here.' Further in the distance a taller pillar seemed to rise, pink and shining, out of the rubble, quite alone.

'Corinthian,' murmured Mrs Venetzia Alabaster as she scanned the shore for her husband.

A small boat with two officials on board hailed the captain. The captain had a grave face as he came to give the women, his only passengers, the news. So great, at the moment, was the disturbance here against foreigners that the British Consul had been withdrawn. An army of Albanians seemed to have overthrown the Turkish Pasha in Cairo. Foreign visitors were unwelcome: they entered Alexandria at their own risk. It went without saying that all women must be covered. Other news followed, arriving on small boats with men in turbans and long gowns who spoke in a strange guttural language and stared at the women with the uncovered heads angrily.

The captain looked at Rose's face. 'Will you go back?' he said gruffly. 'If the consulate is closed I don't know what might happen to people like you. We will unload and return to Leghorn immediately, I'm always glad to get out of this dump.' A terrible smell had started to assail them: from the water, from the shore. 'You better come back with me.'

'Certainly not,' Rose said. She was, literally, trembling.

'Of course not,' said Mattie.

'Are you sure?'

'We are certain.' (But Rose did suddenly glance back behind them, as if for a moment she wanted to see a sign of the civilised world, the world they had left behind on the other side of the Mediterranean. But there was only the sea.)

Mrs Venetzia Alabaster suddenly waved. 'There's Archie, he's seen I'm on board, he's been expecting me for days, he's bringing some boatmen out. You can jump in if you're coming – I'll lend you some long shawls – we're going to the *frank* quarter of course and it is the only place you can go too.' The ship dropped anchor rather hazardously near to the causeway and unloading started at once: they could not wait to get away again.

Still Rose stared, unbelieving. A few dusty date palms stood on the ruined shore of Alexander's great city, Cleopatra's great city, Antony's last dream: the bleak, stinking rubble of a thousand histories including now her own: Alexandria.

Amid hasty introductions to Mr Alabaster the women climbed most precariously down into a small boat and were transported ashore, to a loathsome smell and to sand and huge broken stones and the spires of mosques and unwelcoming faces. They felt some relief to see a French flag flying rather half-heartedly: *The civilised world is still represented*, they thought to themselves (forgot for a moment they were at war with France). Small donkeys were acquired for the short distance to the *frank* quarter: 'Only the Turks and the Mameluks may ride horses,' said Mrs Alabaster disdainfully. 'I believe it is to make us look as silly as possible.'

As they prepared to leave the harbour Mr Alabaster, who seemed rather dishevelled but very energetic, muttered over his shoulder to Rose and Mattie, 'Above all, don't catch anyone's eye. They know I'm a trader, been here years, but I can't guarantee a thing in this atmosphere, you travel with me at your own risk.' Mr Alabaster and a turbaned person who carried a strange sword rode at the head. The three women followed in a line: Rose and Mattie clutching shawls about their faces, followed by Mrs Venetzia Alabaster, her eyes (the only part of her uncovered) looking as disdainful as those of the Arabs. The luggage followed on men's shoulders.

Everywhere a cacophony of alien, foreign sounds disturbed them. Rose held on tightly and precariously to her donkey and looked about her as best as she was able under the long black shawl. Mrs Alabaster had pinned it: it came down to her eyebrows and up to her nose. She was perspiring profusely from her own fear and from the black covering and from the heat that pressed down upon them: water ran down her body. Men in turbans and black-clad women stared, cringing cats that seemed nothing but bones ran under the feet of the donkeys. The incredible heat and the terrible, horrible smell and the warning of such danger increased the wild, unbelieving feelings that suddenly struck Rose over and over almost like blows: *this is the country of knowledge? of hieroglyphs? of the twelve hour water-clock?* The loud, squabbling, guttural sound of Arabs: talking, yelling, trading, calling; the sand everywhere: it was already in her mouth, round her teeth and tongue; the endless piles of broken grey stone, not just along the roads but piled up everywhere about them; the myriad flies and other insects that instantly buzzed about their faces. Blind Arabs stared upwards at them; some seemed to have no eyes at all, as Pierre had told. (She had been warned but it had been no use: secretly she had still imagined *at least* palm trees and rose petals.)

At first it seemed there was, quite literally, nothing at all but ruins, that Alexandria was nothing but a city of huge smashed stones. Then Rose saw that there were indeed houses in among the ruins, made of the old stone or of the kind of mud-dried bricks she had seen in some of the paintings in Paris; they leaned towards each other in small dark alleys, and lines of washing hung between them on wooden poles. The smell everywhere was indescribable, disgusting. She was accustomed to, immune to even, the smells of London, but the heavy foul stench of decay and of other smells she could not even put a name to was almost unbearable in the heat: it was foul, disgusting, loathsome, as if the past itself stank. Flies buzzed everywhere. This was where Harry died, in *these* streets? Her eyes, despite the warning, met directly those of a woman whose face like her body was completely covered except for two small holes: from these holes dark-rimmed almond eyes stared curiously; Rose did not know that her own eyes were blank with disbelief and fear. She stared at the stalls and the traders and the signs in the flowing, alien Arabic markings. And everywhere the hostile faces of the Egyptians, watching the strange little procession of obvious foreigners. Several of the men spat, a yellow thick phlegm landed in the dirt and just sat there as Rose passed, *but I cannot say that I was not warned, I have known about everything*. All this within sight of the harbour. As the sun began to fall downwards and the sky seemed to turn violet and the gates of the *frank* quarter came into view a strange cry suddenly filled the air; it came from more than one direction: *Allahu Akbar . . . Allahu Akbar . . .* they heard. *Allahu Akbar . . . God is Great.*

When they were safely inside the huge *frank* gates (Rose and Mattie hardly able to breathe until they heard the sound of bolts being locked behind them), Mr Alabaster asked Rose if they wanted to rent some rooms in a Turkish *khan.*

'What is that?'

'Big Turkish houses of rooms, mostly used during plague time but it's also where *franks* can go until they get settled. Are you staying, Viscountess?' Rose was sure she had not mentioned a title. 'You can rent a house if you're staying – depending on your business!' and she thought that he seemed to smile.

'I – we are not sure. Rooms here will be fine in the mean time. Thank you.'

Mr Alabaster called in Arabic; a man in a long gown and a turban sauntered over to the Alabasters. Money changed hands (from the Arab to Mr Alabaster). 'Give him half what he asks for!' called Mr Alabaster, and he and his wife disappeared further along the sandy road, while the man in the turban bowed and ushered them in. Rose and Mattie shook off their shawls in relief, dismounted from the asses; Rose fell as her feet touched the ground, but got up at once and brushed the dust away.

The *khan*, a long three-sided dwelling built around an empty sandy courtyard, had accommodation all along the upper floor; they were shown up a single side staircase that led to a long balcony: bare, plain rooms awaited them. Rose looked back as she climbed, stumbling, up the staircase; she stopped a moment, managed to pull the splinter of wood from the ship's rail out of her hand; looked back again at the courtyard and the sand. *I am in Egypt*, she kept repeating to herself in disbelief, *I am in Egypt*. Two ostriches suddenly ran across the courtyard at an amazing speed, and then, looking up at the opposite balcony, Rose saw quite clearly, with her white cap and her spectacles and holding a book in her hand, Miss Constantia Proud, waving and smiling.

'And you actually saw Fanny?'

'I saw Fanny.'

'And is she actually on her way to India?'

'She is on her way to India.' Miss Proud smiled. 'I myself had not of course thought to make one last journey! I find I am rather surprised. I so hoped you would not mind.'

'Mind?' said Rose, half laughing half crying as she embraced Miss Proud. '*Mind!*'

In Rose's bare room a raised platform covered with a carpet was to serve as a bed: it had been laid with pillows and a net to protect her from flying insects; there was nothing else. It opened out like all the rooms on to the long balcony: here they sat. Mattie, beaming with delight at the appearance of Miss Proud, was endeavouring (assisted by some Arabs who spoke no English) to prepare a meal with food they offered and bartered; she was match enough for them at once and Miss Proud advised fresh dates and bread and a kind of cheese, told Mattie how much she had learned to pay for them. It was clear that Miss Proud was infinitely relieved to see them. 'The war has changed everything, I thought you might have been prevented from travelling.'

'Monsieur Montand' – Rose's heart opened for a moment and closed again – 'helped us to get safe passage across France; we were in Switzerland when war was declared. Then we travelled over the Alps, into Italy. Everything is so unsettled, everywhere in Europe – we seem to have been travelling for ever! We finally arrived in Leghorn, and arranged a passage to Alexandria on a trading barque, but the gales had come and the ship had to turn back, twice!'

'No wonder you took so long!'

'But Monsieur Montand gave me a letter. I have a letter for an Alexandrian Copt who was there when the woman was stoned.'

'How will you find him?'

'I am to take it to the Church of St Mark. But,' and she stared at Miss Proud in disbelief once again, 'however did you get here before us?'

'I came from Malta.'

'Malta?'

'I know – one never knows who it will belong to next! But it was not given back to the French as was agreed by the Treaty of Amiens It is still in British hands. You see when Fanny—'

' – oh, my dearest Fanny, how I hated saying goodbye to her –'

'She came to South Molton Street when she got back to England, told me of your time in Paris and that you were going on alone. Those two children seemed very disturbed so I decided to take them to Portsmouth myself – it is a place I know well because of my naval brothers. Luckily they found a ship almost immediately, it was most providential. Almost, Fanny sent the boy back to his father – if they had had to wait another week I think she would have done so. But something seemed to tell her to go on with the journey, that it would be worth it, that if she left that little boy now she would lose him for ever,' *and Rose saw her beloved cousin, pale and determined, waving goodbye with her children from the deck of a small brave sailing ship.*

'So off they went to India! There were many English passengers on board – I saw a group of Quakers embarking, all the women in their grey dresses and bonnets, now that will have pleased dear

Fanny! – and there were other children, and I felt they were in good heart when they left. The children were excited, young Horatio forgot he was angry; I am sure Fanny has made a wise decision. But I felt so sorry that you should be travelling on without her. And then, quite by chance – or at least I *say* it was by chance, who knows if I was not unconsciously looking! – I found a ship that was leaving almost immediately for Malta. Of course everyone knew that war was very near but – on the spur of the moment really – I made hasty arrangements and joined the ship. As soon as I reached Malta I understood war had already been declared. I could only hope you were out of France, for I heard Napoleon made all English visitors prisoners-of-war.'

Rose kept shaking her head slightly: *Miss Constantia Proud was in Alexandria.*

'And in Malta I luckily found a ship leaving for Alexandria almost at once.' Miss Proud recited these extraordinary events as if they were everyday occurrences. 'I arrived here only two days ago: we were advised to turn back because of all the difficulties, and indeed some travellers did so, but I had not come so far in order to leave again! Oh, and I regret to say, dear Rose, that I arrived on the same day as the party of your brother-in-law, Viscount Gawkroger, who would not be turned back either.'

'*Oh no!*' cried Rose. 'He is not here already?' and her voice rang with dismay around the *khan.*

'Three trading boats arrived the day I did. Only a few of us stayed, having been warned that it was so dangerous – three of us stragglers with no plans came here, and I heard that the Viscount's party had rented a house.'

Rose closed her eyes in disbelief. 'We never once met up with them, though we heard they were in Paris. I hoped they had become prisoners-of-war. I hoped and prayed, every single time something went wrong with our journey, that the same was happening to them. Now George will be everywhere!' *I will not cry.* 'Was – did Lady Dolly seem to be – expecting a child?'

Miss Proud looked surprised. 'It did not seem so – but of course we were all so enclosed in our garments. But – dear Rose.' Miss Proud looked suddenly shy. 'Dear Rose, should you prefer to go on with this adventure on your own – I will not be in the least offended. I have already had an enormously exciting time! I was glad to see that I found everything just as interesting as I had when I was younger.' And she smiled at Rose from under her immaculate white cap, and, still making extraordinary efforts not to – for George to be already here was disastrous: for Miss Proud to here was miraculous – Rose burst into tears.

'I am so glad,' she wept, 'to see you! I have been absolutely terrified, and trying not to show it in front of Mattie!'

'I knew, of course,' said Mattie, entering again with some bowls. 'I'm absolutely terrified as well. And we have to buy water. And the Arabs have offered us this stew for a price. I think it's a goat.'

At dawn Rose woke to the strange, harsh calling from the city below. *Allahu Akbar* ... the voice called in the distance ... *God is Great.* She at once smelt heat, and sand, and an alien land. She stepped down from her Egyptian *divan* (looking gingerly at the floor for signs of cockroaches). From her trunk she took the letter Pierre had finally agreed to write for her to bring to Alexandria, to a Copt that he knew. She stopped quite still, the letter in her hand, thinking of Pierre with terrible regret. What it must have cost him, to get them so quickly out of France when his country was preparing for war. He had been so angry, yet he was so kind: despite everything he had remained, as he had promised, a friend; got them all safely away; he did not seem to sleep in those anxious days. But all the time his disapproval had been palpable: she had not been able to break through the barrier he had placed between them. Had he, as she feared, met another person for his heart? She could not tell. He and Rose never again spoke of anything but the journeys, and she knew he thought her spoilt and foolish, had done everything he could bar physically tying them down to stop her journey. Over and over she wanted to say: *I was wrong, I did not understand myself,* but his person that had been so open was closed to her and a cold hand had clamped down over her hopeful heart. For a moment she stroked his incomprehensible Arabic writing: saw him, tall and kind and angry. 'I should be there with you,' he had muttered furiously. 'You cannot get through the streets of Alexandria without a man to accompany you,' and she saw again now his strained face and knew her hopes had come to nothing.

She slowly picked up her journal and went to the balcony, still in the shade. She had been told that the worst of the summer heat was over. But already it pressed down in a way she had never known, already flies buzzed everywhere. In the courtyard outside a rather battered-looking large bird, strange and black, pecked angrily at the dust and she saw that although it was much bigger than any like bird she had ever seen before it was perhaps a species of hawk. The words from her father's old book came back to her: *When they would signify god, or height or lowness or excellence or blood or victory they delineate a HAWK.* The bird seemed to sense her watching: it gave a strange cry as it flew – not away, but straight towards her – diving down towards the balcony angrily (so that she ducked in fright, waving her arms at it) before flying over the wall and away from the *khan*. Although she felt her heart jolting, Rose also felt a tingle of satisfaction. She wrote in her journal that she had, as it were, seen her first real hieroglyph. As she wrote she heard again the harsh Arabic cry in the distance: *Allahu Akbar . . .*

From her balcony she saw Miss Proud across the courtyard. She was under a parasol, brushing flies away quite automatically, and peacefully reading: for all the world as if she had been living in a *khan* in Alexandria all her life. Then the gate to the *khan* opened and Mattie, be-shawled, carrying things that looked like long carrots and a cabbage, sitting quite confidently upon a donkey, called her thanks to some man who went on up the sandy road.

Mattie saw Rose, waved. 'Cornelius Brown is in Egypt!' she called.

Rose leaned over the balcony. 'Wherever have you been?'

'The servants in the *frank* quarter often ride in early to buy food, I was told, so I joined them. One of the traders always comes as an escort, they take turns.' Mattie dismounted. 'I met a sailor who knew Cornelius! Says he's definitely in Egypt, he's a trader too! I told you!' And Mattie laughed and climbed up the side staircase with her vegetables, the shawl still over her head.

She stopped at Rose's room as she passed. 'I asked that Mr Alabaster to call,' she said. 'He speaks Arabic and he can take you to that church with that letter – you can't go anywhere without a man. They don't drink alcohol here apparently, but I warn you, it's only eight o'clock in the morning but he was drunk!' Mattie disappeared again and Rose heard her talking to the Arabs in the *khan*. She seemed to be speaking Arabic.

Allahu Akbar, called the voices in the distance.

'I told you, Archie!' said Mrs Venetzia Alabaster. Dusk was falling but the heat remained; the Alabasters were finally visiting the *khan*, as requested, where Rose had stayed in a fever of inactivity all day, waiting for them. They all sat on the long balcony: the women drank mint tea, Mr Alabaster had brought his own refreshment, drank straight from the bottle.

'I expect that is tropical medicine,' said Miss Proud, 'for I know the Mohammetmen do not allow alcohol.'

'That's what it is, Miss Proud!' he said. 'Tropical medicine!' and he laughed and they smelt the rum. Cries of the alien city could be heard from beyond the gates as darkness came, dark velvet skies of a million stars shone above them, and mosquitoes buzzed everywhere. All the time as they spoke they automatically brushed and fanned mosquitoes and flies away, hit them with their hands.

'It was the name of Fallon,' Mrs Alabaster explained. 'I thought you might be related. Everyone here knows the story; the woman was stoned to death, did you know that?'

'Yes,' said Rose quietly, 'I knew that.' Mattie, coming and going out of the shadows, lit several candles; they glowed and hardly flickered, so still was the night air.

'That new Viscount tried to order me around when he arrived the other day,' said Mr Alabaster. 'He'll regret that. I told him to shove off. I won't be helping him in any matters he might require assistance with, as he will surely find he will in Egypt!'

'Good!' said Rose. 'I want you to help me, but I particularly do not want the Viscount to know anything at all of my plans. I have a letter to take to the Church of St Mark. At once, first thing in the morning.'

'But as for the child,' said Mrs Alabaster, 'there are a thousand such children in Alexandria; it will be like looking for an angel on the head of a pin!' She frowned at her own rather unsuitable metaphor. 'A needle in a haystack, I mean.'

'I have a *letter*,' said Rose doggedly.

'Well,' said Mrs Alabaster, 'we can try, of course.' For a moment they sat in silence. 'Listen,' said Mrs Alabaster.

From the city, outside the gates of the *frank* quarter, a sound drifted. Music – another kind of music – hung in the air: alien, strange, nothing like the music they knew. A distant woman's voice echoed in the dark: throbbing, plaintive. Strangeness entwined them, disturbed them.

'Give us a tune, Vennie,' said Mr Alabaster suddenly. *'Real* music – one of your songs – I'd forgotten how that stuff drifts up here to the *khan* if you're not careful!' He seemed unsettled, got up, stared out at the darkness, sat down again on a marble bench – and then was immediately fast asleep, his empty bottle rolling along the balcony.

'I'll get him carried home soon,' said Mrs Alabaster unconcernedly, and in the silence the plaintive music drifted. 'He'll take you in the morning, translate for you too. It'll cost two guineas. You can give it to me now if you want.' If she saw that both women were taken aback by the enormous amount, she gave no sign. But Rose quickly got up to get the money; the guineas clinked as they changed hands.

'First thing in the morning,' insisted Rose.

'First thing in the morning,' agreed Mrs Alabaster. 'Better to travel at dawn when it is cooler.' And then they sat, silent, listening to the city they were locked away from. Mr Alabaster snored very quietly.

'I expect – once – it was wonderful here,' murmured Miss Proud. 'They say Alexander the Great of Macedonia built the most beautiful city in the world.'

Mrs Alabaster said casually: 'They say Alexander himself thought of the lighthouse and the library and the water cisterns and wonderful buildings – though he died with his army far away, after all. You know how Alexandria was a great city of learning because it once had the biggest and most important library in the whole world? Well, I heard that no ship could land without presenting a book from its country to the library of Alexandria – I quite like that picture, I like to think of a rough old sea captain coming ashore with a precious book under his arm, as well as landing permissions! They say that thousands of years later Cleopatra wooed Julius Caesar, and then Antony, on barges from a palace here so wondrous that both men never really recovered – rose petals and wines and fruits and love songs and wonderful food, never mind that it was laid before them by the most gorgeous woman in the world with lotus flowers and cinnamon oils! I think of that, when the place gets me down.' And she sighed. 'Can't see any sign of it now, can you? You know there are apparently no paintings or statues of Cleopatra. So we can imagine her however we choose.'

'You must have learnt a great many things since you were here, Mrs Alabaster.' Mrs Alabaster only shrugged. Miss Proud hit a mosquito hard with her fan as the buzzing went on and on about their heads. 'Have you perhaps become – fond of Egypt?'

Mrs Alabaster threw back her head and laughed. 'Fond? If you've made your living singing upside down in Ranelagh Gardens while gentlemen threw champagne corks and florins you could learn to be fond of anywhere!' and Rose flushed in the darkness (that she had been with those very gentlemen). 'When Archibald offered me this life I took it like a shot!' and she looked at the snoring man beside them with an unreadable expression on her face. 'I've really only learnt one thing. Poor old Egypt – right back to its Pharaohs – is always being invaded: Greeks, Romans, Arabs, Turks! Even us – passing traders – we've been caught up in so many battles since we've been here – the French came with Napoleon, the English came with Lord Nelson, Lord Abercrombie came. Of course it's because of where it is on the map – on the way to the East – and because of the fertile banks of the Nile – well that's why Archie's here, of course. He trades grain, rice – four harvests a year – you don't see that in Kent! So I suppose in a way I feel – well, not fond, but – protective – even if the strange calls and the music are only Arabic, and don't go right back into their own history and all those wonderful Pharaohs and queens that I wish I could have met.'

Mrs Alabaster leant back, looked up at the stars. 'What music do you imagine those Pharaohs played? That's what I'd like to know. I've seen old ruins all over Egypt with paintings of them playing flutes and lutes but I suppose we'll never ever know the sound of their music. Makes me quite melancholy sometimes, to think of that.' And when Mrs Alabaster was silent the discordant, haunting Arabic music could still be heard from the streets outside the *frank* quarter: drums or tabors drifted upwards and the darkness seemed to rustle with forgotten dreams. 'They became Christian for a while, during the Roman times, still a few of them left, the Copts, like in that St Mark's Church you want to go to, but it's not safe to be a Christian any more than a foreigner. I hear they're mostly living in old ruined temples now, way down the Nile. Most Egyptians have been Mohammetmen for hundreds of years and their ancient ancestors are quite forgot. Now they do stonings and hangings and cut off hands. I can't think the beautiful, dignified Pharaohs were so uncouth!'

Rose and Miss Proud were leaning forward, fascinated; Rose thought how odd it was that they were sitting here talking to one of the heroines of her youth.

'Mrs Alabaster,' she said, 'I saw The Singing Acrobats – not just with my husband before he died, but when I was a child.'

'I dare say you did,' she answered drily. 'We used to say we was as famous as the King! We kept changing, of course – girls got married, or worse, got caught in the family way. They'd try to hide it as long as they could because although we all got that sick to death of it you could make good money if gentlemen took a shine.'

'It was our most favourite thing in the world when we were children – and when we were older! I remember one night they – you – all sang and the audience wouldn't let you go: you were twined around ropes they'd got hanging and swaying in the dark, and there were lamps, and the scarves you wore were fluttering like flags. It was thrilling for children! My cousin Fanny and I kept hoping you would sing Handel, he was our favourite because we knew he used to live in our street!'

Mrs Alabaster leaned back against the wall of the *khan* and quite unselfconsciously began to sing softly.

> *Where'er you walk*
> *Cool gales shall fan the glade*
> *Trees where you sit*
> *Shall crowd into a shade . . .*

Her voice was sharp, yet somehow mesmerising, full of memory or pain; the women leaned forward again slightly without knowing they did so and the discordant music of another culture was no longer heard. Mr Alabaster, inert on a marble bench, seemed perhaps to smile.

At last Mrs Alabaster stood, called in Arabic for a servant. Then she turned to Rose. 'I just wanted to ask you – this is a strange country, as you have already seen. And I find in particular that – things are not always what they seem. There are many lost children of course in such chaos: would you be certain that such a child was your husband's? If you've got money someone is quite likely to give you a child tomorrow.'

Tomorrow? Rose's heart, hearing that word, leapt so extraordinarily that for a split second she could not breathe, or even see. 'You mean,' she managed at last, 'that the child might – might – be actually in the church that we will be going to?'

'Who knows? Perhaps, if the Copts are looking after it. But how would you be certain it was the child you were looking for?'

'I – I hope I would somehow know her. She must be over a year old.' And Rose saw that Mrs Alabaster regarded her almost with pity in the candlelight; then she shrugged.

'Well – I'll come with you tomorrow,' she said. 'I'll dress you, I'll bring all the palaver, and the veil. You won't know yourself!'

'The veil is not an Egyptian concept, surely,' said Miss Proud indignantly. 'The Pharaohs and the queens did not wear veils.'

'Indeed,' said Mrs Venetzia Alabaster, as disapproving as Miss Proud, and she called again in Arabic for servants. 'Those things were brought here by the Mohammetmen and the veil is more important to them, it sometimes seems, than the rest of the clothes. Can you believe? – once Archie and I were sailing along some deserted stretch, miles from Cairo, and some peasant women swam out to our boat to beg *baksheesh*. Some of them were naked, but *all* of them had strips of material tied across their faces!' and Mrs Alabaster suddenly laughed and stretched and seemed to click all her bones as if they somehow needed to be put back into place. Then the servants lifted the sleeping Mr Alabaster on to their shoulders, and they were gone.

Rose could not keep still as the gates of the *khan* closed behind their visitors. She walked up and down the balcony, up and down. Finally she said to Miss Proud, 'Forgive me,' and rummaged for one of her small cigars which she lit at once from the candle. 'I had not understood that maybe so soon . . . tomorrow! Everyone told me it would be impossible but – perhaps it is not impossible at all!' The smoke went up into the darkness. 'Of course, you are most welcome.' She gestured politely to Miss Proud.

'Thank you,' said Miss Proud, and to Rose's amazement she too lighted, with ease, the proffered cigar from the candle. Still Rose walked up and down, up and down, smoking her own cigar, pale and anxious and excited.

'There is nothing we can do until the morning, my dear,' said Miss Proud.

'I know, I know. It is just that – now that the moment has come I – I do not know what to do with my thoughts,' and with an enormous effort she sat down on the marble bench, leaned against the wall of the *khan* as Mrs Alabaster had done. After a moment she too began to sing.

> *Where'er you walk*
> *Cool gales shall fan the glade . . .*

but her voice faded away. 'Imagine being Mr Handel. All that music inside his head. I remember hearing his Water Music with my parents in the Concert Rooms in Hanover Square, and weeping! I was only about ten! Talk to me about something, Miss Proud, I am never going to go to sleep. I feel as if my being will burst!'

'Mrs Alabaster is a quite extraordinary woman,' said Miss Proud calmly. 'She seems to know more about Egypt than most people – including my brothers, who have all been here at some time or another. If Mrs Alabaster had had a chance of a real education, who knows what life she may have had.'

'Her life may not have been so exciting!' said Rose. 'If you never saw them you cannot imagine the excitement of The Singing Acrobats!'

Miss Proud's little white cap, which Rose could just see under the black silk robe that they all wore outside, to have some relief from the flying insects, seemed to shake in a kind of indignation.

'An intelligent woman like that hanging upside down and having champagne corks thrown! She could have done—'

'Done what?' said Rose drily.

'Written books,' said Miss Proud tartly. 'That is the one career that *is* open to all women. To help other women. Rather than either singing upside down or carrying a drunken husband home every night in a foreign country! That is not exactly choice! Do you know, I have been told privately that the King is not in favour of education for women – as if Mrs Alabaster's life should be circumscribed because His Britannic Majesty George III says so!' She banged at insects with her fan; the sound echoed round the *khan*. 'I would like the Royal Family removed, I really believe it would help. I do not of course mean chop off their heads – but – when I was young, you know, I met Captain James Cook. Now *he* has found some places far away that might revere a few royal visitors.'

'But Miss Proud, Captain Cook was – eaten, they say – in the antipodes!'

'Exactly,' said Miss Proud, 'that is what I mean,' and then continued as if she had made a reasonable suggestion. 'We *say* our government is independent of the monarchy, but the King is always interfering.' And Rose had a sudden vision of the old Duke of Hawksfield, adviser to the King, *leaning forward, whispering into the ear of the King: dry, old man's counsel*, and she shivered in the hot darkness.

'And a corrupt, indulgent heir to the throne,' continued Miss Proud, and she shook her head in disgust and stabbed out her cigar viciously on the candle-holder. Rose was mesmerised. 'However!' (Miss Proud was determined to finish her brief polemic on a positive note.) 'Princess Charlotte is next in line and her father will surely one day explode through one or other of his overindulgences – he will quite simply burst! – then a *woman* on the throne, that would surely help!' A large rat or something of its kind ran past their feet. Rose smothered a half-scream, ashamed. Miss Proud seemed not to even notice, stared out at stars. 'Oh, just look up there! No wonder the Ancient Egyptians were astronomers, just look how brightly the stars shine.' A small wind suddenly rose out of nowhere, they felt it gratefully on their cheeks, thought perhaps they heard the sea.

Both sighed, without knowing it. Miss Proud stood. 'I must go to my room.'

'Please stay,' said Rose quickly. 'Just a little bit longer.'

Miss Proud smiled slightly in the darkness but sat down again. 'What would you like to talk of? Shall I tell you about what I am reading?'

'Tell me about your betrothed,' said Rose: the words had burst out before she could stop them. *A sad affair*, the old gentlemen had said. Rose could have bitten off her tongue.

The wind became stronger, stirred and rustled.

At last Miss Proud said, and it seemed inconsequently, 'Did you know that bluebells *en masse* can actually look light purple in colour?'

Rose was so embarrassed that she blushed in the darkness. Miss Proud was of course changing the subject. 'Forgive me, Miss Proud, I do not know what came over me.' The bright stars shone. 'I did not know that bluebells looked purple.' They heard the sound of whispering sand, drifting in the wind over Alexandria as it had always done, being blown in the darkness along old pathways outside the locked gates of the *khan*.

'There was a carpet of purple bluebells under the trees as we rode to the small church where my father was vicar. It was the way the light caught them, I expect. I had a white gown, and a veil – I never thought to wear one again, so far away in Egypt! – only in those days, more than forty years ago, I had ringlets and Napoleon was not even born. We were to live in London, which was my dream.'

'You *did* marry, then?' Rose held her breath, suddenly remembered the glimpse of Miss Proud as someone younger, in the carriage in the rain.

'I was to marry. He was a naval man. He had promised me that when we lived in London I should go to every public lecture, every exhibition – anything we could attend together – for he too found such things interesting. We would learn together. I could not believe how lucky I had been, to find him.'

There was a long silence. Rose waited, still hardly daring to breathe.

'He had arrived in the village for our wedding the previous

evening, and although I had not been allowed to see him, in the custom, he nevertheless had gone out into the valley and picked some of the bluebells for me – and do you know? – the faint scent of bluebells in the spring can remind me still of that evening before I was to be married, when I buried my face in the flowers that were delivered and wept, for pure happiness. As one can, when one is young.' Another long silence. 'My husband-to-be arrived at the little church with my brothers, all in their proud navy uniforms,' *and Rose saw the small church and the bright blue jackets, the gold braid.* 'I walked down the aisle in my white wedding gown on the arm of my oldest brother.' *Rose saw spring sunshine coming in through the small high windows.* 'We stood together, my dear father smiling at the small altar, ready to officiate at the marriage of his only daughter. And my – my betrothed smiled at me, and then – I remember clearly even now – he looked at me so oddly, like a question. And then – he fell.'

'Fell?' echoed Rose stupidly.

'Something had happened – his heart, his head – we could not know – he was almost at once unconscious. The doctor was in the congregation of course, they carried him to the little vestry, they listened to his heartbeat and they cut him and bled him.'

Rose wanted to ask all sorts of questions but could not dare to, could not even look at the person who sat, so upright in her black Arab robe, beside her: *she saw the young bride in white, and blood on the floor, a stain of blood on the white dress; in the small, dark, airless vestry people leaned towards the body and Miss Proud's brothers in their blue uniforms looked at their sister anxiously, trying to persuade her to come away.*

The unexpected wind had blown many of the little flies and insects away for the moment, and the night ruffled and moved with cloud and stars. 'I am – so very sorry,' said Rose, feeling the inadequacy of her words.

'He died within the hour – and the sun was still shining outside. And I remember wishing at the time – this was a most unworthy thought, I know' (and Rose caught a small, wry smile in the candlelight) 'that we had been married, at least, before he fell. For there I was, as I had started: Miss Constantia Proud.' The wind blew along the side of the *khan*.

'What – what did you do?'

'I was so lucky in my family: my brothers bought the house in South Molton Street, but also they had ships, as I told you, and one brother had been made a consul in Spain and said he needed me to accompany him – in truth I do not believe he did, but it made me feel necessary. I was extremely lucky to travel all over Europe for several years. But then my mother became ill and it was required that I live in Wiltshire again, being the only daughter.

'So I determined that – even in Wiltshire – I would do what I would have done with my – husband. I determined that I should educate myself to a high standard – even if I had to do it all by myself. I began reading every single book that I could lay my hands on. Everything. Everything I had ever heard of,' *and Rose saw Miss Proud in her parents' drawing room in Brook Street, how she bent over a book as if she would devour it.* 'Somehow I knew that books would save my life.'

At last Miss Proud stood again. She looked out over the square of the *khan*. 'Do you know, Rose, being here, so far away from our own world, listening to the cry all day long of another religion and another god, I begin to understand why I – daughter of a vicar though I am – have felt so uneasy about our God for many years.' And Rose thought at once of Pierre: *you cannot study old civilisations as I have and believe that Christianity is the only right.*

'Do you not – believe there is a God at all?'

'There are so many wars over religion! People believing in *their* truth, not *your* truth. It is ridiculous.' Miss Proud spoke briskly: she had put the past away. 'I have come to believe that we do with our lives the best we can: perhaps there is a kind of fate, perhaps there is only chaos. But we must not seek help from another, higher being than ourselves: our life is here, on earth, not up in the sky; this is all we have, and we must make the most of it.'

'I wish Fanny was here,' said Rose slowly. 'She is the thoughtful one and I know she has struggled with her ideas of religion. But – perhaps, in the end, the world does not make sense without God.'

'Perhaps in the end the world does not make sense *with* God,' said Miss Proud firmly, and she stared defiantly at the bright stars.

'I am so sorry, dear Miss Proud,' said Rose.

Miss Proud raised her hand in acknowledgement, or farewell,

and the small, upright, dark-robed figure moved into the shadows further along the balcony and disappeared. Drifting on the wind from the city below a tabor sounded, and the plaintive, alien voice sang of love.

TWENTY-TWO

By the time the first dawn cry . . . *Allahu Akbar* . . . echoed up to the *khan* they were ready. Mrs Alabaster had given Rose soft pantaloons, over that a long light gown; on her feet they put small soft leather boots and covered them with slippers. Something like a flat turban was then placed on Rose's head; Mrs Alabaster attached a white veil around this so that only Rose's eyes were visible; over the whole she placed a long black robe that covered her from head to toe. *I feel like a hot nun!* muttered Rose, but Mrs Alabaster said she would get used to it. Mrs Alabaster was similarly attired herself, and infinitely at ease, graceful, in such clothes. The gates of the *khan* were opened, they climbed on to small grey donkeys (Miss Proud and Mattie waving anxiously), and with Mr Alabaster and a sword-carrying Arab in front they set off. Mr Alabaster showed no ill-effects from his rum.

Outside the *frank* quarter blank-faced men stared, shadowy in the early light. For a moment Rose thought she heard, above the pounding of her heart, the sea against the broken shore; then suddenly, from several directions, again the loud sound pierced the morning: from the mosques in among the rubble and the old houses the call to prayer came echoing into the streets, *Allahu*

Akbar! Allahu akbar! The blank-faced men at once disappeared round corners, down alleys. But the cry hung on the still air . . . *Allahu Akbar . . . la ilaha illa Allah! There is no god but God!*

The travellers turned up into the narrow streets of the town; old houses with closed shutters leant nearer and nearer to each other, almost touching it seemed, across dark alleys. Washing – incongruous gay colours – hung out on sticks across the alleys. The fetid smell of the streets again almost overcame Rose. Her layers of clothes were already soaked through; she held tightly to her donkey, who smelt also, but her feet were not far from the filthy paths they traversed *this is where I have come to, to find Harry's child* and the incongruity and wild excitement and fear of her situation as she stared out from the small gap in her veil threatened to overcome her: to make her laugh or cry or scream or simply faint in the heat *but if I faint I will fall on to cockroaches and rotten food and excrement and rats.* She held even tighter to the donkey. They emerged into a wider street: heard the guttural shouts that sounded to Rose, suddenly, bizarrely, like awful old men in the house in Berkeley Square clearing their throats. They saw early morning and the strange bright blue of the sky; and children, and donkeys almost hidden under sheaves of rushes or wheat, and carts piled high with strange fruit. A gate was knocked upon, Pierre Montand's letter was passed across, the gate allowed them entrance and was closed behind them, but when Rose looked to alight, the ground was muddy and wet. *What is this water? Where does it come from? There is no spare water in Alexandria.* And she found that she shuddered at her own imaginings, for the heavy rotten smell in the churchyard was as strong as the smell of the alleys. The animals were led by small, clamouring boys around to the other side of an old building where plaster peeled and, solitary, a Christian cross on the roof. One dusty sycamore tree languished.

After various incomprehensible conversations the foreigners were pointed up some steps and allowed inside the old church. Mrs Alabaster and Rose, in relief, sat to one side on a wooden bench, Mr Alabaster was led away. Rose looked about her: decay, even in here, *I must take the child away at once.*

'This is the church of St Mark in Alexandria,' whispered Mrs

Alabaster. 'They say he brought the Christian religion to Egypt. That'll be him, above us.'

Rose looked upwards. The paint was peeling and the mosaic was cracked and broken, but a man encircled as a saint gazed sadly down, his hand raised. All around him other saints and madonnas hung, in various states of despair. From somewhere came an odd, rhythmic sound: they realised it was a broom being pushed backwards and forwards over the stone floor. Flies buzzed about Rose's eyes; when she raised her hand to hit them away they buzzed about her hands; a few very small candles were lit in a corner, stuck into sand. The idea that she would actually see Harry's child, now, here, made her dizzy with disbelief. She kept trying to breathe deeply, to remain as calm as it was possible to be, but the effort to keep still, not to run screaming after Mr Alabaster, was enormous. Slowly backwards and forwards in the church shadows, they heard the broom, sweeping old stones.

'They say St Mark was tortured and killed by the Romans,' said Mrs Alabaster in a low voice, 'and his head was taken to somewhere in Italy, but it was recovered and returned, so they say, and lies right here in the crypt, with the rest of his body. Still,' she added wryly, 'the same tale is told in Venice!' To Rose, Mrs Alabaster seemed a mystery woman: a Singing Acrobat with all sorts of knowledge.

Suddenly Rose could clearly smell a person somewhere near to her, an unwashed, foreign smell. An Arab had appeared, whispered something to her (she could feel his breath on her ear), held up beads, pushed them into her hand; she felt her heart beating faster, unpleasantly beating. She shook her head, he whispered again into her ear, foreign, insinuating, *you want to buy?* too near, she wanted to push him away, did not dare, *you want to buy?* But just then a door behind the pulpit opened and an old man in a dark turban appeared with Mr Alabaster, and the bead man seized his beads back and disappeared into the shadows. And the broom was suddenly still.

The old man and Mr Alabaster were speaking Arabic, coming towards the women. Rose stood up sharply, forgetting the veil and the heat and the bead man, tripping on her robe, pulling at it from under her feet. 'What does he say?' she called, and her voice echoed in the empty space. St Mark stared down from faded colours and broken mosaic.

If Rose had hoped that Christians would look different, that she would at once feel at home with them, she was disappointed. The Copt in his dark turban and long robe seemed to look very like the Mohammetmen they had passed outside. The old man bowed but Rose saw at once that he was uneasy and they were no more welcome here than anywhere else.

'There has been much troubles,' he said in very heavily accented English, and she had to lean towards him to catch the words. 'Since all the soldiers have gone is not safe. The merchant,' he waved Pierre's letter, 'he has gone, as many.'

'Where is she?' asked Rose urgently. 'Where is the child?' And she looked quickly at Mr Alabaster. 'Does he say she is still alive?' and then found that, having called out the questions, she was terrified of the answers.

'The Turks has been here,' said the old man, in the general direction of Rose and Mrs Alabaster, but not actually looking at them. 'And the Arabs. The child has been gone.' His eyes flickered about the shadows for a moment and then were lowered.

'Do you mean *taken*?'

'I am sorry,' he said, 'may God bless you, the child has been gone.' He spoke in Arabic to Mr Alabaster, pushing Pierre's letter back to him as he did so.

Like a most terrible blow in the middle of her stomach Rose suddenly understood that the long journey from London could all have been in vain. 'No! Please!' she cried loudly to the priest, taking him by surprise, making him look nervously about him, and she moved towards him, put her hand on his arm. 'Please, I must at least know if the child is alive!' The priest spoke rapidly again to Mr Alabaster.

'He wishes you to know that you may, if you wish, see a relic of St Mark,' said Mr Alabaster.

'A relic?' She smelt rum.

'You may not ascend to the grave but you may enter the small room of the finger.'

'The finger?' said Rose stupidly.

'It is a relic.'

'Thank you,' said Rose, panicking. 'That is most extremely kind,' but she looked at Mr Alabaster as if he was mad, or drunk already. 'But surely – are we to know no more about the fate of the child than this?' Fright, loss, clutched at her. 'At least if she is alive, that would be something to know,' she said to Mr Alabaster desperately. 'He must tell us! *Anything!* I will pay!' Somewhere there was the strange sound of a tabor, or a tambourine, being struck over and over again, and over that, faintly, came the cry *Allahu Akbar!* for another god in the old, broken city, and when they looked round the Copt had somehow vanished.

'*Oh no!*' cried Rose. 'Call him back at once! He must tell us where to go, where to look for her, call him back!' and she would have run to the door behind the pulpit if Mr Alabaster had not physically stopped her.

'Listen to me!' he said. The broom started again, brushing across the stone floors: they heard the harsh sound. Mr Alabaster sat down on the bench beside his wife but Rose could not sit. 'The girl your husband met was an Egyptian betrothed to a Turk.'

'I know that, *I know that!*' cried Rose.

'The rulers are Turks. It is very dangerous for Christians to be involved, the priest said he knows nothing more about it and doesn't want anything to do with it.'

'Mr Alabaster, I will pay anything that is required! Anything that I have! I have to know where the child might be, if she is still alive. I cannot just – leave this church and go home again! I will *not* leave, not until I know something; *I must know something!*' and to her own surprise and mortification she seemed to be weeping uncontrollably, she could not stop herself; tears fell inside her veil and her black robe. 'Surely they could tell us where they sent her? Or whether she is at least alive. They must know that much! How can we even *begin* to look if he will not help us!'

Mr Alabaster whipped a small bottle out of his pocket. 'Here, have a swallow,' he said, 'it'll make you calm!' and before she properly understood it she was drinking rum from a bottle in a church. 'Listen, the priest told me that the English trader who took in the mother, I remember him – Cartwright – was forced out of Egypt for his kindness once the British troops left – all his business lost, well, we knew that. And now the Copt merchant that your friend wrote the letter to has gone also.' He gave a grunt of disgust. 'Invading armies come and go, and never think of what they do to people trying to make an honest living in the chaos they leave behind,' and Rose was not sure if Mr Alabaster meant the French or the British or Harry himself, or was merely drunk.

The sound of the broom came nearer. In the shadows they saw a woman holding the broom, sweeping nearer. She wore a shawl over her head but her face was uncovered; she seemed perhaps Rose's age, olive skin, dark eyes. She seemed also to be sweeping very close to Rose, too close to Rose: she looked up suddenly from her labour and into Rose's tear-filled eyes behind the veil, regarding her. She was so near that Rose felt she had to step back, could smell the different smell. (Presumably the Arab woman in exchange could smell the rum.) For a second they stared at one another, Rose still weeping and trying not to. Then, almost without stopping the rhythmical movement of the sweeping, the woman reached up and removed something from her own neck which she put into Rose's hands, rather as the bead man had put his beads. 'No – no thank you,' said Rose; felt something in her hand, warm and oily and dirty, tried to give it back. 'No thank you.' But the woman leaned towards her for a moment and whispered, 'Rashid.' She looked at Rose's eyes, to see if she had understood. 'Rashid,' she whispered again and for just a moment she kept Rose's pale hands in her own and stroked them gently, as if to press in a message and Rose saw kind eyes, holding hers. Somewhere the sound of a door opening: the woman was at once gone back into the shadows like the bead man and the old man, only the whisper echoed back – *Rashid* – and the sound of the sweeping and something from around her neck in Rose's hand.

'Let me see that,' said Mr Alabaster at once. Rose gingerly handed him what the woman had given her, wondered at his agitation. 'Yes,' he said slowly, 'it is the old Coptic sign, the cross from Egypt.' He quickly put it in his pocket. 'Let's get out of here.'

'But who is – Rashid?' said Rose, detaining him. 'What did she mean? Do you think she was trying to tell me something?'

'Yes,' said Mr Alabaster, looking quickly back at the closed door behind the pulpit, 'I think she was trying to tell you something, and I think the priest was lying.' He called something in Arabic in a low voice into the shadows. The woman answered softly and Mr Alabaster disappeared towards her. They heard quiet voices. Then he came back quickly. 'We must leave at once, we are trouble for the girl if we remain.'

'But do you know the Rashid person?' Rose insisted.

'Rashid is the name of a town along the coast,' said Mrs Alabaster, but she said it almost like a whisper and she and her husband were moving Rose as fast as possible from the church as St Mark stared down. They quickly remounted their donkeys and left the churchyard: out in the street the Arab guard was waiting and they turned the animals back towards the *frank* quarter, past the stalls and the dirt and the fetid smells and the alien people and the smashed and broken stones and pillars, travelling as quickly as possible back to safety.

Inside the gates of the quarter Mr Alabaster dismounted, walked beside the donkeys. Miss Proud and Mattie were waiting at the gate of the *khan*, saw that Rose was not carrying any child, helped her down, helped her remove her veil and her turban; waiting to hear everything.

'So much for religion!' said Mr Alabaster. 'That priest was a liar, or probably a coward. The girl heard all that and wanted to help. But – it's no use being too hopeful. In Rashid they could say "Cairo", in Cairo they might say "Aswan". I never let myself forget that my fate in this country is in the hands of the greatest story-tellers in the world, and I advise you to do the same. But we are lucky nevertheless, that girl did know something. She said her brother had taken the baby away from the English merchant's house when the trouble started because they assumed the dead English captain was a Christian, and she had heard it had been taken to Rashid.'

'How do we know it was Harry's child?'

'She said it was the child of the captain who was killed and the woman who was stoned by her people. She heard my conversation with the priest.'

'Then can we go there? Can we go there *now*?' Rose hurried, ungainly, dragged her unwilling donkey, trying to walk level with Mr Alabaster, who was going further up the road. Miss Proud and Mattie followed close behind. 'Is there any way we could go today? Could you please stop!'

'You want me to go with you?'

'*Please!* Please, Mr Alabaster, I cannot of course travel alone but I must go at once!'

He stopped at last. 'A hundred guineas.'

Rose literally blanched. 'A hundred?' *It is nearly one quarter of all the money I have.* It was more than double what Mattie earned in a year. 'It is too much,' she said.

'Not for what you want,' he said slyly. 'The Viscount would give me more.'

'But I will need money to buy the child, to make the journey back to England.'

'I'll not only take you there, I'll stay and help you find out what we can. The cross the girl gave you will be useful, I bet.'

'What do you mean?' She thought he meant to sell it.

'Among other Copts.' He touched the side of his nose knowingly. 'I've learnt to think like *them*, like Egyptians. They won't expect to see a *frank* with a Coptic cross. It'll be a sign.'

Mrs Alabaster called from behind them, still on her donkey. 'How about eighty guineas and no more if we fail; another eighty if we find the child.'

'Fifty!' said Miss Proud unexpectedly, nodding at Rose.

'Seventy!' said Mrs Alabaster. Miss Proud nodded at Rose vigorously.

'Done!' said Rose in a faint voice, biting the side of her cheek in anxiety. 'Can we go there now, this instant?'

Mr Alabaster laughed, again offered her his rum bottle. 'You can't just *go* to Rashid! We'll have to go with a *caravan*.' Rose drank again from the bottle in a kind of madness. 'Maybe early tomorrow. Even travelling to Rashid, which is only a day away, there are Bedouins, thieves, criminals. And there's *firmans* to be obtained – that's the permission to travel. I'll see what I can arrange.'

Rose's donkey pulled at the rope she was holding, gave a loud bray; she saw its large yellow teeth. 'Is it like Alexandria, this Rashid?'

'It has become a more prosperous port than Alexandria, it is a pretty town, you will like it,' he answered her. 'There are more *franks*, more foreigners. Women don't wear the veil all the time – as long as they keep their heads covered and stay out of the back alleys. It's dangerous and wild, but you'll like it better than Alexandria.'

Mrs Alabaster's donkey had come level with them. 'And you will be able to see the place where the stone came from.'

'The stone?' Rose looked back.

'Rashid is another name – the Arab name – for Rosetta. The French or the Italians named the place *Rosette* after the beautiful roses they found there.'

Rose stumbled on her black robe, would have fallen if Miss Proud had not been beside her. '*Rosetta?*' she repeated in disbelief. '*Rosetta?*' She thought at once of her father, dreaming of the town of Rosetta, the place for which she had been named, saw him staring out the window of his study in Brook Street remembering, and she suddenly felt something like joy, as if she had received a sign. *I will find the child. Tomorrow I am going to Rosetta, where my father travelled, the place that gave me my name! And it is the place of the stone. I will find the child.*

'Oh I am so *glad!*' she said to Mr and Mrs Alabaster. And then she suddenly pulled herself up. 'But I must go back.'

'Where? What for?'

'To the kind woman in the church.' She began to pull her donkey round. 'I must pay her. I did not pay her.'

'You must *not* go back,' said Mr Alabaster. 'She asked us to leave!'

And as Rose looked uncertain, Mrs Alabaster said, as if for a moment she could feel Rose's heart: 'She saw you. She will know. That wasn't about money.'

The Alabasters went on up the sandy road. 'See you at the dinner,' they called, and they disappeared where the road turned, he leading his donkey, Mrs Alabaster still riding hers.

Miss Proud explained as they walked back to their *khan*, 'We have all – all the *franks* – been asked to eat with a British trader, a Mr Barber. He stands in apparently for the consul in such difficult times as these.'

'Oh.' Rose was hardly listening.

'I have two hundred guineas for you,' said Miss Proud in the square by the ostriches. 'From Fanny.'

'From *Fanny?*'

'She said you refused to take any of her father's money, that you felt you could be self-sufficient. But that I was to take the money for you.' She pretended not to notice the sudden tears in Rose's eyes. 'I am glad I did even though I could not have imagined myself giving it to you in Egypt! It seems this will be an expensive business.'

'I did have six hundred guineas myself when I left,' said Rose. 'It was as much as I could think of bringing. I still have nearly four hundred but one hundred and forty must now go to the Alabasters!'

'I still have one hundred, and we will manage,' said Miss Proud firmly. 'We will manage, with dear Fanny's help. Now you had better consider this dinner. All the *franks* will be there.'

Rose understood at once. 'George?'

'George probably. One of the traders took Mattie into the town again to buy food and she heard news about George and Dolly and William.'

'*And* more about Cornelius Brown!' said Mattie calmly.

'What did you hear about George?' Rose felt as if her head had so much information in it that it would burst.

'He's still in Alexandria,' said Mattie. 'He's been arranging to go up the Nile, I heard. Antiquities.'

'And Dolly?'

'I *saw* Dolly. I couldn't tell if she was pregnant, of course, she was all covered up. But it was her, she was going round the bazaars like a native! Taller than all the other women. Pale as the moon.'

'It is clear that you cannot avoid your brother-in-law in a place like this,' said Miss Proud. 'I think it is probably only luck that your paths have not crossed already. You have seen how it is – the Alabasters knew everything about the child, Mattie has seen Dolly in the town. I am sure that if the Viscount does not already know you are here, he will certainly know by the end of the afternoon. And Rose dear, I cannot imagine a group of foreigners at a dinner avoiding the subject of the child if they hear the name Fallon – there will be great *frissons* of delight and people only too happy to tell George everything, I expect, if it is anything like the other foreign communities I have known.' They walked up the side staircase of the *khan*. Miss Proud saw Rose's stricken face. 'Perhaps we should just keep our heads down and hope we leave for Rosetta in the morning.'

Rose was silent for a moment, brushed away flies. 'George Fallon does not own Egypt,' she said firmly at last, 'and is not going to make me hide myself in a *khan*. Of course I must see how Dolly is. And tomorrow I will have disappeared to Rosetta to find the child and George can have no way of knowing that!'

'And should the matter of the child somehow arise,' said Miss Proud, 'you can surely pretend no knowledge of it at all. How would you have heard? He knows, you said, of your intense interest in hieroglyphs – that can be the reason for your journey. We could arrive just slightly late so that Viscount Gawkroger will be there already, and will have to make the first move.'

'And I will collect gossip in the kitchen,' said Mattie, 'always the best place.'

Suddenly Rose laughed rather wildly. 'Pierre Montand warned us that most of the Englishmen here would be rogues of one kind or another. We shall adapt and become rogues ourselves!'

'You smell of rum, for a start,' said Mattie.

Allahu Akbar . . . the voices called . . . *la ilaha illa Allah! There is no god but God!*

Mr Barber's old Ottoman house was at the back of the *frank* area of the city. Thin carved grilles that seemed like old brown lace looked down on them from the top of a tall, almost elegant, building. 'That is where the women live,' said Mrs Alabaster, who had come to escort them in Arab dress, pointing upwards with her many scarves. 'They can see you, but you cannot see them. Mrs Barber, the trader's wife, is not of course locked away, but you will find that most Egyptian families live this way still.'

'I wish,' said Miss Proud wistfully, 'that I could meet such women. How do they deal with this life?'

They were late, as planned. Rose, for all her bravado, dreaded seeing George, found she could not swallow properly, was outraged to find that she was shaking. *Surely I have had enough interviews with George over the last year to know that calm is the only weapon.* They walked up a staircase to a big open reception room:

cool, with white stone walls, this room in the centre of the house was open all the way up to the blue sky. Other rooms led off it. Excited English and French and Greek and Swedish and Italian voices roared, speaking of the political situation, the security situation, money: it was clear that much illegal alcohol was available. Rose had a moment of odd relief to see a roomful of people in European dress, except – she suddenly saw – one other. Mr Barber, the host, was speaking to George and Dolly and William: it was the almost comical look of total, unbelieving astonishment on George's face that made Mr Barber turn round, see Mr Alabaster. He welcomed him bluffly, bringing the two parties together.

'Good afternoon, George,' said Rose. 'Good afternoon, William. How good to see you, Dolly.' Dolly was dressed in the clothes of an Arab woman: many layers and shawls, but the shawl from her head had fallen back. She looked somehow stunning, and young, and taller than everybody, and as pale as death itself, and Rose felt her stomach lurch. *Dolly is ill.* Because of the way she was dressed it was impossible to tell whether she was expecting a child or not.

'You said nothing about travelling to Egypt at our last meeting,' said Dolly to Rose, but she spoke as if through glass and the pupils of her eyes were pinpoints of light. 'George has just been informed of a remnant of his brother!'

'*You knew!*' said George, totally discomposed at the sight of his sister-in-law. 'I have just heard – but *you must have known* or you would not be here!'

Mr Barber looked somewhat confused, Mrs Alabaster made introductions, William managed to look as uncomfortable as he always did in Rose's presence since she had burst into a room in the Hotel de l'Empire in Paris.

'Fallon?' said Mr Barber. 'Is the whole family here looking for the child?'

'What child?' said Rose, and there was a sudden silence interrupted by a summons to the table by Mr Barber's Italian wife.

Dolly said loudly, smiling brightly, 'Rose Fallon is the widow of Captain Harry Fallon, of whom you were telling us,' which made Mr Barber, a trader from Nottingham, look visibly embarrassed and try to start a movement to the dinner table in the adjoining room.

But George still stared at Rose. 'You *knew*,' he said, 'and you did not tell me.' And there was terrible danger in his eyes, and his voice was just a little too loud not to be heard by interested guests.

Rose did not answer; turned, although she felt herself trembling, to Mr Barber and praised the beauty of his house. In some relief Mr Barber showed his guests in to dinner, pointing out to Rose the grille where the women could still look down and observe what was happening, showed her the secret stairs in the wall for Mohammetan women to use if an unknown man came unexpectedly to the house.

'In days gone by?' said Rose.

Mr Barber looked surprised. 'No,' he said, 'now. Not *my* wife, of course!'

But as he was ushering Rose into the room with the food George took her arm. 'Allow me to escort my sister-in-law,' he said, smiling a terrible smile at Mr Barber. Thirty guests, eating and talking and drinking alcohol: the babble of noise swelled by the minute. George pushed Rose away from the crowd, out again to the other side of the roofless room and into a smaller room leading off. They seemed to be in a bedroom: silk shawls draped over *divans,* glittering mirrors, some beautiful yellow beaded slippers.

'You *knew*,' said George, and in the small room of other people's lives he actually hit her across the face. She looked at him in amazement, her hand up to her cheek. *George never lost control.* He would never make a public spectacle of himself, never. Had hearing that there was still a part of his beloved brother left in the world after all touched his cold heart?

'You *fool*!' he shouted. 'You stupid, sentimental, dangerous *fool*! Did you think you could keep this from me? Were you thinking of finding this child and bringing it to London, shaming our family, even claiming the title perhaps?' Her hand was still at her cheek in shock: George shouting all these ridiculous things so that others could hear? 'You cannot imagine I am going to let you bring some snivelling black Egyptian brat to London to dishonour my brother's memory, put paid to everything I have worked for all my life! We will not have bastard children sullying us! These thieves and vagabonds here are of no matter, what happens here does not matter, but what happens to the memory of my brother and the honour of our family in England *means more to me than life!'*

'What are you talking about?' At last she could speak. 'I have no idea what you are talking about.' Such was his disarray that George might have hit her again, but Mr Barber and Mr Alabaster arrived in the room, pulled Rose away.

'No, Mr Viscount,' said Mr Alabaster insouciantly – and Rose saw that he was already very drunk – 'we may be vagabonds but we have our standards and we don't hit women,' and Rose just had time to see murder in George's eye before she was half dragged back to the dining room. (Mr Alabaster might not hit women, but he certainly pulled at them rather roughly.) She thanked him, however, raised her eyebrows to Miss Proud to signal she was all right, manoeuvred herself at once to sit beside Dolly; a few moments later she saw that Mr Barber seemed to have calmed George and they both rejoined the party. Underneath all the talking and shouting and drinking an air of heightened excitement now hovered around the table as guests observed the disarray of the Fallon family members, expected revelations and drama. Yet somehow the dinner went on. Next to the pale form of Dolly, a Dutch trader drank rapidly; he was already almost insensible, made grunting noises.

'How are you, Dolly?' Rose said at last. 'You look marvellous in those clothes, they suit you.'

'Did he hit you? We heard him hit you! Well! He is usually so controlled, as I am sure you know. He got a most terrible shock to see you just as he was being told about Harry's child!' and Dolly giggled. 'Here, have some wine!' Rose drank quickly, choked, drank more. Then she spoke softly under the loud conversations.

'You are ill, Dolly. What has happened? What is the matter?'

Dolly looked down. 'Do not speak of it. George still does not know. He would send me home of course. I try every day to lose it.' George Fallon looked across, saw his wife and his sister-in-law, heads together. 'I have taken something from a woman in the bazaar this very morning. I feel – I think,' and for a moment she looked puzzled, 'as if something is happening inside me.' Rose looked horrified, stared back across the table at George and William. *How can they not notice how ill she is?* 'They almost ignore

me now, ' said Dolly, as if in answer to Rose's thoughts, 'even dearest William. I sleep alone. But,' and her young voice, higher than
the others, seemed to pierce the air, 'I like it here.' Her manner was
extremely odd, as if she was somehow floating. 'I love the smell –
of the perfumes and the spices in the bazaars – and all the wild
noise and the music – and that call, that Arab calling sound, it
makes me feel – magical,' and the word *magical* could not have
been more at odds with how Dolly looked, so disjointed, so ill. 'I
want to travel down the Nile.' Dolly drank the Greek wine as if it
was water. 'When this,' she suddenly indicated her stomach in a
kind of rage, then at once held on to the table as if she was giddy, 'is
gone, I will dress not only as an Arab,' she again drank quickly just
like the trader beside her, 'but as a *man*. It will be the only way to
get around safely without,' she glanced across the table in disdain,
'*the English gentlemen.*'

'But they allowed you to come, after all, the English gentlemen?
I thought they would not.' Rose was amazed that she was making
coherent conversation, so strongly was she aware of George's presence at the other end of the big table.

'I would not allow them to come without me, that is all. I said I
would speak to the Duke of Hawksfield, and they knew I would.
You know of course to what I refer?' and she gave a false, strange
little laugh. 'We cannot afford any more *scandale* since the Dowager
and *l'affaire de la Commission de l'Egypte*!'

Roast pigeons were passed up and down the table (Dolly thrust
them away in disgust, seemed to turn even paler) and many kinds
of cheese and olives and wine. Someone started singing an Italian
love song, other voices joined in recklessly. Dolly suddenly got up:
Rose stood to follow, Dolly waved her away, Rose sat again uncertainly. She saw George stand also; all around her noise and
laughter, and she saw that people stared and drank and laughed
and that George was coming towards her, pushing past the table
and the people. It was Mrs Alabaster who stopped George's trajectory: as he passed a wooden pillar she suddenly was there beside
him and in some odd way seemed to wind herself about the pillar
and about him with her arms and her Egyptian scarves. People
cheered at once, here was the entertainment! Everybody knew Mrs
Venetzia Alabaster, late of The Singing Acrobats; she would sing for

them, of course. It was extraordinary: suddenly her feet were no longer on the ground but somehow around the thin pillar, and George was caught in her arms and her flowing scarves. Everybody cheered again at this feat and Rose saw that George could not get away without struggling with Mrs Alabaster in public.

> *Wher'er you walk*
> *Cool gales shall fan the glade*
> *Trees where you sit*
> *Shall crowd into a shade . . .*

As she sang – her voice had that same sharp, mesmerising quality – Dolly slipped back to her seat beside Rose. She had two spots of colour in her cheeks now, and her eyes seemed suddenly to shine. The song finished, the room exploded into vociferous applause; George had no alternative but to sit again beside William, loosen his cravat; the conversation and the laughter rose once more.

'George will kill the child, if there is a child,' said Dolly.

'That is ridiculous!'

'I am not ridiculous,' said Dolly, laughing. 'George will do *anything* to avoid scandal so I hope you do not hold any hopes to have it yourself!' Her words were running together. She held out her glass for more Greek wine, the Dutchman filled it automatically, and his own, spilling wine on to the table. 'Are you going to marry Monsieur Montand?'

'No, Dolly, I am not going to marry him.' Rose looked again around the room, kept talking, anything. 'We were all of us lucky, were we not, not to be imprisoned in Paris when war was declared?' And then she lowered her voice again. 'I see that you are ill, Dolly. Let me take you home. Please, Dolly, you must let me help you somehow.'

'My husband has found a remnant of his brother!' said Dolly loudly to the Dutchman, ignoring Rose. 'This is infinitely more amusing than living in Berkeley Square.' The Dutchman grunted. Dolly suddenly turned back to Rose fiercely, yet her eyes were glazed. 'Did you know about William and George?'

Rose put out her hand to Dolly in despair. 'I wrote to you, Dolly,

I wanted to help. I am so sorry, I could not believe they would force you to marry before you were sixteen. I had thought you might come to live with me in South Molton Street.'

'My husband and' – her voice trembled – 'my brother.' And then she recovered herself and said, *'Answer me, Rose!'* and her voice was suddenly loud enough to be heard all over the room, and George heard her, turned quickly towards them again. Dolly saw that George watched her: at once, pale and disoriented, she nevertheless rose to the occasion. 'And who, after all,' her voice was derisory, 'would want to live in South Molton Street!'

'You are right, Dolly my dear,' George called, and his voice too was loud enough to silence most of the others. 'South Molton Street is certainly not a place for people like us!' And Rose saw he had control of himself again in this wild house in Alexandria where women had once run up secret staircases not to be looked upon, and where forbidden alcohol flowed like water, and Dolly's drugged eyes and the peculiar whiteness of her face. And Rose was suddenly certain: *something is terribly wrong with Dolly.*

'Why, Viscount Gawkroger!' Miss Proud's most sensible voice came across the table. 'You must not impugn the area where many of His Majesty's naval admirals reside when visiting London – even Lord Nelson for a short time I believe. It is a place with an honourable history: did you know Mr Handel composed some of his most beautiful music in Brook Street, just nearby? Perhaps that very song that we have just heard sung so delightfully. Withdraw the remark, sir!' And there was something so respectable and so indomitable and so English about Miss Proud, her white hair so neat under her white cap, the cameo brooch at the lace at her neck, this gentlewoman who had so bravely travelled to where they sat now, that Viscount Gawkroger could only bow in acquiescence.

'I withdraw, Miss Proud,' he said, at his most charming.

And in the moment of silence a young Frenchwoman who was looking for a husband among the foreign population of Alexandria and was dressed accordingly suddenly spoke loudly, drawing attention to herself as she had been hoping to do for some time. 'I hear all of you muttering behind your hands about a child. I would be *enchantée* to be included. *Cet enfant* – are we speaking of an

English child?' Rose saw people exchange glances, expectant, saw George Fallon look across at her: if eyes could kill, Rose would have died there, in that room. And suddenly – in a confused mixture of extraordinary feelings: of real hatred for her brother-in-law and, quite overpoweringly, of fear for Dolly – Rose stood and took a deep breath before George could speak again, and said loudly: 'An English child indeed! George, let me offer you my sincerest congratulations. You will be so glad to have an heir to the title. But I fear you are not taking the care of Dolly that her condition warrants.'

She heard Dolly's intake of breath beside her, and she saw George's face, saw him stand at the table, knocking his glass so that Greek wine ran on to the stone floor.

'Dolly?' he said.

Her pale face stared back.

William stood also; he at once moved to his sister.

'Dolly?' he said.

The two men stared at the girl, perhaps saw for the first time *how she was*.

'I – I think I am not very well, William,' said Lady Dolly, Viscountess Gawkroger, and she put a shaking white hand out to her brother, in a kind of entreaty.

In the night an Arab ran, his long *galabiyya* flapping round his legs, along the sand road of the *frank* quarter, pulled at the bell outside the *khan*. The Englishwomen were urgently called. They hurriedly dressed, pulled shawls about them. Mattie carried towels; Mrs Alabaster, running ahead of all of them from her own house, called orders in Arabic for hot water. Dolly lay on a *divan*, unconscious, on raised cushions, in a pool of blood. Miss Proud and Mattie worked with towels, Mrs Alabaster kept bringing hot water, Rose kept a cool cloth on Dolly's burning forehead, smoothed Dolly's damp hair from her face. Dolly did not move but they saw she breathed still. A drunken Greek doctor had been found in the Arab quarter: he drank coffee and gave orders to the women in bad English. A large cockroach came near, Rose angrily stamped on it, squashing it with her shoe.

'This is your fault!' shouted George at Rose, coming into the room, and Rose shouted back at once.

'No, George, this is not my fault! She took something from an Egyptian woman in a bazaar yesterday morning to try and get rid of the baby; there will be plenty of witnesses to such an unlikely purchase, I am sure. For God's sake, you must find an Arab doctor.'

'What do you mean? No filthy Arab is going near an Englishwoman!'

'Why should she need an Arab doctor?' William's face showed such strain and such concern that Rose wondered again how he could not have noticed the condition of his sister, who loved him so.

'Because she has taken Arab medicine! They hate us – she may have been poisoned for all we know. An Arab doctor might know what we should do. It seems to be our only chance.'

'No filthy Arab—' began George.

'I'll go,' said William, and they heard at once his feet pounding across to the gates of the house in the darkness, heard him calling for them to be opened, the anguish in his voice. Rose stood impotently beside the girl, still smoothing the hot face; she was enraged, distressed, and cold with knowledge. Mrs Alabaster kept calling for more towels, but there were none.

Dolly's eyes flickered open for a moment, saw Rose. Then understood.

'I am frightened,' she whispered, and Rose quickly took her hand. Dolly was trying so hard to say something else. 'Will I go to Hell?'

Rose bent towards Dolly at once. Strange words came to her: Fanny's words. 'I do not believe at all,' she said, 'that you will go to Hell. There is no Hell, Dolly, there is only a calm place, I am sure of it. A calm, peaceful place where you will be happy. God is not a cruel person. God is Love.'

She could feel Dolly's cold, sweating palm as she cried out suddenly to Rose in desolation, *'But I have done terrible things.'*

'No, Dolly. I think you are a very brave person.'

'Am I?' Her eyes flickered, she was going away, yet her eyes longed for something.

'Dolly dearest, you have always been brave, always.'

'Tell me again.' She looked about ten years old, and about a hundred years old, the girl who had a peacock for a friend.

'You are brave, Dolly. You were brave when you were young and tried to educate yourself in your father's study with nobody to guide you. And you were brave with your mama when she was ill and you talked to her. And you were brave in Paris.'

'In Paris?'

'Remember Napoleon?'

The tiniest flicker at Dolly's lips. 'I fainted.'

'And I was so proud of you.'

'Did he – Monsieur Buonaparte – know I was pretending?'

'Of course he did. Napoleon smiled!'

Again the tiniest flicker. Then the hand relaxed, the eyes closed, and then her whole body was overcome with a spasm of terrible pain, and Dolly screamed. The scream echoed out into the Egyptian night.

'Tell dear William . . .' said Dolly, panting, sweating, trying not to scream again – but she could get no further: she clutched at Rose and the scream came one final time. And then the large sad eyes closed and she whispered to the night, '. . . that I am – so sorry to have been a nuisance –' and it was clear she could hardly form words any more, '. . . and that I love him more than anybody in the world.'

The Greek doctor belched and shook his head; Mrs Alabaster, presuming he knew some Arabic, tried to tell him about the Arab medicine, but he looked at her, befuddled. George Fallon stood in the doorway to the room with the dangerous enraged look that Rose knew so well: his plans, his influence in the Torrence family now standing on a knife-edge, and somewhere else a child already born. At four o'clock in the morning, before the dawn cry from the mosques could tell them there was only one God, Dolly died.

When William returned, dishevelled and empty-handed – *not one of the damned foreigners spoke decent English, no one understood me, no one would come with me* – Arab servant women had already begun their alien cry of mourning in the darkness so that the English visitors felt as if they were living inside a nightmare and tried to block the ugly, un-English sound from their ears. The cry was taken up from other *khans* and houses along the road. The women stopped for a moment when George shouted at them, began again as soon as he left them; as dawn broke, the familiar cry *Allahu Akbar* echoed from outside the gates.

In the custom of the country the funeral took place almost at once, brief and cold in the heat. It had to be held in the *frank* quarter, with Mr Barber reading from the Bible, and with the outside gates locked: a rumour had flown that an Arab woman was blamed. Egyptians gathered ominously outside the locked gates, there was the sound of rhythmic banging and a continuing murmur of rage. William looked terrible but did not cry; if George cared that he had lost his wife and child he did not show it. Rose wept. She remembered the tall, ungainly fifteen-year-old standing on the ship to Calais, talking about her mother, asking wistfully about Paris fashions, inventing the Marquis d'X to make her journal interesting for her beloved brother; realised there was nobody in England to mourn Dolly at all. Her mother was dead, her father had never cared for her. The Duke of Hawksfield had seen her as property. Dolly would be quickly buried in a Christian cemetery in Alexandria, without further ceremony, when it was considered safe. Perhaps there were some servants in Berkeley Square who would mind. Perhaps they would look after her peacock.

And then, as Rose turned stiffly away, George came and stood beside her for a moment. He spoke so that only she could hear. She saw his eyes and believed him implicitly.

'Let us be quite clear. There will be no child of Harry,' said George Fallon.

TWENTY-THREE

Rose vomited and discharged into buckets, heard Miss Proud and Mattie doing the same further along the corridor of the *khan*. *George will kill the child, if there is a child*, Dolly had said so insouciantly. As she vomited again and again Dolly's white, dying face was inside her head, and then she saw George: casually killing a fawn simply by breaking its neck with his hands.

Mattie was as ill as the others; the three women had to take turns to empty the buckets when they were able, somehow disposing of their contents at the back of the *khan* where there were open ditches covered with flies, rats as big as cats running everywhere. It was as if they were in some kind of hell; at one moment Rose screamed and vomited at the same time. They received a message that every-one who had been at the fatal dinner party had become violently ill; a French doctor, finally prevailed upon to see if everybody in the *frank* quarter was dying, decreed that it was not a return of the plague but the roast pigeon, or possibly the water brought in to Alexandria, or possibly the Greek wine.

Mrs Venetzia Alabaster arrived at the *khan*, used to these attacks and better able to fight them off; she at once advised them that George, even as he vomited and discharged like everyone else, had come – as if nothing untoward had happened, as if his wife and baby were not dead in Alexandria – to try and persuade her husband to assist him in finding Harry's child. Mr Alabaster was unfortunately inebriated as well as ill, and had taunted the Viscount about a cross. Mrs Alabaster saw Rose's face, clicked her bones angrily. 'Archie is no match for someone like the Viscount, Rose. Especially if he is offered enough money. I am sorry – but that is Archie. I deal with the money when I can, I go to Italy to buy his alcohol, I watch him – but sometimes I lose him. I have brought you a local herb which can help, for you must get better quickly, and here, watch me, rub the inside of your water carrier with almonds, it will help to purify the water.' She pulled something from around her neck. 'I have extricated this for you at least,' and she handed the old Coptic cross to Rose. 'Archie had locked it away with his business papers, but you must have it. And we must try and leave for Rosetta at once. There is a *caravan* planned for dawn tomorrow if you can somehow make it – and I can watch Archie carefully till then. I only came because he is asleep and not abroad spouting your business; you can give me the money now. Do you think you can manage to travel tomorrow?'

'We *will* travel tomorrow,' said Rose firmly, even as she was sick again into a bucket, and in between vomiting she counted out the seventy guineas.

'I saw the brother this morning,' said Mrs Alabaster, 'all by himself along the quay, weeping like a child. I thought Englishmen didn't cry.'

'He left his caring too late,' said Rose bitterly. 'Dolly loved him more than anybody in the world – and he knew it. But he and his uncle sold her to George.'

'I thought that was an Arab custom,' said Mrs Alabaster.

Before dawn, down towards the harbour, traders and foreigners milled with Egyptians and Turks, shouting and bargaining; people from everywhere thronged the *caravanserai*, travellers for Rosetta, Cairo, Aswan. Arab guards were dubiously hired: two Frenchmen had been killed along this route only ten days ago: *Bedouins, Beys, murder*: rumours swirled about them in the darkness. There was the smell of sesame oil from the rags in the lamps that flickered and moved from group to group; sometimes a camel roared, a loud menacing growl from its long, long throat. The Egyptian herb seemed to have done its work: the Englishwomen stood palely in Arab dress, regarding the camels through the small gap in their veils. The camels lay in the sand; Rose wondered if she should pat the one she had decided to ride, as one might a dog, but strange eyes looked at her in the lamplight, unblinking and uncaring. Mattie, to everybody's amazement, had been on a camel when visiting a circus in Deptford with her husband: 'Don't do it, Miss Rose!' she said warningly. 'Ride a donkey! Even Cornelius Brown fell off!'

'Cornelius Brown?' said Mrs Alabaster. 'I know a Cornelius Brown. He is an English trader in Rosetta.'

'So I've been told in the market!' said Mattie triumphantly, and her eyes even sparkled in her pale face.

'Hold on tight, dammit!' shouted Mr Alabaster as Rose clung to the pommel of the carpet saddle and her camel slowly unwound its long spindly legs: she slipped and slid on the saddle and somehow stayed there. The *caravan* at last set off just as the first call came from the mosques, and of Viscount Gawkroger and William, Marquess of Allswater, there was no sign.

They travelled eastwards, at first past long piles of rubble and stone, then they turned towards the sea: if they travelled along the sand all day and no misfortune struck they could be in a safe *caravan* halt before nightfall. There, Mr Alabaster informed the women, they would pick up a small boat to take them on to Rosetta.

Insha' Allah! said one of the Arab guards, looking nervously back behind him, holding his gun in a most awkward and dangerous manner. *God Willing.*

The Mediterranean glistened in the sunshine. The forty or fifty travellers kept close together in a group, suspiciously watching the hills of sand in the distance. Rose had been given a kind of parasol but she felt very odd, and very hot, and finally ill again, swaying backwards and forwards indiscriminately on her camel as it picked its way stoically forward. *I am not going to ask for a donkey*. The landscape blurred before her eyes. *I am going to be sick*. She retched, up there on top of a camel, but there was nothing left to come out. She retched again as the sun beat down. She refused to allow herself to give up, not now: somehow she forced herself to sit up straighter. She could not believe that she would eat anything, ever again, but she was desperately thirsty; she opened her water carrier and drank gingerly, hoping the almonds had done their duty. She looked around: saw Mrs Alabaster and Miss Proud and Mattie trotting along on their small donkeys, all three of them determined and resolute with their black gowns and their parasols, their feet almost touching the sand. The sun beat down. The camel swayed. After a while she somehow found a way of letting her body fall into the camel's rhythm, and they swayed up and down together, and from side to side. As long as she sat up very straight she felt safe, and after a while she stopped feeling sick, and then she smiled to herself in a kind of grim triumph. For an odd moment she felt part of the landscape, riding a camel through the desert in a long black robe, a wooden Coptic cross around her neck. Sometimes they passed date palms. Some were full of ripe fruit, they could see the yellow and red dates in the high branches; some of the trees were wilder, their branches straggling down towards the dry, sandy ground.

When the sun was low in the sky somebody shouted and pointed: they looked across to a distant hill of sand. A lone Bedouin on a black horse was silhouetted against the violet dusk, watching the *caravan*. They could not help it, something caught at their throats. It was like a scene from a great painting. And then he was gone.

'It is only two years since the Battle of Aboukir between the French and the English, when Lord Abercrombie died,' one of the English traders warned the group as they came nearer. 'Aboukir is where we will camp and there are signs of battle still.' Rose stared, startled at that name. 'And of course Lord Nelson's famous Battle of the Nile was in Aboukir waters also, it was not actually on the Nile at all.' Rose shook her head in a kind of disbelief. She thought of Harry's medals, received for being victorious with Lord Nelson: she herself was now in Egypt, on the road where Harry had been.

They arrived at Aboukir, nothing more than a staging post it seemed, before it was dark. Rose's camel decided of its own accord to lie down and if Mr Alabaster hadn't shouted the warning 'Lean back!' Rose would have fallen head first into the sand. She got off very unsteadily. Fires were lit on the shore, tents were raised, food was prepared, buffalo milk was declined. Mr Alabaster pocketed a bottle of rum in a discreet manner and said he would see about a boat to Rosetta. Miss Proud and Rose gazed out to sea, walked gratefully along the sand as the sun went down across the water, relieved to be away from Alexandria.

'What unusual shells everywhere,' said Rose. She bent down to pick up the pretty white shapes buried in the sand, did not hear Miss Proud's warning.

'*Oh God!*' said Rose.

She stood up hurriedly. She was holding a small bleached bone: a finger bone perhaps. She dropped it quickly in the sand, and then as suddenly pulled herself together. She was in Aboukir where terrible battles had been fought. Harry had described the scene so often: the sinking boats on fire; the Mediterranean red with blood and echoing with the screams of men. Miss Proud bent down with her and they buried the finger bone deeper in the sand; saw then in the dusk that there were bleached bones everywhere, bigger bones, part of a skull: bones of Englishmen, they understood, and Frenchmen, and probably Arabs and Turks as well. Rose closed her eyes for a moment, uttered some sort of prayer for the resting of souls even though this place seemed so God-forsaken; just then, as if to mock her, the voice of the *muezzin* came across the sand . . . *Allahu Akbar* . . . the plaintive cry drifting with the sound of the sea.

Back at their camp Arabs had appeared from nowhere and were arguing with the *franks* about camels and donkeys and boats and water and most of all money. Mr Alabaster emerged from the mêlée, smelling strongly of rum: their boat would leave when the moon was properly risen to get them outside the dangerous Rosetta bar in the early morning.

'At the bar water pours in from the ocean and out from the Nile,' said Mrs Alabaster. 'And where the two lots of water meet, whirlpools suddenly appear, and huge waves. We have to have a pilot, to avoid the worst of them.' She saw the anxious faces but did not elaborate.

Waiting for the boat at Aboukir, where her husband had fought with Lord Nelson and become a hero, Rose lay on cushions covered by a net and looked at the shining bright stars in the clear dark sky. Of course the ancient Egyptians would have been astronomers, as Miss Proud had observed, with stars such as these in their eyes. Arab music drifted across the sand from somewhere outside the *caravanserai*. Scorpions burrowed very near but Rose did not know. She felt as if she was in a haunted place; as she heard the sea it was as if the ghosts of thousands of soldiers sighed, to have died here, so far from home, and the music so strange.

But not Harry's ghost, for Harry had died among the ruins and the rubbish of Alexandria. Like Dolly. Poor, doomed Dolly. And Rose felt tears fall lightly from the corners of her eyes past her ears, and perhaps some fell on to the white and shadowed sands of Aboukir.

Lit by the moon they made good time along the coast in their sailboat; waited just outside the Rosetta bar for the first light. The wind came up. A muffled roar could be heard where the fresh water and the salt water battled for supremacy. Rose, bobbing up and down in the boat, kept seeing in her mind the faces of George and William, grim at the hurried funeral: How much did George know? Was he following them, had he gone before them? The pilot called to them as the day dawned and there was much Arabic shouting and gesticulation; suddenly they were off. The boat approached the bar; the roar of water got louder, the sailors prepared to take a run. Everybody held on tight to whatever they could find; the sailboat was gathered up, whirled about, huge waves threw themselves at the small vessel; skilled Arabs with oars seemed to attack the waves as they flew downwards, the boat moved to one side of the bar and then the other. And then, just as suddenly, they exploded out of the battling forces into the calm, welcoming waters of the river Nile, where old wrecks lay on their sides at the river's edge.

Rose, drenched, thought she had never been so frightened, and so excited, in her life; looked anxiously for Mattie, who was lying prone with her eyes closed, and Miss Proud, who sat quite upright, completely soaked also, looking about her with interest. Rose put her hands in the Nile, cupped some water and drank it – they might have just left the sea, but there was no salt at all in the water, it tasted fresh and clean. They sailed calmly on, past small settlements. Soon they passed a battered group of buildings on their right and Mrs Alabaster called to Rose, 'That is the fort of Rashid, where those Frenchmen found the stone!' and Rose felt her heart literally leap in another kind of excitement: stared up at the deserted, squat tower where the Rosetta Stone had lain unnoticed for hundreds and hundreds of years, stared at the crumbling walls where green grass sprouted.

And then, just a little further down the river the town of Rosetta came into view, and just at the same moment the familiar warning cry echoed across to the visitors: . . . *la ilaha illa Allah . . . There is no god but God.*

Rose could hardly believe her eyes. Elegant white buildings. Houses with gardens growing on flat roofs. Beautiful old houses along the quay. Vines growing on trellises, fields of grain, hens running down the street, the inevitable donkeys, minarets shining in the sunshine. But most of all lots of green trees and bright flowers, bowers of roses of different colours, roses everywhere. Other beautiful, exotic, unknown flowers bloomed; fruit was growing: lemons and oranges, pomegranates and limes and bananas.

'It looks so different from Alexandria because it is not so old,' said Mrs Alabaster, seeing Rose's face. 'The river Nile still ran over the land here when Alexander was building his city. And there were no ruins so they had to bring in old stone along the river for their forts and their mosques.' *And Rose saw long flat barges weighed down by huge, damaged obelisks and statues and pieces of palaces, and somewhere, lying among the discarded gods, the broken Rosetta Stone that she had smoothed with her own hand.* She shivered in the heat. She thought of her father, smoking his exotic tobacco in Brook Street and dreaming of *here,* of this very place, and naming his daughter. She looked for men grinding coffee on the shore, and a small boy, and an old Arab man singing.

Along the shore the masts of hundreds of other boats stood up like trees in forests, and they heard a cacophony of voices and languages and bargaining and business amid the masts: trade. The women on the boat in their black robes had removed their veils out on the Mediterranean Sea; the women on the shore – were they foreign women? – were wearing no head coverings at all. One of them,

Rose saw, was *smoking*. Were they to be free then, in Rosetta? She felt a weight lift from her.

But then they heard the sound of horses, saw the tobacco at once thrown away, saw the women on the shore hurriedly cover their heads; the women on the boat quickly attached their own veils. A troop of turbaned men approached a jetty, drew up, shouted.

'It is the Mameluks,' muttered Mr Alabaster anxiously. 'But the Mameluks need traders too, after all.' He held his *firman* from the Governor of Alexandria and, washing out his mouth with river water, stepped across other boat decks to get ashore. He gave the *firman* to the man who seemed to be in charge, greeting him in Arabic: a long conversation ensued, horse's bridles shook and rang small bells. From the sailboat anxious faces stared upwards at the stern expressions of the men in the huge bright turbans with shining scimitars at their hips: were they to be allowed to enter this paradise? Softly from the shore came the scent of limes.

By midday they were ashore; Rose easily rented a house that had a long garden and Mr Alabaster immediately went enquiring after the St Mark's Church of Rosetta. He did not return. Mrs Alabaster clicked her bones and went to look for him; by late afternoon Rose and Miss Proud and Mattie were confident enough – heads covered but without veils, without a man to accompany them – to walk along the bank of the Nile and into the noisy, crowded town to perhaps find him. It seemed to them that *franks,* especially foreign women, moved about unmolested, uncovered, along the quay and in the wide, elegant streets: there appeared to be people here from every country on the globe. It seemed friendly, safe. Rose looked into the face of every child she passed. There was no sign of Mr Alabaster with news. There was no sign of George: they would surely have seen him easily in this place. The women walked past the strange signs in the unreadable, flowing Arabic writing: Rose felt the stirrings of old thoughts in her head, of the different marks that made different languages that had puzzled her so long ago. They even saw an English word on an ornate old building: BATHS, where steam wafted up into the sky from windows in the roof and men loitered outside, laughing together.

And then Mattie saw her husband.

'There he is,' she said quite calmly. 'I knew I'd find him.'

But the person Mattie pointed out was not quite as Rose and Miss Proud had imagined Mr Cornelius Brown. This man was (or, rather, seemed to be) an *Arab*. He hadn't seen Mattie, he was talking English to a man who sounded like a Frenchman: they were deep in conversation. But the Frenchman, who had the eye disease and looked ill, was talking to an *Arab*. For a moment Mattie stared at the Arab, brushing away mosquitoes from her face, oblivious. 'Look what he's wearing!' she said, not bothering to lower her voice. 'He must have become a Musselman!'

'Mattie!' Rose and Miss Proud stared in deep alarm. The man Mattie was sure was her husband wore a turban, and pyjama trousers (so it seemed to them), and a silk jerkin over a cotton open-necked garment like the top of a *galabiyya*. They stared and stared. He looked sunburnt and rugged and – they were somehow taken aback – handsome, and he was smiling cheerily at the Frenchman. 'What will you do?' Rose found she was whispering, but Mattie's face was quite calm.

'I've always told you what I'd do,' said Mattie, not bothering to whisper at all. She walked towards her husband, leaving Rose and Miss Proud speechless.

'Hello, Cornie,' said Mattie.

If men fainted, Cornelius Brown would have fainted. His mouth opened but no words came out. His French companion looked bemused. The last time Cornelius Brown had seen his wife Mattie Brown had been in another world, years ago, on Ludgate Hill, off Fleet Street. It was not possible for him to turn his mind round quickly enough to understand that he was seeing her in Rosetta wearing the black robe of Arab women. He thought she must be a ghost, but she had no such misapprehensions about him. Which was why it was so easy for Mattie to punch him in the face, twice.

'That's for walking out without saying,' she said, 'without even telling anyone of your plans. I was glad you went, you knew that, but you should've said, because your mum was that upset and thought you were dead. You're a coward, Cornie.' And then she walked back to her female companions and they, as if in a dream, allowed themselves to be swept along, to turn up further into the town. None of them mentioned at first this extraordinary incident, but at last Rose could not help it: she laughed. Mattie was smiling slightly and the corner of Miss Proud's mouth twitched. Above them they saw the sun, a huge gold disc in a dark violet sky, sinking behind the horizon.

'Well,' said Mattie. 'Just look at that!' She stared in amazement at the setting sun. 'And imagine me finding Cornelius Brown in such a place after all these years! Just as I said I would,' she added with great satisfaction.

'Shall you see him again?'

'I didn't come here to see him again,' said Mattie calmly. 'I always told you, he behaved very badly to his mum. I came here to punch him. I always do what I say.' Rose and Miss Proud exchanged bemused glances. And the sun began to disappear behind them. They walked further into the centre of the town.

But Mrs Alabaster had warned them not to go into the *bazaar*, the back streets and the fetid alleys of this town; even as they stared down narrow openings the stench was again unbearable; there were the mysterious doorways: perfumes, jewels, filth, spices, medicines, and they thought of Dolly and the *bazaars* of Alexandria and were silent. As dusk fell the forbidden alleys where they glanced nervously were crowded with Egyptians buying and selling: there women walked completely covered, and men in turbans and long *galabiyyas*, no foreigners. But there – as they walked carefully by, only looking, pulling their shawls up about their faces – there, just near the entrance of the forbidden place, Rose's eye was suddenly caught by something. She gasped suddenly and her mind whirled, even as she looked about her nervously.

'*Of course!*'

Hurriedly she covered her face, motioning to the others to do the same, still looking around. No one paid them any attention at all: there seemed no danger. Then they heard a whispering, ticking, swishing sound, and an Arab suddenly appeared from behind a beaded curtain; he smiled and beckoned. *Come . . . come,* he called out in English. *I make tea. You want to buy?* There seemed no danger. Rose moved towards the exotic dark doorway quickly: they could smell cinnamon and orange.

'Look!' said Rose again, and she pointed.

It was a small, exquisite blue cross of lapis lazuli, the same bright blue stone that Pierre had had on his desk in Paris. And in the centre a smaller cross still was set in jewels. It was so beautiful that all three women put out white fingers from under the black robes: felt it, smoothed it. He saw their eyes.

'You want to buy?' he said again.

'How much?' said Rose. The others looked astounded.

'Is beautiful. From Pharaohs' tombs. We discuss. Drink tea.' He held the curtain open, the beads rattled, they saw darkness beyond.

'How much?' said Rose again sharply. Miss Proud could not imagine what she was doing, in the forbidden bazaar, looking at something so obviously valuable and expensive.

'Why are you doing this?' she asked, and they saw Rose's impatient face.

'George knows there is a cross!' she said. 'If it is valuable, he will forget it was ever supposed to be a Coptic cross!'

Mattie at once understood and took over. 'How much?' she said, in Arabic.

'Fifty guineas.'

Rose was so surprised, so alarmed, that for a moment her shawl fell as she stared at the man. Mattie seized her arm at once and pulled her further into the *bazaar*. 'Say nothing. Come quickly.'

The Arab saw them leaving. 'Forty guineas,' he said. 'We drink tea.'

Over her shoulder Mattie called, 'Five!'

Outraged Arabic curses followed them, and also 'Thirty,' in English. The alley became darker, they saw men begin to light their lamps.

Mattie suddenly looked around, realised they had come the wrong way. 'Can we afford fifteen guineas?' she whispered. 'It is much, much too much but I think we should get it quickly and get out of the *bazaar*.'

Rose scrabbled at her money inside her robe. At once she felt other Arab eyes staring, heard a murmuring, she thought, in the crowd. 'Quickly,' she said, glancing about her.

Mattie negotiated. The money was handed over: the cross was given to Miss Proud, it shone bright blue, jewels sparkling in her old hand as they turned away. The murmuring in the crowd grew louder; suddenly they felt people shoving, pushing, peering forward, but it was not the foreign women just then that had caught their attention. Down that narrow dark alley where they were lighting the lamps two Arabs dragged a screaming, dirty Arab woman; her skirt became caught, her bare legs dragged behind her, her feet had begun to bleed. Nobody stopped them. The woman cried out in desperation to the crowd, they saw her uncovered, terrified face, but the crowd were spectators merely: they watched in silence. Almost, the English women could have touched her as she was dragged past them. One of the Arab men called out something: the crowd then murmured angrily, moved forwards, someone threw a stone at the screaming woman.

'We must do something!' Miss Proud cried, in English: the crowd turned towards her at once, she saw their faces. Rose and Mattie hurried her away, pushing her between black-robed women towards where they saw the lighter streets, but not before several stones had hit them; one caught Miss Proud on the head. They did not wait, they did not argue, they did not save the Arab woman: the feeling of violence in this paradise was unmistakable. Frightened and sickened the Englishwomen pulled their black robes completely over their faces, closed their ears to the woman's cries, and hastened back towards the harbour, towards their house, the scent of the roses. Back there in the dark alleys of the *bazaar* the figures of the unknown story, the Arab men dragging the woman, grew smaller in the distance; the woman's cries could at last hardly be heard, and people went about their business.

Miss Proud's face, back in the elegant house with the marble pillars, was as white as chalk: 'I should have intervened,' but there was blood on her old, fragile head and she knew they were powerless. Rose felt panic rising. They had turned away, just as Pierre Montand had had to do, impotent. *I must find the child and take her away from this dangerous place.* And then suddenly she cried, 'But where is the blue cross?' Miss Proud painfully opened her old, still shaking hand: the exquisite cross lay there still.

Rose put it around her neck. It lay there against her skin, next to the old wooden cross of the Copts, hidden under Egyptian gowns.

In the house only Arab servants moved, sulkily, stealthily, in the kitchen: no lamps had been lit, no Mr and Mrs Alabaster. Silence echoed at them. They suddenly felt their foreignness, their aloneness in an alien land. They shook themselves, as if they had been bewitched; Mattie lit oil-lamps, Rose found precious water, bathed Miss Proud's head, realised how the bones of her old skull were so near the surface, so vulnerable; felt again panic. Anything could happen here, only the Alabasters stood between them and chaos. *I must find the child quickly.* The door banged open and one of their guardian angels staggered in and fell against the door.

'Where's my Vennie?'

'We don't know. We were all out looking for you.'

Mr Alabaster made his way windingly to a *divan*, fell across it, did not look at the ladies as he spoke to them. 'There's a St Mark's church here,' he said. 'Down behind the Turkish Baths. It's all locked up and dark now, I banged and banged on the gate but nobody came. Except a passing Copt told me there is a service there tomorrow afternoon.' He seemed even more inebriated than usual, if such a thing were possible. Rose closed her eyes in impatience.

From the streets they heard the *muezzin* and the door banged again as Mrs Alabaster came in carrying pomegranates and bananas and long white flowers.

'There you are, Archie,' she said at once, relieved. 'Where have you been all this time?' but Mr Alabaster seemed to be asleep.

They told her of being attacked in the *bazaar* and she clicked her bones angrily at the danger they had been in, looked carefully at the cut on Miss Proud's head, insisted on giving her one of her herbs. 'Why ever would you go there when you know it is so dangerous?' But they looked across at Mr Alabaster sprawled on the *divan*, said nothing. Mrs Alabaster began very gently stroking Miss Proud's head and shoulders.

'Oh!' Miss Proud was surprised to be touched. 'Thank you,' and colour slowly returned to her face.

'There is an Arabic word: *mass*,' said Mrs Alabaster. 'It means to touch delicately. And so the English word: *massage*.' Gently her hands went backwards and forwards and Miss Proud closed her eyes. And for a moment Rose remembered another life and how Pierre had held her hand across the table so gently and asked her to marry him. She too closed her eyes.

They told Mrs Alabaster of finding Mattie's husband.

'So it is the same Cornelius Brown!' she said, astonished. 'He's your husband?' She opened her mouth to say something else and then stopped, her hands still gently stroking Miss Proud's shoulders. 'We know him, of course we know him. He's one of the English merchants here. We all know one another!' She looked at Mattie, amazed. 'And you just appeared from his past and went up and hit him, by the river Nile in Egypt? He must have been very surprised!'

The bell rang outside the door.

'*It's George!*' whispered Rose at once.

'It's Cornie Brown,' said Mr Alabaster, who turned out not to have been asleep after all, peering into the night. He opened the door. 'How are you, Cornie? Long time since I've seen you. Have a drink!' And then, almost as an afterthought: 'You've got a black eye, man!'

'That's right and all!' agreed Cornelius Brown. 'You've got my wife here, Archie, so I'm told.'

'Your wife? Your wife wouldn't come here without you, Cornie, it's against the custom, you know that. Have a drink! Actually I'm wanting to have a good talk with you about the state of things here. Lot of changes going on in Cairo, we hear. Have a drink.' A bottle of rum was in his hand.

'Now you know I don't drink these days, Archie! Rashid is settling, *insha' Allah*, but first I need to speak to my wife.' The women in the household were listening, fascinated.

'Perhaps you didn't hear, Archie,' said Mrs Alabaster. 'Mattie is Cornelius's wife, it seems, or,' and she looked apologetically at Mattie, 'one of them!'

'Mattie?' repeated Mr Alabaster. 'Our Mattie? You mean our Mattie is Cornie's wife? What about the other one?'

'Well!' said Mattie, coming forward herself. 'You've got another wife, Cornie?' And she began to laugh. 'Are you bringing her back to Ludgate Hill then? Your mum'll be surprised! Oh, look at your eye!' And Mattie stood, leaning against a marble pillar (for it was a very old and elegant house) and laughing. Rose and Miss Proud, when it was clear that Mattie was in no way distraught, stared at the sunburnt, handsome Englishman with a black eye dressed, it seemed, in pyjamas, and started laughing too. Cornelius Brown took it like an Englishman.

'Fair enough, fair enough, but I would like to talk to you, Mattie,' he said at last. 'I know I owes you an explanation, but you knew I couldn't come back once I jumped ship. And you owes me an explanation, turning up like this, enough to give a man a heart attack.'

'Like the one you gave your dad.'

'I hope that old bat is long gone to his grave!'

'Cornelius Brown, what a thing to say about your own father!'

'Me own father was a bully and a drunkard and well you know that, Mattie.'

'It's true,' nodded Mattie to the entranced audience.

'He's dead then?'

'He's dead, crying for you at the end.' This seemed to make no impression on him.

'I bet. And me mother?'

'She's still going strong, like she always did.'

'Good!' And Cornelius Brown's face managed a smile. 'Come on then, Mattie? Just a bit of a talk?'

And Rose nodded at Mattie. 'Go on!' she whispered.

'After all these years!' said Mattie, rolling her eyes; she automatically reached for her black robe, then stopped. 'Do I have to wear all this paraphernalia, even walking with my own husband?'

'Rashid has always been a more free-and-easy place,' said Cornie. 'But it's unsettled just now.' The women thought of the *bazaar*. Mattie, stolid in her black robe, disappeared out into the sandy street with Cornie in his pyjamas, for all the world an Arab couple, but from Ludgate Hill.

Mrs Alabaster started laughing again. 'He may have skipped the navy and become a Mohammetman and married an Arab woman,' she said, 'but Cornelius Brown is an Englishman right down to his toes. He *walks* like an Englishman. He's quite handsome now I come to think of it! She never wanted him back?'

'I really think she did not. But she felt he had behaved badly, she really very much wanted to give him a piece of her mind.'

'Well she certainly did that,' said Mrs Alabaster.

'However, I am sure,' said Rose, 'that he will never come back to England now, so Mattie is properly free of him at last.'

'Who knows?' said Mrs Alabaster. 'In my opinion the human

heart is so strange and so complicated that we hardly know ourselves,' and Rose heard her humming Handel as she went into the kitchen.

Mattie reappeared, her cheeks pink.

'Well, listen to this,' she said. 'He's invited us all to his house, to meet his other wife and' – Mattie herself looked bemused at her information – 'his five children!' *Allahu Akbar* . . . came the cry across the town.

'What? When?'

'Now. Tonight. He says it all must be explained. He's told his other wife.'

'Oh Mattie!' said Rose. 'Are you all right?'

'Do you want to go, Mattie?' asked Miss Proud sensibly. 'Do you mind about all this?'

Allahu Akbar . . . cried the voices.

'Mind?' said Mattie. 'Course I don't mind! Once I'd given him that punch I felt really satisfied.' She saw that they all looked at her. 'D'you think I've been pining all these years? I didn't want twenty children! I missed him, course I did, he was lively and we knew each other so well – that's why I always knew I would find him, eventually. I know Cornie, I knew he would have survived. But I saw my mother and his mother, always expecting another baby and another, and I made a vow not to be the same. And you were enough of a daughter, Miss Rose, in a way,' and she gave Rose a very old-fashioned look and then somehow they both began to laugh. 'And his horrible dad was enough to put anyone off!' Mrs Alabaster put a cup of tea down beside Mattie and Mattie looked up, surprised. 'Well – everything *is* in a muddle today,' she said, drinking the tea gratefully. And then added: 'And he's become quite rich it seems! Cornelius Brown! He's a merchant, he buys rice in Rosetta – Rashid he calls it. And he's become a Musselman because it made it easy to have two wives!' and she started to laugh again. 'What a very strange world. I knew I'd find him though.'

'I would feel *so privileged* to meet an Egyptian woman in her own house,' said Miss Proud longingly.

'Well then – tonight,' said Mattie. 'We can't begin to look for the child tonight, Miss Rose.' Rose nodded but moved away uneasily, looked out of the window, felt the two crosses against her skin.

'Unless, of course' – Mattie looked at Miss Proud – 'we have been travelling so long, and you were hurt – are you tired?'

'TIRED!' said Miss Proud, outraged. 'TIRED! I have the rest of my life to be tired, Mattie! I will put on my best gown if it is dry from its adventures at the Rosetta bar.'

So Mr Alabaster led his party of robed women in a small procession to Cornelius Brown's house. They were glad to understand it was nowhere near the *bazaar*. But the Rosetta night was alive and noisy: rows and rows of small shops lit with candles: fruit, vegetables, sailmakers, maize, tailors, bakers, money-changers; people of all nations milled about, shouting and laughing, *bonjour*, said the Arabs, *ciao, hello hello hello, you want to buy?* Everywhere Rose looked for George. Sheep and goats appeared round corners, disappeared down alleys, skittering in slimy rubbish. The women asked Mr Alabaster about the second wife of Cornelius Brown, were disappointed to know that he had never met her. They all saw her in their imaginations: young and beautiful with dark, mysterious eyes, and they pulled their robes about them, to hide failings. Away from the river there were tall old Ottoman houses such as they had visited that fatal day in Alexandria. Cornelius Brown lived in such a house: they saw the decorated grilles (did not know that unseen eyes looked down, voices whispered). They walked up stairs into a cool stone house with part of it open to the night sky; they saw the shining stars. In the main room there were servants but no Egyptian women.

'Where's your wife, Cornie?' said Mattie at once. 'We're all impatient, you better introduce us!' and there seemed to be a fluttering of birds' wings above them.

'You'll excuse us then, Archie, I'll get them to make you a pipe,' and Cornelius led the women up another floor. 'This is their way!' he said fiercely to Mattie, 'I don't want you making no fun of them,' and he called in Arabic to announce their presence, and then they passed through a curtain. Four women sat shyly on cushions in a room of carpets and hangings and silver; and although the room was lit with oil-lamps it was the scent of oranges and cinnamon that drifted in the air. The women wore wonderful flowing scarves but no veils; they were not young beautiful Arab women at all:

they were no longer young, certainly, and they were rather plump in the way that Mattie was plump.

'Are these *all* your wives, Cornie?' asked Mattie in amazement. Two olive-skinned young girls, daughters obviously: one aged four or five, one ten perhaps, had been playing with what looked like marbles as the Englishwomen entered; at once the smallest girl ran to the women, hiding behind them, pulling her mother's shawl across her face. The older girl stayed where she was, stared.

'I would leave youse,' said Cornelius, clearing his throat rather loudly, 'it would be the custom, and you'd love to have a good old converse about me I'll be bound, but I'll have to act as interpreter.' And he introduced his first wife, Mattie, to his second wife, Layla: in the religion he had embraced many years ago having two wives was quite acceptable so he gave no indication of feeling himself a bigamist, but his face looked rather hot. Rose quite unexpectedly felt her fingers itching in the way they had so many years ago, to write down what she was seeing. 'And these are Layla's sisters,' said Cornelius, and the other women smiled and bowed their heads.

'*Salamu 'aleikum,*' said Mrs Alabaster.

'*Aleikum as-salam,*' they answered

Mattie and Layla eyed each other, seemed almost immediately to take comfort in the fact that they looked, especially in their long robes, rather alike. Layla's robe was rich blue; she wore flowing blue trousers underneath, they saw, and the most exquisitely beautiful scarf that was as blue as the Egyptian sky. Shawls about her head were decorated with silver and she wore silver earrings and bangles which jangled sweetly as she moved. Mattie removed her black robe. Underneath she was wearing her very best dress, all the way from London on land and sea and the river Nile: high-waisted and low-cut and oddly enough blue also. She had ribbons wound round her hair and she wore a gold chain at her neck. The Arab women were spellbound. Cornie's expression was unreadable. For a moment everyone was silent. And then, talking to each other in seeming amazement, the Arab women got up and began feeling Mattie's dress, shyly stroking her white arm.

'I'll leave you for a bit,' said Cornelius at last, pulling at his shirt. 'Flo, come here.'

'*Flo?*' said Mattie, looking questioningly at Cornelius; then they saw the older of the two young girls step shyly towards her father. 'Oh,' said Mattie approvingly, 'he's named her after his sister, she will be glad. Pleased to meet you, Flo.'

'Flo speaks English, like her older brothers. She pestered and bamboozled me until I said yes – I said there was no need to learn English, her brothers need it for business, but she of course will not. But she wouldn't take no for an answer. And, devil's luck, she's better than any of them! Flo,' he said again, 'will you look after the ladies and translate for them?'

'*Aywa*, Papa,' said Flo. 'I will do the best.' And she sat on the floor in an odd way, one leg tucked underneath her. She looked at the guests shyly but also proudly, and waited. Her English was slow but clear, and the visitors heard that she had the Ludgate Hill sound to her voice, like Cornie and Mattie. Cornelius Brown pulled the curtain to, and went downstairs. He was sweating.

The hostesses saw at once that Miss Proud was the oldest, neat and upright in her best gown and her white cap, and they immediately made room for her on the cushions first, before the others, settled her comfortably. They stared at the Englishwomen's stylish clothes; the Englishwomen stared back at the beautiful silks and cottons. A servant girl brought mint tea. Mrs Alabaster made polite remarks in Arabic, the oil-lamps that smelt of oranges cast soft shadows. But it was clear Layla had something on her mind: she kept whispering to Flo, who kept shaking her head, staring at the floor. Tea was poured, gowns were observed and stroked, only Layla did not smile now that Cornelius was gone.

'I know your auntie,' said Mattie to Flo, 'she'll be that pleased that Cornie has remembered her.'

'Is she beautiful?'

'Well – in a way,' Mattie answered diplomatically. 'She's good for a laugh. Used to sing,' she muttered to her companions. 'Had lots of cheek.'

'What is *cheek*?' said Flo at once, and Mattie was discomposed.

'Well – energetic – like your father,' she said rather feebly.

'Where are your brothers, Flo?' asked Rose. Flo at once stood and beckoned Rose to follow her, but even as Rose stood Flo would not leave until Mattie followed also. As they left the women's room they could hear men's voices. Directly above the main room below there was a small passageway. Flo put her finger to her lips and gestured to Rose and Mattie to follow her. Delicate wooden handiwork decorated the open part of the wall with a lattice screen, and through the holes in the handiwork the women looked down, as mutely instructed by Flo. There was Mr Alabaster, smoking a strange, complicated pipe that seemed to lead down to a jar of water. Cornie sat opposite him, smoking like this also, and beside Cornie four young Arab boys, not quite men: were these Cornie's sons?

'They say Mohammed Ali takes charge in Cairo – we don't know what will happen here.' The men leaned forward: Rose felt uncomfortable, as if somehow she was spying.

Just as they were going back into the room of the women Flo put her hand very shyly on Rose's arm. 'The short boy is the son of my aunt. For my husband.'

'Oh – but you are very young. For marriage.'

'It is important to arrange husband for joy,' said Flo. She did not seem very joyous and Rose saw just how very young she was, thought of Dolly, closed her eyes in an unexpected flash of pain. But Flo was now patting Mattie's arm. These gestures each time were very tentative, but very urgent. 'Please,' she said softly to Mattie as they entered the women's room, 'my mother she is frighten. Speak kind to her.'

Mrs Alabaster was keeping up a half-Arabic conversation, and Miss Proud was laughing as the women wound colours about her: 'No, no! *Shokran*, thank you,' as Layla insisted that the beautiful blue scarf she had been wearing stay around Miss Proud's shoulders, that it was now hers. Mattie spoke quietly to Mrs Alabaster. Mrs Alabaster spoke directly to Layla in Arabic, slowly and clearly. The Arab women were suddenly silent, there was a little chattering and fluttering and then they all turned to Layla, who suddenly poured out a torrent of Arabic that seemed as if it might not stop.

Mrs Alabaster turned to Flo. 'Can you help me, dear?' she said. 'My language is not good enough.'

Reluctantly Flo turned again to her mother, spoke in Arabic. Layla nodded her head, over and over again, and her sisters also.

Mrs Alabaster said quietly, 'I think she is afraid you will take him away, Mattie.'

'Take Cornelius Brown back to London in his pyjamas? Is she insane?'

Flo turned to Mattie and took a big breath, and Rose suddenly saw that the girl's hands were shaking. 'My mother,' Flo said, 'asks me to speak that she begs you not to take Papa away, for he is' – she struggled for the words – 'her lifetime and all of our lifetimes,' and there was something touching about the dark girl and her London accent far, far away from London. 'She thinks it is devil's luck that you have come.' She spoke very politely and very shyly so that 'devil's luck' had a gravity about it. 'She knows you are very angry because she has seen his face when he had meeted you.' Flo suddenly ran out of words, turned quickly to her mother, spread her shaking hands, and all the women understood that Flo was frightened too.

'Heavens!' said Mattie at once. 'This is ridiculous! You poor girl. And your poor mother. I don't know what Cornie has been saying to you about me, but of course I am not going to take him away! Of course I'm not! Flo!' Flo looked at Mattie. Mattie spoke very clearly, and very slowly. 'Flo, tell your mother that I have no intention of taking Cornie anywhere. And what is more, I am very glad to see that she has kindly given him many children. Which I would never have done!' and Flo translated and Layla's face, unbelieving at first, was at last wreathed in smiles; all of them smiled, all the Arab women, smiling and smiling at the English ladies who had suddenly appeared in their midst in their strange and beautiful clothes, but who would not, after all, take away Cornelius Brown.

Rose lay awake in the town of Rosetta, the town her father had named her for, writing. She had been awake for so long since they left Alexandria with the *caravan* that she could not sleep. Outside her net mosquitoes and flies buzzed around her head, like her thoughts. So many other things happening: Dolly dead, everyone so ill, George threatening the child, the journey to Rosetta, the crosses she was wearing, the family of Cornelius Brown. But she had come to Egypt to find a family of her own. *A young Arab girl,* she wrote, *will have to learn to be an Arab woman. She will be locked away like Flo and Layla and her sisters. If I can find her and take her away then by the time she has grown up all Englishwomen will be free to be educated, to have a profession, to travel the world, I would make sure she learned absolutely everything, I would be good for her.* And a sudden swift pang of loneliness caught at her. *I would love her so much. I would love her with all my heart.*

She closed the journal, lit one of her small cigars.

She thought of Cornelius Brown. Had he ever thought of Mattie in all those years? *Does he sometimes think of England?* But if she took a young child away from Egypt now, it would remember nothing. Smoke drifted. *Of course she will be better off in England, I will bring her up as an Englishwoman.* At last she lay down on the *divan*, tried to sleep, kept trying to sleep, *I must sleep*, kept thinking of the child, fell asleep for a moment then was strongly awake again, panicking: *where is George?* She tossed and turned in the heat: *there will be no child of Harry*, George had said. *Where is he?* She shook her head over and over, as if a sound was buzzing there and she must get rid of it, and then she knew she could not wait one moment longer. Quickly she put on her gown, attached the white veil and the small turban, put the black robe over everything, and left the house on foot, completely covered now like one of the women in the narrow alleys of the bazaar.

The streets were still full of Arabs and foreigners, the stalls seemed to be closed now but sounds of laughter brayed out, and music, under the bright stars of Rosetta. High flutes and nasal voices made their strange song. Mr Alabaster had said the church was near the Turkish Baths. No one seemed to take any notice of her. She kept to the side of the main streets and did not look up, hurried like a dark shadow through the handsome roadways, past white buildings, heading for the one English sign she had seen: BATHS; looking all the time for some sign of a Christian church; found, behind the baths, a white cross on an old broken-down building. The gate to the Coptic churchyard was locked. She waited for a moment, looking about her uneasily, and then, holding her gown and cloak and shawl about her, quickly climbed over the gate and into the yard.

The church was in darkness but light shone from a narrow path opposite and she followed the light, telling herself firmly she was in a Christian place now: she was surely safe. She crossed broken stones, then went through an archway and down the narrow path; things scuffled: people? animals? she could not tell. She smelt the sesame oil of lamps, and food, and spices and filth. *She saw the screaming Arab woman with her feet bleeding being dragged down the dim and dangerous alley.* A man – a priest? – was relieving himself against a wall. Rose waited and when he was finished took a deep breath and spoke loudly. *'Salamu 'aleikum,'* she said. He nearly jumped out of his skin. But he had heard her voice. He looked at her carefully, understood that she was a foreigner, and it seemed to Rose that he sighed.

'Français?' he said. *'Italiano?'*

'English,' said Rose. 'Do you speak English?'

'A little,' he said.

'Oh I am so glad,' said Rose. 'I need your help.'

'Of course,' he said, and she supposed that if she climbed over a gate in the middle of the night she must indeed need help. 'A child?' he asked.

Rose was stunned. How did he know? Had he heard of her search? Did everyone in Egypt know of Harry's child? *Where is George?* She simply nodded.

'Come back tomorrow,' he said gruffly, and turned away and would have disappeared inside the doorway.

'No, no! Wait!' Her loud cries echoed about the narrow, acrid pathway; the priest turned back irritably. She tried to take one cross, the wooden cross, from around her neck, it got caught up with her white veil, like two religions fighting with each other. Finally, dishevelled, she got the veil off, and then the Coptic cross, and held it out to the priest. His face changed, he looked at her again, more carefully.

'You are boat girl?'

'What is "boat girl"?'

'Why are you here, the Church of St Mark?'

'As I said, I am searching for a child.'

'You are *searching* for child?' Rose nodded, and he asked her again, 'You are *searching* for child that is living?'

'Yes,' she said. 'A child who is half Egyptian and half English. I am looking for the child of the English captain.' He seemed to study her face, her manner.

'This?' said the priest, holding up the wooden cross. She told him. He seemed to be making up his mind about something. 'Come,' he said finally. He still held the wooden cross in his hand.

They went through the doorway and down a dark passage *I am not frightened I am not frightened* and she was led to a small room. Several men sat around a table. An old man was sitting cross-legged among some cushions on the floor; he was smoking the kind of Arab water-pipe that she had seen Mr Alabaster smoking. They interrupted their conversation in some surprise as Rose followed the priest into the room: Rose's heart beat like a loud drum; she told herself firmly that they were Copts not Mohammetmen, they would not stone her. The priest from the church held out the wooden cross for the men to see.

'*Salamu 'aleikum,*' she said carefully.

The priest spoke rapidly in Arabic. The old man on the floor drew in the sweet-smelling tobacco from the water-pipe, blew it out through half-closed eyes, looked at Rose. It soon became clear that although he could not speak English, the conversation would be with him. The priest acted as translator.

'What child is this?' the old man asked.

'A child that was born to an Egyptian woman after the British troops left here – the father was a captain in the English navy and was killed in the streets of Alexandria. I believe the woman was stoned to death, by her own people. I believe you have the child here.' And she looked around the dark, dingy room expecting a child to suddenly appear and she felt as if her heart would burst.

'What do you want with the child?'

She took a deep breath. 'She is my husband's child. My husband is dead, as you know.'

Dark eyes regarded her. 'You know the story?'

'I do.'

'You still want to see the child?'

'I do.'

'What will you do with the child?'

'Whatever is best, for the child. Is it *here*?' She tried to keep the sound of hysteria from her voice; her heart was beating so painfully she could not. 'I believe the child is in danger! *Is it here?*'

He did not answer the question directly. 'Are you Christian?'

She knew this must be some kind of test, thought of the Reverend Horatio Harbottom and hoped God would not strike her down. 'I am English. In England we are Christians, and my cousin is a vicar of good renown.'

'Do you think you are the same?'

'I beg your pardon?' It did not make sense, she had not understood, she was dizzy with lack of sleep but she must pass the test.

'This is the place in the world where Christianity began. And the Mohammetan faith. And the Jewish faith. You know Moses?'

'Of course.' Her eyes had become quite wild. *Where is the child have they got the child here am I near at last to the child?*

'It was here in Egypt that his basket was found in the bulrushes. By the Nile. In our country there is a Jewish synagogue where Moses was found, and a Christian church nearby. And a mosque beside. Once we were entwined, now we are enemies. We all live in the land of our forefathers and our religion, our history, lives here, with us. Do you think you are the same?'

She still wasn't sure what he meant. 'The same as you?' She could not imagine what he wanted her to say. 'I think, in England, we are – more removed from our religion.' She used her hands: *apart, separate.* 'Here in Egypt it seems as if – as if you all – inhabit it.' She placed her hands together. She had no idea what the translating priest would make of that but the old man nodded as if the answer satisfied him. The other men were listening to this exchange of views with interest.

Suddenly she knelt down to the old man who sat cross-legged on the floor. 'Please tell me if the child is here! She is not safe!' She held his arms, she could not help it. 'I must take her away at once!'

He regarded her hysterical manner with interest and emitted what Rose took to be some Arabic curse so that she leaned away from him at once and his terrible breath. But he repeated it and she saw that it was a kind of cackle. 'You do need not to shout, God will answer, if He wishes!' and now all the men, passing the water-pipe amongst them, laughed too and Rose bowed her head seemingly submissively, waiting tensely. 'But you have been given Coptic cross by one of us, and we do not expect them to be in hands of *franks*. If one of us gave it to you, this is sign to us that you are to be believed and trusted.' Rose thought of the woman, sweeping and listening. She stayed there, on her knees.

'This has all become mountain,' said the old man. Rose looked at the translating priest: *mountain?* but he only shrugged. 'It is only girl, and half-English. She would be dead. We only hide her because English merchant in Alexandria who had money. But they tried to kill him – some Turk did – and he had to run away – there is no money now. If you have money you can easily buy her from monks. She is in monastery with monks.' The old man was quite matter-of-fact and the water-pipe went round and round as they watched her carefully.

We cannot know one another, thought Rose. *Who knows if they are telling the truth? Yet they are the only people in the whole world who can help me. And so I must trust them.* It was only then, as he stretched towards the water-pipe, that Rose saw that the old man was not sitting cross-legged among cushions: he had no legs. She looked away, quickly.

'Where is the monastery?'

The old man looked at her slyly and answered her himself. 'I,' he said in English, pointing at his chest. 'I!'

It was early morning when she arrived back at the house.

Inside the house everybody was up, everybody was talking, except Mr Alabaster, who snored slightly with his mouth open on the *divan*. 'There you are,' said Miss Proud in relief. 'Where have you been? Did you go for an early morning walk? You have missed the deputation.'

She froze. 'George?'

'No, Cornelius and Layla and the sons.'

'What is it? What is it, Mattie?' for Mattie's cheeks were red.

Mattie went very quickly into the kitchen to the Arab servants. 'You tell them, Mrs Alabaster, if you would,' she said over her shoulder. 'I need to watch these people or who knows what you'll be eating for breakfast, them thin cats probably!'

Mrs Alabaster clicked her bones in that way she had and

entwined herself into one of the marble pillars with her long scarf. 'Well, I don't know what you'll make of this, Rose,' she said. 'Mattie got a visit from the house of Cornelius Brown very early this morning. Cornelius and Layla, and the sisters and the sons, and Flo and Flo's betrothed – everyone!' and Mrs Alabaster laughed. 'Listen!' she said as if Rose was not listening most intently. 'Cornie and Layla and the whole family have asked Mattie to stay in Rosetta. That is' – she paused for a delicate moment – 'to live with them permanently.'

Rose's mouth fell open. 'What do they mean, live with them?'

'It seems they would like her to take her place in the household as the first wife.'

'Mattie – *first wife*? Are they quite mad? How dare they?'

'Perhaps Mattie would be happy,' said Miss Proud. 'Perhaps you should let her decide, Rose.' Rose stared, felt her cheeks redden.

'As far as we could understand, it was Layla's idea,' said Mrs Alabaster, entwined still. 'She is, I think, more in charge of that household than it would first appear and she did most of the talking. She believes it would be good for Cornelius to have someone who is English, and who knows his original family, to be with. After all, Layla has her sisters. They all feel it would make him happy. And Cornelius seemed to agree with them despite his black eye.' She observed Rose's shocked face. 'I told you the human heart holds many surprises,' she finished wryly.

The main door was quietly pushed open. Into the big room with the beautiful marble pillars came Flo, Cornelius Brown's young half-Arab, half-English daughter, her face almost covered: a girl of ten, accompanied by one of her young brothers. She was carrying a very large bunch of yellow roses as if she came from her father's garden; their scent at once filled the room. '*Maati?*' she said uncertainly. Mattie appeared at the kitchen door. Flo thrust the roses at her. 'Please, *Maati*,' she said. 'Stay with us, please, oh please live in our house. I will look after you.' And the brother bowed, embarrassed, awkward in front of the women, and then the two children – for they were only children – turned and left as quickly as they had come. Mattie stared after them, expressionless, holding the roses in her arms. Rose felt tears stinging her eyes. Mattie, of course, did not belong to her.

'Mattie,' she said very quickly. 'If you wish to go and live with Cornie, you must do so. You must do what would make you happy. I will, of course, let you go but – I am going down the Nile to get the child.' Everybody stared at Rose. 'I know where the child is. As soon as it is dark I am going down the Nile to get her.'

TWENTY-FOUR

In the distance the sound of the brass bells from the Hindu temple could be heard, a light, jingling noise, as if children played with friendly gods. Fanny sat in a swing chair on the shaded *varanda*. Gently the chair moved to and fro, gently Fanny fanned herself in the late-afternoon heat. Strands of red hair escaped from underneath a wide-brimmed hat. She had been walking around the large garden with her brother's wife but she had given up in the heat. Her mother had had beautiful gowns of Indian silks and cottons and embroidered muslins made for her, Fanny had never in her life had so many beautiful clothes. Today she wore cool blue Indian cotton, the second gown she had worn today, for the heat pressed down. She had even taken off her shoes. This was the 'cold' season, India's winter; Fanny nevertheless found the heat oppressive, imagined snow. Silent servants brought cold drinks at regular intervals: they may have thought Fanny was asleep, her eyes were closed, certainly.

But Fanny was thinking.

The beautifully kept gardens spread out before her in all their wondrous profusion of colours, bright reds and yellows and golds. Several Indian gardeners moved slowly among the flowers in their long *dhotis*. The turbaned old man who was in charge of them sat in the shade afforded by the big banyan tree whose branches fell to the ground. Fanny could hear the voices of her children calling and laughing with their cousins and with the Indian servants who looked after them.

An hour passed. Fanny opened her eyes, swung backwards and forwards. But she had not been asleep.

Her father emerged on to the *varanda* in his white suit, carrying some papers. He sat near to her at a small table. Servants brought glasses of tea.

'You look a picture, my dear!' he said in his usual cheery manner, smiling at her. 'You should wear blue more often.' He sipped his tea in silence for a few moments. 'There is mail,' he said.

'From Rose?' Fanny jumped up so eagerly that her hat fell on to the swing chair, she came to sit at the other side of the table, smoothing her hair back. 'There is a letter from Rose! Is she on her way? Has she found the child?' She put out an eager hand for the letter.

'Not from Rose, dear girl.'

'Oh.' Fanny's face fell. 'I miss her so much, I was sure she would come if she was able. She would love it here, Papa – she may still be searching for the child, of course. Oh, if only we could know.' He did not speak.

She turned some Indian bangles that her sisters had given her round and round on her arm. She had of course heard his silence. She asked at last: 'From Horatio, then?'

'From Horatio and others.'

'What do you mean?'

'Well, well, dear girl, we knew that this was bound to happen. We knew, in the end, that we would hear from Horatio.'

'Yes, of course.'

'He has a lawyer, and he has involved the Company.'

'The East India Company?' He saw the dismay on her face.

'Yes, Fanny.'

'Oh Papa! I had not considered that, I am so sorry.'

'Well, well, do not be sorry. They do not alarm me on my behalf, but on yours. You know I have contacted many lawyers, but there is no alternative open to you, as we have discussed over and over.

If you want to keep the children you must go back.' He saw her face. He wished his wife was here, instead of bustling about indoors. 'It could be even worse, Fanny my dear, Horatio could have insisted that the children be returned at once, without you, and it would have to be done. With some' – Mr Hall raised his eyes to the Indian heavens 'Christian magnanimity, he has agreed that you may return – *at once* – also.'

Fanny sat very still.

In the silence they heard the chatter of birds returning to the trees in the garden, saw colours flash. The sky became a wild, streaked flame of sunset. A small snake slithered across the *varanda*: Fanny could not help it, raised her bare feet, though she knew there was no danger from this one; her father pushed it away with his stick, smiled at her. He wished he could be of more assistance to his eldest daughter, who was obviously distressed in some way; his wife was better at this than he. He and his wife doted already on their two new grandchildren, had seen their blossoming, did not want them to leave again so soon. Somewhere a dog barked.

'Do you believe in God, Papa?'

He looked surprised at the turn in the conversation, and then he laughed his hearty laugh. 'Well, well, you now know much more about such things than I do!' he said. 'It has never been my field of enquiry. Perhaps there is some kindly gentleman in the sky watching over us, et cetera, what do you think?' He was smiling again, he had always felt more comfortable smiling. 'That's what I used to tell you when you were young!'

'I know. And I used to talk to him very happily. Horatio, however, sees a vengeful force if we do not do his bidding.'

'God's bidding, or Horatio's?'

Fanny laughed despite herself. Her father smiled again and she was suddenly reminded of Rose's childish hieroglyph for him: no face, just a smile.

'I have checked the sailings from Bombay,' he said at last. 'There is one at the end of the week—'

'No!'

' – that we could send letters by: to Horatio; to London just in case Rose has returned there. Then there are several more sailings – they are not entirely reliable of course, having to detour and backtrack sometimes because of Napoleon, et cetera – at the end of the month.'

When night comes to India it comes quickly. There is a beautiful dusk, and then it is night, and cooler in the cold season. They heard the young people being gathered up to go inside, children's clear, high voices filled with regret. Soft-footed servants lit candle-lamps; some were carried outside, but Mr Hall waved them away: the light brought mosquitoes and huge moths and other large insects, there was enough light flickering from inside the house where they could hear Fanny's mother giving orders to servants, and the sisters calling to each other. The birds were quiet now, but not so far away jackals barked and monkeys chattered: this house was an oasis of civilisation like other houses in the district, but when darkness fell the wilderness seemed very near. There was a beam of candlelight, then darkness again as a door closed and a skirt rustled. Fanny's mother came to sit beside them; she had three glasses on a tray, good Spanish sherry. Mr Hall had ways of acquiring almost everything they required; his wife did not enquire too closely. But even as they drank there were flickering lights far along the road and the sounds of horses, they would come to the other side of the house. Mr Hall sighed, half relieved, half exasperated: business.

As he drained his glass he said, 'Well, Fanny, wear blue, my dear, it suits you. And whatever plans you make, you know I will help you financially in any way you require.'

'Thank you, Papa.' The door into the house closed behind him.

Mrs Hall had brought a light shawl; she placed it round Fanny's shoulders. 'Your papa has told me, Fanny dearest, about the letters.'

'I will go back to England at the end of the month, Mama.' Frogs croaked across the garden, over and over.

'We have been so lucky to see you, but it has been such a short visit,' said Mrs Hall sadly. 'I will miss the children most painfully. And you, my dearest Fanny.' Mrs Hall had never once voiced to Fanny her feelings about Horatio Harbottom, had always called him 'dear Horatio', but as she sipped her sherry in the darkness on the Indian *varanda* she remembered Fanny's wedding day and the rather sanctimonious voice saying *God's pure water will be my choice* as the guests drank fine sherry, very like this one. And how a little shiver of unease at such unconviviality on such a day had struck her, such foreboding only heightened when Horatio had forbidden Fanny to come to London even when her family left for India. Mrs Hall was grieved at the change in her daughter. She thought of her, large with child, standing beside the scented honeysuckle bushes at the gate of the vicarage in Wentwater, saying goodbye to her family, telling them not to worry, crying and waving and smiling. There had always been something pure – it seemed an odd word, but Mrs Hall used it nevertheless – about Fanny: her quick mind, her certainty of God, and above all her simple goodness. She still had that goodness, of course, it shone from her. But – something had changed in her daughter. A wry, dry manner – as if the world had proved less wise than she expected.

'Fanny, dearest . . .'

'I have a plan, Mama.' Someone had now placed a lamp at a window inside the house, the light from the lamp caught the side of Fanny's face and Mrs Hall saw that her daughter was frowning. Fanny's Indian bangles tinkled as she finished her sherry rather quickly and put her glass back on the table. 'It will take skill, and all my courage, but I have a plan.' The wry, almost smiling tone. 'Do you believe in God, Mama?'

Mrs Hall puzzled at her daughter's face in the half-light. Over long years she had found it best to chatter on: her family expected it and solutions sometimes showed themselves; they thought she did not notice. She said: 'To tell you the truth, Fanny dear, I have been rather taken with the Hindu religion. They have lots of gods and lots of festivals and bright parades and cheeriness. But, is it they who expect wives to immolate themselves upon their husbands' graves? – that will never do, a very barbarous custom. Oh, and I do like Buddha – such a peaceful-looking, well-fed god, and they believe we have been butterflies or elephants in previous lives. It seems to me that there are very many lovely religions and we should all live happily together. But Fanny dear, these are things you should discuss with your father, not me, for I have little education, as you know. We go to the English church here, of course, but I find I am too busy in this world to worry too much about the next – oh, forgive me, Fanny – dear Horatio is of course a man of the Church, and although you do not now mention God as you used to as a child – remember how you often spoke to him? – I expect you are settled in your mind about that matter at least. It would be extremely inconvenient' – she finished her sherry – 'for a vicar's wife not to believe in God!' She looked obliquely at her daughter in the half-light but Fanny's face was unreadable. 'But if you have any difficulties you should perhaps talk things over with those *very* nice Quakers who were with you on the boat; they were much nicer than that pinch-faced young curate!'

Fanny laughed. 'Dear Mama. You are of course cleverer than all the rest of us put together!' Her bangles jangled as she picked up the tray and the empty sherry glasses. 'If I am to go back to being Mrs Horatio Harbottom I need to have a plan, certainly.' She stood on the *varanda* with the tray, listening to the frogs. After a moment she said: 'Those very nice Quakers you mention say God is Love, Mama. If God does exist I am sure he will forgive me for what I am about to do.' She did not elaborate.

Mrs Hall knew her daughter well enough not to question her further; saw that Fanny had settled something in her mind. 'As long as you are not planning to murder dear Horatio, I am sure the Lord will understand, Fanny dearest,' she said, and saw again the wry smile and in a few moments they walked arm-in-arm together back into the house where they could hear the children playing and Fanny's sisters quarrelling – ostensibly over a card game, but actually over an officer of His Britannic Majesty's Indian Army.

In the night Fanny came to her mother's room carrying a candle. Mrs Hall, wearing a large white nightcap, popped up from the realms of sleep at once.

'What is it, dear girl? Is anything amiss?' Fanny was in her nightdress, her red hair falling. 'Sit here with me, as you always used to.'

'I want to say something to you, dearest Mama.' Fanny placed the candle on a small table and sat on the side of her mother's bed. 'And then I will never say it again and I will deny I have said it, even to Papa, and I will never tell even Rose until the day I die, for I can only manage if I tell no one, but I find I must tell someone, after all.'

Mrs Hall waited very quietly, not adjusting her nightcap, not pulling at the bedcovers, almost as if she was not really there at all. Outside frogs still croaked across the lawn.

'I have decided to become a Quaker, Mama. And not only a Quaker but a preacher, for they use women also in that way without discrimination and they say I have a talent.'

'You do indeed have a talent, Fanny. You are one of the world's "good" people and it cannot be hidden.'

Fanny sighed. 'But you see' – and her mother saw the intense face in the candlelight – 'I can no longer believe in God, Mama. If he does exist he is extremely badly served by many of his stewards. He may still come to me one day, he may not; in the mean time I am in a very difficult position, as you say, being married to a vicar. So I have decided to take what I have learned from Horatio – and what I have learned, I am sorry to say, is that the Church is full of hypocrites – and put it to my own use.' If Mrs Hall was surprised, or shocked, she did not make any sign that this was so. 'The Quakers will look after me: I do not of course mean that I need "looking after" as such, but they are to become very ubiquitous, it has been decided, in Wentwater.'

'That will make dear Horatio very cross,' said Mrs Hall, in something of an understatement.

'Dear Horatio,' again that new, dry tone, 'has always had difficulty being anything but obsequious in the presence of dukes and duchesses, and my – my mentor, you would perhaps call her, is a duchess. I would not bet on the outcome for Horatio's soul in a combat between religion and the aristocracy! He will, indeed, be furious. But it means I will have support in Wentwater – and I have been sorely in need.'

'Oh, my dearest child . . .'

'No, Mama, you could not have helped me, not this time.' For a moment she smoothed her mother's bedcover. And she gave a small laugh. 'Mama, my work as the vicar's wife has always been to speak to women, to try and help them with their difficulties. But in my advice I would never in a hundred years have thought of making such a wild leap of ideas as the Duchess of Brayfield made for me.' Again Mrs Hall gave no sign of surprise at her daughter's confidante, although she was in truth surprised indeed, for everyone knew of the Duchess of Brayfield. '*I shall* do good – I believe in goodness in the world. But I do not believe any longer that there is a Christian God, that man in the white beard I used to speak to as a child. But the Duchess said: *Why not just do good then? Who would know the difference except you and me?*' In the distance a jackal, or a fox, howled at the moon; it was a melancholy sound and it fell away and the night was silent. 'But no one will ever guess.'

'I am no one,' said her mother comfortably, 'and all I have to say is that a person with as true a heart as you will always bring kindness to other people, and – really – it does not matter what you wear.' And in the tropical night they both laughed, perhaps a melancholy laugh like the cry of the jackal, but a laugh nevertheless at the way of the world, and how it must be dealt with.

TWENTY-FIVE

Mr Alabaster sat on the *divan*. All day he had not been able to go out because his wife guarded him like a dragon; all day he had not been able to find his rum because his wife had secreted it. He felt extremely unwell and his hands shook. He had finally admitted under Mrs Alabaster's angry, suspicious questioning that the Viscount had arrived in Rosetta and that they had met.

'What did you tell him?'

'Only that we were going to go to the church; what else was there?' He had begun a kind of blustering but his wife's look withered him into a whisper. 'Four times as much he paid me, Vennie! Four times as much.' She had refused to speak to him after that. Now he listened in disbelief to their planning. He needed a drink. His face was creased both with pain and incredulity. 'She can't go alone, Vennie,' he muttered. 'Foreigners are killed without any thought. The Copts can't protect a foreign woman.' The late-afternoon sun shone brightly in the exotic bright blue sky.

'Take Flo,' said Mattie. 'She can translate and you will be less conspicuous, a woman and a girl. A woman on her own is not safe.'

'I am not in the least frightened any more.' Rose had slept for three hours, she was intoxicated with success. 'I have walked round Rosetta at night, completely unmolested, completely unnoticed. I believe we exaggerate the danger.'

Miss Proud's face was very white. 'Have you forgotten the woman in the alley?'

Rose thought: *The child needs me now: George must never find her. I will not allow anything to frighten me now.*

'There are pirates and madmen on the Nile.' Mrs Alabaster spoke calmly. 'Any passing stranger will see that you are a foreigner and may take it into his head to kill you. That is the reality of setting out along the river in the night with complete strangers.'

'Take Flo,' said Mattie again. 'She could help. They won't notice a child.'

'She cannot just *take* Flo!' Miss Proud was appalled.

'The Egyptians love their children,' said Mrs Alabaster. 'I don't think they would hurt a child. And Flo will understand how to be safe, she is an Arab.'

'They said I was to come alone. That nobody was to be with me. I know where the boat is moored, they will wait for me.'

'It is true that she must trust someone,' said Mrs Alabaster, 'and she must go now, tonight, for no doubt that bloody Viscount,' she regarded her husband derisively, 'will turn up here at any moment babbling about crosses.'

'But she should not take foolish, terrible risks!' said Miss Proud, her old face so white.

But there was something about Rose's face that made their words trail away. She had reached her destination: she could not go back. 'At last I have found her, she is alive, this is what I have made the long journey for. For more than a year almost everything I have done has been directed towards this moment. I thought George would try and stop me because he would want her because she was Harry's child, but he sees a child as a threat! You all think me melodramatic, but I know George in a way you do not and I believe he is capable of killing her. What would it matter to him? What would it really matter to anyone in the world – except to me? *I must go*. And I *have* to go alone or they will not take me. *This is why I came to Egypt!*'

'I'm going to get Flo,' said Mattie. 'I will impress upon Cornie that you are a viscountess. He is still an Englishman, underneath his pyjamas,' and she hurried off in her black robe.

'There are probably twenty monasteries, or fifty,' muttered Mr Alabaster. Everyone ignored him. Rose was counting money, filling her water bottle from a pitcher: the money went into an inside pocket, everything else into a small reed basket which she would carry inside her robe.

'Archie is right,' said Mrs Alabaster finally, and she shrugged. 'And also you should know that there are a thousand children fathered by *franks* here, English, French, Portuguese, whatever. How will you know? You could be palmed off with anything. Why do you think they want you to go alone?'

'I keep telling you, I felt it was true, what they said!' Rose was aware of tears at the back of her eyes, began to shout. 'I keep telling you, it seemed to me that they were taking risks to help me, and I feel grateful to them. They talked among themselves about what was the best thing to do. It is a small boat, just the old man with no legs will go, and his nephew. One extra woman who seems to be an Arab woman would not cause suspicion. If all of us went, everybody in Rosetta would know.'

'Then take Flo,' said Mrs Alabaster. 'Nobody will be suspicious of a young girl like her.'

'People will blame me, said Mr Alabaster. 'That I let you go.'

'You are not *letting me go*, Mr Alabaster!' cried Rose in anger, any sign of tears immediately gone. 'I am going of my own volition and I beg that you stay sober enough not to inform the Viscount of my movements, no matter what financial reward he offers you!'

'Don't you worry. Archie won't be going anywhere at all,' said Mrs Alabaster.

And from the end of the long garden George and William came, late afternoon shadows through the trees and the rose bushes, and up to the still open door of the house.

'Here you are then,' said George calmly. 'As we were informed.' And he threw a bag of money at Mr Alabaster. 'Give me the cross, Rose.'

Mrs Alabaster stared at her husband, at the little bag of money. And then she sighed, and in that sigh in the house in Rosetta they saw her life, the life she had chosen with Archibald Alabaster, to save herself from growing old with The Singing Acrobats.

The wheels of Rose Fallon's mind spun. 'You have been a bad friend to me, Mr Alabaster,' she said in a low voice. She bowed her head, made herself stare at the marble floor. She must get rid of George quickly. She could feel the jewelled blue cross around her neck.

'Never employ a drunk, Rose,' said George. 'He has told us everything. You came all the way to Egypt just to look for the child.' He gave a short laugh and did not notice that Miss Proud took a little reed basket from Rose, took it out of the room. 'It is surely a little – pathetic – looking for your dead husband's baby, since you were unable to have one of your own.' He spoke so seemingly lightly. 'I have already told you – Harry's child has nothing to do with you. He is an illegitimate child, a half-caste, a bastard, nothing. He is not an heir, he would not enable you to make claims on the Fallon family. And he will never get to England, I will make quite certain of that!'

Rose felt anger, danger. Very slowly she turned away slightly from George, saw then the silent, pale-faced William. His sister had been dead only three days. 'I am so sorry about Dolly,' she said to William. 'One day I will give her last words to you, as she asked me to.' It was as if she had hit him. And then she looked at the sky and the setting sun. She turned away again and unfastened the jewelled cross. She saw George's eyes widen and gleam: he therefore did not see the surprised look on Mr Alabaster's face.

'Give that to me,' said George, quickly putting out his hand. He looked at it intently. 'You would not know, but this is not a Coptic cross,' he said at once. 'But it is beautiful! And worth a great deal of money. You were lucky indeed, *Rosetta mia*. Go away, everybody except Rose,' he added sharply. 'I have a proposition to put to her. In private.' And he stood and stared at them all, the blue cross dangling from his hand. Miss Proud stood unmoving, Mrs Alabaster only had eyes for her husband to stop him saying anything.

'*Get out!*' shouted George. Rose nodded at them anxiously, telling with her eyes to go quickly. There was a great deal of embarrassed moving about round the marble pillars. George would not continue any further conversation until only he and

Rose remained in the house. 'I want to speak to Rose *alone*,' he insisted loudly. They all looked back uneasily, except William, who made his stoic way towards the river with hunched shoulders as the sun set.

In the doorway of the empty house she turned to him at once. Immediately she could smell the snuff, as she had always been able. He saw tears in her eyes, thought they were because he held the cross in his hand; did not know that they were tears of frustration and rage that she was being kept from her journey. 'What do you want, George? Why do you not leave me alone now? There is nothing else I can give you.' He stood holding the blue, shining piece of lapis lazuli in his hand.

'I want you to consider marrying me,' said George.

There was an astounded silence.

'I surprise you? But it is an idea that has a lot to recommend it if you think about it.' Rose sat, speechless, on the nearest thing available, a small marble bench just outside the door of the house. George sat himself down beside her in the garden in a companiable manner. 'Why should you be surprised?' They could smell roses and lemons and the river. 'Look how well we know each other. There would be no secrets: how many married couples can say that? We only have to keep up appearances. You know I am very rich: that wealth would give you much independence, and you are, as I know, *Rosetta mia*, a woman who likes her independence! And there is one thing that we have in common: we both loved Harry. I once told you that he was the only person I have ever loved in my life, and it is so. I know what the word means although I know you think I do not.'

He got up suddenly, walked through bushes of bright flowers, turned, came back again. And Rose thought how extraordinary it was that George of all people found it hard to talk about his dead brother, even now, yet could not bear the thought of his child.

'You cannot possibly imagine that the Fallon family would allow the existence of a snivelling half-caste oily Arab to cast doubt on the heroic death of Harry, to sully his name?' (As if he had persuaded himself that Harry had died heroically saving England after all.) Rose understood then that the myth of Harry, the medals and the portrait, would live on in the Fallon family for ever. 'Do you imagine we would allow a filthy foreigner to use *our name*? This brat is nothing, and I will deal with it.' A pigeon rustled in a tree just above them and for a moment they both looked upwards. 'You know too much, of course, *Rosetta mia*.' He stood very near to her, too close, that way of his, looking down at her. 'I do not want you babbling on for the rest of my life about some bastard foreign child. Marry me and we will forget that.'

Marry me and you cannot testify against me, Rose translated. She waited.

'The Duke of Hawksfield and his family are too deeply in my debt now, Rose, to be able to live without me, despite Dolly's death. And by the way, Dolly was a very silly and hysterical girl, as you know perfectly well, but she left me with some very – interesting – memories. The point of all this is: the Duke of Hawksfield for some reason values you, so our marriage would hopefully soften the blow of the death of his niece. And finally, Rose – I think this will please you – after tonight, when I have dealt with this matter once and for all, I am leaving for Cairo: the pyramids, the Sphinx; and the places beyond Cairo on the Nile, the places of the old Pharaohs, of which the more I hear, the more I know will be exciting and to our benefit a thousandfold. I know about antiquities more than I know about most things. I know how they become "fashionable" – I can smell this fashionableness in England now. It is said that Bedouins already roam the streets in Cairo selling jewels, and that you can buy ancient skulls and bones for next to nothing, and decorated pots, and slabs from tombs – I cannot wait to be there! You know there is tremendous interest in the hieroglyphs, but no knowledge. You are so enamoured of these things – you could be in a position to find more examples.'

Rose closed her eyes for a moment so that he would not see how much that would have been the fulfilment of her oldest dream: that she could help solve the mystery of the hieroglyphs after all.

'Perhaps there will be more trilingual or bilingual stelas,' he continued, 'or there may be clues in the papyrus paper which is apparently to be found inside the cases of the mummies, and the mummies they say are literally everywhere, we could get at them easily.' (Into Rose's mind flashed a picture of George *getting at* mummies.) 'You could make a genuine contribution to a solving of the hieroglyphs by at least collecting more examples, which you must know that as an unaccompanied woman here you cannot possibly even begin to do.'

George knew he was offering her a world that would change her life. Yet he must know there would be no heir. *What would he do with me, a few years on from now, when the matter of this child was forgotten?* There would be some way or other, no doubt, for her to be dispensed with.

'Now tell me one thing. What exactly were you to do with this?' He held the cross lovingly, turning the beautiful blue stone over and over; the jewels caught the last light. 'I am certainly not going to give it to any priest, of course. But Alabaster – a tedious man, is he not! – muttered about a sign, that this is the only thing that will get you an audience with the priest who has the child.'

'He has told you then – all that I know.' She suddenly actually put her head in her hands as if it would help to hide her thoughts. *It is almost dark. I must get rid of him.* Nevertheless she looked up again for just a moment. 'George, why does this matter upset you so? Why do you not just go to Cairo? Your friend the Prince of Wales and all his brothers have scores of illegitimate children. Surely, for you, this child simply *does not matter.*'

'When I am part of the *beau monde* it may not matter. To be part of the *beau monde* Harry must be a hero. He died in battle, not in a brawl! Your ignorance of social matters even though you were part of our family astounds me.' His agitation was extraordinary, so far away from England. 'Did you have an appointment?' She smelt the snuff, her mind raced. She took a deep breath.

Very slowly she began. 'Because of the danger,' she said softly, so that he had to lean towards her to hear, 'we were to wait until the *bazaar* closed. I was to present myself in secret, with the cross, late tonight.'

'Alabaster said nothing of that.'

'Go earlier then,' said Rose, shrugging. 'I understood they felt it safer to hand over the child when the town was asleep, but you may be able to persuade them differently. The Copts are apparently in danger for protecting and harbouring the child of a woman who brought such shame.'

'Alabaster told me nothing of this.'

Rose suddenly shouted at him: 'How do I know what Mr Alabaster was planning! Perhaps he wished to retrieve the child himself and auction it to the highest bidder! I thought he would help me! Go and ask him yourself!' Tears had sprung into her eyes again. *I must leave. And surely Mrs Alabaster will have locked Archie up somewhere by now, where George cannot get at him.*

'Very well, very well.' She felt him smile, knew he was watching her carefully; at once she lowered her eyes, stared at the roots of rose trees in the sand. 'That will suit me. I have something to attend to first. I will come back to you when the whole business is dealt with and we will leave for Cairo immediately. For now' – and a different kind of smile flicked across his face – 'I have a – meeting – in Rosetta and my meeting – since I have no desire to keep any secrets from you – is with a very pretty young Arab boy. So you need not fear that I will bother you in that way, *ever.*' He was still smiling, this bereaved widower. 'I will wait till the *bazaar* closes and the town is quiet. I suppose it makes sense that they cannot hand it over in front of the whole population of Rosetta. I will come back for your decision when I have dealt with the whole matter, and we will not discuss the child again.'

She closed her eyes. *Why doesn't he go!* He began to walk away. Then for a moment he stopped. And he turned and looked at her, and there he was, the old George, dangerous in the way she knew so well.

'I never feel quite that I can trust you, *Rosetta mia*. I think you can do nothing now, but with you one can never be sure. You will make' – he paused for the words – 'an interesting wife. But let us resolve one thing whether you accept my offer or not. There is no way in the world, so do not even consider it, even if you found the boy rather than myself that the law would consider him as *first*: having any rights in my family, and *second*: belonging to you. I will not, under any circumstances, allow this – this nuisance – to exist, even if by some wild miscalculation of mine that I cannot conceive of I do not find him tonight.' He disappeared towards the centre of the town. He did not look back.

For several moments Rose sat completely motionless. *He really means to – do away with this child, **as if it is nothing**.* She got up quickly and went inside the house. *He is offering me Egypt in exchange for the life of the child.* And again she closed her eyes just for a moment, saw the hieroglyphs: the magical, mysterious writing that waited to be unravelled. Something else pounded at her head. *Always George will be there: always. Even if I find the child before him I will never be able to get away from the Fallon family: they will always be there, such a child will never be safe.* And the empty house with the marble pillars seemed to echo her words: *always . . . never . . .*

Finally the others drifted back. It was as if an agreement had been reluctantly reached: nobody spoke about the child any more. She heard Mr Alabaster pleading for rum. Miss Proud fetched the little basket of food and water, came and sat silently beside Rose, and together they watched the darkening sky.

Just as Rose put on her veil and her robe and picked up the basket there was a loud knocking at the door. Such was the tension in the marble-pillared house that everyone stood stock still and stared at the door without answering. Then they heard Cornelius Brown's voice, calling over and over for Mr Alabaster.

'Quickly, Archie!' he called again. 'There's big trouble.'

'Where?' Mr Alabaster was already on his feet.

Cornie put his head round the door. 'At the baths. They say an Englishman is being attacked by a group of Mameluks – *in* the baths, would you believe? We must at least go near, we will take care, but anything could happen.'

'Right,' said Mr Alabaster. And Rose and Miss Proud saw that they placed knives inside their clothes.

'No, Archie!' cried Mrs Alabaster to her husband. 'You cannot go, you know what happened to that French trader down by the river in broad daylight! Nobody could help at all! I don't want you to go anywhere at all!'

'We can't just leave an *Englishman*!' said Cornie. 'Hurry, Archie!'

'For heaven's sake, Cornie,' said Mrs Alabaster, 'you left England years ago, you're one of *them* now!'

'Archie and I both speak Arabic,' said Cornie doggedly, setting off into the road, 'and I might be one of them, as you say, but I don't leave Englishmen to fight by themselves if I can help it.'

Mattie and Flo suddenly appeared but Cornie was too distracted to do more than pat his daughter's head as the men hurriedly turned towards the public baths.

'Then I am coming too,' called Mrs Alabaster. 'I speak Arabic.' But as she left, pulling her robe over her head, she looked back at Rose and made a motion with her hand that she should go. And the heavy door closed behind her and suddenly the room was very quiet.

'Quickly,' said Mattie. 'I have stolen Flo, God help me.' She looked at Rose very strangely. 'I know what this means to you.' She turned to Flo. 'Remember what I told you, you are a Copt now, Flo, you hear me, and you and Rose must look after each other. Remember the bargain we have made.' They all saw that the little girl's eyes sparkled with excitement.

'*Aywa*, Maati,' she said, and placed herself at Rose's side like a small sentry.

'Go then!' said Miss Proud. 'Go, go! You make me wish I believed in a God, so that I could pray!'

Outside the house as the two shawled figures went towards the river, they saw people running towards the town.

At the Turkish Baths all was pandemonium. A naked young Arab was thrown down the steps, lay where he fell; it was clear he was dead. A man wrapped in towels that had blood dripping from them was finally brought roughly out to the street amid much gesticulation and yelling. 'They've cut off his hand,' someone cried. The crowd milled around the foreigner, tried to see who it was, what was happening; they heard an English voice vowing that this would be reported to the British monarchy, but the Mameluks who rushed out behind the bathers seemed intent on murder. They shouted in Arabic about infidels and sodomisers, waving scimitars; quickly Cornie went in towards them, followed by Mr Alabaster. Mrs Alabaster watched, her heart in her mouth. As somebody dragged the dead Arab away, somebody else (she could have sworn it was Cornie) hit the Englishman, and he fell to the ground. Towels fell apart, people yelled, scimitars were brandished, Mrs Alabaster could hear Cornie's loud voice shouting, closed her eyes as she saw what seemed to be Cornie kicking the body on the ground over and over. Then just as suddenly she saw that the Beys were calling for their horses; they swaggered down the broken stone steps, leaving the English to fight it out. It was clear, as they clattered away, that the violence was over, for now. She did not know if the Englishman was dead or alive. Cornie and Mr Alabaster picked him up, tried to cover him with towels, carried him off down the alley and disappeared.

'Good God!' said Mrs Alabaster to nobody in particular. 'It's George Fallon! It's that bloody Viscount!'

In the darkness at the far end of the harbour the girl and the woman swiftly crossed the decks of bigger boats, climbed down into the *felucca*, which slipped out into the night, south along the Nile. The Copts were a little surprised to see Flo, but as Mattie had surmised did not complain: small Arab girls did not count. Flo glanced about her in the dark in great excitement as her home slipped by. She had never been on the river before.

'We seem as boat girls,' whispered Flo giggling, and then at last Rose understood what the priest had thought in the churchyard: that she was going to *have* a child, that she was one of the foreign women who laughed down by the river. The wind or the current seemed to take the boat incredibly quickly, the nephew at the helm was skilled; soon Rosetta was almost out of sight, but for a long time Rose constantly looked behind them, as if George might suddenly appear.

It became very cold. Sometimes the old man with no legs asked Rose questions; Flo translated haltingly. He wanted to know if she had ever met Napoleon, seemed flabbergasted to hear that she had, and not entirely believing. For a while he sang, strange music of his own. At last he fell asleep. Rose and Flo huddled together for warmth under a big shawl, stared out at the night: at the moon and the stars over the Nile; heard the call sometimes of some wild animal. A heavy dew fell over them. Sometimes they passed other boats slipping past in the shadowy currents; sometimes the nephew steered with his foot. Sometimes Rose and Flo would doze against each other. Rose's exhausted half-sleep was full of falling, she would fall and then wake again to stars and the moon and the quiet, dark water. And then a river wind rose and the nephew unwound more rope: the boat sped along and they could hear the sails. Once a sudden squall turned them, blew them off course, and it seemed the boat would overturn; then just as suddenly the river was still again. Sometimes they could see both sides of the riverbank, sometimes they seemed to be sailing into eternity. When dawn broke they saw the shadows of peasants, the *fallaheen*, Flo said, already at work in their green fields. There was a new sound: waterwheels turned by blindfolded buffaloes, just as Rose's father had recounted, the wooden wheels covered with earthen pots that poured water from the Nile into wooden troughs. The melancholy sound of the unoiled wheels turning round and round became part of the morning, and then the *muezzin*'s cry from somewhere along the bank floated over the water . . . *Allahu Akbar* . . . *Allahu Akbar*, all things strange, exotic, unforgettable.

The old man woke, muttered to his nephew, and the *felucca* was guided in to a deserted spot on the riverbank. The nephew picked up the old man and disappeared: Flo indicated to Rose that they were to do their ablutions here. They washed at the edge of the Nile, feeling the cold, clear water on their faces as the sun rose, filled their water bottle. The Copts came back and they set off immediately; all shared hard-boiled eggs and bread from the little reed basket. As they sped along in the early morning – the Copts sometimes calling now to other craft, or lifting an arm in greeting – the sun sparkled across the water from the east and the sky became deep blue and they saw women washing clothes and clay pots by the side of the river, and again the buffaloes turning the creaking waterwheels that took the precious water for the fields. The Nile became busier and busier, small boats, large boats, all sorts of fruit and vegetables and boxes and sacks of unknown matter and people. *As if it is a road, not a river*, thought Rose. It became very hot; there was a small mat covering part of the *felucca*; here Rose and Flo sheltered from the sun and shared a watermelon the Copts had brought. The sun was high in the sky when the *felucca* turned in to one of the innumerable canals that were cut into the riverbank; silently they sailed away from the river, at first at speed, taken by an odd wind, then slower as the water became lower. Sometimes the nephew used an oar, now, to push them away from the sides, then the canal stopped altogether. There was no more water.

The nephew woke the old man, lifted him on to his shoulders, began at once to walk through dark palm groves and sand, motioned the others to follow him. They could feel the sun, screwed up their eyes, just kept walking: 'he says we must reach monastery before sunset,' Flo told Rose. The palm trees became fewer and the sand higher, then the terrain became dry and cracked and the green was gone altogether: it was as if, as soon as the water stopped, the desert rolled back again. They were walking in the desert. Rose, exhausted beyond any feeling she had ever known, could not allow herself to ask them to stop: *if I die, I die,* she had dropped the woven basket further back, kept nothing but money and water; now she lifted her black robe to make it easier to walk and only concentrated on putting one foot in front of the other; she could see nothing ahead of her but more sand. Occasionally she stopped to drink the precious water, made Flo drink it, for even Flo stumbled. But the nephew, carrying the old man, walked on and on hour after hour *we are in eternity this is the meaning of eternity.*

The sun at last turned downwards: still they walked on. And then Rose heard a sound from Flo ahead of her and raising her eyes from the sand she saw something shimmering in the distance; as they got nearer and nearer it seemed to be the ruins of an ancient temple rising up before her: *is this what they call a mirage?* But the ruins stretched out into the sand, broken pillars and stones: *could this be a monastery?* It was completely deserted. A bird of prey suddenly swooped upwards with a great flapping of wings as if it had been disturbed: otherwise there were just the empty ruins and the sand. They reached the first of the broken stones. The nephew put down the old man and grunted and lay down before the ruined temple and was, at once, asleep. Literally out of nowhere several Arabs appeared, squatted down by the old man and the sleeping nephew. Rose was used now to conversations sounding like arguments: shouts, gestures, laughter. They did not seem to be monks or religious men. She squatted on the sand as the Arabs did, averted her face, longed to just lie down in the sand like the nephew. Unfortunately a large scorpion came running towards her: she screamed, got up quickly, everybody stared at her. She walked away from the group of men; Flo followed her, a small, thin shadow in the sand.

'They ask who are you,' said Flo. 'You should not scream. You scream like a *frank*.'

'I am sorry,' said Rose humbly. They walked further along the side of the temple, curious pieces of broken and cracked stone lay everywhere. Rose bent down to look at them more carefully; suddenly she gasped. 'Here is a *cartouche*!' she said. 'Here is an owl! This is hieroglyphic writing! Here, in this sand, by this temple. I am looking at hieroglyphs in the sand!'

Flo seemed unimpressed. 'You are to find child?' she asked.

'I hope so,' said Rose, holding some of the stones in her hand, turning them over and over.

'Girl?'

'I think it is a girl,' said Rose.

'You take girl to your country?'

'I do not know, Flo,' said Rose. 'Would you like to go to my country? Mattie's country?'

'Best I like *Maati* stay in Rosetta.'

'Of course.'

'*Maati* said if you get child, then she can stay. So I must come with you to help you get child.'

Rose stared at Flo uncomprehendingly. The nephew called.

'We go back,' said Flo.

'But . . .' Rose stared at Flo, then pulled herself together. 'I must take these stones,' she said.

Flo shrugged. 'I would not.'

Rose looked up then; stood quickly. There were more Arabs gathered round the Copts. All of them were men. All of them were staring sullenly at where Rose and Flo were standing. Rose pulled her black robe about her face, took Flo's hand as they made their way back. 'If they ask, you must not say why I am here. You must say I am a very religious lady.'

'What is *religious*?'

'You must say I wish to see the monastery.'

'What is *religious*?' Flo skipped beside her on the sand.

'Caring about God.'

'Allah?'

'No, the God of the Copts.' She saw that Flo looked confused.

The nephew had already put the old man on his shoulders and had begun walking onwards. Rose and Flo followed behind, Rose actually braced herself for the first stone but the men just stood, watching her silently. When she looked back they had disappeared. *We cannot know one another. I could never know them, and they would never know me, in a thousand years.*

They walked along the side of the temple: tall, crumbling. Rose could hardly comprehend what she was seeing. There were more broken pillars; she saw statues whose heads and arms had been smashed: large broken pieces lay scattered everywhere, she stumbled against a big stone foot. The sun was low down now, and the sky was deep, dark violet. They moved along beside high, crumbling walls, moved at last into the shade of the walls, the nephew put the old man down again. The old man began to ring a bell that had lain in the bottom of the boat, he rang it backwards and forwards under the ruins. The nephew just lay down in the sand and was immediately asleep again.

'Look!' said Flo.

Something – a shadow, a pinpoint of light – seemed to be slowly ascending towards them from a dark underground opening, and a faint bell rang. *Could it be the child?* As it came nearer they saw it was an old man, a monk; he was carrying only a small candle and he too was ringing a similar bell, the sounds hung on the air. The monk emerged and he and the old man with no legs began a long conversation, in which Rose was pointed to several times. The entrance deep into the earth looked like a cave or a tomb, it stretched dizzyingly back to nothing at all: darkness. Flo was staring at it open-mouthed.

'Must we – go in there?' asked Rose anxiously, and just as anxiously Flo translated her words into Arabic, but nobody answered: the two old men were talking and the nephew was asleep. Sometimes the bells rang by mistake as the old men gestured to one another and the sound jagged the air for a moment. Rose looked about her. Just the sand stretching into the distance, and the ruins silhouetted against the sky, and darkness falling.

At last they turned to her, and Flo translated.

'We are to sleep above the wall tonight, in the temple. There is a place.'

'But the child? I must see the child.' In her distress Rose moved towards the monk in the doorway of darkness; she thought she saw behind him other dim figures, and perhaps more behind them, stretching back, an army of faces. 'Please,' she said, 'I have come so far to see the child, but – surely – it is not living under the ground, it should be in the light!'

But the face in the doorway, all the faces, if indeed they were faces, stared impassively and turned away. The man with no legs had disappeared – perhaps he had been carried into the tomb. The nephew lay asleep on the sand.

Flo took Rose's hand. 'Come,' was all she said. It was colder now. The two made their way slowly back through the sand along the crumbling wall of the ruins to an opening. Flo took them through. They climbed upwards and upwards over stones. The temple was partly open to the elements but parts of it were covered still. Flo walked on ahead uncertainly, and then in the gloom Rose saw a small brown hand, waving to her. She followed Flo and there, in a corner, cushions lay, and shawls, and beside the cushions, incredibly, food lay on leaves, and a pitcher of water. Rose looked around quickly, there must be people here, but among the broken pillars she heard only a scuffling of small animals, and their own breathing. Did people stand in the darkness with stones? Then she saw large figures carved into the wall above her. Flo sat quickly on one of the cushions at last, in small-child exhaustion, then said that she had been told that someone would come to them in the morning.

'Who told you?'

'I do not know. It was monk maybe?'

'Where did they all go to?'

'I do not know. I saw only one.'

'Only one monk?'

'Yes.' *Did I dream the faces stretching backwards to infinity inside the cave? Am I so tired that I see ghosts?*

'Where did all those men come from earlier, when we first stopped? From this temple?' She looked around fearfully, dimly saw the carved figures.

'I do not know.'

'Who made this food?'

'I do not know.'

Flo ate quickly: when she had finished she lay down near to Rose and fell asleep at once, as if she always slept in ruined temples. Rose tried not to panic, tried not to think she was in an ancient temple in the middle of Egypt and night had fallen. She looked upwards and saw bright stars shining through the broken roof, in the starlight the figures on the walls seemed to stare down at her. She moved nearer to Flo, listened to her soft, even breathing. It was very cold. She marvelled at this small ten-year-old girl: never once had she complained, or shown fear, except perhaps at the underground tomb, if it was a tomb. *Will Harry's child be as this child is?* Something drifted round her mind: Rose had come to Egypt to find a child, with Mattie, as she had always been, at her side. But it was Mattie who had found a child, after all. And Mattie would stay, Flo said, but only if Rose found Harry's child. Rose did not understand.

At last she lay down next to the sleeping girl, pulling all the shawls over them for warmth, wondering what would happen next. There was something comforting about the girl's slow even breathing beside her. She had to believe the Copts were looking after them, like the woman in the church who had given her the cross and murmured *Rashid*. She stared into the darkness. The walls of the temple gazed down; somewhere something ran and burrowed; she was too tired to care. How did these people live here? Perhaps many people lived near here. Where was everybody? Who had cooked the food and so kindly laid out the cushions? It would seem to be women, but she had seen no women . . . But nothing was as it seemed, that was all she knew about Egypt . . .

When she suddenly woke from a deep, deep sleep the first light had touched the open sky above her and the air was chill. She heard Flo pouring water from the pitcher outside. She sat up suddenly, saw that there were indeed figures all around the temple, figures carved on the walls. Huge, ancient damaged figures looked down, some fading colours still. As she looked at them more carefully she saw beautiful women. Not one of them had covered her face.

And beside and underneath the figures she saw the writing, the hieroglyphs: incredibly, after all, she was seeing what the scholars saw, what Pierre had seen. She got up and walked to the walls, looked carefully at the figures. Some of them were carrying pitchers like the pitcher of water that had been left in the temple; some carried fruit, some kneeled near large black dogs. And everywhere the hieroglyphs. She stood running her fingers over the lettering, feeling the shapes, trying as she had when she was young to breathe in the meaning. But there was only the smell of ancient dust. The more she looked, the more she saw. She began to see that many of the huge figures and much of the lettering had been disfigured, it seemed deliberately; in many places the Coptic cross had been carved right across the figures and the writing in the stone. Something about the splendid ruin of the figures, and the damaged writing, made tears come into her eyes: somebody had carved and written so painstakingly of life and death and battles and joys, and here it was, scratched out, discarded. She remembered long ago, her father's description of the hieroglyphs: *the olden days, talking to us*. And she stared again at the muscular perfect men and the beautiful long-nosed women with their high headdresses, and the boats and the animals. *If writing dies there is nothing, for we cannot understand*.

Flo came back into the temple; she had washed her face and done her hair.

'There is nobody,' said Flo uncertainly, 'not even man who carried old man and went to sleep.'

'They will come,' said Rose bravely. She ran her hand over the lettering and up over the damaged figures just once more. 'They will come,' she said again to Flo, 'I know they will come,' and Flo looked at Rose with her little enquiring face, but said nothing. At last Rose picked up the pitcher of water and climbed downwards over stones to the sand. She looked slowly about her. Only the ruins, shadowed in the early morning, silent and empty. And the sand, stretching away for ever. She found a private place further away; it was behind an ancient smashed stone leg but it could not be helped. She poured some of the precious water to wash herself with her robe. When she stood again she saw the first ray of the sun rise over the edge of the horizon and to herself she said *now I am going to see the child.* But all she could see was stone and sand: nothingness. Her father had said: *Egypt is the ancient world. I felt I was inside the Bible.*

'They will come, of course,' said Rose again to Flo. 'We know there must be someone here, somewhere.' Flo now sat on the sand, one leg tucked under her, her shawl about her head, silent. She looked like a small ancient monument herself. Part of the landscape. No bird, or animal, or human stirred as they waited.

The sun began to rise.

And then, like an apparition, a lone figure dressed in black could be seen in the far distance, walking towards them out of the sand: how he had suddenly appeared there they did not know, perhaps he had emerged out of a ruin or a tomb or a cave: he was there anyway, a priest in black, carrying something, shimmering in the rising sun, walking towards them and suddenly Rose thought *this is like a scene in the Old Testament, this is what my father meant, the sun rising and the figure in the distance and the bare desert landscape of the ancient times* and then at last she knew: the man in black was carrying the child. She wanted to run towards him, but her legs would not move; she stood as if paralysed, her arms aching with loneliness, the rising sun blinding her view.

He arrived beside them at last, breathing heavily; they could smell his sweat. They saw then that he was not a priest, or even a monk, but more like the hundreds of Arabs who walked about Rosetta every day. He had the eye disease so common to those who lived beside the Nile.

He passed the child across to Rose: it was wrapped in a shawl the colour of the sand: she could not immediately see its face.

'You want to buy?' he said.

TWENTY-SIX

In the darkness at Aboukir Rose shivered, heard the sea, walked once more with Miss Proud along the shore among the bones of dead men. Tonight a strong wind blew across the sand that covered the bones; blew the sand at the women, into their eyes and their mouths: they held their robes about their faces. They murmured together: Miss Proud had just arrived at Aboukir from Rosetta. She was accompanied by Cornelius Brown with his turban and his *galabiyya*: he had come at Mattie's insistence to assist with their departure: he took a risk, Rose knew; they all took a risk. There were other travellers, waiting for camels to Alexandria or for sailboats to go to Rosetta or Cairo; there was the usual bargaining and shouting of a *caravanserai*. The moon was behind cloud tonight along this coast, there was only the light from a few stars, and the fires along the shore, and the occasional lantern, flickering and smoking with polluted sesame oil. Camels lay on the shifting sand; sometimes in the darkness one of them roared from its long, dry throat. Tomorrow morning, early, they would join a small *caravan* back along the road to Alexandria, back at once to the blocked, crowded 'new' harbour; by nightfall they must find a boat to Malta, to Italy, to anywhere where it was safe, or safer than here.

Rose had not dared to stop at Rosetta, the beautiful, dangerous town of her name: Turks and Egyptians would be very interested in a foreign woman with a child, as well as George Fallon. Flo had slipped silently away into the darkness bearing messages; the Copts had taken Rose further on to the Rosetta bar. She had travelled as an Arab woman; as they crossed the Rosetta bar and out into the Mediterranean Sea she had hidden the child in a shawl inside her robe and prayed to any god of any faith who might be listening.

Now Miss Proud told her of Flo arriving back at the marble house in the dead of night where her father waited, full of alarm; of how he, Cornelius Brown, had saved George's life by seeming to be, himself, murdering the Viscount to save the outraged Beys the bother. And of George's injuries, and how George and William, in great danger now in Rosetta, had simply disappeared.

'Does George know I have the child?'

'We do not know.'

'Does Mr Alabaster know?' Miss Proud nodded gravely: Mr Alabaster had been there when Flo returned with secrets.

'Could they be already waiting in Alexandria?'

'We do not know.'

In Aboukir in the darkness now a donkey complained somewhere along the sand. The sound of a donkey sometimes echoes like a malicious laugh.

*

My dearest and most missed Fanny,

I know nothing of you, nothing at all. You live in my Mind, I so often think of you and wonder what is happening to you and the Children. This letter is being written on the Mediterranean Sea, we believe we can send Letters from Leghorn where we should arrive this evening which is the first time since I left Europe that I have been able to send anything. I am not on my way to India as we Planned, dearest coz, but back to somewhere where I hope I can get proper Assistance for Harry's child – my child as I shall call her now. She needs Medical help most urgently – I could not have travelled with her where we might have been even further away from the help she needs. I have called her Rosetta.

*I found Rosetta. She was in a Coptic Monastery in the ruins
of an ancient Temple somewhere far up the Nile from Rosetta
town and across a desert; they would only permit me to buy her
if I left Egypt Immediately, for the Egyptian Christians suffer
very much from the Turkish Rulers as it is, and the child, as we
always knew, is one that the Turks as well as the Egyptians
would like to find . . . And, Fanny, the child is as if blind. I say
'as if' for this may be partly Cured, she suffers from an advanced
state of what is called Ophthalmia, the Disease of the Eyes that
Pierre told us of. A dubious passing Greek doctor told me to
bathe the eyes with Clean water – as if such a Commodity were
freely available; it pains the child and she cries a great deal,
poor mite. Oh Fanny, she is so tiny and fragile, and ill with
many things besides the Ophthalmia. I am so frightened, Fanny.
I am frightened that she will die before we get back to England.
She is so thin that I feel her bones, they are like the bones of a
small bird.*

*George Fallon will Follow us I have no doubt: he wants this
child, this reminder of Harry's unheroic End – but he does not
want her alive, in England. He is afraid of Scandal, he is afraid
of a Reminder that Harry did not die a Hero, that the whole
story of his Death may unravel. But I cannot think of that now,
all I can think of is to find help, and surely the Law of England
will not allow him to damage her? Luckily – for us – George
has been attacked – he almost died of foolishness in Egypt,
like his brother – something happened in the Turkish Baths in
Rosetta that caused great Offence: he has disappeared, they
say, but I cannot hope we have seen the Last of him and – oh,
of course you cannot know. Fanny, Dolly is dead. In childbirth
is what we say. I used your words, Fanny, to comfort her. I told
her there is no Hell. Oh my dearest coz, the world is indeed
Strange and Terrifying and how I long to know that you are
safe in it. For nothing in the World, I know now, is
necessarily as it seems.*

*Miss Proud is travelling home with me – it is she who sits with
Rosetta now as I write – did you know that she came to find
me? – Never was I so pleased to see a Familiar Face as I was to see
hers the day I first stepped Ashore in the Egypt of my Dreams –*

*which was not, of course, like my Dreams at all. But Mattie has
stayed in Egypt – for how long I do not know – for she has found
a Family, her Husband's Family (she found Cornelius Brown, and
punched him, as she had always said she would, but then other
things unravelled). She had promised me long ago that she would
not leave me until I had my first child . . . and Mattie as we know
is a woman of her Word. Because of Mattie we met Egyptian
women in their own Houses – oh, dearest Fanny, how I wish I
could have Shared all this with you. But I must hurry now
because they call that the Port is now in sight and because of
Napoleon there is so much that is uncertain, we have no idea of
our plans, nor even if Italy is safe or whether we will ever get back
to England unharmed with Napoleon's Armies everywhere they
tell us, and talk of coastal Blockades and no certainty anywhere
and the child so ill.*

*I have not seen the whole of Egypt, as I used to dream. I have
not seen the great Pyramids, floating – as Pierre described
seeing them from the Nile – in the morning light. But I have
seen Egypt nevertheless. I have seen the ruined city of
Alexandria, city of old memories; I think I learned there the
meaning of desolation. I have seen the river Nile just as Papa
told of so long ago, and the Life that it brings. And I have seen
the desert stretching out to eternity and I have had a glimpse
of how the ancient world must have been. I have even seen
Hieroglyphs, decaying in the desert. I have seen great kindness
and great cruelty – but I had seen that in the world we grew
up in also.*

*Now they call me again. I will try to find a way to get this
to you. I send all my love to the Family, and especially to you,
how I long to hear news of your Journey – how I miss you all,
and especially you my dearest, dearest Fanny, you can never
know.*

*Ah, but there is one more thing, because I know that –
although I tried – I cannot seal this letter without it. People
asked how I could be sure this was Harry's child. But there
was no doubt, the Ophthalmia cannot hide it, her fragility
cannot hide it. She does not look like Harry but she is instead
the image – oh Fanny, can you believe this? – the same long*

patrician nose, the same piercing blue eyes, however damaged. There is no doubt at all.

I wanted to find this child so much. It is only a God with a bizarre Sense of Humour who therefore led me to a small, ill, Egyptian version of the Dowager Viscountess Gawkroger.

Rose

TWENTY-SEVEN

Sometimes sun streaked in around the wooden shutters, trying to insist there was life and joy outside; the knife sharpeners and the pedlars called as usual, but inside the house in South Molton Street they did not hear. Nightingales sang in the trees in Hanover Square: they did not hear.

'We found her in Egypt,' they had said to the London doctors, as if such matters were routine.

But the summer days in South Molton Street brought no safety, after all. It was as if the house was still empty; doctors came into sad, dark rooms where the shutters were so often closed against the sunshine; they wished to attend Rose and Miss Proud but the women would say nothing of themselves, only of the child. Sometimes watchful, damaged blue eyes stared up intently, following any movement in the room painfully: but then the eyes would close. After only a few days the doctors said they believed there was no more that they could do, for the child was dying.

'Children die every day,' said the doctors to Rose gently, 'you know that. Children die in the greatest families in England, in the family of the King himself. It is quite extraordinary that she did not die on the journey. But there is nothing more that we can do.'

Miss Proud insisted she sit upstairs so that Rose could get some sleep; Rose could not bear to sleep but sometimes she drifted for an hour: she fell downwards in her dreams, dreamed of hieroglyphs that became more menacing.

She refused to give up. It seemed to Miss Proud that Rose became almost mad: day and night whispering gently to Rosetta *they said you would die in Milan and you did not, they said you would die in Cologne, you have come so far and survived, you must not give up now, take this tiny drink of milk, this tiny spoon of medicine.* Sometimes the damaged blue eyes opened, sometimes the child swallowed, but then the eyes would close again, almost it seemed in relief, almost as if the child said at last: *let me go.*

You must not die, Rosetta, whispered Rose.

*

Darkness comes late on summer evenings in London: those who travel under cover of darkness therefore have less time. Miss Proud, the strain of her long journey showing in her face, her spectacles magnifying her eyes, saw the visitor in absolute astonishment; hurriedly ushered him inside. She had a vision of the old naval gentlemen coming to pay their respects and finding a *Frenchman*: she locked the door carefully. 'I am so very glad to see you, *monsieur* – but any Frenchman is surely in great danger here!' She brought him into her book-filled, newspaper-strewn room.

'*Oui, madame,*' he answered wryly, 'at Dover I thought my last hour had come. One of my compatriots – on what business I do not know – was shot dead, for they heard his voice. I cannot risk staying long, I must leave again before first light. But – I am here.' He regarded her. 'You are safely returned, *Dieu merci*! But – you are very thin, *madame.*'

'We have been back only ten days, Monsieur Montand, we are hardly organised, we are too concerned with the illness of the poor child. We have no maids, nothing at all, we carry our own coal up and down the stairs – and no doubt it is good for us! It does not matter – we are home at last. But' – and she suddenly regarded him in puzzlement – 'how did you know? You could not have known.'

'Mattie arranged a letter to be delivered to me by a French merchant who was travelling to Paris.

'*Mattie* did?'

'She told me of all that has occurred. And your part in it, *madame* – you are an incredible woman to cross the world alone in such an extraordinary manner! And – you are, all three, safe?'

'Safe?' Again she stared at him. 'We are so grateful to be home, but . . .' Miss Proud suddenly sat down at her table as if she could no longer sustain her own small weight. She rubbed her hand across her face. '*Monsieur* – the long journey back was like a terrible dream of foreign ports and foreign doctors and war. The child is so ill – as well as the ophthalmia which Mattie will have told you of.' He nodded. 'And soldiers always, and the worry of George Fallon at the back of us! I believe I could not live through that journey again. But Rose has been extraordinary. She hardly leaves the child's side: it is my belief that on that journey she *willed* the child to live, to hold on, to survive – some strength of character I hardly recognised she had. We have seen English doctors at last, thank God, they come each day, but – *monsieur*, they are very grave. Her life seems to me, and I know to Rose, a small flame that might still flicker out. It is *terrible* for Rose. And she of course worries all the time at every knock on the door. George was determined the child should not live as a reminder of his brother's shame and Rose somehow whisked her away from under his eyes. I believe he will not forgive her.' Miss Proud's magnifying spectacles fell to the floor among the books and papers everywhere. Pierre bent, picked them up.

'I am glad to see that some things do not change, *madame*,' he said smiling slightly. 'I remember this room of books and newspapers from my earlier visit when they tried to set fire to your kitchen!' and they both tried to laugh but their laughter was anxious as they looked upwards.

'Monsieur Montand.'

'*Oui, madame?*'

'I think – I think Rose will be so very glad to see you.'

He went up alone and unannounced. He walked into the empty drawing room, for a moment looked about him, remembering a summer night like this when he had asked her to marry him and she had refused.

'*Rosette*,' he called gently.

She appeared from the small room next door, unbelieving, as though she had heard a ghost call. He was shocked by her appearance. Her face was so thin and white and strained that she looked much older.

'*Pierre!*' She stared, held on to the wall to support herself. 'How? – how did you . . .' She tried to find words, could not. 'That is . . . the war . . . you are . . .'

'Rose. *Rosette.*'

'But . . .'

'Mattie found someone to bring a letter into Paris for me.'

'Mattie *wrote* to you?' *She saw Mattie, sitting in Brook Street long ago, learning letters.*

'There was a Monsieur Cornelius Brown, who I understand is her husband, who assisted her to tell me of all that has happened.'

'Where is George?'

'I do not know, *Rosette.*' As he came towards her she made no move at all, as if she could not; she noted yet did not that he was dressed all in black, his hair tied back in the manner of an English captain; he saw the curve of her long thin neck, her hair was longer, there were red blotches on her dry white skin. He simply put his arms around her. For a moment she stood still, nothing yet said, then she put her arms around him also, felt his tall, warm body next to hers, smelt the sweat of a man who had been riding. He felt a long sigh leave her body and then for a brief moment she relaxed, leaned against him, and he could smell her hair. And so they stood, in a room in South Molton Street.

At last she led him back into the small room next door. There the child lay, with a lamp burning nearby: tiny, olive-skinned, emaciated: like the child of a gypsy or a beggar. And Rose heard his involuntary intake of breath as he moved closer. The child was not asleep, lay listening to the sounds of London perhaps, or perhaps to sounds of another life altogether that existed only in her head. It was clear the ophthalmia had damaged one of her eyes for ever. Yet she suddenly stared intently at him.

'But – *of course* . . .'

'Yes,' said Rose.

For although the child's skin was dark, and although one of the eyes was so damaged and she looked so tiny and so ill, there was no doubt that this was Harry's child, for Pierre Montand would never forget Harry's mother, wearing the ancient Egyptian ring in Berkeley Square. The child looked up at him: a tiny, damaged version of the Dowager.

'I have named her Rosetta,' said Rose.

Pierre continued to stare, amazed. *'La pauvrette!'* he said. 'She is so small, yet she must be – nearly two years old,' and his voice caught, just for a moment, and she knew he thought of Alexandria and the stoning of the mother in the dark alleys.

'She seldom eats. I do not know if she sleeps, or just lies there still breathing.' Rose shook her head wearily. 'And she has never smiled. I think that is the saddest thing of all.'

He was silent for a long time: he saw Egypt in his mind. 'She lived in the desert in another world; now,' and at last he turned and looked at Rose, and she saw from his eyes that he loved her still as he moved towards her, 'now she lives in *la rue* South Molton, with a beautiful and brave lady who is scented with lemons.' The child watched them.

'Pierre.' She took a deep, unsteady breath. ' Pierre, whatever is to happen – I know you are the wisest, kindest – the kindest man that – forgive me, I am not clear-headed and I know this is not the right time and not the right place, everything is different now . . .' She stumbled, gestured towards the child, but made herself go on. 'Pierre, I did not understand myself when you – I was not brave, and I was not wise. Of course so much has changed now – both our lives – but I want you to know that I have thought very much of my foolishness. I did not mean to hurt you. I thought of this so many times in Egypt. I came – I *ran* – to look for you in the French Ambassador's house the next morning. But you were gone.' She did not know if she was making sense. The blue eyes moved painfully from Pierre to Rose, and then closed. Perhaps the child slept at last, she made tiny breathing sounds. Rose kissed the small forehead. *'Ma'assalama,'* she said softly, as she always said, her face close. 'I am here, I will always be here, and we are both named Rosetta.'

They watched the child, the tiny breathing.

'I tell myself,' said Rose, 'that while she has that look you saw, of watching and listening, *she will not die*. It is *life*, that look,' and he saw that her eyes had filled with tears but they did not fall; she busied herself about the cot, about the room. The child breathed gently. They went back into the drawing room, leaving the door between the two rooms open. For some time they sat in silence: he on the soft sofa, she on the tall chair, listening for the slightest sound. At last he put out his hand, to take her hand gently as he had done once before. It was as if she heard Mrs Alabaster's voice: *mass: to touch delicately.* He felt her shaking. This time she got up and came to sit beside him.

'It is my turn,' he said, 'to make my apologies.' Gently he touched the deeper frown mark on her forehead. 'You have proved me wrong, and I am amazed and glad. You did what you said you could do – you, and Miss Proud, and Mattie. Because I know so well how it must have been, I can still hardly believe you have done this, and I – I am filled with admiration. If you wish to know of my weakness – I wept when I received the letter of Mattie.' Then, at last, he held her, he held his love, and there, suddenly, they wordlessly came to some decision, and at last Rose Fallon let go: tears poured down her face in exhaustion, in joy, in desire, in despair, in relief, and then, finally, in abandon: in absolute abandon of the years of learning to be restrained; felt the same yet differently, her whole body on fire in the way she knew so well and yet had almost forgotten *again again again* as if a river had at last overflowed, the Nile river, the sand, the ruins, the child, the lamp in South Molton Street.

They heard a coachman call to another in the street outside. Relentlessly the old clock from Genoa told them of each quarter of the hour that was quickly passing.

'*Je t'aime, Rosette.*'

'I love you, Pierre. I am so glad to see you again! But – I know you should not be in England! You cannot be safe here!'

'For a very short time I am safe.' He stroked her hair, her exhausted, now flushed, face, her thin bare shoulder, but Rose suddenly leapt up guiltily, for the child, as if for a moment the child had been forgotten *what if she has died and I was not there?* The tiny chest still moved. Rose stood in the doorway, between the two rooms as if she did not know where she should be.

'Tell me of Madame Fanny,' said Pierre gently. 'What of her journey?'

'There was a letter waiting here.' Rose slowly did up buttons. 'She is returning – we think it will be soon, but of course how can we know, with war affecting everything and the journey so long? The Reverend Horatio Harbottom has pursued her with the law – he made some disturbance, I believe, with the East India Company – Fanny must be terrified of losing the children now.'

'Madame Fanny will return to Monseiur Harbottom?'

'I expect she must. The letter said nothing of that.'

'Do you regret Mattie?'

'I miss Mattie more than I can say – and it is *not* – you must not imagine that I cannot carry coals upstairs or chamberpots downwards, and of course there shall be new maids. But Mattie was . . . Mattie was part of my life, I did not think to lose her.' She turned back to the child for a moment and then she moved quickly to sit beside him again as if she could hold it back no longer; took hold of his hands as if he had the answers. 'What is to happen? If she will live after all it is George who has the right to her, not me!'

'You have always known that, *Rosette*.'

'I have always known, but I *could not* do things differently. George would have killed her if he had found her first – Pierre, it would have been so easy, he would not have had to do anything at all, he could have just laid her in the sand somewhere and – walked away. When I close my eyes I almost see him doing it.' And for a moment she did close her eyes, as if she could not get rid of the image. 'I understand,' she looked at him with difficulty, 'as you accused me, that there was a great deal of romance and foolishness in my heart about this child. But once George was there and I understood how he felt, then it was simply a matter of her life!'

Pierre nodded, stood. He too looked in at the sleeping child, listened for the small breathing, looked at the hands of the old clock from Genoa. He walked to the window and stared out at South Molton Street.

'Rose, one of the reasons I came at once, when I received the letter of Mattie – I have news for you.' He handed her some sheets of paper; she saw Mattie's round, laborious letters, there were many blots of black ink.

AND MR PIERRE YOU MUST WARN MISS ROSE – WE DIDINT NO BUT
THE VISCOUNT SNEEKED BACK INTO ROSETTA AND TOOK THE BLUE
CROSS TO THE CHURCH AND THE PREESTS APARANTLY LARFED
AND HE WAS ANGRY. HE CAME TO THE ALABASTERS HOUSE IN THE
NITE AND NOW MR ALABASTER IS DEDE.

WHATEVER THEY SAY I THINK HE DID IT HE IS AS MAD AS A
CAMEL WE THINK HE HAS GONE FOR OBELISKS BUT ONE DAY MISS
ROSE MUST LOOK OUT FOR HIM FOR HE MUST NO SHE HAS THE
CHILD THAT MUST BE WHY HE DID IT.

Then there was added, in a different handwriting:

There is no proofe it is onley what we think, They said Archie
had a Fall and was Dronke but Mrs Alabaster knows, She said the
viscount was ropable like a bull when he knew about the trick with
the blue cross, and Miss Rose leaving.
>   *Yours faithfully*
>   *Cornelius Brown (esq)*
>   *and his wife Mattie Brown*

Pierre saw that Rose kept reading the words, over and over. He came back to sit beside her. 'If you are prepared to come to France there will be special dispensations made for you, an English-woman. I have his word.'

'Whose word? George's?' She looked at him, not understanding.

'Napoleon's Buonaparte's word. I have told him your situation. Remember when Mademoiselle Dolly – ah, *la pauvre*, I am so sorry for her story, which Mattie recounted me.'

Rose's eyes were suddenly like stone. 'He killed Dolly as surely as if he had stabbed her with a knife. George. And William and the disgusting old Duke of Hawksfield, adviser to the King! To them she was a pawn, nothing more!'

Gently he went on, as if explaining to a child. '*Ecoute-moi, Rosette*. Napoleon remembers you and the day of the fainting. If you – if you decide you will come to me, we will go now. We will be mar-ried in Paris with his permission. George cannot safely come there.'

She stared, uncomprehending. 'But I must stay with Rosetta.'

'Rosetta will come with us, of course!'

'*But Rosetta cannot travel!*' He did not speak. 'And our countries are at war,' she added stupidly, as if he did not know, as if he had not ridden through danger, in the night, a lone Frenchman on horseback: the enemy. She still had the letter in her hand, looked at him as if she did not quite see him, as if she was still back there with Mattie.

'Our countries are certainly at war,' he repeated, and his face hardened, and his voice. 'The French tried, through much diplomacy, to avoid this further war. The conditions of the Peace of Amiens were broken by your government and your King over and over. I fear that this time it will be a war to the death.'

'Whose death?'

'Your treacherous King. Your boastful Lord Nelson. Your fat Prince of Wales.' And then he said: 'Napoleon is to become Emperor of France.'

She looked shocked then; out of shock, perhaps, laughed. Then just as suddenly stopped, appalled at herself. 'But what was the Revolution for?'

He sighed. 'That *different* men may be rulers, perhaps. Something of this nature is urgently needed – this I do understand, for the royalists attack him constantly. We must make the *République* secure and it is Napoleon who stands for the *République*. For myself I will be glad,' he added drily, 'if this war only means we will repossess the Rosetta Stone,' and she saw that he tried to lighten the feeling between them.

'Is there any progress?' Now she touched his face: he knew that she had come back to him.

'With the hieroglyphs? *Non. Rien d'importance. Hélas.*'

'Oh Pierre, I saw them, the hieroglyphs! I saw . . .' But she could not go on and her eyes again seemed somewhere else. 'I – I sleep so strangely, Pierre. I am with Rosetta in the night, of course, but when I fall asleep, I fall downwards in a dream, it is always a dream of falling and the strangeness is – the dream is not Rosetta – not even George – I dream, night after night, of them – of the hieroglyphs.' The words poured out. 'In my dream I see the hawk and the owl and the foot and the strange shapes, they go round and round and round in my head, as if they would not have me forget them. When I saw them in the ruined temple, damaged and scratched and covered with Coptic crosses, I wanted to weep!' Her white face was still flushed. 'And in my dreams I am always waiting, waiting for the key to the hieroglyphs to be found, as if it is *just there*, beyond my reach.' She gave a half-laugh. 'Why ever should I dream such a dream? I am not a scholar!'

He smoothed her hair. 'Come to Paris,' he said. 'We shall look at the hieroglyphs together, every day!' and he smiled at her. 'But, *ma chérie*, I have been thinking as I rode here, perhaps you could learn more of the Arabic language in France, having heard the sound in your ear – there are many good professors in Paris – and one day we could return to Egypt, with Rosetta. Arabic is not the language of the hieroglyphs, but the more languages you learn, the more you can understand how languages *form*. And so perhaps you one day will understand the old Egyptian languages – who knows!' She felt such intense love for him, for his words and ideas and plans and dreams, that she had to look away.

'And your volumes?' she asked in a moment.

'We work, night and day. He insists that it is continued, even in wartime. But – *écoute-moi maintenant* – you must come back with me. And once we marry, if Napoleon becomes King of England – which is of course a possibility – nobody will be able to take from you Rosetta.'

'Napoleon, King of England? King of my country? Of course not!' She was so surprised that she stood up.

'It is at least possible, *ma chère*.' She stared at him, disbelieving.

'This – this is not how we think in England. We never even imagine such a thing!'

He stood, regarded her wryly. 'It is how we see things in France, *ma Rosette*. But now we must hurry, for there is much to arrange.'

She looked at him in total astonishment. 'Do you mean – now? You cannot mean *now*? Tonight?'

He smiled, as if every moment he spent in England was not full of danger. 'I cannot come every week! But Napoleon agreed to this one journey. Just this one.' And as he spoke, the old clock from Genoa chimed again. 'We must set off before it is light.' He looked down into the street, and then turned back urgently. 'It is later than I thought – it is now. We must leave now!'

She stared at him in incomprehension. 'But Pierre – Rosetta – I cannot – it is not just the ophthalmia, it is her *life*. Surely you understand that?' She took hold of both his arms. 'I love you – do not mistake me this time, I love you, Pierre, and I would be so glad to marry you,' and she looked up into his dear face. 'I would be so glad. I dreamed you would come back, dearest Pierre – but I never thought my dream would come true!' Suddenly she pulled him back into the small room. 'Look at her,' she whispered.

Pierre knew it was true: something about the child frightened even him. He looked away quickly. *They had to do it this way. They had to take the risk.* 'She can do it! She has travelled all the way from Egypt! Rose, I will take you both through the darkness: we must take a risk, just one more, *ma chérie*. For all we know, George is already on his way. Once we are out of England and back in France I have Napoleon's authority and we will be safe. And once we reach Paris I can look after you both. In France doctors know well of ophthalmia, of course, from the returning soldiers: she will be very well cared for.'

'But' – she was puzzled that he had not understood – 'it is not just ophthalmia – her life hangs by a small thread, you must see that!' And then she seized his arms again. 'If it was just me I would come! I would not fear anything, for no journey can frighten me now. But you *must* see: I am Rosetta's chance of life. If she had stayed where she was she would be dead by now. If George had found her she would be dead by now. *I am going to make her live!*'

'And George Fallon?'

'I will not let him have her!'

'Then we must take her away tonight. This is our only chance.'

And she saw his face, and her heart contracted with fear. 'Oh Pierre, you must not make me *choose*! Give me time!'

'In war there is not time, Rose.'

'Listen to me, listen to me! I will not move the child *one more step* until she has – has turned the corner back into life! But I cannot bear to lose you a second time, not now – you will never be rid of me now, for I love you too much,' and then she felt his hands on her body, as if he too could not bear to let her go a second time. '*Pierre!*' she whispered, and at once now she was on fire again, as if something inside her was unquenchable, felt his hands and his mouth upon her and again abandoned herself to his heart as he whispered, 'We must go now, *Rosette.*'

'Ah – *please,*' she said, *'please,* my darling,' and perhaps it was not clear what she was pleading for: him? his understanding? his hands? for time to decide? – but the child next door heard perhaps: stirred anyway, and cried out over and over, a small, dry, exhausted cry, the tiny child with her damaged blue eyes and the clock chimed and dawn light threatened London.

He saw then that she would not pick up the child and come. There was love, but there was steel.

Slowly he took up his dark cloak. 'Goodbye, *Rosette.* There is no more time left.' And he seemed to be speaking to both of them. 'I am more sorry than you will ever know that you will not come with me, for – *je regrette que* – I think you do not understand – it is impossible for me to return.'

Her anguished eyes. 'You cannot do this, Pierre. You know now how much I love you! You have seen the helplessness of Rosetta. It is wrong of you to make me choose – it is an impossible choice!'

'There will not be a third time, *ma Rosette,*' said Pierre Montand. She saw most terrible pain in his eyes. 'For sometimes we must be brave enough to make impossible choices.'

In the last darkness of the night the sound of a horse on the cobblestones echoed, and then died away.

TWENTY-EIGHT

The wars of Napoleon spread. More young men disappeared to war. There was no chance at all of movement between England and France. Ports were blockaded. There was no word from the man to whom she had given her love. Frenchmen were shot on English soil: *Napoleon's spies,* they said: she understood Pierre had taken his life into his hands to come to her *but I hold the life of Rosetta in mine.* Trees began to shed their leaves around Hanover Square, the leaves rattled and danced down Bond Street. In the small room she continued her determined, unwavering vigil.

And then, one day, Rosetta lived.

Infinitely slowly the small body turned some corner, came back to the world, took the milk and the medicine. The doctors called it a miracle. But out of Rose's hearing they conferred gravely. The damaged eyes might have opened again, but of damage to the mind: they shook their heads, they could not tell. Day after day Rose spoke to her of life. Infinitely slowly the child sat up, turned her head to survey the room, was carried into the drawing room, to light, to autumn leaves. She had a doll that she stared at, unblinking, and an old worn cushion called Angel. One extraordinary day, watching a ray of autumn sun fixedly, she somehow slid down from the sofa where she had been placed beside Rose, to be nearer to the sun. Another day she tried to pull herself along the floor, again towards sunlight. She watched everything about her intently. And as Rosetta came back to life, so did Rose. She understood that George Fallon had not yet come chasing after her. And she understood there had been no message from France, no sign of validation of what had happened between her and Pierre that night. *Just a word. Just one word.* But nothing came. The ports might have been blockaded, but Pierre would have found a way. And so she understood.

Pierre Montand was gone from her life.

But Rose knew that George Fallon would come. She knew that he would eventually have to face the Duke of Hawksfield with news of Dolly's death. She knew that he would not tell anybody else of the child, that one night – she knew it would be in the night, he always came at night – he would just slide ominously into her life again like fog off the river. She knew very well she could not keep Rosetta locked away in South Molton Street indefinitely.

She told the doctors she was planning to move from London: 'Not yet,' they warned, 'not yet. This has been a long, long battle for her small body. You must promise us that for six months she will be here where we can help her.'

'Perhaps then,' said Rose, 'I could take her away to – to another country,' saw the look of shock on the doctor's faces.

'That would be most unwise!' they said sternly. 'You are in the safest country in the world in these troubled times of war. You could not easily get medical care for her in foreign places.'

Rosetta began to take delicate, fragile steps sometimes, but her legs were not strong enough to hold her; she would fall. Sometimes now she would pull herself upwards and hold on to chairs or doors with an odd determination.

Rose planned their new life. 'As soon as it is spring we will go,' she said to Miss Proud. 'I will find a quiet place where we will be safe. And if he comes when we have gone you must tell him the child is dead.'

'And if he comes *before* you have gone?' Night after night Miss Proud lay awake in South Molton Street, listening anxiously for George Fallon.

'I will tell him the child is dead myself,' said Rose firmly, and every evening when Rosetta, always unprotesting, had been put into her bed, she would look about the drawing room for any signs: the doll, the worn old cushion called Angel, small spoons.

And thus they lived, locked in South Molton Street, taut as bows, waiting for Rosetta to be strong.

'You should wear black, Rose,' said Miss Proud one day. 'In case he comes.'

The old naval gentlemen were finally allowed, in great secrecy, to come and visit. They tried to hide their shock at the appearance of all of them: of Rose, of Miss Proud, of the scrawny, olive-skinned, damaged Fallon child. They looked (the old gentlemen told themselves afterwards) as if they were wraiths, or ghosts, not quite substantial: as if they came from elsewhere. But the old gentlemen made jolly conversation, reminded them there was a world, gave Rose and Rosetta (and even Miss Proud) sweets. They listened to the adventures, their grey heads shook in relief and disbelief as they listened: 'It seems there will soon be women travelling everywhere! We will have to make up our minds to it!' they exclaimed, hardly able to believe their ears.

'One day Rose shall write books telling them how!' said Miss Proud. And the old gentlemen laughed, defeated, but proud of them, knowing the world was changing. The child sat beside Rose on the old soft sofa and listened and stared.

'And – the Fallon family?'

'I do not know,' said Rose coldly. 'We do not go about.'

'You cannot' – they looked perplexed – 'keep her locked up here.'

'I know.' She said nothing more. They caught Miss Proud's eye but they were too kind and concerned for Rose to at that moment press her, and sat in anxious silence.

'Have you' – Rose did not look at them – 'can you say, perhaps, how long this war will be?'

'Ah, my dear.' They sighed and shook their heads. 'This time it will not end until Napoleon is dead.' Pierre had used the same word about the King of England. 'He unsettles the world. It cannot be allowed to continue.' Again silence. The old gentlemen cleared their throats. 'Her eye. Is there something . . .?'

'I fear there is not. I was too late, the damage was done. But they assure me, now, the doctors, that she will slowly become well in other ways.'

The old gentlemen smiled benignly. 'We shall love her. And – will she speak?'

'She does not speak and she does not smile and I have no way of knowing what goes on in her small head. So – I talk to her. I have told her that she shall wear a black eye-patch like a pirate – and one day she will know what *pirate* means, for there were plenty in the Mediterranean, we heard such stories!' But Rose sighed. 'We are hoping her cousins will soon be home from India and I have thought perhaps – with other children . . .' They nodded wisely (although Rose was the only little girl they had known).

'Oh my dears, look! Rain!' The old naval gentlemen pointed to the windows, disappointed. 'We had hoped we might persuade you to walk in the square, a breath of air perhaps . . .' Rose and Rosetta and Miss Proud looked, saw sudden autumn rain falling past the window. Rosetta, astonished, somehow slid down from the sofa and tried to inch her way across the rug, determined; Rose gently picked her up and carried her to the window.

'It has hardly rained since we returned,' said Rose, 'and she has been so much confined to her bed. She will never have seen such a thing in the desert.' And Rosetta looked solemnly up to the sky, to see from whence the water might have come.

'That is *rain*,' said Rose to Rosetta gently, smiling at her. 'You will see a great deal of it in this country! It is *rain*.'

The old gentlemen and Miss Proud went on talking; Rose stood at the window holding the child. She looked at Miss Proud's thin, pale face; at the grey heads of the old naval gentlemen; at these people she knew loved her. Anxieties pulled at her: *they will die*.

And then Rosetta reached up with her hands and pulled Rose's face round to the window. Rose felt the small warm hands on her cheek.

'*Rain*,' said Rosetta clearly. She turned back to Miss Proud and the old gentlemen, and then she looked at Rose. And then suddenly something happened out of nowhere: that old, charming Harry Fallon look appeared, for Rosetta smiled.

Next day there was a great banging on the door: Rose with Rosetta in her arms looked out of the top window in terror: *Is it the whole Fallon family?* Suddenly, seeing who it was, she ran down the stairs just as Fanny and the children and Miss Proud were running up. Fanny had not received a letter from Rose. She did not know Miss Proud had travelled to Egypt. She did not know the child had been found. She saw her cousin dressed in black with a gaunt white face, and the small thin child. Just for a moment they all stopped on the stairs and stared at one another, for apart from these matters Jane and young Horatio were taller and their faces glowed with their adventures. And Fanny was neatly dressed all in grey and just undoing a small grey bonnet.

'Who is dead?' said Fanny, staring at her cousin.

'No one is dead, dear Fanny,' said Miss Proud. 'We will explain.'

'Why are you dressed like that?' said Rose, staring at her cousin.

Fanny laughed. 'And I will explain also!'

Then everyone hugged and wept and asked questions. Fanny's children at once studied Rosetta's watchful, damaged eyes and asked about her olive skin. Then (used now to the company and fun of cousins) they wanted to play with her but they saw she was odd, like a thin doll, so they lifted her infinitely carefully as they had the new baby in India, and talked nonstop to her, and occasionally poked her very gently with interest, and smiled at her a hundred times and told her things about India until, understanding or not, Rosetta smiled. (And Fanny saw at once: *Harry Fallon's smile.*) Then the children fell asleep on the sofa as they had always done; Rosetta, who always lay awake, staring and watchful, was so exhausted that she fell asleep beside them, one small thin arm resting on her cousin Jane's arm as evening slowly drifted down over London. Just before he fell asleep small Horatio (not so small now) said: 'I am going to join the navy and fight Boney,' and smiled, and Rosetta seemed to be heard to say *Boney* in her sleep.

Now Rose and Miss Proud stared at last at Fanny in her grey

gown, their eyes full of questions. And Fanny stared at the white-faced old woman and her gaunt, pale cousin.

'Tell me,' said Fanny. 'Everything.' And so at last she heard the story of the search for Rosetta: Miss Proud following Rose to Egypt; Alexandria; Dolly; travelling to the town of Rosetta; Mattie and Cornelius Brown; every detail of the adventure along the Nile, and the Copts, and Cornie's daughter Flo, and the ruined temple, and the desert. 'Ohh,' Fanny breathed, entranced. 'Ohh.' And she took her cousin's thin hands, and saw her strained face, concealed her concern. 'And the drawings and the lettering carved into the walls, the sand stretching far into the distance? Was it – as you dreamed?'

'Yes,' said Rose, strangely. 'Yes. In the desert it was – at last – as I had dreamed.'

'And it is certainly clear there is no mistake! She looks exactly like the Dowager, only – she smiles as Harry smiled.'

Rose nodded. 'She smiles as Harry smiled.'

Fanny looked away for a moment at the small, sleeping girl; shook her head in a kind of wonderment at what Rose had done. Then she stood and walked to the window and the darkening sky, looking out over the city where she had been born. 'Oh, how much I love these crisp autumn evenings.' She turned back to them. 'You have said nothing of George.'

'We know nothing of George. He has been involved in many scandals in Egypt.' Rose's voice was dismissive. 'How can he easily come back here? How can he show his face to the Duke of Hawksfield? He is a murderer! And can you believe, he asked me to marry him!' She spat the words out. 'He cannot bear the idea of her existence, I thought he might love her, as part of Harry, but he thinks only of scandal affecting Harry's heroic memory.' And then her voice shook. 'One day he will try to take her from me.'

'So what shall you do?'

'I shall keep her. I shall go to France.' She saw Fanny's puzzled look. 'Or Norfolk. Or I shall come to Wentwater.'

'Of *course*, if that would help.'

'If George ever comes back while we are still here, I shall tell him his brother's child died on the journey. That is why I am wearing black.' The tremor in her voice was gone, and she spoke coldly. 'I shall kill him rather than let him have her.'

'*Rose!*' And Fanny laughed. But her cousin did not laugh with her. Fanny caught Miss Proud's eye, then quickly looked away, out over their city. *Poor Rose. It is not over yet.*

Rose and Miss Proud stared at Fanny in her grey dress, longing to ask a hundred questions of their own, but something about Fanny's manner deterred them. The room was silent except for the breathing of the three children. The conversation had halted: there was still too much to say. At last Rose and Miss Proud lit candles, poured hot water into red wine as Mattie had done a hundred times. Rose hesitated slightly as she handed the glass to Fanny *if Fanny has really become a Quaker, do Quakers drink wine?* but Fanny smiled and took the glass. 'In my heart I am not a "plain" Quaker, Rose, I am very much a "gay" Quaker, for no one shall take from me the enjoyments of life! But it will do my husband good to believe I am holier than he!'

'Fanny' – for now at last Rose and Miss Proud could ask the questions – 'you cannot *really* have become a Quaker? Have you, Fanny? But you are dressed as one!'

She looked down at her grey gown, smiling slightly, ran her hands over the material. 'There are wonderful cloths and wonderful tailors in India. This is the most beautiful cloth I have ever worn – it was hard to bring home only grey!' And then she looked at the two women gravely. 'Yes. I have become a Quaker.'

Miss Proud looked at dear, clear-thinking Fanny, nonplussed: she had expected her back speaking of Hindus, and Mohammetmen, and Buddha perhaps – but the grey sober dress of a Quaker was totally inexplicable. 'You have been to *India* – surely that is a land of other religions! I had expected you in a *sari* at least!'

'I was absolutely fascinated by the other religions. But – this is to be mine. By great good luck a party of Quakers were travelling to Africa and India on the ship I sailed on from England.'

'Ah.' Miss Proud suddenly remembered the group in grey at Portsmouth.

'I had so much time on that long journey to consider my life. And of course, Horatio.' She came back to sit beside them. 'I married him above all other things because I thought he had the key to *knowledge*, the key to my education, which I so longed for. And because I was not educated enough I did not at first understand that' – she paused and drank some of the wine slowly – 'that Horatio does not have the key. And yet I understood, even as I travelled further and further away from him, that there is no law for me, that I would lose my children if I did not return to their father.' Still they stared at Fanny in her grey dress in disbelief. *What has all this to do with Quakers?*

'One of the things that has drawn me to the Quakers is that they believe in *change*. They believe that one day the law that says children are owned only by their fathers will be changed, and if that is to be so, for other women, I am glad.' She paused. 'But for me and for Jane and for small Horatio it will be too late. If I want my children,' and she gave an odd little laugh, 'my husband is part of the arrangement.'

Rose looked across at the sleeping children, thought of them wild and unhappy in Paris. 'They seem very – they have become . . .'

'Improved. They are much *improved*. They are happier. They have grown a hundred times without Horatio there to dominate their growing, to tell them what they must think. And in India they found cousins, they found a grandfather and an uncle who lived wonderfully exciting lives that had nothing to do with sin and retribution, and who *listened* to them! They do not even fight any more – Jane has long given Horatio to understand that if he pinches her, she will pinch him back! And Horatio wants to join the navy, he spent so much time with sailors on our journeys: pulling ropes, polishing brass – he even helped to sew a sail!

'And – *India*. Oh, if only I could begin to describe such a place to you!' And Fanny ran her hands through the red hair for a moment and it fell back across her round face in the way they knew so well. 'It is – it is such a place, such sights and smells and warmth and beauty. I saw a flower, just the day I arrived, it was such a deep red that it felt as if my eyes themselves were learning. And my dear, dear family at last,' and tears sprang for a moment into her eyes and she got up quickly, went back to the window. 'And then – we were *forced* to return. So' – and they heard a new hardness in her voice – 'I was *forced* to find a way of dealing with a situation that my lack of education and knowledge had got me into.' Still Rose and Miss Proud were silent, not understanding.

'And here we are!' And Fanny gave them an odd look, as if to say *do you follow me so far?* 'I did wonder if we should see England again, for the journey back was so truly perilous that I thought my problems were to be solved by the Lord in another way altogether! But – we survived! – and today I saw an English autumn day, the golden leaves on the trees – so different from the heat in India – and English people, and the familiar sights as we came into London – the bridges, the people, St Paul's, the church spires of our own churches, I heard our *own* church bells ringing! – the feeling of my own dear country. And I knew that I was glad to be home, whatever my return may bring.'

'Are the Quakers – are they coming to Wentwater then? Are you going to attend Quaker meetings there?' Nothing made sense.

'Listen to me,' said Fanny again. 'This is the difference. The Quaker faith sees no difference in the talents of men and women.'

'What do you mean?'

'There are very many calls – the unspeakable conditions in the prisons, the terrible business of slavery which our country supports. I will do what I am good at.' She paused for a moment. 'What God sees fit,' said Fanny. And Rose realised that this was the first time her cousin had mentioned God at all.

'Do you mean – that you shall you preach to others?' asked Miss Proud, puzzled.

'Perhaps,' said Fanny, 'if that is my strength.'

'Dearest, dearest Fanny,' said Rose, confused. *Something is odd. Something does not make sense.* She got up slowly, put down her glass. Then suddenly she threw her arms around her cousin. 'Oh, Fanny – dearest, dearest Fanny, I am so glad to see you! And I am so glad to see – to see that you feel confident that all will be well. But' – Rose stepped back, looked hard at her cousin's face, still holding her arms – 'you have been away and you have forgotten! Horatio will never agree. That you, a woman – *his wife!* – should be a Quaker – even perhaps a preacher? In opposition to him? For that is how he will see it – he will not see it as further proof of God's goodness, he will see it as a challenge to his authority – which you have already so sorely tried. He will *never* agree!'

Fanny gently disentangled herself from her cousin's loving embrace, turned again to the window that looked over her city.

When she turned back to them she had an odd look on her small, round face again: an ironical, wry look, almost as if she would laugh at them.

'Sit down for a moment, Rose darling.' Rose did so, perplexed. 'First of all, Papa has made me a large allowance that is tied legally so that Horatio must obtain my signature in order to get access to it. Horatio is extremely fond of money. Secondly,' and Fanny still looked at them obliquely, seeming almost to smile, 'the other thing that Horatio is inordinately fond of, as you know, is – what shall we call them? – people of rank! Lords and ladies, dukes and duchesses. The Quakers have some very powerful friends, and they have agreed to – to assist and protect me. This will impress itself upon Horatio.' She saw their doubtful faces and she went on in the same dry tone. 'Horatio and I spent many long hours in prayer together – oh, how *many* hours! – asking God to come to me, and guide me. Well, my dears, his prayers have been answered. Surely he will be grateful! It is just that it is perhaps not *quite* in the way he expected.'

There was a silence in the room as they looked at her, and Rose thought: *she is doing this for the children, not for God: to keep the children, a way of keeping the children.*

Suddenly Miss Proud began to laugh. The others looked at her, surprised. 'I cannot help it,' said Miss Proud, and her eyes filled with tears that were definitely laughter, and her little white cap shook. 'I do not in any way laugh at your decision, Fanny, and I do believe you will be able to help people, that is the kind of person you are. But – you have found the one way to defeat Horatio! God and the Aristocracy!' And her little cap shook again as she struggled to contain her laughter. Then she said to Fanny, 'I have something for you.' From the voluminous pocket of her black gown something appeared. It was a floating Egyptian scarf that was as extraordinarily blue as the Egyptian sky, and Rose remembered Layla and the women winding it around Miss Proud upstairs, in the *haramlek*, and insisting that she keep it, and she heard the soft laughter, and the rustle of the scarves and silks, and for a moment she seemed to catch the scent of oranges.

'Oh, how *beautiful*!' Fanny stared at the colour, entranced.

'Wear it, Fanny,' said Miss Proud, 'to show that your heart is "gay", not "plain". It belonged to a woman from another religion where they say *la ihala ill' Allah* – there is no god but God – and I am sure you heard in India other such claims to singularity. But you can wear this to say that perhaps there are many gods, and perhaps they all mean well.' And Miss Proud shook her head slightly and the bright blue scarf glittered in the candlelight.

'Ah, my dear young friends, I am so proud of you both, however the world may turn.' And she got up, stiffer now they saw, and slower, and – unusually for Miss Proud – she kissed them both. 'Of George Fallon we do not yet know. Of the Reverend Horatio Harbottom we do not yet know. But here we are again, sitting safely in South Molton Street drinking wine on a beautiful autumn evening as if the world has not changed; as if you were not, the two of you, brave adventuresses who have done the most extraordinary things: you have had an education, after all, and I am infinitely proud of you!'

As they heard her descending the stairs and moving about quietly in her own rooms Rose felt a sharp pain, suddenly. And she saw herself, moving quietly in lonely rooms, because she did not take the chance of happiness that had been, so dangerously, offered.

'What is it, Rose?' Fanny asked gently. 'Talk to me properly.'

Rose's thin face was painful to observe. 'Do *not* think I would not do everything the same, all over again. But – Pierre Montand rode through the night and the enemy lines and the south of England where no Frenchman is safe, to ask me to marry him and to take Rosetta and go and live in France. We – he and I when he came . . .' but she could say no more, she shook her head. 'I love him, Fanny.' There was a long silence as Fanny took in all the implications. *'La belle France,'* and Rose's voice shook slightly, 'as we always called it. It meant too of course a way of escaping from George, until the end of this war, however long – or short – it may be. Oh – how *much* I wanted to be like one of the heroines of the new novels and put Rosetta under my arm and ride off with my lover into the night!' She bit her lip. 'It is much harder in real life – Fanny, I could not know for certain that Rosetta would live! She could not have made one more journey! And now' (and Fanny saw what strength it required for Rose not to break down) 'this *war* – I cannot write to him, I cannot go to him, I cannot tell him that Rosetta is so much better. Oh Fanny! I had to choose. And I *had* to choose this way. But

I have lost him a second time!' Fanny dared not move to comfort her cousin, saw the desolate, older face. 'And now I sit and wait. For George Fallon.'

They sat there, the two cousins: in grey, and in black. The shining blue scarf lay beside them on the sofa. The candles flickered, the room became darker, their children slept. Fanny gave a deep sigh from somewhere far inside of her. She took her cousin's hand in hers, turned it over gently, intently. Instinctively they knew that they were there, for this moment, with each other again, as close as they had been long ago.

'We are both, in the end, caught by the same cruel law after all,' Fanny said slowly, glancing across at the children, then staring again at their entwined hands. 'Rose, we *have* to find a way because of the children' – she looked up at Rose as if she might say something else, and then away again – 'to bear things the best way we can. You too, Rose, must find a way, however difficult, as I have done.' And Rose knew, suddenly, that Fanny would not speak tonight of God. It was not about God. They sat in silence. Then Fanny spoke again. 'Who would have thought it could possibly turn out this way when we were seventeen, and the world shone?' And she seemed to stare into the distance. 'Remember Vow Hill, and the bathing machines?'

'I remember.'

There was a movement beside them. Horatio and Jane were still fast asleep. But they saw that Rosetta was regarding them – and the bright, glowing blue colour beside them – with her damaged, watchful Fallon eyes.

TWENTY-NINE

To say that the loins of the Reverend Horatio Harbottom were (to use biblical language) aflame is hardly to describe his state as he approached South Molton Street. He would, of course, maintain cool dignity for the moment of reunion but he would demand, at once, privacy to speak to his wife and there – his mind aflame now as well as certain parts of his anatomy as he contemplated the moment – his marriage would re-begin.

How he had *suffered*. The ladies of the parish of Wentwater had done their best, of course, but how he had suffered. Nobody could know how he longed to see his dearest Fanny, how much he had missed her. A small voice told him he could have loved her better: *I will*, he told himself painfully, *I will*. He longed to see her beloved face everywhere in the vicarage again: cooking, stirring things as her red hair fell about her dear face, calling to the children, her cheeks flushed as she bent over the fire in her long yellow gown (the loins gave another lurch). His life would be properly organised again: her calm manner, seeing to things, his meals ready, listening to his sermons, everything as it used to be; and (once again his body leapt) Fanny more penitent now for the terrible thing she had done, more – he searched for the appropriate word – pliable in his arms than she had ever been before.

Some of the more heightened of these thoughts were perhaps due to the fact that in his wife's absence the Reverend Horatio Harbottom, while in the throes of missing his wife and her support most terribly, had become acquainted with certain French publications that had stimulated his imagination in ways that had not previously occurred to him. These publications had been made available to the vicar late one evening over the whisky bottle by a fellow cleric so that, having perused them at length, they could both denounce them from the pulpit. (Curiously, they were copies of the same publications that had been available to Dolly in her father's study: like Dolly, Horatio had studied them avidly.)

It was therefore as something of a man possessed that the Reverend Harbottom, lavender-scented, stood banging on the door of South Molton Street. He had not considered it necessary (in the circumstances he had considered it might have been a hindrance) to be accompanied by his uncle the bishop to the reunion with his wife.

Miss Constantia Proud opened the door to him herself and ushered him into her drawing room with its newspapers and periodicals and books balanced everywhere. Horatio expected Fanny: to his great surprise the room was full of ladies and gentlemen.

'Ah, Harbottom,' they said and extended their hands.

'Reverend Harbottom, do you know Lord Stone; the Duchess of Brayfield; Sir Reginald Makepeace?' Miss Proud made introductions while Horatio's eyes nearly popped out of his head. First one white-haired lord and then another nodded their heads graciously.

'Congratulations, Harbottom,' they said.

Other gentlemen shook his hand. 'Congratulations, Harbottom,' they echoed, 'our very best wishes.' The aforementioned Duchess of Brayfield smiled in so civilised a manner that he was quite undone. *The Duchess of Brayfield*. Everybody knew of her and her influence. She was *famous*. He pulled his shoulders back, made himself even taller. They must know he had forced the return of his wife as any man would have done, and he had forgiven her too, for he loved her. He too became gracious, he felt himself among equals as never before, his white clerical collar simply shone.

The door opened and Mrs Horatio Harbottom appeared, holding the hands of Jane and young Horatio. The Reverend Harbottom hardly saw that his children had grown tall and straight, hardly saw Rose in the background with an odd-looking child in her arms, for in front of him stood his dear wife, Fanny. But – she was dressed, he realised at once, in the demure grey dress and bonnet of the Quakers.

'Good afternoon, Horatio,' said Fanny.

'Good afternoon, Papa,' said Jane and young Horatio.

'Congratulations, Harbottom,' said the gentlemen.

'What – what is this?' Horatio looked at Fanny, looked about him, bewildered. He saw now that some of the other ladies were dressed as Fanny was – though not the Duchess of Brayfield. Some of the gentlemen also, he noticed now, were dressed in grey – though not Lord Stone. *It could not – it could not surely? – be a meeting of Dissenters?*

'Let us pray,' said one of the gentlemen, and without further ado God was thanked for sending his spirit to Fanny Harbottom, encouraging her to do his good work.

'She speaks with true feeling and understanding, Harbottom,' said Lord Stone, 'as of course you are aware. We feel that Wentwater can only profit from having her there, to speak of our Lord. We shall visit often,' and Horatio felt his mind tumbling. *What can they mean? It is I who speak of our Lord in Wentwater. Fanny is my wife!* He looked at her.

'You cannot be a Quaker! That is to be a misfit in God's Church! I am a vicar in the Church of England where my uncle is a bishop, and you are my wife!'

'I thank God,' Fanny said clearly and simply, looking at Horatio, 'that He has come to me and spoken to me at last. You know, Horatio, how you and I have longed for that. I will do everything in my power to use His spirit for the good of the world.' She seemed calm, not penitent at all. He began to bluster and thunder.

'You are my wife!' He looked about him for support. 'She is my wife! Her duty is to me, not to anybody else. I am God's representative on this earth and my wife's duty is to me alone! To me! She is a woman!' And to his great discomfort pictures of the Frenchwomen in the books burst into his mind at this most inconvenient of moments.

'We are all children of God by faith in Jesus Christ,' Lord Stone said to Horatio kindly, 'where there is neither male nor female but we are all one in Jesus Christ.'

'That is *blasphemy*!' exploded Horatio. Silence echoed around him in Miss Proud's drawing room as the group of people stared at him, and from a small table a precarious pile of periodicals, disturbed, fell to the floor. Looking about him again, suddenly realising the enormity of the situation, the reason he was surrounded by such powerful people, Horatio sat down quickly on the soft sofa. These people were supporting Fanny, not himself. They would not be intimidated by his uncle the bishop.

'I want Fanny,' he cried piteously.

'I am here, Horatio.' She came, with the two children, towards him. They all sat beside him on the soft sofa: a family. He could smell her clean, fresh skin.

'I want it like it was,' he said to her. 'I have *suffered*.'

'But God has called Fanny,' Lord Stone said gently, 'and even in the Church of England you surely cannot deny God's calling.'

'God does not call *women*!'

'We believe he does.'

Horatio jumped up again. 'Never a Quaker, a Dissenter in my house! Never, *never*! No servant of the Church of England can allow a Dissenter near. My uncle is a bishop, he will see to it.'

'Why, Harbottom, I know your uncle,' said Lord Stone. 'He has asked me, only recently, to put his name forward as a member of my club.'

'Horatio.' Fanny held out her hand; he sat back on the sofa, he felt her soft skin. 'Horatio,' she said gently, 'you too wanted God to speak to me, to enter my heart. How many times did we pray together for this miracle? Can you not be pleased that the miracle has occurred?'

'We prayed for him to enter your heart *from the Church of England*!'

'We cannot choose the conduits of our Lord,' said the Duchess of Brayfield softly, 'for the Lord moves in mysterious ways, Reverend Harbottom, his wonders to perform.'

The Reverend Horatio Harbottom, surrounded by his family again, his inflamed loins quite diminished, put his head in his hands. In the silence Lord Stone said, 'Let us contemplate God for a few moments, in the stillness of our own hearts.' And for a little while, in Miss Proud's drawing room, there was a calm quiet: just the sound of breathing, the odd cough. After some moments Lord Stone said to the Reverend Horatio Harbottom, very gently, 'Know thyself, man.'

'Papa,' said young Horatio kindly, seeing his father's distress, 'I have ridden an elephant, and I am going to join the navy and return to India, to keep India safe, for England's sake.'

'And Papa,' piped Jane, 'in India, where the tea grows, I have learned to make tea. I will make tea for you.'

In a little while the visitors prepared to leave.

'We shall, of course, visit Wentwater often,' said Sir Reginald Makepeace, 'to see that all is well. I look forward to productive discussions with you concerning the slave trade.'

'I hope you will always make us welcome in Wentwater,' said the Duchess of Brayfield, 'for we are so proud of Fanny, and will come very often.' And she smiled at him. 'To see that all is well.'

'Congratulations, Harbottom,' said Lord Stone.

THIRTY

There was no warning. He came one night as November winds blew the last dry leaves into stinking gutters from the trees round Hanover Square. Miss Proud and Rose were playing chess in Rose's drawing room, listening for the child; they heard the knocker bang. They heard the new maid answer, they heard George's voice. There was only time to close the door of the small room: Rose quickly sat again and moved a bishop, as the footsteps came upwards.

For a moment all three stared at one another. It was months since the day in Rosetta when they had last met, and all three were different. He only ever saw Miss Proud as an old woman, but George was startled by the change in Rose. *Now she is old too*, he thought. *She has red lumps on her skin. She is scrawny, scraggy, she looks terrible. She is dressed in black as old women dress.*

George looked different himself, and burnt by the sun; his adventures had aged him also. There was a long scar down one side of his face. He leaned on his swordstick as he had always done so fashionably, but one arm seemed impaired in some way, he held it oddly as he stood there: the Mameluk Beys had done him much damage with scimitars before Cornelius Brown could get to him to kick his ribs.

'This is a surprise, George,' said Rose, as she had said so long ago. 'When did you return?'

He stared at the women at the chessboard, he took in the quiet house. *Where is it?* He did not sit. Finally he said: 'I am just arrived from Portsmouth. William and our belongings are already ahead of me at Berkeley Square. I believe, though, that there is one more belonging for me to collect.'

Silence in the drawing room. The knife sharpener called and carriages rolled past.

'Could you kindly leave us, Miss Proud?' He made an attempt at gallantry.

'Do you know, Viscount Gawkroger, I believe, if you will excuse me, that this time I will not.' She moved a knight.

He gave up gallantry. 'Where is it, Rose?'

Silence in the drawing room. George looked about, looked at the stairs leading to the rooms upwards, as if he would go there.

'You have not heard, George?'

'I have heard that this was a very expensive decoy.' From his jacket he brought the blue jewelled cross, and despite themselves both women caught their breath. The blue lapis lazuli looked so beautiful, the jewels shone so exotically in South Molton Street; it carried somehow the scent of cloves, and the shifting sand, and the *muezzin*'s cry. 'I must congratulate you at least on your taste,' said George. 'This will sell for a fortune.' He placed it back amongst his clothes: the hint of Egypt disappeared as quickly as it had come, and they heard coach wheels and someone laughed along the street and called of meat pies. 'I have heard that you went down the Nile and found some child. I have heard that you were both seen with some child in Milan.'

'But you have not heard, George.'

'What?'

Rose took a deep breath. 'The child is dead. He died on the journey back. He was – too frail, too ill, to make the long and difficult journey.'

'Where did he die?'

'He died' – Rose bowed her head. *We were seen in Milan. So he died after Milan* – 'he died as we travelled across Switzerland; we had to avoid France of course. We buried him there.'

Still he cocked his head, as if listening to the house, to the sounds of this silent house. He regarded her black gown. *Is she in mourning for a bastard?* 'Where are the witnesses?'

'I am witness, Viscount Gawkroger,' said Miss Proud gravely, 'to everything that has happened. Your sister-in-law is one of the bravest women I have known.'

'She is also one of the most wily!' he snapped back at once. 'For all I know you have him hidden right here under the floorboards, ready to sidle out and cause trouble for my family!'

'I had him christened in a Swiss church before he died,' said Rose quickly, 'There will be a record.'

'Of his death?'

'Of his *name*. I named him Harry Fallon.'

'How *dare* you! *How dare you!*' He actually seemed as if he would strike her, as he had in Alexandria. 'A bunch of oily stinking Arab rags carrying the name of my brother?'

Miss Proud stood at once. Both women knew the shouting of a man's voice might frighten the child, she would cry.

'It is all over, George,' said Miss Proud quickly. 'It is finished.'

Again he looked at Rose: something terrible had happened to her, he could see that. For a few moments he stood there, regarding the women. 'Perhaps it is true,' he said softly. 'But perhaps it is not.'

'Perhaps you would like to search the house, George,' said Rose coldly, 'like some kind of common bailiff.' She saw conflicting emotions cross his face.

At last he said: 'I will be back. I will have people put to watch you. I will be back when you least expect me.' He moved towards the door. 'I sent William on ahead of me, to explain about Dolly's death, but' – and he grimaced – 'I must now face the Duke of Hawksfield. I will expect you both to bear witness to her death in childbirth if it is necessary.' And Rose thought: *So there it is: he needs us still. That is why he has not torn the house limb from limb.* 'But I will be back, Rose, for I do not trust you. And do you know: I do not believe I could bring myself to marry you after all. You look like an old maid, as I always said you were once Harry died. Your life is over. You should take up spinning!' And George Fallon turned and went down the stairs; the door into South Molton Street banged loudly.

Rose quickly went into the small room. Rosetta lay awake, watchful and silent.

The next afternoon there was hardly time for Miss Proud to call in warning up the stairs, hardly time for Rose to lift Rosetta quickly, put her into her small bed.

'Stay there quietly,' she whispered, as if Rosetta ever did anything else: Rosetta always stayed quietly, waiting.

Miss Constantia Proud brought them upwards.

The Dowager Viscountess Gawkroger held a handkerchief very obviously to her nose. With every step up towards the top half of the house, heavy disapproval emanated from her person, along with a rather strong eau de Cologne. Her skirts and her demeanour rustled and flounced and criticised. The Duke of Hawksfield came behind: upright, stern, silent. Then William appeared, sunburnt like George, but thinner, gaunt in the way that Rose was gaunt: something had happened to their lives that had changed them. The Duke had saved William's patrimony but the price had been his sister, and William knew it. Finally, reluctantly, there was George again, carrying with him a feeling of such suppressed rage that Rose understood at once that he must have been compelled by the Duke to join this gathering: she saw that George and the Duke could hardly bear to look at one another.

Everybody (including Rose) was dressed in black.

Rose greeted them politely, felt shock at once to see the Dowager: saw the long nose, the piercing, still-blue eyes that were replicated so exactly on the small face of the child in the next room. She flinched slightly at the touch of the old Duke of Hawksfield as he bent over her hand, impeccable as always: she smelt bergamot, and a hint of almonds, and pomade from his white hair. She indicated that they should sit down; eau de Cologne preceded or followed the Dowager to the most upright chair in the room. Although the fashion still decreed a modicum of simplicity, her mourning dress carried broad hints of other times, and a rather large hat perched, with feathers. The gentlemen sat uncomfortably: George made the mistake he always made, sitting on the sofa, forgetting how soft it was. Rose felt the drawing room full of alien presences, old memories. The new maid brought tea; Miss Proud poured. George refused tea, abruptly stood again in an ungainly manner, hampered by his injured arm. She saw his impatience: forced here by the Duke, anger radiated from him.

'William advises us that you too have been in Egypt.' The Duke's voice was full of gravel, or sand; Rose suddenly remembered the dark hawk that flew over her, the first morning in Alexandria.

'Miss Proud and I have only recently returned.'

'You know then, perhaps,' said the Duke, 'of a matter of which I have only just been apprised. The death of my niece.'

'I do know,' said Rose. 'I am so very sorry.'

'You are in mourning for her?'

Rose bowed her head, as if assenting. She did not look at George.

They sat in silence. Outside there were shouts and argument as all sorts of coachmen exchanged insults: nothing could pass the coach that bore the Hawksfield coat of arms and South Molton Street was completely jammed.

Rose waited: *Do they know anything of Rosetta?*

'I wish to hear something more of Dolly's death,' said the Duke harshly. Rose looked at him coldly. *She saw the pale, strange face of Dolly in the merchant's house, telling of going to the market to buy something to get rid of the baby, and her body in the Turkish khan and George saying, 'No filthy Arab,' and William's anguished face and the high buzzing of the mosquitoes in the darkness, and the heat, and the death.* She wondered which of these matters he would like to know of.

It was Miss Proud who spoke. 'All of us were there, Your Grace. Whatever else had happened, there was nothing any of us could do at the end.' Nobody would ever have disbelieved Miss Proud, and indeed she spoke the truth.

'There, Your Grace,' said the Dowager Viscountess, 'that is what my son has already told you.' She made as if to rise, as if the unpleasant interview in the unpleasant house was over, but the Duke of Hawksfield quelled her just by staring at her. The feathers on her hat shook. The old clock from Genoa informed them all in its Italianate manner that the hour was fifteen minutes past three. The Duke looked at Rose.

'What do you know of this matter?' he said. 'I wish to learn more.' Rose felt the eyes of George and William boring into her. She also heard an infinitesimal sound and turned abruptly. In the doorway of the small room Rosetta stood, holding on to the door and staring at the visitors, all of whom, for various reasons, were too shocked to speak.

The Dowager Viscountess stared, transfixed. She put a hand to her throat as if she could not swallow; she put her hand to her heart as if it would not beat. Her face drained completely of colour; some sound began to come out of her as she stared at the small, dark, damaged version of herself. Rosetta stared back.

'Get it away! *Get it away!*' The Dowager breathed as a dying fish breathes, her mouth gasped. '*Get it away!*'

Rosetta stared.

The Duke, George and William had all risen.

'This – this cannot be Dolly's child?' The gravel voice. Rose caught a glimpse of George's appalled, bright red face.

'No, Your Grace.' Rose quickly picked up Rosetta, stood with her in the doorway. 'Dolly's child died with her. This is my late husband's child. I knew about her, she was the reason for my journey to Egypt.' Rosetta seemed quite unmoved by the Dowager's hysterics, but stared at the feathers on the old lady's hat, which were dancing wildly now. But her small olive hand rested at Rose's neck, for safety. For some time the only sound in the room was the Dowager's strangulated breathing.

George had not spoken, Rose did not look at him. Finally the Duke said, and it was now a statement, not a question: 'This is Harry's child.'

'Yes, Your Grace. He had a child by an Egyptian woman in Alexandria. She was born after his death. I found her in a monastery along the Nile.' Rosetta stared at the people, put her hand now into the hand of Rose.

There was a long, terrible silence. Finally the Duke said: 'What is the matter with the eye?'

'When I found her she was suffering from an eye disease very prevalent in Egypt; it is called ophthalmia.' The Dowager made a sound of disgust.

Miss Proud spoke. 'When we arrived in Egypt the British Embassy in Alexandria had been closed, such is the danger to English people there in these difficult times. When Rose found the child it was imperative to leave the country at once, for Captain Fallon's actions have had long and dangerous consequences. We got what medical help we could but it was not only the oph-thalmia – the child was so weak she would have died if Rose had not found her. It was not until Milan that a decent doctor was found, and not until we got to England that she was able to be treated satisfactorily. She is still, of course, recovering, the doctors still come most days. But it was Rose who saved her life.' The Italian clock ticked loudly.

At last George Fallon, Viscount Gawkroger, was recovered enough to speak, but his face was still bright red. 'This child, Your Grace, is of course, mine. My brother's widow did not see fit to tell me of its existence in London. I heard of the child when I got to Egypt – and would have found it myself if I had not been attacked by foreigners.' Now Rose did look at him but he avoided her eye. 'Of course my family would want to make claim to, and find safety for, any child of my brother.' Rose saw how the words came out of his mouth like lead. 'My sister-in-law thought to find the child on her own, but she has no claims, no right to it at all. It is my plan to take the child: she will be placed in a suitable convent where she will be well attended to.'

'No!' Rose was unable to stop her cry, even with the child in her arms; she felt Rosetta jump in alarm at the sound. 'You cannot do that! You cannot take her away from me. This child has been trav-elling for most of her life, dragged from one place to another, ill, not old enough to understand at all what was happening to her. Please, you must let her feel settled first, whatever is to finally become of her. I beg you, if you have any feeling for this child, or for me, for we have been through many dangers together, let her get properly well, let her feel safe.' Her face was whiter than the Dowager's. 'The doctors say she must not be moved, she is recovering from death!'

The Duke of Hawksfield cleared his throat. 'The law is quite clear, my dear,' he said to Rose, not unkindly. 'You have no rights at all to a child of Harry's. George is the legal guardian. He would not, one expects, forbid you to visit the convent. I am sure,' and he looked at her with that same unreadable expression she remem-bered, 'that you have done a brave thing, if somewhat reckless nevertheless, to bring her all the way to England, through countries at war. But: she does not belong to you,' and Rose felt something in her heart breaking.

'You were always melodramatic, Rose,' said George, some sense of equilibrium restored to him. 'She will be removed to a convent within the week. She is mine, and we shall take her now. She will be quite safe, there is a nurse, for William is a father now.' He moved to stand behind his mother's chair, one hand resting lightly on her shoulder as if to say, *It is almost over*. The shouting of the coachmen in the street worsened, ascended to the windows. There seemed to be some sort of small riot. Inside the room the silence went on and on as if no one knew quite how to take the final step.

It was Rosetta who moved. Something about the Dowager intrigued her: the dress or the jewellery perhaps. She slithered from Rose's arms, made her odd, slow way across the rug. Everyone in the room seemed for a moment hypnotised by the child, for everybody stared. Perhaps it was the scent of eau de Cologne. Perhaps it was the feathers on the hat, the way they moved: certainly she looked up at them. Or did she know, as she crawled very slowly but determinedly across the room; across the room to her grandmother? And then, as if a ghost hovered with them in the room, Rosetta smiled at the old lady: Harry's smile.

The Dowager stared at the scraggy echo of her beloved son, clutched at air, and fainted. This was a large occurrence of feathers and petticoats and rather swollen legs which Rosetta regarded with much interest. Rose leapt to Rosetta and whisked her out of the way, George leapt to his mother, Miss Proud called to the maid for smelling salts. When these arrived they were wafted under the Dowager's nose and faint noises emanated. At this point the Duke, who had not moved, took charge.

'Take your mother to the coach, George, perhaps Miss Proud and William will assist you. We will make arrangements regarding the child later, not at this moment.'

George immediately stood up. 'Your Grace, forgive my impertinence, but you do not own my family. I will not leave the child here one more moment!'

'You will leave her for the present, George,' said the Duke icily, 'for we have not yet finished discussing the death of my niece.'

Something in his voice made even George pause: he stared with unconcealed anger for a moment at the old Duke, at Rose, and finally at Rosetta. Then he turned back to his mother. She was eventually angled down the narrow staircase and only the Duke and Rose and Rosetta were left in the room, and the aroma of eau de Cologne and perspiration.

The Duke said, 'I would be glad if you would sit down.' Rose sat slowly; she was white enough to have fainted herself. *If he insists on asking about Dolly I will tell him the truth.* Rosetta wanted to be put down, but then leaned against Rose for safety, watching the Duke carefully with her damaged blue eyes.

The Duke stood, upright, stern: something unbending about him, and again Rose remembered the hawk; there was something repugnant to her about this man and his power. She looked away from him in despair.

'I have observed you, Rose,' he said quietly, 'since the lives of our families were conjoined. You are an intelligent woman. Many of the women about me,' he added drily, 'are not. I believe you thought it was wrong of me to allow George Fallon to marry my niece,' and he put up his hand before she could speak. 'Without that marriage Dolly's family, William's inheritance, were ruined: too many generations of fools. Dolly's sisters married well, but not well enough. Ann's family has money, of course, but also sons. You do not understand the business of old English families, nor do I expect you to, but I did what I thought to be for the best.' This man walked with kings, this man standing in a house in South Molton Street was powerful in the land and power emanated from him now and she wanted to turn away, such was her almost physical disgust at his presence. She became reckless.

'I was with Dolly when she died in Alexandria. She died in great pain and unhappiness, much of it brought about by her husband, whom you forced her to marry, and by her brother, your nephew, whom she loved with all her heart.' He bowed his head slightly: it was impossible to tell whether he cared or not. She thought to say more, to make a crack in the old man's stern countenance, but did not; heard once more the high buzzing of the mosquitoes in the hot dying Alexandrian night. Rosetta watched the silence. The Duke remained motionless, impervious. At last he gave what may have been the trace of a sigh.

'My dear – these things are over. Dolly is dead. As for you: the Viscount seems to want the child. It is a girl, and it is damaged, but it is – obviously' – and he glanced again at Rosetta – 'a child of the Fallon family and they will not let you keep her, nor would the law allow it. For myself,' the gravelly voice went on, 'I would not care, for my time with the Fallon family has at last, thank God, run its course. William now has a son, the first of many I hope – and we pray that the Torrence line is now as safe as the Torrence fortune, which I have – secured. I understand,' he saw again the child regarding him, 'that you and the child have shared many things, and I think what you and Miss Proud did was extremely foolhardy, but also remarkable. The child seems – fond of you. I would like to make a suggestion.'

'Your Grace,' Rose burst out passionately, 'the Fallon family have ruined one young girl's life, that of your own niece!' and she felt the child flinch again from the sudden tension. 'I do not think George wishes this girl well. I believe' – she bit her lip and then continued – 'I believe George would have killed her if he had found her first.'

His face remained blank. 'That is a strong accusation.'

'Your Grace, George's brother – my late husband – did not die a hero. This child is a reminder. The Viscount, as you no doubt understand, wishes to be part of – of the kind of circle you, and Dolly, were born into. This child is not part of that plan.' She looked away. She had said it all: she did not care. When at last she looked back the Duke of Hawksfield was regarding her with a kind of patronising forbearance.

'You cannot think we did not know of this.' The word *we* encompassed the world he inhabited: the King, the Government, the Power: England. 'You surely do not imagine that somebody like George Fallon could ever become a real part of the world I live in? The child is nothing.'

She spoke coldly, lifting Rosetta up into her arms again. 'She is not nothing to me, Your Grace.' And then, again, she could not contain herself. 'The Fallon family must not be allowed power over yet another young girl! A *convent*! Why should she end her days in a convent? When I . . .' she stumbled and then said quietly, saw the girl watching her face so carefully, 'when I love her.'

'I am afraid the law says that the Viscount does have power over this child and he may place her in a convent if that is what he wishes.' He watched her carefully. 'But – in an area where,' he coughed slightly, 'the law does *not* walk – I have power over the Fallon family. I could have the Viscount turned away from every door in London society if I chose. I would like to ask you if you would consider becoming my wife.'

She looked at him as if she had misheard.

He smiled. It was a wintry smile, but it was a smile. 'You would change your position, and the girl's, for ever, for I believe I do not need to tell you of the Hawksfield family, and of our – prominence. My own wife died some years ago. We did not have children of our own but I am unable to pass my title and my estates to William, my sister's child, as I have a younger brother, with sons. That is why William's patrimony was so important to me: his estate had to be made safe by whatever means available. And now my business is done and the Torrence family is safe.'

And Dolly is dead, thought Rose.

'I have sometimes thought I should like a companion, and as I say, I have observed you for some time. If you married me you would be able to stand in lieu of the girl's mother – I would see to that. She would be brought up in one of the proudest families in England, and you would be the Duchess of Hawksfield, intimate of the King and Queen of England. The old Queen would be glad no doubt of the company of someone young like yourself in her troubled life. There would be no difficulty from George, I can assure you of that, for I blame him for the death of my niece and he shall know it, and shall – providing you agree to my proposal of course – concede legal guardianship of the child to me, and so to you also. If he wishes to live in society.'

Rose did not speak but she found that her hands were shaking, and that the Duke had observed this.

'We will not live with the Fallon family. As I say, the long business is concluded safely at last: William's inheritance is safe. I do not care for London any longer, it has become vulgar: I can go back to Hawksfield Castle with a clear mind at last: I have done my duty as I see it. And – should you do me this honour – I give you my word that the child,' again he observed Rosetta for a moment, 'would legally become my daughter. I also give you my word that she would have an excellent education. You would expect that, I am sure.' He shrugged. 'As for her health, we can of course take her doctors with us to Hawksfield Castle, if that is necessary.' Still Rose did not speak. 'On the other hand, should you feel unable to accept my offer, I am afraid you must say goodbye to her.'

Rose mumbled something along the lines of 'Your Grace, you do me great honour,' staring all the while at his old, cold face. The merest, merest hint of a threat drifted somewhere above them.

'It seems that I might, despite my age' – again the wintry smile – 'offer you a solution to your difficulties. I understand that you may need time to think over my offer, but in the circumstances I feel we should not be tardy. I shall expect to hear from you by the end of tomorrow. We would be married at once.' And he bowed and took her hand and dry lips brushed her skin: the bergamot, the pomade. Then he turned and left: she heard his footsteps going down the stairs.

Rosetta looked up at Rose's face and stared. After some time she put one of her small hands into the hand of Rose, and continued observing her. The only sound in the room was the old Genoa clock. It chimed a quarter-hour. And then a half-hour. Then Rosetta, staring at Rose still, noticed a change in her face.

'Rain?' she said, uncertainly.

Miss Proud came and went, she tried to comfort the weeping, white-faced woman; her heart ached but there was no advice she could profitably give. Rose must decide.

At last Rose put Rosetta to bed as she always did, then sat beside her in the darkness. *'Ma'as salaama*, Rosie,' she said, as she always said when she kissed the tiny head. Rosetta stared at the figure sitting beside her bed for a long time; finally fell asleep clutching the worn, frayed cushion called Angel.

Rose walked slowly back into the drawing room. She lit one of her cigars. Over and over in amongst the smoke of the cigar she heard Fanny's enigmatic words: Fanny, who had gone back to Wentwater with the Reverend Horatio Harbottom: *We have to find a way to bear things. You too, Rose, must find a way, however difficult, as I have done.*

On the old, soft sofa where she had once lain with Pierre Montand and declared her love, she drifted into a kind of sleep: dreamed of ruins in the sand and crumbling, lost hieroglyphs defaced with Coptic crosses; mysterious, shadowy dreams of keys and unlocking and secrets. No sign, no message had ever come from Pierre after that night: *there will not be a third time*, he had said. She heard the nightwatchman lying, *lying*: declaring that all was well.

Next morning, watched gravely by Rosetta, Rose picked up the quill, dipped it into the ink and made the marks on paper that she had learnt so long ago, the marks that had so delighted her, that told what was in her head. Of what was in her heart she gave no sign. *To the Duke of Hawksfield*, she wrote. Her skin was drawn tightly over her cheeks, like pale parchment.

> *My Lord, I must thank you for your generous offer to take Rosetta and myself as part of your family, and I am most grateful to accept.*
> *We will await your instructions.*
> *Rose Fallon*

When the letter had gone Rose walked, quite alone in the cold November day, around the neat, gravelled paths in Hanover Square that she knew so well.

She was determined to make this change with grace; she kept trying to count her blessings over and over: most of all, she had Rosetta, for George could not harm them now. They would never want for anything, Rosetta would have the best medical help that money could buy, and a real education, as men received. It would surely be a very small wedding, far from London. Perhaps they would even enjoy living away from the hurly-burly of London. Perhaps this was, in a way, a happy ending after all.

The thin winter sun tried to shine across the gravel through the railings and the trees: broken half-shadows as if from a dream, her own dreams. She allowed herself to think of Pierre's face, just one more time.

And alone on the path in Hanover Square she closed her eyes in longing.

Pierre's loved face changed into the old, cold face of the Duke of Hawksfield.

THIRTY-ONE

A private service had been held in the chapel in the grounds of Hawksfield Castle, then a formal dinner in the castle hall for perhaps a thousand guests. King George III of England, supported by numerous courtiers, sat at a table on the raised dais together with the Duke and the new Duchess of Hawksfield; Rose had been presented by the King with a pendant of diamonds and emeralds: it glittered now, around her neck.

Huge tapestries and priceless paintings hung above the guests: the paintings were framed in gold. Chandeliers sparkled with hundreds and hundreds of candles, servants scurried about replacing the lights, removing wax. Ceilings were painted and moulded: saints and princes stared down from trailing clouds, intertwined with angels. Cold draughts blew along floors, came in under huge old doors, ruffled at rich rugs and carpets. Several large orchestras played, there was a regal rendition of Handel's Royal Fireworks Music: there would be actual fireworks later.

The royal party ate from gold. Much fine food and wine was served by hundreds of bewigged footmen. Fanny, regarding the food all around her, assumed whole villages belonging to the Duke would have been plundered, sheep and pigs and cows, but she saw that people who were fortunately, or unfortunately, sitting near to the King, as she and Horatio were, did not stuff chicken legs and cow's ribs into their mouths or gurgle down wine as they had at Berkeley Square: this was obviously not done in the presence of the King of England in the castle of the Duke of Hawksfield.

The Duke's family, among them William and Ann, the Marquess and Marchioness of Allswater, were also near to the royal dais (still adjusting to the idea that Rose Fallon had suddenly become their *aunt*). But Ann knew enough about the society she moved in not to make any voluble criticisms of the old Duke's actions. She consumed huge quantities of brandy and did not care: had she not produced one son and was she not pregnant with another? Her place was secure and her front teeth were to be replaced by new, bright, white porcelain. William caught George's eye. (George sat further down the hall with his mother, where his position as ex-nephew-in-law to the Duke warranted. His anger made his face very red.)

'*Whore!*' he had managed to whisper to Rose, privately, earlier. 'You have prostituted yourself. And I will always, always know it!'

Now George scanned the tables nearer to the King: it was here, tonight, when the dancing and the fireworks were in full flow, that he would approach a duchess's daughter he had ascertained earlier: he must turn his presence at this – his mind could not bear to think the word – *illustrious* wedding to his advantage. The duchess's daughter had an unfortunate face, a little like a cow: big eyes, fat cheeks and lips; but her ducal father was distantly related to His Majesty: with this family perhaps he would be luckier. He was once more looking for a suitable wife.

The Reverend Horatio Harbottom was hungry. He could not eat. He had tried small mouthfuls, but to be this close to the King of England almost made him choke. His wife, *his own wife*, had stood beside the King of England, as witnesses in the chapel. It brought him out in terrible perspiration. Fanny was now beside him in her grey dress. He felt humble in her presence, she seemed above him, she moved with royalty. She again organised his life, she again cooked his meals: he knew how lucky he was to be married to such a person, who welcomed lords and ladies to his lowly vicarage. Sometimes he felt very confused. He did not quite understand what had happened. His children now, he realised, had become very – he searched for a word – forbearing. When he blustered and thundered and said travelling had ruined them, everybody was – what were they? – indulgent, as if he had been ill. The Reverend Horatio Harbottom gave a small sigh. He spent a lot of time in his garden now: somehow that was where he was happiest. The other day he had picked a large bunch of winter flowers and brought them in to Fanny, and she had looked at him a little as she used to, long ago. He sighed again. He could still thunder from the pulpit on Sundays; and Fanny was returned to him, however strangely. He did not allow the French publications to enter his mind very often, for Fanny was very kind.

He watched Fanny now, surreptitiously, but Fanny was staring at her cousin. In a simple yellow gown, wearing the exquisite royal pendant, Rose listened to some words of His Majesty; she was pale still, and thin, Fanny saw, but she was smiling politely and sat very straight; contained, it seemed, now that the step had been taken. Only her clenched hands which Fanny could see beneath the table gave her away. The King smiled benignly. The Duke of Hawksfield watched his new wife. The orchestra played a mazurka now, but nobody, of course, danced, not in front of the King.

Miss Proud, having for Rose's sake bowed perfunctorily to King George the Third of England, had escaped. She had made her way up the magnificent marble staircase from the hall and along vast, dim corridors, as soon as was decently possible; candles flickered, noblemen stared, Greek figures posed whitely, old Roman urns looked at her malignly. Several times she had got lost, and footmen and maids had guided the sweet old lady (they assumed her sweet, not being privy to her thoughts) along further ghostly corridors, up further stairs; now she sat with Rosetta and her nurse, stifling as best she could those thoughts she had harboured in the hot Egyptian night on the balcony of the *khan* about disposing of the Royal Family in the antipodes. The nurse bustled away for tea; Miss Proud actually wiped her brow with a small white handkerchief and then sat stiffly beside the child, who had been placed in a very large ornate cot, a Hawksfield family heirloom.

'Well, Rosetta,' said Miss Proud. 'Well.' She stared about the large, dark, ancestor-hung room. 'Your life has changed very much and I will withhold my prejudices, for the sake of necessity, you understand?' Rosetta seemed to consider this, observed Miss Proud carefully, and then smiled at her. 'You will have many, many wonderful chances. Your mother has,' Miss Proud leaned closer, spoke more softly, 'found a way, as your Aunt Fanny has done. You must always be proud of them, Rosetta. I, on the other hand, a foolish old woman, will do my very best to make sure you do not lose touch with the real world. But – most of all, my dear, I hope – *oh*, I shall miss you most dreadfully,' and suddenly Miss Proud was busy with her handkerchief, 'I hope that you and your dear, dear mother will somehow be able to be happy.'

All at once fireworks lit up the room. The nurse bustled back, lifted Rosetta carefully to the windows overlooking the Duke's long, ornate gardens filled with mazes, and white statues, and perfectly shaped trees. They stood at the window open-mouthed as great patterns of lights burst into the sky, over and over, in every colour of the rainbow. Rosetta's blue eyes were wide, as best they could be. They heard the fireworks exploding into the night.

The Royal Coach had gone.

Over the dancing and the music Fanny saw that the Duke of Hawksfield would speak. He stood. The guests coughed into silence, the music died away: everybody attended His Grace. He gave a brief oration, he thanked the assembled guests for their good wishes. Then he bade them goodnight and he turned towards the grand staircase, indicating to his new wife that she should follow.

Rose looked back once. Fanny saw that she smiled at the assembled guests with blank, empty eyes. She did not see them at all, any of them, not even Fanny.

'Come, Rose,' said the Duke of Hawksfield.

THIRTY-TWO

And so Rosetta lived: in splendour and safety; in a castle; not in the Egyptian desert and not in a convent. She became Lady Rosetta Hawksfield, to whom her real uncle (George, who had wanted to kill her) and her real grandmother (the Dowager Viscountess, who had cried *Get it away!*) had, for the sake of their social survival, to give obeisance. And Rosetta smiled at them: and they saw Harry. When she came to London they showed her the huge painting of her father and his medals in the entrance hall of the house in Berkeley Square: she observed it expressionlessly. And against all their principles, they found – to their utmost humiliation – that they began to want to see more of the foreign, olive-skinned, damaged child; that to their horror they began to *yearn* to see the child who watched them so carefully, as if she knew them.

George Fallon's greatest humiliation of all was that, in the presence of the Duke of Hawksfield at least, he had to address his mortal enemy, Rose Fallon as: *Your Grace*. He did it through murderous, gritted teeth.

Rose, Duchess of Hawksfield, smiled and smiled and understood that the nights of her life were the price she had to pay for Rosetta (for Rosetta was her love, and her life). It was Rose who taught Rosetta to read and write before she was given to the best tutors in the land; it was Rose who taught her the joy of words and the miracle of how she could take the thoughts from inside her head and place them on paper.

Rose paid the price, and smiled and smiled. She was an exemplary wife and became a hostess of great renown, and she knew that she had done what she had vowed on that cold morning, alone in Hanover Square, to – with grace – do.

But words uninvited haunted her mind: the old description in her father's book of hieroglyphs: *the bird of prey swoops directly down upon anything beneath it . . . and its opponent, unable to do the like, is overcome.* The requirements of the nights – the moment when her husband, the Duke of Hawksfield, turned to her with his cold eyes and said, 'Come, Rose' – meant that the life that had once danced in her soul finally fragmented, and froze.

1817

Time present and time past
Are both perhaps present in time future
And time future contained in time past.

T. S. Eliot
(*Burnt Norton*, 1935)

THIRTY-THREE

First it was a rumour: men in crowded, smoky coffee-houses passed it from mouth to mouth with other gossip, took it home to their wives. Had it been any other member of the Royal Family – especially the Prince Regent, even the King himself, now locked away mad – there would have been laughter; or something more than laughter perhaps, a sense of disdain. But the young Princess: *she will be different*, the people had said.

Finally the newspapers gave confirmation:

Her Royal Highness Princess Charlotte is no more. This young, beautiful and interesting Princess died at half past two o'clock in the morning of Thursday November the sixth 1817 having survived the delivery of a still-born child but a few hours.

Miss Proud's body was knotted and bent as she pored over the newspapers beside the fire in South Molton Street. She had grown smaller and her magnifying spectacles had grown larger: her spectacles were so strong now that she looked like an old owl.

'No Queen of England then, after all,' said Miss Proud to the empty room. 'If only a *woman* had become monarch, English-women would have become free. And now our chance is lost.' She was so engrossed in the report that she singed her slippers, did not notice this until she caught the smell of burning. She moved back clumsily, brushed at her slippers in an absent-minded manner, still reading.

> . . . looking to Her Royal Highness as the mother of a long and illustrious line of British Kings, but little attention has been paid to what must be the state of the succession on the contingency of her premature demise. But now the consideration has been forced on our attention, and the prospect is by no means flattering. The sons and daughters of our present monarch are all without lawful issue . . .

Miss Proud's maid (who had been having a quiet weep for the young Princess down in the kitchen) was suddenly aware of burning, came running up into the drawing room, found discarded singed slippers and Miss Proud painfully putting on her coat and hat. Already bells tolled all over London.

'You must not go out, Miss Proud, not with your rheumatics: it is too cold, and it is too dangerous, there will be crowds everywhere and all them soldiers roaming about with one leg, and drunk!' Miss Proud smiled but seemed not to hear; the maid sighed and helped Miss Proud with her boots, put on her own cloak and bonnet also. The two women went out into the grey November day, made their way slowly in the direction of Whitehall.

Public grief seemed to strike London in a most unusual way: crowds appeared, people wept along the streets as if their hearts would break for the loss of their Princess; past the new gas street lamps in Piccadilly, past the new, grand statues of the Duke of Wellington; wept at their loss. *Such a saintly princess . . . ill-treated by her degenerate father.* They tried not to see the degenerate unemployed soldiers and sailors who roamed the streets also, shouting and begging for halfpennies or work; who vomited, from too much gin and not enough food, over the extravagant new memorials celebrating the Battle of Waterloo and Victory Over Napoleon. Dragoons on horseback kept an uneasy eye on the huge crowds, roughly pushed them back with their horses. Troublemakers had been complaining: of the ridiculous cost of the oriental palace in Brighton; of the sight of so many Victory Memorials when the soldiers who had gained that victory were starving; of the government itself. The government had rounded up those rebels who they believed encouraged the unemployed in their misery, and they were hanged. Napoleon might be captured on St Helena, but revolution was only too obviously in the air in England, and today the officers on horseback were looking for any similar rabble-rousers. Miss Proud could not have looked less like a rabble-rouser, but as a young man who had been addressing part of the crowd was hustled roughly past she managed to slip a sovereign into his hand: saw surprised, grateful eyes. She was grateful too: the Dowager Duchess of Hawksfield insisted on giving her money. Miss Proud often spent it in this way.

But today in Whitehall most people turned their heads away from the unemployed soldiers, and grieved for the lovely Princess. After some time Miss Proud and her maid made their way slowly home.

Odes and elegies to the dead Princess (of varying quality) were instantly composed in their thousands, all over the Kingdom of Great Britain.

The Established Church was terrified, even as it prepared for the Royal Funeral. People wept, yes, but there was too much unease in the air, some people even thought of Napoleon, the defeated enemy, as a hero! What if such huge crowds in the street, weeping now for the Princess, turned against the monarchy and the Church? As had happened in France? *It was not to be contemplated!* And so Words of Warning, commanding people to turn back to Religious Principles or Expect the Lord to Punish them, thundered about the countryside, were printed as innumerable pamphlets. Churchmen distributed two hundred and forty-nine thousand, nine hundred and thirty-two Bibles.

George Fallon, Viscount Gawkroger, was disgusted. Churchmen throughout the land lectured unendingly on the need to give up frivolous pleasure and immorality and extravagance, to embrace instead abstinence and domesticity: such sentiments seemed somehow to be creeping into his own life. His wife the Viscountess, who looked just slightly like a cow, informed him sweetly that she had heard – now that there was no heir to the throne – that all the King's sons, all the raddled, immoral dukes, were hurriedly paying more attention to their formal, approved marriages and earnestly trying to impregnate their legal wives: domesticity reigned, the Viscountess said, however briefly, even in royal circles – and perhaps could reign in theirs? (For they only had one child, a son of course.)

'Ye gods!' cried George in a rage, throwing a newspaper across the room.

On the day of the Royal Funeral at Windsor, Miss Proud, again, slowly put on her boots and her cloak. She wanted to hear what was being said in the churches: sermons were to be delivered on the death of the Princess all over the nation, and Miss Proud suspected the Church would make its own use of this sad occasion. Accompanied by her maid, she sat in the front row of a church near Piccadilly. It was a long time since she had been in a church. She closed her eyes for a moment as she listened to the organ playing, remembered her long-ago childhood in the vicarage in Wiltshire and the spring afternoon when she had walked down the aisle in a white wedding gown.

The Dean began, deceptively quiet,

'My dear brethren, look upon the protracted agony and premature dissolution of an illustrious, amiable and truly excellent Princess in her twenty-second year.' And then the voice, already, started to rise; the sermon began in earnest. 'When it is our Almighty Creator's will to say to the Sword of the Destroying Angel: *'Sword! Go through the land, for the iniquity of them who dwell therein!'* who is able to abide his coming? All ye who have sinned: Repent! Where are the Egyptians, the Persians, and the Great Assyrian monarchies?' He was shouting now. 'They are swept away by the besom of destruction; they are overwhelmed! But they were previously long sunk and buried' (the voice lowered to a whisper) 'in the whited sepulchre of luxury and voluptuousness.'

Here Miss Proud got up and very slowly walked back down the aisle, her maid following behind. Miss Proud looked like such a sweet old lady that the weeping congregation presumed she was overcome by emotion, and in a way they were right. The voice of doom pursued her.

'The fleets and armies of our fiercest enemies were all unable to effect our destruction! Let not our own national offences then, our own enormities, accomplish that terrible event! Repent!'

'Repent yourselves!' said Miss Proud loudly.

When she got home she found in her newspaper a woman writer of some renown calling on the Women of England: In these Alarming Times Women Must Show the Way. They must give up all else, all thoughts of self, and devote their whole lives to their families; they must give themselves wholeheartedly: as a helpmeet to their husbands, as an example to their children; they must raise the depressed tone of public morals and awaken the drowsy spirit of religious principle, and the Hearth must be their Tabernacle.

'Ye gods!' said Miss Proud in a rage, throwing (as far as her terrible rheumatism would allow) the book across the room. *The Hearth must be their Tabernacle!* For women, the world is going backwards!'

Everywhere excitement for things Egyptian, started by Napoleon, had grown to immense proportions: there were Egyptian exhibitions in Piccadilly, and all over the country women wore turbans as a fashion accessory. Antiquities from Egypt now arrived at Marseilles or Portsmouth on every ship: huge granite legs and hands, obelisks, heads of Pharaohs found lying in the sand. In Egypt the French and the English bargained with one another, tricked one another, scrawled graffiti on one another's treasures, divided Egypt's sites of antiquity between them or curried favour with the new Pasha, Mohammed Ali, whom they had once dismissed as a mad Albanian. (The mad Albanian had, by force and by cunning, obliterated the Mameluk Beys.) With the disappearance of those Mameluk Beys who had chased him from the Baths in Rosetta, George Fallon would have amassed another fortune – if he had not crossed Mrs Venetzia Alabaster, now one of the most powerful traders in Egypt and married to a fierce Bedouin sheikh. Even now George was not safe around the ports of Alexandria and Rosetta: he could not therefore oversee the shipping of antiquities to Europe. He nevertheless acquired some smaller treasures by creeping into old tombs far away up the Nile. He found gold cups, and stunning jewellery (pieces of which his old, mad mother sometimes wore). It was whispered that the Viscount Gawkroger walked with the dead: smashed mummy cases in the darkness to find the valuable papyri that had been buried with the bodies, so that he could sell the ancient writing. George obtained these treasures but he stared at them, uncomprehending.

However, at the seaside in Worthing, Thomas Young, an English doctor and linguist, had been sitting beside the sea with some ancient papyri and a copy of the Rosetta Stone: his holiday reading.

'The Egyptians kept detailed records of their rulers and they had many *foreign* rulers,' he said to his wife as they sat in the shade of an old oak tree in the garden of their hotel. 'Surely they would have had to write at least the foreign names down with an alphabet or phonetics, so we must first find and compare foreign names like *Ptolemy*, *Alexander*, *Cleopatra* with more than one similar letter.' At last he was able to prove he had found five examples of the name PTOLEMY: in the hieroglyphs, spelt alphabetically, inside the cartouches on the Rosetta Stone.

The English government, thrilled by his findings (and most anxious to find the key to the hieroglyphs before the French), advised their consul-general in Egypt to urgently find and send other specimens of ancient Egyptian writing. ('But please do not send whole obelisks,' they instructed firmly.)

The arrival in London of all these exciting antiquities decided a new young poet, Percy Shelley, and his accountant, Horace Smith, to view these treasures at the Museum, and then see which of them could write the best poem about them. Miss Proud, through her friendship with them, acquired copies of both poems – but declined to be the judge. ('One is a poet,' she said to Rosetta drily, 'and one is a stockbroker.')

Mr Smith (the stockbroker) had written a poem entitled: ON A STUPENDOUS LEG OF GRANITE DISCOVERED STANDING BY ITSELF IN THE DESERTS OF EGYPT WITH THE INSCRIPTION BELOW:

In Egypt's sandy silence all alone,
Stands a gigantic Leg, which far off throws
The only shadow that the Desert knows.
'I am great Ozymandias,' saith the stone,
'The King of Kings; this mighty City shows
The Wonders of my hand.' The City's gone!
Nought but the leg remaining to disclose
The sight of this forgotten Babylon.

Mr Shelley (the poet) had written a poem entitled: OZYMANDIAS.

I met a traveller from an antique land
Who said: Two vast and trunkless legs of stone
Stand in the desert. Near them, on the sand,
Half sunk, a shattered visage lies, whose frown,
And wrinkled lip, and sneer of cold command,
Tell that its sculptor well those passions read
Which yet survive, stamped on these lifeless things,
The hand that mocked them and the heart that fed:
And on the pedestal these words appear:
'My name is Ozymandias, king of kings:
Look on my works, ye Mighty, and despair!'
Nothing beside remains. Round the decay
Of that colossal wreck, boundless and bare
The lone and level sands stretch far away.

Fifteen-year-old Lady Rosetta Hawksfield read the poems carefully and then visited the British Museum to see these treasures from her country for herself. She reported back to Miss Proud at once.

'There are plenty of big stone legs in the Egyptian collection to write poems about – should one so desire! But I do not believe that Mr Shelley has actually seen that beautiful granite head of the young Pharaoh.'

'Why?'

'Oh, Miss Proud, you should see it, it is huge, and thousands of years old, and it has crossed oceans and it is still smiling! It is so beautiful! It was apparently found buried in the sand far up the Nile by a mad Italian who used to be a strongman in the Circus and is now working for the British Consul in Cairo. It is called the "Head of Young Menon" and it was loaded into an Egyptian boat on the Nile – I expect the strongman just lifted it up all by himself – and floated all the way down the river to Alexandria and then put on a barge and it came all the way across the sea to England and it nearly drowned several times. Fancy writing a poem about a *leg* when you could write a poem about such a head!' Lady Rosetta Hawksfield was a cool and collected young lady: Miss Proud regarded her extraordinary outburst of enthusiasm with interest.

'And so I do not believe that Mr Shelley *saw* the head in the Museum,' said Rosetta again to Miss Proud.

'Why do you say that?'

'Because the face that has crossed oceans does not have a sneer of cold command! It is beautiful, and so kind.'

Miss Proud, to her chagrin, had been confined to her rooms by doctors since the day of the funeral of the Princess and so could not verify Rosetta's words. But she said: 'Mr Shelley is writing of something else, I believe.'

'What do you mean?' asked Rosetta.

'He is very angry with the government. And the Church.'

'About the poor soldiers and sailors, and the memorials?'

'And unfair laws. And money being spent instead on the Prince Regent and his pavilion in Brighton. And Mr Wordsworth, once a revolutionary, accepting the appointment of Distributor of Stamps – that has upset Mr Shelley. And people being hanged. And how the Church supports the monarchy and does not criticise.

And how history may judge our leaders differently. I believe he is using the poem to write of these things.'

Rosetta smiled her father's smile, in her blue dress that matched her eyes. She was wearing, as Rose had always promised, a patch over one eye, like a pirate, and she regarded Miss Proud fondly. 'You always make sure I see *underneath*.'

'I only want you to know the world, dear child.'

They heard the rustle of skirts and Fanny, who always lodged with Miss Proud when she came to London, ran downstairs. She kissed Rosetta. 'I am so sorry to keep you waiting.'

'Mama will meet us there,' said Rosetta.

'We will report everything,' they said to Miss Proud as they ran out into the falling snow and into the carriage that was blocking South Molton Street, as usual.

Despite the weather the hall was crowded with people, as if the approach of the date of the birth of Jesus made them more thoughtful than usual. There were angry wounded soldiers next to pensive middle-class men in waistcoats, and ladies in hats and shawls, and children too, huddling next to their parents for warmth.

When Fanny spoke there was silence. She spoke very simply in her grey dress; the people took to her and knew her because her red hair was never quite neat under her grey bonnet and she seemed like them, someone who had hurried here despite the snow because it somehow seemed important to do so. And there was one other thing that the people liked about Fanny. At her waist, shining against the grey of her Quaker gown, she wore a startling blue scarf the colour of the Egyptian sky. And people smiled without realising, because it was so beautiful, and so joyous, and made them feel hopeful.

Fanny said: 'In this busy city we have come together to reflect, in quietness, about our lives. Let us all be silent for a moment. Let us take this moment to quieten our hearts and listen – in the stillness perhaps a voice will speak to us, or perhaps the solution to difficulties in our lives may simply become clearer.' And the hall shuffled, and became quiet, and some people coughed, and some people closed their eyes, and some people looked about them in an uneasy manner as if taken aback to be left with their own thoughts.

It was out of the quietness (perhaps it was because of the quietness) that an outraged voice suddenly called from somewhere in the hall: 'You should be home looking after your husband and your children! It says in the Bible: *I do not permit a woman to be a teacher, nor must woman domineer over man; she should be quiet!* First Epistle to Timothy, Chapter Two!'

A ripple ran around the hall, people turned towards the voice in anger, saw it belonged to a soldier in a torn and dirty uniform, and that he had no arms. The people in the hall murmured among themselves, not knowing then whether to be angry or ashamed, but Fanny put out her hand towards the soldier in a conciliatory gesture.

'My friend,' she said gently, 'such anger as yours in any heart can only lead to sadness. One of my assistants will come to you at the end of this meeting – perhaps we can help you in some way. You have fought for our country and we are grateful to you, and proud of you.' And the soldier was silent, stared up at Fanny. And the men in waistcoats too, and the women, and the other soldiers, were all quiet again for a time, as if the lady in grey with the flying red hair and the wonderful blue scarf brought them, however briefly, a kind of calm.

Fanny spoke of hope and of good. Because she was dressed in her grey Quaker gown, and because she spoke so kindly, and of love, the people in the hall assumed they were hearing of God. Only Rose, Dowager Duchess of Hawksfield, noticed that, actually, His name was not mentioned.

Later that evening the red-haired Quaker woman was to be seen entering the Hanover Square Concert Rooms; not for a recital of Mr Haydn's music, which was often the fare at the moment, but for a special meeting arranged by the Trustees of the British Museum. Such was the interest that carriages arriving outside the concert rooms were blocking traffic. With the red-haired woman was a dark-haired woman in a beautiful fur-lined cloak, and an odd-looking young girl. Odd-looking because she had olive skin, not quite like Londoners, and wore a black patch over one eye as if she was the daughter of a pirate. They took their seats: the hall was buzzing with anticipation.

Rose looked about her; the Director of the Trustees of the British Museum raised his hand and she smiled. Rose was hostessing his dinner afterwards, in her large house in Grosvenor Square, for the philosophers and the linguists and the members of Parliament: she smiled at many people. She saw George Fallon, Viscount Gawkroger, antique hunter *extraordinaire*, standing with his wife; they nodded coldly to one another but no machinations of his could harm her now, for now she walked with royalty. And George Fallon was where he had always been: richer and richer, but outside the magic circle.

Standing with George were William and Ann, the Duke and Duchess of Torrence. Ann had had all her front teeth out long ago, safe with three sons; she used her fan a great deal, for the porcelain paste teeth were not entirely satisfactory. She was still a social dragon, but an enigmatic rather than a voluble one because the porcelain teeth clattered rather loudly when she spoke. William caught Rose's eye, raised his hand in greeting: Ann saw, did not care. Whatever might be between them did not bother her: let the saintly Dowager deal with his wine-sodden reluctance.

Ann misunderstood.

Long ago William and Rose had found themselves one evening, the Duke of Hawksfield called suddenly to Windsor, alone in the long ornate garden where mimosa now grew and where the Duke and William had once planted a frankincense tree, to see if it would flourish. William had looked about him in embarrassment as he always did in Rose's proximity, wanting to get away from the one woman who knew too much about him, but Rose had laid a hand lightly on his arm. 'There is no need to avoid me William, I am not in the least interested in discussing you with my husband,' she said coolly. 'But – I said that one day I would give you Dolly's message.'

She saw his startled face: light and shadows fell across the garden where Greek statues held burning torches, but at once they both saw the hot Alexandrian darkness and the mosquitoes and the wailing of the women, and Dolly. William would not look at Rose, suddenly paid great attention to a statue of Athene, Goddess of Wisdom.

'She asked me to say something to you.' She saw that he could not bear it.

'Whatever else you may think of me, Rose, please do not think that I do not know that I failed' – and he could not say her name – 'my sister.' Rose was silent. 'I know she loved me,' he said into the marble folds of Athene's flowing robe. 'From a small child she loved me most, and I did not love her enough. I thought when she married George that he would look after her, I told him that she needed – great care. But – he got bored. And – I saw what I wanted to see.' He still stared ahead at the white shape in the darkness; finally his hand smoothed the marble, as if to somehow comfort himself. 'I know, however, the price of my patrimony, Rose, I do not need you to remind me. And I will know it for the rest of my life.'

'She asked me to say something to you,' she repeated. 'At the end.' He reluctantly turned to her at last. 'She asked me to say that' – Rose remembered Dolly's desolate, dying face, so long ago, and swallowed hard – 'that she was sorry to have been a nuisance to you, and – and that she loved you more than anybody else in the world.'

She saw his face, heard the sound in his throat, saw his shoulders crumple; before he could turn away she put her arms around him for a moment and wept also: at last then, for a short moment, Dolly was properly mourned in the middle of the dark and flickering garden of her uncle, where there was now no sign at all of the frankincense tree. It had died, as she had done, in a foreign land.

So Rose raised her hand now, in the Hanover Square Concert Rooms, and saluted Dolly's brother wryly.

With them all now, in the concert hall, was George's new friend, Charles Cooper, back from the wars, a man with a mission: he needed urgently to marry an heiress or he would have to go into the Church. His cold, handsome face surveyed the room as George's had once done (except that Charles Cooper would sacrifice class for money). Rose had made it extremely clear to George that Rosetta was not for sale.

'If she was *mine*,' George had said in reply, old anger surfacing, 'she would marry him!' But Lady Rosetta Hawksfield did not belong to George.

When Rose, Dowager Duchess of Hawksfield, still looking about the crowded concert hall, caught sight of Pierre Montand buttoning the shoe of a young boy, the room turned and spun; she made a small sound and held the back of the chair in front of her. She did not see Rosetta stare; in a moment she had contained herself. Pierre Montand, his hair marked with grey now, indicated to the boy to sit beside a woman and another older boy. He smiled down at them all.

Only this. This is the only pain in the world now that I knew I could not bear.

Pierre Montand left his family and went up on to the platform, where the speakers were now gathering. He went across to some very large flat parcels at the back of the platform and a young man helped him to unwrap them and display the contents. Fanny then suddenly saw him also, turned quickly to look at Rose, saw her face. Fanny said nothing at all, but took Rose's gloved hand into hers, and held it tightly.

'What is the matter, Mama?' asked Rosetta, observing everything, seeing her mother's face.

'Nothing, my dearest. A ghost.'

As the platform became suddenly alight with many lamps, both Rose and Fanny gasped. One of the strange and beautiful paintings they had seen long ago in the Commission de l'Egypte in Paris illuminated the stage: a painting of the Nile river and the lush vegetation and the blindfolded buffaloes turning the waterwheels, and the sails of the *djerms* and the *feluccas* caught in the sunlight, and Rose remembered, out of the past, the early-morning river with Flo, and the haunting sound of the waterwheels – and the finding of Rosetta. She looked at Rosetta. The girl stared at the painting: something there in her face; it could not possibly be memory Rose thought, yet something intent, private.

The other painting was of the hieroglyphs: the hawk and the lion and the sun and scarabs. Rose quickly looked down at her hands: somebody watching might have thought the hieroglyphs were of no interest to her.

There was applause. Dr Young, the Englishman who had taken the Rosetta Stone for holiday reading in Worthing, spoke to the illustrious gathering of his thoughts on the hieroglyphs, and the small triumphs as scholars slowly moved towards knowledge, deciphered some of the words. They knew definitely now that there was a connection between the two Egyptian inscriptions on the Rosetta Stone, and that the hieroglyphs were at least partly alphabetic. The audience audibly stirred and rustled with excitement. But knowing there were Frenchmen in the hall, Dr Young did not say what he had now come to believe: that the hieroglyphs were partly phonetic sounds also. 'The British Consul sends us evidence all the time,' he told the audience. 'But we are still, after twenty years, only at the beginning of unravelling the meaning of the writing of Ancient Egypt.' He glanced at the French visitors.

Pierre Montand, sitting on the stage with his precious paintings, those paintings that had been obtained with the loss of so many Frenchmen who were now only memories, listened to the prosperous Englishman standing before him. He would not say that in France a brilliant, impecunious student of linguistics, Jean-François Champollion, who had somehow managed to avoid conscription into Napoleon's voracious armies, had found an old Coptic monk, in Paris, to teach him the Coptic language. Monsieur Champollion knew that this language was the nearest anybody would find to the ancient Egyptian languages; this young man studied long into the night in defeated France and believed he was on the way to solving the mystery. Pierre's head was bowed and his thoughts were unreadable. When it was his turn to speak, he told of the *Description de l'Egypte*, of the meticulous work that for so many years had gone into the preparing of the sections for publication, and of the volumes still to come. The audience, many of whom had seen – even owned – the magnificent books, listened, mesmerised. Pierre spoke of how they had come about: of the work of the *savants* in Egypt under Napoleon, of Napoleon's fascination for all things Egyptian, as if Napoleon Buonaparte was still leader of France and not languishing in the South Atlantic under British guard. And he ended by saying that it was one of his greatest dreams that the hieroglyphs would be solved in his lifetime and thus allow everyone to know more about the priceless treasures found in that ancient and fascinating land.

Afterwards guests arrived at Rose's house in Grosvenor Square exhilarated, delighted and fascinated with the evening's entertainment; they came into the huge chandelier-lit hall: the philosophers and the doctors and the linguists and the writers and the politicians. When Pierre Montand arrived he introduced his wife. Rose, the Dowager Duchess of Hawksfield, who had had many years of practice at hiding her feelings, smiled and smiled her hostess's smile, including in her smile the attractive woman by his side.

'*Bonsoir*, Madame Montand,' she said. '*Bienvenue à Londres*.'

The museum's Director of Trustees whisked them away. More people arrived. Footmen glided with trays and Rose mixed with the guests, smiling and smiling.

The evening was a great success, the interest in Egypt was everywhere, clamouring among the chandeliers and the wine; all sorts of people spoke of their desire to travel to Egypt, to sail the Nile, to walk the desert, to see the treasures.

'I wish to see the Pyramids by moonlight,' cried one lady in an awed voice.

'I wish to see,' said another lady dramatically, striking a pose so that the flowers in her hair shook violently, 'where the little baby Moses in his little basket was found by the Pharaoh's wife on the banks of the Nile. Or – was it his daughter?'

Pierre Montand nodded pleasantly to Fanny in her Quaker dress, did not attempt to speak to her. Dr Young, the English linguist, was also a Quaker and spoke to Fanny at length. Rosetta spoke to her Uncle George, whom she did not like particularly but whom she had long, long ago learnt to twist round her little finger: she only had to smile. She treated her old grandmother (now confined to her bed crowing about the ascension of Louis XVIII in France) in exactly the same way, with a kind of exasperated intimacy which Rose, observing, admired: as if Rosetta understood them, being of their blood. They were appalled by her existence, and adored her despite themselves, and understood her not at all.

'You must travel, *Rosetta mia*,' said George Fallon to his niece, 'you must see your homeland. I will arrange everything.' He had said this to her twenty times and twenty times, Rosetta had answered, 'England is my homeland,' as if she meant it.

'Of course England is her homeland, George,' said his wife heartily, although privately she knew an Englishman would have to be desperate for money to marry a one-eyed, olive-skinned bastard: even Charles Cooper, who was desperate, was surely not that desperate.

When the carriages were called and Pierre Montand left with his wife, he bowed again to the Dowager Duchess of Hawksfield.

'This is my daughter, Rosetta,' said Rose. And saw, for a fleeting moment as he bowed to Rosetta with her jaunty eye-patch and her confident smile, that Pierre's composure slipped. He looked back at Rose. And she saw that he, too, remembered the child in the cot in the next-door room and the windows looking out over South Molton Street and the candle guttering out in the night, and the turmoil and the love and the danger. Neither of them saw that Rosetta stared at them both, as she had stared so long ago.

And then he was gone.

THIRTY-FOUR

Rosetta walked from Grosvenor Square to South Molton Street. The uneven surfaces of the dangerous streets ran with slush and mud and the usual filth: turds, orange peel, newspapers, bones, dead rats, broken bottles, fish-heads. Neither Rose nor Miss Proud liked Rosetta to walk alone even on this short journey: there were beggars and soldiers and street children even in Mayfair. But Rosetta insisted that people were frightened of her and her eye-patch, not she of them. She wore a cloak and stout little boots; it was still snowing softly but Rosetta, intent on her own thoughts, did not notice. The maid met her at the door, took her cloak, ushered her in to the bent old lady and the fire. Miss Proud, sitting at her table among books and newspapers, was frowning over the work of a new poet she had begun recommending to people, a young man called John Keats. He had just published his first book of poetry but no one but his friends was buying it.

'People cannot recognise new talent when it is in front of their eyes,' she said severely to Rosetta, 'just because he has trained as an apothecary,' and then she blinked and smiled. 'Good morning, dear girl. I forgot for a moment where I was.'

Rosetta laughed and kissed the old lady. 'Have I missed Aunt Fanny?'

Miss Proud looked through her latest, very magnifying, spectacles. 'She has already gone back to Wentwater. You know how she feels she must hurry home, and Jane's impending marriage calls!'

'Of course. I should have been earlier. I had an Arabic lesson with that mad old professor Mama found at the museum.'

'Is he mad?'

Rosetta considered. 'Yes,' she said. 'He is an Englishman but he thinks he is an Arab – he wears Arab clothes and a small turban, but he still looks like an Englishman! They say he has a *shisha* – a water-pipe – in his house and there is much interest in what he puts inside it. However his knowledge of the language is wonderful. But I am sorry I missed Aunt Fanny, I was so interested to hear her last night. People like her because she is so simple and direct.'

'She says the Reverend Horatio Harbottom has taken to his bed again.'

'As he does whenever she goes away! But Jane and Horatio told me that as soon as she gets back he says, "I think I could take a little soup."' And Miss Proud laughed with Rosetta through her spectacles but saw that the girl was distracted about something. Miss Proud had learnt that Rosetta would come to what was on her mind in her own time.

'Poor Reverend Harbottom,' said Miss Proud. 'He was outmanoeuvred long ago. He never knows when the Duchess of Brayfield may call – as she and Lord Stone apparently do most frequently. It greatly enhances Horatio's position in Wentwater when the fine carriages draw up to the vicarage, but such continuing unexpected visits keep him on his toes!' Rosetta giggled, reminding Miss Proud that she was clever and educated and articulate but she was also, still, a young girl. 'And you have snowflakes in your hair, young lady.'

'And you have red cheeks from the fire!' Rosetta sat down among Miss Proud's books.

'I see Miss Jane Austen has died,' said Miss Proud, folding up a newspaper. 'I wanted to talk to her and now I never shall.'

'What should you have said to her?'

'Many things. I am an admirer of her writing. But in particular I would have raised the subject of her heroines. I would have liked to know how the creator of Elizabeth Bennet could later give us a heroine of the dimension of Fanny Price in *Mansfield Park*. Is *that* the new woman, that somewhat insipid personality of such – or so I see it, I may be wrong – self-effacing virtue?' Miss Proud suddenly and most unexpectedly banged both her hands angrily on the table. 'I keep having the most extraordinary feeling that the world for women is going *backwards* instead of bravely into the future! I cannot bear to think that, for I grew up in an age of enlightenment and new thought and hope. If women are to be . . .' For once in her life Miss Proud was lost for words. She rested her face into her hands for a moment, and Rosetta saw the old, wrinkled fingers that wore no jewellery. 'If women are to be forced back by sections of society to make the *hearth* the centre of their lives – then our brave new future is doomed.'

'I will be your new woman,' said Rosetta.

'My dear, I know you will. It is not individuals that I mean. There will always be brave individuals. It is – oh, I sense an ominous feeling in the air, a feeling that all the women's freedoms we have actually seen approaching – with our own eyes: look at the adventures of your mother and your Aunt Fanny when they were younger! look at Mrs Venetzia Alabaster! – may be over before they have properly begun.'

Rosetta regarded the old lady solemnly with her piercing blue eye. 'Miss Proud,' she said, 'I met, last night, a Frenchman called Monsieur Pierre Montand.'

Her words hung there in the shocked air. 'Did you indeed?'

'Do you know him, Miss Proud?'

'I have met him.'

'He was at the lecture with his wife and children.'

Miss Proud looked away suddenly. 'I see.'

'Did my mother know him once?'

'That is a strange question.'

'Is it?' Rosetta had an odd, unladylike way of sitting sometimes, with one leg tucked under her. When Mattie and Flo came to England for a visit, Miss Proud remembered that Flo sat in exactly this same way. The two girls seemed to be able to sit like that for hours, hardly moving, as still as stone; Rosetta sat that way now, among the books.

'There is a part,' Rosetta said slowly, 'that Mama keeps hidden from me.' She looked carefully at Miss Proud. 'She has always told me my story, and how she found me, and how the Duke asked Mama to marry him so that she could become, with him, my legal guardian, but – Miss Proud – I was wondering – how did she know that I had been born?'

Miss Proud looked taken aback for a moment. Rosetta's strange instincts always disconcerted her. 'My dear – it – it was known that your father had—'

'Yes, yes, I know all that. But afterwards, my father was dead. He never knew. How then could *she* have possibly known, in the middle of London, that I had been born. *To come looking for me?* She even knew that I was a girl! Who told her?'

Miss Proud did not answer. Rosetta left the question in the air.

'Was there a price?' she said. She seemed to speak casually, but took off her eye-patch, which she hardly ever did in front of anyone, even Miss Proud; the damaged blue eye blinked.

'Do you mean money?'

'No, no, I know she had to buy me, Flo told me all that. I mean another sort of price.'

Miss Proud smiled. 'You have been reading too many novels!'

'And in novels, you know, there is *always* love.'

Miss Proud thought how like her grandmother Rosetta was sometimes: the direct manner, the strange sharpness, the blue eyes. She said nothing, and after a moment Rosetta went on, as if she was again changing the subject, as if her words were chance, had no plan.

'Last night when I saw the painting of the Nile I felt – I know this does not make sense – homesick.'

'Oh, my dear.' There was silence for a moment. 'But, of course, that is natural. We have always spoken to you of Egypt. Although it is, as we have told you, a difficult place for women.'

'Of course. Egypt is a very difficult place for women, as I have learnt all my life. However, covering my face will not be a problem to me.' And she replaced her eye-patch. 'But all is not as it seems there.'

'What do you mean by that?'

'In Egypt, Flo's English is so good that she actually *works* with Cornie and Mattie and Mrs Alabaster in the business. Yet Uncle

George, in this freer world, England, would never take *me* into the family business – even though he knows how clever I am with figures – in a million years.'

Miss Proud nodded wryly. 'You are quite right, alas.'

Rosetta seemed to be peering at the bookshelves. 'Flo – when she visited – I could speak to her in a quite different way, even though she is older than me, and married and locked away – *seemingly*. And the first thing I used to do with Flo was take off my eye-patch – ophthalmia is nothing to her, she is surrounded by it. I never take it off in front of Horatio and Jane. *I felt as if I was like Flo*.' Rosetta frowned. 'As if she was my family, even though every-thing about her upbringing and education was different from mine.' She picked up a book, turned the pages, seemed to be perus-ing it. 'I think – I do not much wish to be an English heiress. All the girls I know want only one thing. To marry and have a family. To not marry is a disgrace.' (She forgot she was talking to Miss Proud, who had not married.)

'All young girls would like to marry and have a family. It is nat-ural.'

'And it is even natural to me, believe it or not! But I have eyes. One eye,' she amended bitterly. 'I see how things are in the world that I live in. Who will marry me – a one-eyed Arab? Only someone like my Uncle George, to whom money would be everything. Uncle George brought a man to see Mama, Mr Charles Cooper – he is in urgent need of an heiress. He was in the army and very handsome. Luckily Mama and I both agreed that he was most unsuitable!' Again she was not looking at Miss Proud, turned the pages of one of the volumes beside her. 'I think my cousin Horatio would marry me out of kindness – as long as I would go to India!'

'He is a dear boy.'

'He is. But I do not want to marry him.' And then the words burst out. 'I want to go to Egypt! I feel as if I *know* it.'

'But my dear – your mother has always talked to you about Egypt, she was fascinated by the idea of the place since she was a child when her father told *her* of it, just as she has told you. It is nat-ural you should think of it too.'

'It is something else. I know I have had many, many advantages and I am so grateful. But – I am not an Englishwoman. Not really.'

'Dear girl.' Miss Proud took off the spectacles and rubbed her eyes. Rosetta became merely a shape in the room 'There are many things of the human heart that one does not necessarily understand fully. But my dear, I am absolutely certain that Rose would never stop you doing what you wanted to do. She knows that Mattie and Flo are there. And the wonderful Mrs Venetzia Alabaster, the Singing Acrobat, with her Bedouin sheikh and now one of the most powerful traders in Egypt! Your mama knows how Egypt captures people. She knows you would have many people who would help take care of you if you wanted to visit.'

'Oh no – you do not understand! It is not *me* that I worry about, but *my mother* – about what would happen to her! If I left her after all she has done for me. What if I wanted to stay there? So I must know if there was a price' – she stood up suddenly, struggled to find the right words – 'if she had to – give up something for my sake. And last night, for the first time, I believe I understood that there was.'

Again Miss Proud was confounded by Rosetta's perception. 'But – what has that got to do with you going to Egypt?'

Rosetta said slowly: 'I want to go to Egypt more than anything in the world. But I realise that now it might be my turn. I might have to give up something also.' She moved for a moment through the books. 'I can, of course, be an English heiress if I have to.' And Miss Proud saw that Rosetta would give up her own life for her mother, and her heart contracted for the girl; and for Rose, who had meant so well.

'Rosetta, these – these matters are hard to measure.' Rosetta shook her dark curls, the way she did when she was exasperated: to Miss Proud without her spectacles she seemed an impatient shadow moving now about the room.

'Miss Proud, I am nearly sixteen. I understand things. I know French and German like many young girls, but I have been educated in Greek and mathematics and natural philosophy like a man. I have had the best tutors of any girl in England. I know how to *think*.'

'Nevertheless' – Miss Proud replaced her spectacles – 'there are many other – intangible – things to understand also. I think you should talk of these things to your mother, not to me,' but she saw Rosetta's sharp Fallon eyes.

'I know, I *know* there are other things to understand in life also,' said the girl in exasperation. 'My education has *taught* me there are other things, even if I am not – that is – even if I am not to experience them myself. And I know how much my mother wanted me, what she did to find me.' Rosetta stared out at the snow that was falling heavily now past the windows in South Molton Street. 'I have only odd memories of when I was young, but – I remember my mother as – as a quite different person. Now she is so polite, such a good hostess, so kind to people, so infinitely calm and smiling that it is hard to know if there is any longer that other person underneath. I saw more things in her face last night than I have seen there for a long time.' She quickly came and sat across the table from Miss Proud. 'Mama loved teaching me to read, I remember that part; I started to learn how to read before I was three years old! So I know – and you and Aunt Fanny have always told me too – how much my mother loved *words*. She was fascinated by words since she was a child – I know that was what began her interest in the hieroglyphs – that they were *words* that someone had written. And – that is Monsieur Montand's interest also, is it not?' Miss Proud did not answer. 'And for many, many years she kept a journal.'

'It is true I had hoped she would write more. For so many things have happened to her, she was always observing and writing and growing – she is a most intelligent woman – she could have been of great assistance, I felt, to others.'

'And then she stopped.'

The old lady collected together some quills on her table with great concentration.

'Miss Proud, those precious journals are in an old trunk gathering dust. She writes nothing now. She sits at her mother's desk – and writes only invitations to tea! *Maybe there is nothing underneath any more!* Do you know I have never seen her cry since I was a young child? One day she wept – it is one of my earliest memories, and it was here in this house, I am certain. She stood at that window upstairs and wept and – and I think I thought it was rain coming down her face.' Miss Proud could not trust herself to speak. 'So – was there a price? Did she have to put something away with the journals when she married the Duke?'

The old lady in black knew the fifteen-year-old girl opposite so well. Rosetta's heart was like melting gold underneath her manner; Rosetta loved Rose deeply, for Rose had, as she had once promised, been there, always. But there was steel in Rosetta's fifteen-year-old soul, just as there had been in Rose's.

'There was – a price, Rosetta, yes.'

'Was it the Frenchman, Monsieur Montand?' And as Miss Proud looked away Rosetta added, 'I *saw* them. I saw how they looked. I have never seen my mother look like that. It was *so* . . .' Miss Proud thought Rosetta would say *romantic*, but instead she said slowly, '*terrible.*'

Miss Proud sighed. 'Very well then. But I had rather your mother told you than me, for I was merely an observer. It was terrible, yes. They loved each other very much, I think.' As Miss Proud recounted the events, she saw Rosetta's face grow stern.

'Did she cry that day, making the decision? Is that the day I am remembering?'

Miss Proud seemed to stare into the distance, saw Rose's desolate face as she waited for a word from France, her inconsolable, desperate weeping after the visit of the Duke of Hawksfield. 'Yes. Yes, that is the day you remember.'

'Did she hear again from Monsieur Montand?'

'I believe she never heard from him again.'

'And she had chosen me?'

'She had chosen you, yes, dear girl, because she loved you so much.'

Pierre Montand could not have been more astonished when Lady Rosetta Hawksfield was announced at the house of the French Ambassador in London. Brushing snow from her shoulders she entered the small, elegant room with yellow satin curtains where he was working at a desk. The girl with the eye-patch and the olive skin had haunted him in the night, as he lay awake haunted by her contained, smiling mother.

'*Bonjour*, Mademoiselle Rosetta,' he said, rising to take her hand.

'*Bonjour*, Monsieur Montand.' He was so tall, and he looked down at her so kindly. She wasted no time, fixed him with her intense stare. 'Have you known me before, Monsieur Montand?'

'Please, *mademoiselle*,' he said, smiling a little, 'will you not be seated?' and he drew one of the dark, delicate chairs towards the fire that was burning in the grate. He stood on the other side of the fire. And then when she had sat he answered her question. 'Yes, Rosetta. I met you one night many years ago. I saw you when you arrived first in England.'

'My mother, I understand – I only found out today – chose me, over you.'

If he was thrown by her direct, almost impolite manner he did not let it show. '*Oui, Rosette*. That is correct.' Suddenly something in her reminded him of the fifteen-year-old Dolly, so long ago. It was not the recklessness of Dolly, but it was just that same intensity, as if it was life or death. And then he remembered: for Dolly that was true. He looked at the girl sitting before him most carefully.

'Are you married, *monsieur*?'

'You saw my wife and sons last night, I believe.'

'So you cannot marry my mother now?'

'*Non. Je regrette*. I cannot marry your mother now.' His voice was immensely kind and Rosetta suddenly felt an odd lump in her throat: she turned from him, brushed at her skirt.

He said then, puzzled: 'Does your mother know that you have come to see me?'

'I am almost sixteen! I have my own carriage, *monsieur*. I have servants waiting for me below. She does not know, of course.' And then she was silent for a moment, he saw that she was choosing her next words carefully. 'Could you – could I ask of you an enormous favour? Could you – would you come with me just once? It would take no more than an hour.'

Very gently he said, 'I do not wish to meet your mother again, Rosetta.'

'Why?'

'Because – because we both have different lives now.'

'Only one hour.'

'*Non, ma petite*. It is too – long ago. It is in the past, *le chemin perdu*. A meeting can serve no purpose, for we have taken other pathways. One day you will understand.'

'Please. I beg you.' The blue eye stared up at his face. 'She does not know. She will not be prepared. I need you to do this so much.'

Again he looked puzzled. 'I do not understand.'

Rosetta looked for the words. 'Something in her has – gone away. Or died. I think it needs to come back. Monsieur Montand, you are a Frenchman.' She took a deep breath. 'If you cannot marry her, you could be her lover.' He was so surprised that he did not know whether to laugh, or to weep: she gave him time to do neither. 'In novels,' she insisted, *'love always wins.'*

'In real life,' he said slowly, 'there are many kinds of love.' And he looked towards the window, where snow was falling: at the elegant yellow curtains, at rooftops, at an English church spire through the snow in the distance. 'I cannot help your mother, Rosetta. I have my own children now, and I love them. Just as Rose loves you.'

'Monsieur Montand, *I beg of you,*' she said again. 'Just one hour.' She saw his closed face. 'Listen to me, *monsieur*. My mother has become one of the most well-known and admired hostesses in London in her beautiful house in Grosvenor Square. She is charming and she smiles all the time and is very good at listening to people, and very kind, and the old Queen is always asking for her. But I know she was once somebody else. She used to care, they have told me, passionately about the hieroglyphs. She was *wild* about them.'

He gave the briefest of smiles at Rosetta's choice of words; he could not help it, heard Rose's voice: *They have written their lives. They are trying to tell us.* And the way she ran her fingers so intently over the markings, trying to understand. And out of the past the old memory sprang: Rose leaning her dark head against the damaged face of an ancient piece of stone.

'Oui, mademoiselle, yes. She was that way, as you say, which was unusual for a young woman at the time.'

'She cared wildly, passionately about the act of writing, the importance of writing. I know of this because she taught this to me when I was very, very young, before I was given to – to real tutors.'

'Yes.'

'Now what does she write? Social invitations! The nearest she gets to hieroglyphs is to smile in Grosvenor Square at the people who are fascinated by the new fashion that is Egypt: they would be shocked and unbelieving to know that she has actually been there, alone in the desert. *Where has it all gone?*'

'We change, Mademoiselle Rosetta,' he said gently.

'Not about things like that.'

'You speak very – assuredly – for one who is so young.' Again he spoke kindly, so that she would not feel he was making fun of her.

'*Monsieur*, I know she has something locked inside her. It is so cruel. You can unlock her.'

But he only shook his head and then walked back and sat at his desk. The meeting was over.

She stared at him intently until he looked back at her, and then she said: 'Was it you, *monsieur*, as Miss Proud said to me this morning, who told her of my existence in the world? So that all this' – and she spread her hands to include him and herself and the world – 'has happened?'

She saw that he was shocked and he looked down at his desk, at the papers, straightened the papers. 'Yes,' he said finally. 'It was I who told her about you.'

'So you could say, perhaps,' Rosetta spoke very slowly and very simply, 'that it is all because of *you*, because of your own actions, that I am here talking to you. Begging for your help for just one hour.'

He was silent. She saw he could not speak.

'Did you love her, Monsieur Montand?'

After a long time he said, 'Yes. I loved her more than I can say.'

In the carriage he saw that Rosetta was shaking. 'You also love her very much,' he said.

'Yes. And she chose me. I wish to be worth her love.'

The cold December afternoon was darkening and the candles in the crystal chandeliers were already lit in the hall of the huge house in Grosvenor Square. Footmen had run outside with large umbrellas at their arrival, other servants moved smoothly, doors opened, coats were removed; the candles flickered.

'She will be at her old desk that she loves,' said Rosetta. 'Writing nothing.' And took him into the room.

She watched her mother turn white, and then red, in front of their eyes, and then stand clumsily at the old mahogany desk that could change into a card table. All of them heard the old Genoa clock take a deep breath and strike the hour of four. Very faintly, cigar smoke drifted.

Rosetta watched Pierre move towards Rose, and Rose move towards him. She walked slowly into his arms, he held her and he seemed to bury his face in her hair, and then they did not move, and they did not speak. Rosetta thought she heard a sigh.

She left the room, closed the door quietly. There was an antique chair in the large hall and Rosetta waved away the hovering servants and sat there like a sentry, one leg curled underneath her, that odd way she had; the patch over one eye, the blue, high-waisted dress, a cashmere shawl. The light faded from the sky completely and night fell over London.

And in the darkness and the flickering candlelight Rosetta remained. She was as unmoving as the ancient, damaged figures on the walls of the ruins in the desert, where she had been found.

THIRTY-FIVE

That summer, early one morning, Rose drew open the curtains in her room. She looked out at the beautiful square and the green leaves on the trees and the flowers beyond. It was so early that she could hear birds singing, before the sounds of London properly began. She walked quietly down the stairs of the big house, past the ancestors and the Roman urns and the Grecian statues, and into the room that contained the desk that could become a card table. She put on her new magnifying spectacles. Rosetta's first letter, sent from Calais, lay there to be read again many times. Rose held it in her hands for a moment, as if to catch the girl once more. Then, from the secret drawer in the desk she drew a sheet of blank paper as she had done so often when she was young. Miss Proud had waited so long; she had long ago given up saying *when will you begin writing?*

Rose dipped her quill into the ink and began at once to write, and soon she did not hear the old Genoa clock or the sounds of servants or the carriages that began to move round the square.

That summer [she wrote] *the old men appeared at the top of Vow Hill as usual, carrying small telescopes. They were waiting, they* said, to see His Britannic Majesty's glorious fleet appear in the English Channel, returning from heroic battles against the French and the new general that everyone had begun to speak of, General Buonaparte. Sometimes there was no sign of any fleet at all, yet the old men with their telescopes were still to be seen on Vow Hill, arriving early on fine mornings for the best position. Just above the bathing machines.

AFTERWORD

It has very recently been suggested that Arab scholars, too, decoded the hieroglyphs, hundreds of years before the Rosetta Stone was found by the French troops, but that the information had been lost, or hidden, when Egypt was invaded by Islamic armies.

The story is told that on 14 September 1822, Jean-Françoise Champollion, working in his attic room in Paris, checking his work from the first clue – the Rosetta Stone – with some recently discovered hieroglyphs, suddenly, twenty-three years after the stone had been rediscovered, understood at last how things fell into place. He ran out of his attic and along the street to the Institute of France where his brother was working. He rushed in shouting his news: *I've got it!* and then fainted quite away. The Frenchman, helped by the earlier work of the Englishman, Dr Thomas Young, had at last found the key and unlocked the mysterious writing, the hieroglyphs of Ancient Egypt. There was much more to be done, but the key had been turned.

The hieroglyphs were found to be alphabetic letters; phonetic sounds; syllables; and both symbolic and actual pictures of things.

Since 1822 they have told more and more: of battles and kings and ancient gods; of love and death and shopping lists and poetry. They were not magic symbols; they did not, after all, hold the secrets of the world; but they proved to be, nevertheless, the olden days, talking to us.

SELECT BIBLIOGRAPHY

I am indebted to the writers of the following books:

The Pleasures of the Imagination: English culture in the 18th century by John Brewer (HarperCollins, London, 1997)

London: a Social History by Roy Porter (Hamish Hamilton, London, 1994)

Jane Austen and the French Revolution by Warren Roberts (Macmillan, London, 1947)

Extracts from the Journals & Correspondence of Miss Berry 1783–1852, edited by Lady Teresa Lewis (Longman & Co, London, 1866)

Letters from England by Don Manueal Alvarez Espriella, pseudonym of Robert Southey (Longman, Hurst, 1807)

Witnesses for Change: Quaker Women over Three Centuries, edited by

Elizabeth Potts Brown and Susan Mosher Stuard (Rutgers University Press, 1989)

Letters on Egypt, Claude Etienne Savary, translated from the French (London, 1787)

Travels in Various countries of Europe, Asia & Africa: Part 2: Greece, Egypt and the Holy Land by the Rev. Edward Daniel Clarke (T. Cadell & W. Davies, London, 1816)

Voyage to the Cape of Good Hope and up the Red Sea; with travels in Egypt, through the Deserts, etc. by Richard Renshaw (J. Watts, Manchester, 1804)

Journal of a Tour in the Levant by William Turner, Esq. of the Foreign Office (London, 1820)

Original letters from India 1779–1815 by Mrs Eliza Fay, introduced by E. M. Forster (Hogarth Press, London, 1925)

The Great Belzoni by Stanley Mayes (Putnam, London, 1959)

The Hieroglyphs of Horapollo Nilous, Greek version with an English translation by Alexander Turner Cory (William Pickering, London, 1839)

Cracking Codes: the Rosetta Stone and Decipherment, edited by Richard Parkinson (British Museum Press, London, 1999)

The Rosetta Stone: the story of the decoding of the hieroglyphs by Robert Sole and Dominique Valbelle, translated by Steven Rendall (Profile, London, 2001)

The Rosetta Stone: introduction and translations by Stephen Quirke and Carol Andrews (British Museum Publications, London, 1988)

The Warning Voice: a Sermon Preached on the Occasion of the Death of Princess Charlotte, 1817 by Weedon Butler, A.M., Rector of Woolston Magna (Nichols, Son, and Bentley, London, 1817)